The Queen's Cup

by

G. A. Henty

Double 9
BOOKS

The Queen's Cup
by G. A. Henty

ISBN: 978-93-59395-92-0

Published by

DOUBLE 9 BOOKS

2/13-B, Ansari Road
Daryaganj, New Delhi – 110002
info@double9books.com
www.double9books.com
Tel. 011-40042856

ABOUT THE AUTHOR

English author and war correspondent George Alfred Henty lived from 8 December 1832 to 16 November 1902. He is most well-known for his historical fiction and adventure books, including The Dragon & The Raven (1886), For The Temple (1888), Under Drake's Flag (1883), and In Freedom's Cause (1883). (1885). He was a British journalist who served as G. A. Henty's war correspondent. He was raised in Cambridge and finished his education there at Gonville and Caius College. He continued to cover important wars that followed, such as the Italian and Austro-Italian Wars. He wrote 122 books, most of which were geared toward young readers. He also wrote non-fiction, adult fiction, and short tales. In Henty's stories, the main character is a boy or young man who is going through a challenging situation. His characters are consistently low-key, astute, courageous, truthful, and resourceful with a lot of "pluck." The date was put at the bottom of the title page of each of Henty's 122 historical fiction works in their first printings.

CONTENTS

Chapter 1

A large party were assembled in the drawing room of Greendale, Sir John Greendale's picturesque old mansion house. It was early in September. The men had returned from shooting, and the guests were gathered in the drawing room; in the pleasant half hour of dusk when the lamps have not yet been lighted, though it is already too dark to read. The conversation was general, and from the latest news from India had drifted into the subject of the Italian belief in the Mal Occhio.

"Do you believe in it, Captain Mallett?" asked Bertha, Sir John's only child, a girl of sixteen; who was nestled in an easy chair next to that in which the man she addressed was sitting.

"I don't know, Bertha."

He had known her from childhood, and she had not yet reached an age when the formal "Miss Greendale" was incumbent upon her acquaintances.

"I do not believe in the Italian superstition to anything like the extent they carry it. I don't think I should believe it at all if it were not that one man has always been unlucky to me."

"How unlucky, Captain Mallett?"

"Well, I don't know that unlucky is the proper word, but he has always stood between me and success; at least, he always did, for it is some years since our paths have crossed."

"Tell me about it."

"Well, I have no objection, but there is not a great deal to tell.

"I was at school with—I won't mention his name. We were about the same age. He was a bully. I interfered with him, we had a fight, and I scored my first and only success over him. It was a very tough fight—by far the toughest I ever had. I was stronger than he, but he was the more active. I fancied that it would not be very difficult to thrash him, but found that I had made a great mistake. It was a long fight, and it was only because I was in better condition that I won at last.

"Well, you know when boys fight at school, in most cases they become better friends afterwards; but it was not so here. He refused to shake hands with me, and muttered something about its being his turn next time. Till then he had not been considered a first-rate hand at anything; he was one of those fellows who saunter through school, get up just enough lessons to rub along comfortably, never take any prominent part in games, but have a little set of their own, and hold themselves aloof from school in general.

"Once or twice when we had played cricket he had done so excellently that it was a grievance that he would not play regularly, and there was a sort of general idea that if he chose he could do most things well. After that fight he changed altogether. He took to cricket in downright earnest, and was soon acknowledged to be the best bat and best bowler in the school. Before that it had been regarded as certain that when the captain left I should be elected, but when the time came he got a majority of votes. I should not have minded that, for I recognised that he was a better player than I, but I fancied that he had not done it fairly, for many fellows whom I regarded as certain to support me turned round at the last moment.

"We were in the same form at school. He had been always near the bottom; I stood fairly up in it, and was generally second or third. He took to reading, and in six weeks after the fight won his way to the top of the class and remained there; and not only so, but he soon showed himself so far superior to the rest of us that he got his remove to the form above.

"Then there was a competition in Latin verses open to both forms. Latin verse was the one thing in which I was strong. There is a sort of knack, you know, in stringing them together. A fellow may be a duffer generally and yet turn out Latin verse better than fellows who are vastly superior to him on other points. It was regarded as certain that I should gain that. No one had intended to go in against me, but at the last moment he put his name down, and, to the astonishment of everyone, won in a canter.

"We left about the same time, and went up to Oxford together, but to different Colleges. I rowed in my College Eight, he in his. We were above them on the river, but they made a bump every night until they got behind us, and then bumped us. He was stroke of his boat, and everyone said that success was due to his rowing, and I believe it was. I did not so much mind that, for my line was chiefly sculling. I had won in my own College, and entered for Henley, where it was generally thought that I had a fair chance of winning the Diamonds. However, I heard a fortnight before the entries closed that he was out on the river every morning sculling. I knew what it was going to be, and was not surprised when his name appeared next to mine in the entries.

"We were drawn together, and he romped in six lengths ahead of me, though curiously enough he was badly beaten in the final heat. He stroked the University afterwards. Though I was tried I did not even get a seat in the eight, contrary to general expectation, but I know that it was his influence that kept me out of it.

"We had only one more tussle, and again I was worsted. I went in for the Newdigate—that is the English poetry prize, you know. I had always been fond of stringing verses together, and the friends to whom I showed my poem before sending it in all thought that I had a very good chance. I felt hopeful myself, for I had not heard that he was thinking of competing, and, indeed, did not remember that he had ever written a line of verse when at school. However, when the winner was declared, there was his name again.

"I believe that it was the disgust I felt at his superiority to me in everything that led me to ask my father to get me a commission at once, for it seemed to me that I should never succeed in anything if he were my rival. Since then our lives have been altogether apart, although I have met him occasionally. Of course we speak, for there has never been any quarrel between us since that fight, but I know that he has never forgiven me, and I have a sort of uneasy conviction that some day or other we shall come into contact again.

"I am sure that if we meet again he will do me a bad turn if possible. I regard him as being in some sort of way my evil genius. I own that it is foolish and absurd, but I cannot get over the feeling."

"Oh, it is absurd, Captain Mallett," the girl said. "He may have beaten you in little things, but you won the Victoria Cross in the Crimea, and everyone knows that you are one of the best shots in the country, and that before you went away you were always in the first flight with the hounds."

"Ah, you are an enthusiast, Bertha. I don't say that I cannot hold my own with most men at a good many things where not brains, but brute strength and a quick eye are the only requisites, but I am quite convinced that if that fellow had been in the Redan that day, he would have got the Victoria Cross, and I should not. There is no doubt about his pluck, and if it had only been to put me in the shade he would have performed some brilliant action or other that would have got it for him. He is a better rider than I am, at any rate a more reckless one, and he is a better shot, too. He is incomparably more clever."

"I cannot believe it, Captain Mallett."

"It is quite true, Bertha, and to add to it all, he is a remarkably handsome fellow, a first-rate talker, and when he pleases can make himself wonderfully popular."

"He must be a perfect Crichton, Captain Mallett."

"The worst of it is, Bertha, although I am ashamed of myself for thinking so, I have never been able to divest myself of the idea that he did not play fair. There were two or three queer things that happened at school in which he was always suspected of having had a hand, though it was never proved. I was always convinced that he used cribs, and partly owed his place to them. I was jealous enough to believe that the Latin verses he sent in were written for him by Rigby, who was one of the monitors, and a great dab at verses. Rigby was a great chum of his, for he was a mean fellow, and my rival was always well supplied with money, and to do him justice, liberal with it.

"Then, just before we left school, he carried off the prize in swimming. He was a good swimmer, but I was a better. I thought myself for once certain to beat him, but an hour before the race I got frightful cramps, a thing that I never had before or since, and I could hardly make a fight at all. I thought at the time, and I have thought since, that I must have taken something at breakfast that disagreed with me horribly, and that he somehow put it in my tea.

"Then again in that matter of the Sculls at Henley. I never felt my boat row so heavily as it did then. When it was taken out of the water it was found that a piece of curved iron hoop was fixed to the bottom by a nail that had been pushed through the thin skin. It certainly was not there when it was on the rack, but it was there when I rowed back to the boathouse, and it could only have got there by being put on as the boat was being lowered into the water. There were three or four men helping to lower her down—two of them friends of mine, two of them fellows employed at the boathouse. While it lay in the water, before I got in and took my place, anyone stooping over it might unobserved have passed his hand under it and have pushed the nail through.

"I never said anything about it. I had been beaten; there was no use making a row and a scandal over it, especially as I had not a shadow of proof against anyone; but I was certain that he was not so fast as I was, for during practice my time had been as nearly as possible the same as that of the man who beat him with the greatest ease, and I am convinced that for once I should have got the better of him had it not been for foul play."

"That was shameful, Captain Mallett," Bertha said, indignantly. "I wonder you did not take some steps to expose him."

"I had nothing to go upon, Bertha. It was a case of suspicion only, and you have no idea what a horrible row there would have been if I had said anything about it. Committees would have sat upon it, and the thing would have got into the papers. Fellows would have taken sides, and I should have been blackguarded by one party for hinting that a well-known University man had been guilty of foul practices.

"Altogether it would have been a horrible nuisance; it was much better to keep quiet and say nothing about it."

"I am sure I could not have done that, Captain."

"No, but then you see women are much more impetuous than men. I am certain that after you had once set the ball rolling, you would have been sorry that you had not bided your time and waited for another contest in which you might have turned the tables fairly and squarely."

"He must be hateful," the girl said.

"He is not considered hateful, I can assure you. He conceived a grudge against me, and has taken immense pains to pay me out, and I only trust that our paths will never cross again. If so, I have no doubt that I shall again get the worst of it. At any rate, you see I was not without justification when I said that though I did not believe in the Mal Occhio, I had reason for having some little superstition about it."

"I prophesy, Captain Mallett, that if ever you meet him in the future you will turn the tables on him. Such a man as that can never win in the long run."

"Well, I hope that your prophecy will come true. At any rate I shall try, and I hope that your good wishes will counterbalance his power, and that you will be a sort of Mascotte."

"How tiresome!" the girl broke off, as there was a movement among the ladies. "It is time for us to go up to dress for dinner, and though I shan't take half the time that some of them will do, I suppose I must go."

Captain Mallett had six months previously succeeded, at the death of his father, to an estate five miles from that of Sir John Greendale. His elder brother had been killed in the hunting field a few months before, and Frank Mallett, who was fond of his profession, and had never looked for anything beyond it save a younger son's portion, had thus come in for a very fine estate.

Two months after his father's death he most reluctantly sent in his papers, considering it his duty to settle down on the estate; but ten days later came the news of the outbreak of the Sepoys of Barrackpoor, and he at once telegraphed to the War Office, asking to be allowed to cancel his application for leave to sell out.

So far the cloud was a very small one, but rumours of trouble had been current for some little time, and the affair at least gave him an excuse for delaying his retirement.

Very rapidly the little cloud spread until it overshadowed India from Calcutta to the Afghan frontier. His regiment stood some distance down on the rota for Indian service, but as the news grew worse regiment after regiment was hurried off, and it now stood very near the head of the list. All leave had not yet been stopped, but officers away were ordered to leave addresses, so that they could be summoned to join at an hour's notice.

When he had left home that morning for a day's shooting with Sir John, he had ordered a horse to be kept saddled, so that if a telegram came it could be brought to him without a moment's delay. He was burning to be off. There had at first been keen disappointment in the regiment that they were not likely to take part in the fierce struggle; but the feeling had changed into one of eager expectation, when, as the contest widened and it was evident that it would be necessary to make the greatest efforts to save India, the prospect of their employment in the work grew.

For the last fortnight expectation had been at its height. Orders had been received for the regiment to hold itself in readiness for embarkation, men had been called back from furlough, the heavy baggage had been packed; and all was ready for a start at twenty-four hours' notice. Many of the officers obtained a few days' leave to say goodbye to their friends or settle business matters, and Frank Mallett was among them.

"So I suppose you may go at any moment, Mallett?" said the host at the dinner table that evening.

"Yes, Sir John, my shooting today has been execrable; for I have known that at any moment my fellow might ride up with the order for me to return at once, and we are all in such a fever of impatience, that I am surprised I brought down a bird at all."

"You can hardly hope to be in time either for the siege of Delhi or for the relief of Lucknow, Mallett."

"One would think not, but there is no saying. You see, our news is a month old; Havelock had been obliged to fall back on Cawnpore, and a perfect army of rebels were in Delhi. Of course, the reinforcements will soon be arriving, and I don't think it likely that we shall get up there in time to share in those affairs; but even if we are late both for Lucknow and Delhi, there will be plenty for us to do. What with the Sepoy army and with the native chiefs that have joined them, and the fighting men of Oude and one thing and another, there cannot be less than 200,000 men in arms against us; and even if we do take Delhi and relieve Lucknow, that is only the beginning of the work. The scoundrels are fighting with halters round their necks, and I have no fear of our missing our share of the work of winning back India and punishing these bloodthirsty scoundrels."

"It is a terrible time," Sir John said; "and old as I am, I should like to be out there to lend a hand in avenging this awful business at Cawnpore, and the cold-blooded massacres at other places."

"I think that there will be no lack of volunteers, Sir John. If Government were to call for them I believe that 100,000 men could be raised in a week."

"Ay, in twenty-four hours; there is scarce a man in England but would give five years of his life to take a share in the punishment of the faithless monsters. There was no lack of national feeling in the Crimean War; but it was as nothing to that which has been excited by these massacres. Had it been a simple mutiny among the troops we should all be well content to leave the matter in the hands of our soldiers; but it is a personal matter to everyone; rich and poor are alike moved by a burning desire to take part in the work of vengeance. I should doubt if the country has ever been so stirred from its earliest history."

"Yes, I fancy we are all envying you, Mallett," one of the other gentlemen said. "Partridge shooting is tame work in comparison with that which is going on in India. It was lucky for you that that first mutiny took place when it did, for had it been a week later you would probably have been gazetted out before the news came."

"Yes, that was a piece of luck, certainly, Ashurst. I don't know how I should be feeling if I had been out of it and the regiment on the point of starting for India."

"I suppose you are likely to embark from Plymouth," said Sir John.

"I should think so, but there is no saying. I hardly fancy that we should go through France, as some of the regiments have done; there would be no very great gain of time, especially if we start as far west as Plymouth. Besides, I have not heard of any transports being sent round to Marseilles lately. Of course, in any case we shall have to land at Alexandria and cross the desert to Suez. I should fancy, now that the advantages of that route have been shown, that troops in future will always be taken that way. You see, it is only five weeks to India instead of five months. The situation is bad enough as it is, but it would have been infinitely worse if no reinforcements could have got out from England in less than five months."

"Is there anything that I can do for you while you are away, Mallett?" Sir John Greendale asked, as they lingered for a moment after the other gentlemen had gone off to join the ladies.

"Nothing that I know of, thank you. Norton will see that everything goes on as usual. My father never interfered with him in the general management of the estate, and had the greatest confidence in him. I have known him since I was a child, and have always liked him, so I can go away assured that things will go on as usual. If I go down, the estate goes, as you know, to a distant cousin whom I have never seen.

"As to other matters, I have but little to arrange. I have made a will, so that I shall have nothing to trouble me on that score. Tranton came over with it this morning from Stroud, and I signed it."

"That is right, lad; we all hope most sincerely that there will be no occasion for its provisions to be carried out, but it is always best that a man should get these things off his mind. Are you going to say goodbye to us tonight?"

"I shall do it as a precautionary measure, Sir John, but I expect that when I get the summons I shall have time to drive over here. My horse will do the distance in five and twenty minutes, and unless a telegram comes within an hour of the night mail passing through Stroud, I shall be able to manage it. I saw everything packed up before I left, and my man will see that everything, except the portmanteau with the things I shall want on the voyage, goes on with the regimental baggage."

A quarter of an hour later Captain Mallett mounted his dog cart and drove home. The next morning he received a letter from the Adjutant, saying that he expected the order some time during the next day.

"We are to embark at Plymouth, and I had a telegram this morning saying that the transport had arrived and had taken her coal on board. Of course they will get the news at the War Office today, and will probably wire at once. I think we shall most likely leave here by a train early the next morning. I shall, of course, telegraph as soon as the order comes, but as I know that you have everything ready, you will be in plenty of time if you come on by the night mail."

At eleven o'clock a mounted messenger from Stroud brought on the telegram:

"We entrain at six tomorrow morning. Join immediately."

This was but a formal notification, and he resolved to go on by the night mail. He spent the day in driving round the estate and saying goodbye to his tenants. He lunched at the house of one of the leading farmers, where as a boy he had been always made heartily welcome. Before mounting his dog cart, he stood for a few minutes chatting with Martha, his host's pretty daughter.

"You are not looking yourself, Martha," he said. "You must pick up your roses again before I come back. I shall leave the army then, and give a big dinner to my tenants, with a dance afterwards, and I shall open the ball with you, and expect you to look your best.

"Who is this?" he asked, as a young fellow came round the corner of the house, and on seeing them, turned abruptly, and walked off.

"It is George Lechmere, is it not?"

A flash of colour came into the girl's face.

"Ah, I see," he laughed; "he thought I was flirting with you, and has gone off jealous. Well, you will have no difficulty in making your peace with him tomorrow.

"Goodbye, child, I must be going. I have a long round to make."

He jumped into the dog cart and drove away, while the girl went quietly back into the house.

Her father looked up at the clock.

"Two o'clock," he said; "I must be going. I expected George Lechmere over here. He was coming to talk with me about his father's twelve-acre meadow. I want it badly this winter, for I have had more land under the plough than usual this year. I must either get some pasture or sell off some of my stock."

"George Lechmere came, father," Martha said, with an angry toss of her head, "but when he saw me talking to Captain Mallett he turned and went off; just as if I was not to open my lips to any man but himself."

The farmer would have spoken, but his wife shook her head at him. George Lechmere had been at one time engaged to Martha, but his jealousy had caused so many quarrels that the engagement had been broken off. He still came often to the house, however, and her parents hoped that it would be renewed; for the young fellow's character stood high. He was his father's right hand, and would naturally succeed him to the farm. His parents, too, had heartily approved of the match. So far, however, the prospect of the young people coming together was not encouraging. Martha was somewhat given to flirtation. George was as jealous as ever, and was unable to conceal his feelings, which, as he had now no right to criticise her conduct, so angered the girl that she not unfrequently gave encouragement to others solely to show her indifference to his opinions.

George Lechmere had indeed gone away with anger in his heart. He knew that Captain Mallett was on the point of leaving with his regiment for India, and yet to see him chatting familiarly with Martha excited in him a passionate feeling of grievance against her.

"It matters nought who it is," he muttered to himself. "She is ever ready to carry on with anyone, while she can hardly give me a civil word when I call. I know that if we were to marry it would be just the same thing, and that I am a fool to stop here and let it vex me. It would be better for me to get right out of it. John is old enough to take my place on the farm. Some of these days I will take the Queen's shilling. If I were once away I should not be always thinking of her. I know I am a fool to let a girl trouble me so, but I can't help it. If I stay here I know that I shall do mischief either to her or to someone else. I felt like doing it last month when she was over at that business at Squire Carthew's—he is just such another one as Captain Mallett, only he is a bad landlord, while ours is a good one. What made him think of asking all his own tenantry, and a good many of us round, and getting up a cricket match and a dance on the grass is more than I can say. He never did such a thing before in all the ten years since he became master there. They all noticed how he carried on with Martha, and how she seemed to like it. It was the talk of everyone there. If I had not gone away I should have made a fool of myself, though I have no right to interfere with her, and her father and mother were there and seemed in no way put out.

"I will go away and have a look at that lot of young cattle I bought the other day. I don't know that I ever saw a more likely lot."

It was dark when George returned. On his way home he took a path that passed near the house whence he had turned away so angrily a few hours before. It was not the nearest way, but somehow he always took it, even at hours when there was no chance of his getting the most distant sight of Martha.

Presently he stopped suddenly, for from behind the wall that bounded the kitchen garden of the farm he heard voices. A man was speaking.

"You must make your choice at once, darling, for as I have told you I am off tomorrow. We will be married as soon as we get there, and you know you cannot stop here."

"I know I can't," Martha's voice replied, "but how can I leave?"

"They will forgive you when you come back a lady," he said. "It will be a year at least before I return, and—"

George could restrain himself no longer. A furious exclamation broke from his lips, and he made a desperate attempt to climb the wall, which was, however, too high. When, after two or three unsuccessful attempts, he paused for a moment, all was silent in the garden.

"I will tackle her tomorrow," he said grimly, "and him, too. But I dare not go in now. Bennett has always been a good friend to me, and so has his wife, and it would half kill them were they to know what I have heard; but as for her and that villain—"

George's mouth closed in grim determination, and he strolled on home through the darkness. Whatever his resolutions may have been, he found no opportunity of carrying them out, for the next morning he heard that Martha Bennett had disappeared. How or why, no one knew. She had been missing since tea time on the previous afternoon. She had taken nothing with her, and the farmer and his two sons were searching all the neighbourhood for some sign of her.

The police of Stroud came over in the afternoon, and took up the investigation. The general opinion was that she must have been murdered, and every pond was dragged, every ditch examined, for a distance round the farm. In the meantime George Lechmere held his tongue.

"It is better," he said to himself, "that her parents and friends should think her dead than know the truth."

He seldom spoke to anyone, but went doggedly about his work. His father and mother, knowing how passionately he had been attached to Martha, were not surprised at his strange demeanour, though they wondered that he took no part in the search for her.

They had their trouble, too, for although they never breathed a word of their thoughts even to each other, there was, deep down in their hearts, a fear that George knew something of the girl's disappearance. His intense jealousy had been a source of grief and trouble to them. Previous to his engagement to Martha he had been everything they could have wished him. He had been the best of sons, the steadiest of workers, and a general favourite from his willingness to oblige, his cheerfulness and good temper.

His jealousy, as a child, had been a source of trouble. Any gift, any little treat, for his younger brothers, in which he had not fully shared, had been the occasion for a violent outburst of temper, never exhibited by him at any other time, and this feeling had again shown itself as soon as he had singled out Martha as the object of his attentions.

They had remarked a strangeness in his manner when he had returned home that night, and, remembering the past, each entertained a secret dread that there had been some more violent quarrel than usual between him and Martha, and that in his mad passion he had killed her.

It was, then, with a feeling almost of relief that a month after her disappearance he briefly announced his intention of leaving the farm and enlisting in the army. His mother looked in dumb misery at her husband, who only said gravely:

"Well, lad, you are old enough to make your own choice. Things have changed for you of late, and maybe it is as well that you should make a change, too. You have been a good son, and I shall miss you sorely; but John is taking after you, and presently he will make up for your loss."

"I am sorry to go, father, but I feel that I cannot stay here."

"If you feel that it is best that you should go, George, I shall say no word to hinder you," and then his wife was sure that the fear she felt was shared by her husband.

The next morning George came down in his Sunday clothes, carrying a bundle. Few words were spoken at breakfast; when it was over he got up and said:

"Well, goodbye, father and mother, and you boys. I never thought to leave you like this, but things have gone against me, and I feel I shall be best away.

"John, I look to you to fill my place.

"Good-bye all," and with a silent shake of the hand he took up his bundle and stick and went out, leaving his brothers, who had not been told of his intentions, speechless with astonishment.

Chapter 2

Frank Mallet, after he had visited all his tenants, drove to Sir John Greendale's.

"We have got the route," he said, as he entered; "and I leave this evening. I had a note from the Adjutant this morning saying that will be soon enough, so you see I have time to come over and say goodbye comfortably."

"I do not think goodbyes are ever comfortable," Lady Greendale said. "One may get through some more comfortably than others, but that is all that can be said for the best of them."

"I call them hateful," Bertha put in. "Downright hateful, Captain Mallett—especially when anyone is going away to fight."

"They are not pleasant, I admit," Frank Mallett agreed; "and I ought to have said as comfortably as may be. I think perhaps those who go feel it less than those who stay. They are excited about their going; they have lots to think about and to do; and the idea that they may not come back again scarcely occurs to them at the time, although they would admit its possibility or even its probability if questioned.

"However, I fancy the worst of the fighting will be over by the time we get there. It seems almost certain that it will be so, if Delhi is captured and Lucknow relieved. The Sepoys thought that they had the game entirely in their hands, and that they would sweep us right out of India almost without resistance. They have failed, and when they see that every day their chances of success diminish, their resistance will grow fainter.

"I expect that we shall have many long marches, a great many skirmishes, and perhaps two or three hard fights; but I have not a shadow of fear of a single reverse. We are going out at the best time of year, and with cool weather and hard exercise there will be little danger of fevers; therefore the chances are very strongly in favour of my returning safe and sound. It may take a couple of years to stamp it all out, but at the end of that time I hope to return here for good.

"I shall find you a good deal more altered, Miss Greendale, than you will find me. You will have become a dignified young lady. I shall be only a little older and a little browner. You see, I have never been stationed in India since I joined, for the regiment had only just come home, and I am looking forward with pleasurable anticipation to seeing it. Ordinary life there in a hot cantonment must be pretty dull, though, from what I hear, people enjoy it much more than you would think possible. But at a time like the present it will be full of interest and excitement."

"You will write to us sometimes, I hope," Sir John said, when Mallett rose to leave.

"I won't promise to write often, Sir John. I expect that we shall be generally on the move, perhaps without tents of any kind, and to write on one's knee, seated round a bivouac fire, with a dozen fellows all laughing and talking round, would be a hopeless task; but if at any time we are halted at a place where writing is possible, I will certainly do so. I have but few friends in England—at any rate, only men, who never think of expecting a letter. And as you are among my very oldest and dearest friends, it will be a pleasure for me to let you know how I am getting on, and to be sure that you will feel an interest in my doings."

There was a warm goodbye, and all went to the door for a few last words. Frank's portmanteau was already in the dog cart, for he had arranged to drive straight from Greendale to Chippenham, where he would dine at an hotel and then go on by the mail to Exeter.

It was three o'clock when he drove into the barracks there. Early as the hour was, the troops were already up and busy. Wagons were being loaded, the long lines of windows were all lighted up, and in every room men could be seen moving about. He drove across the barrack yard to his own quarters, left his portmanteau there, and then walked to the mess room. As he had expected, he found several officers there.

"Ah, Mallett, there you are. You are the last in; the others all turned up by the evening train, but we thought that as you were comparatively near you would come on by the mail."

"I thought I should find some of you fellows keeping it up."

"Well, there was nothing else to do. There won't be much chance of going to sleep. We all dined in the town, for of course the mess plate and kit have been packed up. We are not taking much with us now, just enough to make shift with. The rest will be sent round to Calcutta, to be stored there till we settle down. The men had a dinner given to them by the town, and as they all got leave out till twelve o'clock, and the loading of the wagons began at two, there has been a row going on all night. Most of us played pool till an hour ago, then we gradually dropped off for an hour's snooze."

"There will be a chance of getting breakfast, I hope?"

"Yes, there is to be a rough and tumble breakfast at a quarter to five. We fall in at a quarter past. We got through the inspection of kits yesterday. The mess sergeant and a party will pack up the breakfast things, and the pots and pans will come on by the next train. There is one at eight. It will be in plenty of time, as I don't suppose the transport will be off until the afternoon, perhaps not till night. There are always delays at the last moment.

"However, it will be something to be on board ship. That is the first step towards getting at those black scoundrels. We are all afraid that we shall be late for Delhi; still there is plenty of other work to be done."

"Any ladies with us?"

"No, there was a general agreement among the married officers that they had best be left behind. So for once the regiment goes without women."

"There is a levity about your tone that I do not approve of, Armstrong," Frank Mallett said, reprovingly. "There were no women when we went out to the Crimea, at the time when you were a good little boy doing Latin exercises."

"Well, altogether it is a good thing, Mallett, and we shall be much more comfortable without them."

"Speak for yourself, Armstrong. Lads of your age who can talk nothing but barrack slang, and are eminently uncomfortable when they have to chat for five minutes to a lady, are naturally glad when they are free from the restraint of having to talk like reasonable beings; but it is not so with older and wiser men. How about Marshall?"

"He has been away on leave for the last ten days. He has not come back here. There have been two fellows inquiring after him diligently for the last week. There was no mistaking their errand, even if we did not know how he stood. I expect he is on board the transport. I fancy the Colonel gave him a hint to join there. No doubt the Jews will be on the lookout for him at Plymouth, as well as here; but he will manage to smuggle himself on board somehow, even if he has to wrap up as an old woman."

"He deserves all the trouble that has fallen upon him," Frank Mallett said, angrily. "I have no patience with a young fool who bets on race horses when he knows very well that if they lose there is nothing for him to do but to go to the Jews for money. However, he has had a sharp lesson, and as it is likely enough that the regiment won't be back in England for years, he will have a chance of getting straight again. This affair has been a godsend for him, for had he remained in England there would have been nothing for him to do but to sell out."

So they chatted until the mess waiters laid the table for breakfast, when the other officers came pouring in. The meal was eaten hastily, for the assembly was sounding in the barrack yard. As soon as breakfast was finished, the officers went out and took their places with their companies.

There was a brief inspection, then the drums and fifes set up "The Girl I Left Behind Me," and the regiment marched off to the station, the streets being already full of people who had got up to see the last of them, and to wish them Godspeed in the work of death they were going to perform.

The baggage was already in the train that was waiting for them in the station, and in a few minutes it steamed away; the soldiers hanging far out of every window to wave a last goodbye to the weeping women who thronged the platform. Two hours later they reached Plymouth, marched through the town to the dockyard, and went straight on board the transport.

There was the usual confusion until the cabins had been allotted, portmanteaus stowed away, and the general baggage lowered into the hold. A tedious wait of three or four hours followed, no one exactly knew why, and then the paddle wheels began to revolve. The men burst into a loud cheer, and a few minutes later they passed Drake's Island and headed down the sound.

They had, as expected, found young Marshall on board. He kept below until they started, although told that there was little chance of the bailiffs being permitted to enter the dockyard. As he had the grace to feel thoroughly ashamed of his position, little was said to him; but the manner of the senior officers was sufficient to make him feel their strong disapproval of the position in which he had placed himself by his folly.

"I have taken a solemn oath never to bet again," he said that evening to Captain Mallett, who was a general favourite with the younger officers; "and I mean to keep it."

"How much do you owe, young 'un?"

"Four hundred and fifty. What with allowances and so on, I ought to be able to pay it off in three or four years."

"Yes, and if you keep your word, Marshall, some of us may be inclined to help you. I will for one. I would have done so before, but to give money to a fool is worse than throwing it into the sea. As soon as you show us by deeds, not words, that you really mean to keep straight, you will find that you are not without friends."

"Thank you awfully, Mallett, but I don't want to be helped. I will clear it off myself if I live."

"You will find it hard work to do that, Marshall, even in India. Of course, the pay and allowances make it easy for even a subaltern to live on his income there, but when it comes to laying by much, that is a difficult matter. However, so long as the actual campaign lasts, the necessary expenses will be very small. We shall live principally on our rations, and you can put by a good bit. There may be a certain amount of prize money, for, although there is nothing to be got from the mutineers themselves, some of the native princes who have joined them will no doubt have to pay heavily for their share in the business."

"Well, you won't give me up, will you, Mallett?"

"Certainly not. I was as hard as anyone on you before, for I have no patience with such insane folly, but if you keep straight no one will be more inclined to make things easy for you."

The voyage to Alexandria was unmarked by any incident. Drill went on regularly, and life differed to no great extent from that in barracks. All were glad when the halfway stage of the journey was reached, but still more so when they embarked in another transport at Suez.

Here they learned, according to news that had arrived on the previous day, that at the end of August Delhi was still holding out; and that, although reinforcements had reached the British, vastly greater numbers of men had entered the city, and that constant sorties were made against the British position on the Ridge.

Excitement therefore was at its highest, when on the 20th of October a pilot came on board at the mouth of the Hooghly, and they learned that the assault had been made on the 14th of September; and that, after desperate fighting extending over a week, the city had been captured, the puppet Emperor made prisoner, and the rebels driven with tremendous loss across the bridge of boats over the Jumma.

The satisfaction with which the news was received, in spite of the disappointment that they had arrived too late to share in the victory, was damped by the news of the heavy losses sustained in the assault; and especially that of that most gallant soldier, General Nicholson.

Nor were their hopes that they might take part in the relief of Lucknow realised, for they learned that on the 25th of September the place had been relieved by Havelock and Outram. Here, however, there was still a prospect that they might take a share in the serious fighting; as the losses of the relieving column had been so heavy, and the force of mutineers so large, that it had been found impracticable to carry off the garrison as intended, and the relieving forces were now themselves besieged. There was, however, no fear felt for their safety. If the scanty original garrison had defied all the efforts of the mutineers, no one doubted that, now that their force was trebled, they would succeed in defending themselves until an army sufficiently strong to bring them off could be assembled.

Not a day was lost at Calcutta. General Sir Colin Campbell, who was now in supreme command, was collecting a force at Cawnpore. There he had already been joined by a column which had been despatched from Delhi as soon as the capital fell, and by a strong naval brigade with heavy guns from the ships of war.

All arrangements had been made for pushing up reinforcements as fast as they arrived, and the troops were marched from the side of the ship to a spot where a flotilla of boats was in readiness. The men only took what they could carry; all other baggage was to be sent after them by water, and to lie, until further instructions, at Allahabad. As soon, therefore, as the troops had been packed away in the boats, they were taken in tow by two steamers, and at once taken up the river. Officers and men were alike in the highest spirits at finding themselves in so short a time after their arrival already on the way to the front, and their excitement was added to by the fact that it was still doubtful whether they would arrive in time to join the column. Cramped as the men were in the crowded boats, there was no murmuring as day after day, and night after night, they continued their course up the river.

At Patna they learned that the Commander in Chief was still at Cawnpore, and the same welcome news was obtained at Allahabad; but at the latter place they learned that the news of his having gone forward was hourly expected.

They reached Cawnpore on the morning of the 11th, and learned that the column had left on the 9th, but was halting at Buntara. Not a moment was lost. Each man received six days' provisions from the commissariat stores, and two hours after landing the regiment was on the march and arrived late at night at Buntara, being received with hearty cheers by the troops assembled there.

They learned that they were to go forward on the following morning. Weary, but in high spirits at finding that they had arrived in time, the regiment lighted its fires and bivouacked.

"This has been a close shave indeed, Mallett," one of the other captains said, as a party of them sat round a fire. "We won by a short head."

"Short indeed, Ackers. It has been a race all the way from England, and it is marvellous indeed that we should arrive just in time to take part in the relief of Lucknow. A day later and we should have missed it."

"We should not have done that, Mallett, for the men would have marched all night, and, if necessary, all day tomorrow, to catch up. Still, it is a wonderful fluke that after all we should be in time."

"There is no doubt that it will be a tough business," one of the majors said. "Havelock found it so, and I expect that the lesson he taught them hasn't been lost, and that we shall have to meet greater difficulties than even he had."

"Yes, but look at our force. Sixteen guns of Horse Artillery, a heavy field battery, and the Naval Brigade with eight guns; the 9th Lancers, the Punjaub Cavalry, and Hodson's Horse; four British regiments of infantry and two of Punjaubies, besides a column 1,500 strong which is expected to join us tomorrow or next day.

"I hope in any case, Major, that we shan't follow the line Havelock took through the narrow streets, for there we cannot use our strength; but will manage to approach the Residency from some other direction. We know that it stands near the river, and at the very edge of the town, so there ought to be some other way of getting at it. I consider that we are a match for any number of these scoundrels if we do but get a fair ground for fighting, which we certainly should not do in the streets of the town."

"I don't care how it is, so that we do get at them," another officer said. "We have heard such frightful details of their atrocities as we came up that one is burning to get at close quarters with them. I suppose we shall go to the Alumbagh first, and relieve the force that has so long been shut up there. I only hope that we shan't be chosen to take their place."

There was a general exclamation of disgust at the suggestion.

"Well, someone must stay, you know," he went on in deprecation of the epithets hurled at him; "and why not our regiment as well as any other?"

"Because I cannot believe that after luck has favoured us so long she will play us such a trick now," Frank Mallett said. "Besides, the other regiments have done something in the way of fighting already while we have not fired a shot; and I think that Sir Colin would be more likely to choose the 75th, or, in fact, any of the other regiments than us. Still if the worst comes to the worst we must not grumble. Other regiments have had weary times of waiting, and it may be our turn now. Your suggestion has come as a damper to our spirits, and, as I don't mind acknowledging that I am dog tired with the march, after not having used my legs for the last seven or eight weeks, I shall try to forget it by going off to sleep."

Making a pillow of his cloak, he lay down on the spot where he was sitting, his example being speedily followed by the rest of the officers.

The next morning the troops were on the march early, but they were not to reach the Alumbagh without opposition, for on passing a little fort to the right they were suddenly attacked by a small body of rebels posted round it.

But little time was lost. Hodson's Horse, who were nearest to them, at once made a brilliant charge, scattering them in all directions. A short pause was made while the fort was dismantled, and then the column proceeded without further interruption to the Alumbagh.

There was some disappointment at its appearance. Instead of finding, as they had expected, a palace, there was nothing but a large garden enclosed by a lofty wall, and having a small mosque at one end. It had evidently been a place of retirement when the Kings of Oude desired to get away from the bustle and ceremony of the great town.

The Commander in Chief was thoroughly acquainted with the situation in the city, by information that he had received from a civilian named Kavanagh; who had at immense risk made his way out from the Residency, and was able to furnish plans of all the principal buildings and the route which, in the opinion of Brigadier General Inglis, was the most favourable for the attack.

In the evening the reinforcements arrived, bringing up the total force to 5,000. When the orders were issued, the officers of the —th found to their intense satisfaction that, as Captain Mallett had thought likely, the 75th was selected to remain in charge of the baggage at the Alumbagh.

The force moved off, early on the morning of the 14th, but, after marching a short distance along the direct road followed by Havelock, struck off to the right, and, keeping well away from the city, came down upon the summer palace of the Kings of Oude, called the Dilkoosha. It stood on an eminence commanding a view of the whole of the eastern suburbs of the town, and was surrounded by a large park.

As soon as the head of the column approached this, a heavy musketry fire broke out, and it was at once evident that their movements had been watched and the object of their march divined. The head of the column was halted for a few minutes until reinforcements came up. Then they formed into line, the artillery opened on their flanks, and with a cheer the troops advanced to the attack.

"The beggars cannot shoot a bit," Frank Mallett said to his subaltern, Armstrong. "I expect they are Sepoys, for the Oude tribesmen are said to be good marksmen."

Keeping up a rolling fire at the loopholes in the walls, the infantry pressed forward. The fire of the enemy slackened as they approached, and they soon forced their way in, some helping their comrades over the wall, others breaking down a gate and so pouring in. A halt was made until the greater portion of the troops came up, and then the advance was continued.

The defenders of the wall had been considerably reinforced by troops stationed round the Palace itself, but they were unable to withstand the British advance, and soon began to retreat towards the city; stopping occasionally where a wall or building offered facilities for defence, but never waiting long enough for the British to get at them. In two hours all had been driven down the hill to the Martiniere College. Here again they made a stand, but were speedily driven out, and chased through the garden and park of the college, and thence across the canal into the streets of the town. Here the pursuit ceased, the —th being told off to hold the Martiniere as an advanced position. Sir Colin established his headquarters at the Dilkoosha, the rest of the troops bivouacking around it or on the slope of the hill between it and the college.

After seeing that the men were comfortable, and getting some food, most of the officers gathered on the flat roof of the college, whence a fine view was obtainable over the town. The Residency had been already pointed out to them, and the British flag could be seen floating above it. Several very large buildings, surrounded for the most part with walled gardens, rose above the low roofs of the native houses in the intervening space.

"The way is pretty open. A good deal of the ground seems to be occupied with gardens, and most of the houses are so small that they could not hold many men."

"I agree with you, Mallett. It is evident that we shall be passing through an open suburb rather than the town itself. Those big buildings, if held in force, will give us a good deal of trouble. They are regular fortresses."

"I don't think that any of them are built of stone. They all seem to be whitewashed."

"That is so," the Major agreed, as he examined them through his field glass. "I suppose stone is scarce in this neighbourhood, but it is probable that the walls are of brickwork, and very thick. They will have to be regularly breached before we can carry them.

"It makes one sad to think that that flag, which has waved over the Residency for the last five months, defying all the efforts of enormously superior numbers, is to come down, and that these scoundrels will be able to exult in the possession of the place that has defied all their efforts to take it. Still one feels that Sir Cohn's decision is a necessary one. It would never do to have six or seven thousand men shut up there, when there is urgent work to be done in a score of other places. Besides, it would need a vast magazine of provisions to maintain them. Our force, even when joined by the garrison, would be wholly inadequate for so tremendous a task as reducing to submission a city containing at least half-a-million inhabitants, together with thirty or forty thousand mutineers and a host of Oude's best men, with the advantage of the possession of a score or two of buildings, all of which are positive fortresses." .

"No, there is nothing for it but to fall back again till we have a force sufficient to capture the whole city, and utterly defeat its defenders. With us away, this place will become the focus of the mutiny. Half the fugitives from Delhi will find their way here, and at least we shall be able to crush them at one blow, instead of having to scour the country for them for months. The more of them gather here the better; and then, when we do capture the place, there will be an end of the mutiny, though, of course, there will still be the work of hunting down scattered bands."

"We may look forward to very much harder work tomorrow than we have had today," Captain Johnson said. "With these glasses I can make out that the place is crowded with men. Of course, today we took them somewhat by surprise, as they would naturally expect us to follow Havelock's line. But now that they know what our real intentions are, they will be able to mass their whole force to oppose us."

"So much the better," Frank Mallett said. "There is no mistaking the feeling of the troops. They are burning to avenge Cawnpore, and little mercy will be shown the rebels who fall into their hands."

"I should advise any of you gentlemen who want to write home," the Colonel said, gravely, "to do so this evening. There is no doubt that we shall take those places, but I think that there is also no doubt that our death roll will be heavy. You must not judge by their fighting today of the stand that they are likely to make tomorrow. They know well enough that they will get no quarter after what has taken place, and will fight desperately to the end."

Most of the officers took his advice. Captain Mallett sat down on the parapet, took out a notebook, and wrote in pencil:

"Dear Sir John:

"Although it is but four days since I posted you a long letter from Cawnpore that I had written on our way up the river, I think it as well to write a few lines in pencil. You will not get them unless I go down tomorrow, as I shall of course tear them up if I get through all right. I am writing now within sight of the Residency. We had a bit of a fight today, but the rebels did not make any serious stand. Tomorrow it will be different, for we shall have to fight our way through the town, and there is no doubt that the resistance will be very obstinate. I have nothing to add to what I wrote to you last. What I should like you to know is that I thought of you all this evening, and that I send you and Lady Greendale and Bertha my best wishes for your long life and happiness.

"Yours most sincerely,

"Frank Mallett."

He tore the page from his notebook, put it in an envelope and directed it, then placed it in an inner pocket of his uniform.

"So you are not writing, Marshall," he said, as he went across to the young ensign who was sitting on the angle of the parapet.

"I have no one particular to write to, Captain Mallett, and the only persons who will feel any severe sorrow if I fall tomorrow are my creditors."

"We should all be sorry, Marshall, very sorry. Ever since we sailed from Plymouth your conduct has shown that you have determined to retrieve your previous folly. The Colonel himself spoke to me about it the other day, and remarked that he had every hope that you would turn out a steady and useful officer. We have all noticed that beyond the regular allowance of wine you have drunk nothing, and that you did not touch a card throughout the voyage."

"I have not spent a penny since I went on board at Plymouth," the lad said. "I got the paymaster to give me an order on London for the amount of pay due to me the day we got to Cawnpore, and posted it to Morrison; so he has got some fifteen pounds out of the fire. Of course it is not much, but at any rate it will show him I mean to pay up honestly."

"Well done, lad. You are quite right to give up cards, and to cut yourself off liquors beyond the Queen's allowance; but don't stint yourself in necessaries. For instance, fruit is necessary here, and of course when we once get into settled quarters, you must keep a horse of some sort, as everyone else will do so. How much did you really have from Morrison in cash?"

"Three hundred; for which I gave him bills for four fifty and a lien on my commission."

"All right, lad, I will write to my solicitor in London, and get him to see Morrison, and ask him to meet you fairly in the matter. He will know that it will be years before you are likely to be in England again, and that if you are killed he will lose altogether; so under these circumstances I have no doubt that he will be glad enough to make a considerable abatement, perhaps to content himself with the sum that you really had from him."

"I am afraid that my letter, with the enclosure, assuring him that I will in time pay the amount due, will harden his heart," Marshall laughed. "I am much obliged all the same, but I don't think that it will be of any use."

However, on leaving him, Mallett went downstairs, borrowed some ink from the quartermaster, and wrote to his solicitor, enclosing a cheque for 300 pounds, with instructions to see the money lender.

"You will find that he will be glad enough to hand over young Marshall's bills for four fifty for that amount," he said. "He has already had fifteen pounds, which is a fair interest for the three hundred for the time the lad has had it. He will know well enough that if Marshall dies he will lose every penny, and that at any rate he will have to wait many years before he can get it. I have no doubt that he would jump at an offer of a couple of hundred, but it is just as well that the young fellow should feel the obligation for some time, and as the man did lend him the money it would be unfair that he should be an absolute loser."

Chapter 3

The next morning three days' rations were served out to the troops, and the advance begun; the movement being directed against the Secunderbagh, a large garden surrounded by a very high and strong wall loopholed for musketry. To reach it a village, fortified and strongly held, had first to be carried. The attack was led by Brigadier Hope's brigade, of which the regiment formed part. As they approached the village, so heavy a musketry fire was opened upon them that the order to advance was changed and the leading regiment moved forward in skirmishing order. The horse artillery and heavy field guns were brought up, and poured a tremendous fire into the village, driving the defenders from their post on the walls.

As soon as this was accomplished, the infantry rushed forward and stormed the village, the enemy opposing a stout resistance, occupying the houses and fighting to the last. The main body of them, however, fled to the Secunderbagh. The 4th Sikhs had been ordered to lead the attack, while the British infantry of the brigade were to cover the operation. The men were, however, too excited and too eager to get at the enemy to remain inactive, and on leaving the village dashed forward side by side with the Sikhs and attacked the wall. There was a small breach in this, and many of the men rushed through it before the enemy, taken by surprise, could offer a serious resistance. The entrance was, however, so narrow that very few men could pass in, and while a furious fight was raging inside, the rest of the troops tried in vain to find some means of entering.

There were two barred windows, one on each side of the gate, and some of the troopers creeping under these raised their shakos on their bayonets. The defenders fired a heavy volley into them, and the soldiers, leaping to their feet, sprang at the bars and pulled them down by main force, before the defenders had time to reload. Then they leaped down inside, others followed them, the gates were opened, and the main body of troops poured in.

The garden was held by 2,000 mutineers. With shouts of "Remember Cawnpore," the troops flung themselves upon them; and although the mutineers fought desperately, and the struggle was continued for a considerable time, every man was at last shot or bayoneted.

In the meantime a serious struggle was going on close by. Nearly facing the Secunderbagh stood the large Mosque of Shah Nujeef. It had a domed roof, with a loopholed parapet and four minarets, which were filled with riflemen. It stood in a large garden surrounded by a high wall, also loopholed, the entrance being blocked up with solid masonry. The fire from this building had seriously galled Hope's division, while engaged in forcing its way into the Secunderbagh, and Captain Peel, with the Naval Brigade, brought up the heavy guns against it. He took up his position within a few yards of the wall and opened a heavy fire, assisted by that of a mortar battery and a field battery of Bengal Artillery; the Highlanders covering the sailors and artillerymen as they worked their guns, by a tremendous fire upon the enemy's loopholes. So massive were the walls that it was several hours before even the sixty-eight pounders of the Naval Brigade succeeded in effecting a breach.

As soon as this was done the impatient infantry were ordered to the assault, and rushing in, overpowered all resistance, and slew all within the enclosure, save a few who effected their escape by leaping from the wall at the rear.

It was now late in the afternoon, and operations ceased for the day. The buildings on which the enemy had chiefly relied for their defence had been captured, and the difficulties still to be encountered were comparatively small. The next day an attack was made upon a strong building known as the Mess House. This was first breached by the artillery, and then carried by assault by the 53rd and 90th regiments, and a detachment of Sikhs; the latter, single handed, storming another building called the Observatory, in the rear of the Mess House.

At the same time the garrison of the Residency had, in accordance with the plan brought out by Kavanagh, begun operations on their side. The capture of the Secunderbagh and Mosque had been signalled to them, and while the attack on the Mess House was being carried out they had blown down the outer wall of their defences, shelled the ground beyond, and then advanced, carrying two large buildings facing them at the point of the bayonet.

All day the fighting continued, the British gaining ground on either side. The next day the houses still intervening between them were captured, and in the afternoon the defenders of the Residency and the relieving force joined hands. The total loss of the latter was 122 officers and men killed and 345 wounded.

Frank Mallett's letter to Sir John Greendale was not sent off. He received a bullet through the left arm as the troops advanced against the

Secunderbagh, but, using his sash as a sling, led on his company against the defenders crowded in the garden, and took part in the desperate fighting. Three of his brother officers were killed during the three days' fighting, and five others wounded.

"Well, Marshall," he said on the evening of the day when the way was open to the Residency; "you have not cheated your creditor, I see."

"No, Captain Mallett. I thought of him when those fellows in the mosque were keeping such a heavy fire upon us as we were waiting to get into the Secunderbagh. It seemed to me that his chance of ever getting his money was not worth much. How the bullets did whizz about! I felt sure that we should be all mown down before we could get under the shelter of the wall.

"I don't think I shall ever feel afraid in battle again. One gets to see that musketry fire is not so very dangerous after all. If it were, very few of us would have got through the three days' fighting alive, whereas the casualties only amount to one-tenth of the force engaged. I am very sorry you are wounded."

"Oh, my wound is a mere trifle. I scarcely felt it until the sergeant next to me said, 'You are wounded in the arm, Captain Mallett.' The doctor says that it narrowly missed the bone, but in this case a miss is as good as a mile. I am very sorry about Hatchard and Rivers and Miles. They were all good fellows, and when this excitement is over we shall miss them sadly. It will give you your step."

"Yes, I won't say that it is lucky, for one cannot forget how it has been gained. Still it is a good lift for me, for there are two or three down for purchase below me, and otherwise I should have had to wait a long time. It puts you one higher on the list, Captain Mallett."

"I am going to clear out altogether as soon as the fighting is all over, so whether I am fourth or fifth on the list makes no difference whatever to me."

"Still it is a great satisfaction to have been through this and to have taken one's share in the work of revenge. It was a horrible business in the Secunderbagh, though one did not think of it at the time. The villains richly deserved what they got, but I own that I should not care to go into the place again. They must have suffered tremendously altogether. The Colonel said this afternoon that he found their loss had been put down as at least six or seven thousand."

The regiment took its full share in the work that followed the relief of Lucknow, portions being attached to each of the flying columns which scoured Oude, defeated Kunwer Singh, and drove the rebels before them wherever they encountered them.

In the beginning of February the vacancies in the ranks were filled up by a draft from England. The work had been fatiguing in the extreme, but the men were as a rule in splendid health, the constant excitement preventing their suffering from the effect of heat or attacks of fever.

Two companies which had been away from the headquarters of the regiment for six weeks, found on their return a number of letters awaiting them, the first they had received since leaving England. Captain Mallett, who commanded this detachment, found one from Sir John Greendale, written after the receipt of his letter from Cawnpore.

"My Dear Mallett:

"We were all delighted to get your letter. Long before we received it we had the news of the desperate fighting at Lucknow, which was, of course, telegraphed down to the coast and got here before your letter. You may imagine that we looked anxiously through the list of killed and wounded, and were glad indeed that your name in the latter had the word 'slightly' after it.

"Things are going on here much as usual. There was a terrible sensation on the very morning after you left, at the disappearance of Martha Bennett, the daughter of one of your tenants. She left the house just at dusk the evening before, and has not been heard of since. As she took nothing with her, it is improbable in the extreme that she can have fled, and there can be little doubt that the poor girl was murdered, possibly by some passing tramps. However, though the strictest search was made throughout the neighbourhood, her body has never been discovered.

"We lost another neighbour just about the time you left—Percy Carthew. He went for a year's big game shooting in North America. We don't miss him much, as he lived in London, and was not often down at his place. I don't remember his being there since you came back from the Crimea. Anyhow, I do not think that I ever saw you and him together, either in a hunting field or at a dinner party; which, of course, you would have been had you both been down here at the same time. If I remember right, you were at the same school."

And then followed some gossip about mutual friends, and the letter concluded:

"The general excitement is calming down a little now that Delhi is taken and the garrison of Lucknow brought off. Of course there will be a great deal more fighting before the whole thing is over, but there is no longer any fear for the safety of India. The Sikhs have come out splendidly. Who would have thought it after the tremendous thrashing we gave them a few years back?

"Take care of yourself, lad. You have the Victoria Cross and can do very well without a bar, so give someone else the chance. My wife and Bertha send their love."

Two or three of his other letters were from friends in regiments at home bewailing their hard fortune at being out of the fighting. The last he opened bore the latest postmark. It was from his solicitor, and enclosed Marshall's cancelled bill.

"Of course, as you requested me to give 300 pounds for the enclosed, I did so, but by the way in which Morrison jumped at the offer I believe that he would have been glad to have taken half that sum."

Mallett had gone into his tent to open his letters in quiet. He presently went to the entrance, and catching sight of Marshall called him up.

"I have managed that affair for you, Marshall," he said; "and have arranged it in a way that I am sure will be satisfactory to us both. You must look upon me now as your creditor instead of Morrison, and you won't find me a hard one. Here is your cancelled bill for four hundred and fifty. I got it for three hundred, so that a third of your debt is wiped off at once. As to the rest, you can pay me as you intended to pay him, but I don't want you to stint yourself unnecessarily. Pay me ten or fifteen pounds at a time at your convenience, and don't let us say anything more about it."

"But I may be killed," Marshall said, in a voice struggling with emotion.

"If you are, lad, there is an end of the business. As you know, I am very well off, and the loss would not affect me in any way. Very likely you will light upon some rich booty in one of these affairs with a rebel Rajah, and will be able to pay it all off at once."

"I will if I can, Mallett, though I think that it will be much more satisfactory to do it out of my savings, except that I shall have the pleasure of knowing that if I were wiped out afterwards you would not be a loser."

A few days later Frank Mallett was sent with his company to rout out a party of rebels reported to be in possession of a large village twenty miles away. Armstrong was laid up by a slight attack of fever, and he asked that Marshall should be appointed in his place on this occasion.

"One wants two subalterns, Colonel," he said, "for a business like this. I may have to detach a party to the back of the village to cut off the rebels' retreat, and it may be necessary to assault in two places."

"Certainly. Take Marshall if you wish it, Captain Mallett. The young fellow has been behaving excellently, and has gone far to retrieve his character. Captain Johnson has reported to me that he is exemplary in his duties, and has shown much gallantry under fire, especially in that affair near Neemuch, in which he rushed forward and carried off a wounded man who would otherwise have certainly been killed. I reported the case to the Brigadier, who said that at any other time the young fellow would probably have been recommended for a V.C., but that there were so many cases of individual gallantry that there was no chance of his getting that; but Marshall was specially mentioned in orders four days ago, and this will, of course, count in his favour.

"Take him with you by all means; your ensign only joined with the last draft, and you will certainly want someone with you of greater experience than he has."

Marshall was delighted when he heard that he was to accompany Captain Mallett. In addition to his own company, a hundred men of the Punjaub infantry and fifty Sikh horse were under Captain Mallett's command, the native troops being added at the last moment, as a report of another body of mutineers marching in the same direction had just come in.

Frank spent a quarter of an hour in inspecting some maps of the country, and had a talk with the native who was to act as guide. When the little force was drawn up, he marched off in quite another direction from that in which the village lay. Being in command, he was mounted for the first time during the campaign. The lieutenant in command of the Sikhs presently rode up to him.

"I beg your pardon, Captain Mallett, but I cannot but think that your guide is taking you in the wrong direction. I looked at the map before starting, and find that Dousi lies almost due north. We are marching west."

"You are quite right, Mr. Hammond, but, you see, I don't want any of the natives about the camp to guess where we are going. None of these Oude fellows bears us any goodwill, and one of them might hurry off, and carry information as to the line we were following.

"We will march four miles along this road, and then strike off by another leading north. We must surprise them if we can. We don't really know much about their force, and even if we did, they may be joined by some other body before we get there—there are numerous bands of them all over the country. And in the next place, if they knew that we were coming, they might bolt before we got there.

"Besides, some of these villages are very strong, and we might suffer a good deal before we could carry it if they had notice of our coming. However, you were quite right to point out to me that we were not going in what seemed the right direction."

The column started at four o'clock in the afternoon. It had been intended that it should move off at daybreak on the following morning, but Frank had suggested to the Colonel that it would be advantageous to march half the distance that night.

"Of course, we could do the twenty miles tomorrow, Colonel," he said, "but the men would hardly be in the best fighting trim when they got there. Moreover, by starting in the afternoon, the natives here would imagine that we were going to pounce upon some fugitives at a village not far away."

The permission was readily granted, and accordingly, after marching until nine o'clock in the evening, the column halted in a grove of trees to which their guide led them, half a mile from the road. Each man carried four days' cooked provisions in his haversack. There was therefore no occasion for fires to be lighted, and after seeing that sentries were placed round the edge of the grove, Frank Mallett joined the officers who were gathered in the centre.

"What time shall we march tomorrow?" the officer in command of the native infantry asked.

"Not until the heat of the day is over. We have come about twelve miles, and have as much more to do; and if we start at the same hour as we did today we shall get there about nine. I shall halt half a mile away, reconnoitre the place at night, and if the ground is open enough to move without making a noise, we will post the troops in the positions they are to occupy, and attack as soon as day breaks.

"In that way we shall get the benefit of surprise, and at the same time have daylight to prevent their escaping. Besides, if we attacked at night a good many of the villagers, and perhaps women, might be killed in the confusion.

"Tomorrow morning we will cut down some young saplings and make a dozen scaling ladders. We have brought a bag of gunpowder to blow open the gate, and if the main body enter there while two parties scale the walls at other points we shall get them in a trap."

At about nine o'clock the next evening the guide said that they were now within half a mile of the village, and they accordingly halted. The men were ordered to keep silence, and to lie down and sleep as soon as they had eaten their supper; while Mallett, accompanied by the two officers of the native troops and the guide, made his way towards the village.

It was found to be larger than had been anticipated. On three sides cultivated fields extended to the foot of the strong wall that surrounded it, while on the fourth there was rough broken ground covered with scrub and brushes.

"How far does this extend?" Captain Mallett asked the guide.

"About half a mile, and then joins a big jungle, sahib."

"This is the side they will try to escape by; therefore, Mr. Herbert, you will lead your men round here with four scaling ladders. You will post them along at the foot of the wall, and when you hear the explosion of the powder bag or an outburst of musketry firing, you will scale the wall and advance to meet me, keeping as wide a front as possible, so as to prevent fugitives from passing you and getting out here. The cavalry will cut off those who make across the open country. I would give a good deal to know how many of these fellows are inside. Four hundred was the number first reported. They may, of course, have already moved away, and on the other hand they may have been joined by others. They were said to have some guns with them, but these will be of little use in the streets of the village, and we shall probably capture them before they have time to fire a single round."

At three o'clock the troops stood to their arms, and moved noiselessly off towards the positions assigned to them. Captain Mallett led his own company to within four hundred yards of the wall, and then sent Marshall forward with two men to fix the powder bag and fuse to the gate. When they had done this they were to remain quietly there until warned that the company was about to advance; then they were to light the fuse, which was cut to burn two minutes, to retire round the angle of the wall, and join the company as it came up. The troops lay down, for the ground was level, and there was no spot behind which they could conceal themselves, and impatiently watched the sky until the first gleam of light appeared. Another ten minutes elapsed. The dawn was spreading fast, and a man was sent forward to Lieutenant Marshall to say that the company was getting in motion.

As soon as the messenger was seen to reach the gates, Mallett gave the word. The men sprang to their feet.

"Don't double, men. We shall be there in time, and it is no use getting out of breath and spoiling your shooting."

They were within a hundred yards of the gate, when they heard a shout from the village, and as they pressed on, shot after shot rang out from the wall. A moment later there was a heavy explosion, and as the smoke cleared off, the gate was seen to be destroyed.

A few seconds later, the troops burst through the opening. Infantry bugles were sounding in the village, and there was a loud din of shouting, cries of alarm and orders. From every house the mutineers rushed, musket in hand, but were shot down or bayoneted by the troops. As the latter approached a large open space in the middle of the village a strong body of Sepoys advanced in good order to meet them, led by their native officers.

"Steady, men, steady," Captain Mallett shouted. "Form across the street."

Quickly the men fell in, though several dropped as a volley flashed out from the Sepoy line.

"One volley and then charge," Mallett shouted. Some of the guns were already empty, but the rest poured in their fire, when the word was given, as regularly as if on parade.

"Level bayonets—charge!" And with a loud cheer the soldiers sprang forward. The Sepoys, well commanded though they were, wavered and broke; but the British were upon them before they could fly, and with shouts of "Cawnpore," used their bayonets with deadly effect, driving the enemy before them.

As they came into the open, and the fugitives cleared away on either side, they saw a long line of men drawn up. A moment later a flash of fire ran along it.

"Shoulder to shoulder, men," Captain Mallett shouted. "Give them the bayonet."

With a hoarse roar of rage, for many of their comrades had fallen, the company rushed forward and burst through the line of mutineers as if it had been a sheet of paper. Then they divided, and Captain Mallett with half the company turned to the right. Marshall took the other wing to the left.

Encouraged by the smallness of the number of their assailants, the mutineers, cheered on by their officers, resisted stoutly. A scattering fire opened upon the British from the houses round, and the shouts of the mutineers rose louder and louder, when a heavy volley was suddenly poured into them, and the Punjaubies rushed out from the street facing that by which the British had entered. They bore to the right, and fell upon the body with which Marshall was engaged.

The Sepoys, taken wholly by surprise, at once lost heart. Cheering loudly, the British attacked them with increased ardour, while the Punjaubies flung themselves into their midst. In an instant, that flank of the Sepoys was scattered in headlong flight, hotly pursued by their foes. There was no firing, for the muskets were all empty; but the bayonet did its work, and the open space and the streets leading from it were thickly strewn with dead.

The Sepoys attacked by Captain Mallett's party, on the other hand, though shaken for a moment, stood firm; led by two or three native officers, who, fighting with the greatest bravery, exhorted their men to continue their resistance.

"Would you rather be hung than fight?" they shouted. "They are but a handful; we are five to one against them. Forward, men, and exterminate these Feringhees before the others can come back to their assistance."

The Sepoys were now the assailants, and with furious shouts pressed round the little body of British troops.

"Steady, men, steady," Captain Mallett shouted, as he drove his sword through the body of one of the rebel leaders who rushed at him. "Keep together, back to back. We shall have help here in a minute."

It was longer than that, however, before relief came. For three or four minutes a desperate struggle went on, then Marshall's voice was heard shouting:

"This way, men, this way!"

A moment later there was a surging movement in the ranks of the insurgents, and with a dozen men Marshall burst through them, and joined the party. These at once fell furiously upon the mutineers, and the latter were already giving way when some fifty of the Punjaubies, led by their officers, fell upon them.

The effect was decisive. The Sepoys scattered at once, and fled in all directions, pursued by the furious soldiers and the Punjaubies. Reaching the walls, the fugitives leapt recklessly down. Forty or fifty of them were cut down by the cavalry, but the greater portion reached the broken ground in safety. Here the cavalry could not follow them, for the ground was covered with rocks and boulders concealed by the bushes. In the village itself three hundred and fifty lay dead.

"Thanks, Marshall," Frank Mallett said, when the fight in the village was over. "You arrived just in time, for it was going very hard with us. Altogether it was more than we bargained for, for they were certainly over a thousand strong. They must have been joined by a very strong party yesterday."

"I ought not to have gone so far," Marshall replied, "but I had no idea that all the Punjaubies had come to our side of the fight. The men were so eager that I had the greatest difficulty in getting them off the pursuit. Fortunately I met Herbert, and learned that all his men were with us. Then I gathered a dozen of our fellows, and rushed off, telling him to follow as soon as he could get some of his men together.

"You can imagine what agony I felt when, as I entered the open space, I saw a surging mass of Sepoys, and no sign of any of you; and how I cursed my own folly, and what delight I felt, as on cutting our way through we found that you were still on your feet."

"Yes, it was a close shave, Marshall; another two or three minutes and it would have been all over. The men fought like lions, as you can see by the piled-up dead there. Half of them were down, and twenty men cannot hold out long against four or five hundred.

"We owe our lives to you beyond all question. I don't see that you were in the least to blame in the matter, for naturally you would suppose that some of the Punjaubies would have joined us. Besides, it was of course essential that you should not give the Sepoys time to rally, but should follow them up hotly.

"Where is Anstruther?"

"I don't know. I have not seen him since we entered the square."

"Have any of you seen Mr. Anstruther?" Captain Mallett asked, turning to some soldiers standing near.

"He is lying over there, sir," one of the men said. "He was just in front of me when the Pandies fired that volley at us as we came out of the streets, and he pitched forward and fell like a stone. I think that he was shot through the head, sir."

They went across to the spot. The ensign lay there shot through the brain. Four or five soldiers lay round him; one of them was dead, the others more or less seriously wounded.

"Sound the assembly," Captain Mallett said, as he turned away sadly, to a bugler. "Let us see what our losses are."

Chapter 4

The bugle sounded, and in a short time the infantry fell in. They had been engaged in searching the houses for mutineers. The Punjaubies had lost but five killed and thirteen wounded, while of the whites an officer and eighteen men were killed and sixteen wounded; nine of the former having fallen in the bayonet struggle with the Sepoys. Nine guns were captured, none of which had been fired, the attack having been so sudden that the Sepoys had only had time to fall in before their assailants were upon them.

"It is a creditable victory," Mallett said, "considering that we had to face more than double the number that we expected. Our casualties are heavy, but they are nothing to those of the mutineers.

"Sergeant, take a file of men and go round and count the number of the enemy who have fallen.

"Ah, here comes a Sowar, and we shall hear what the cavalry have been doing outside."

The trooper handed him a paper: "Fifty-three of the enemy killed, the rest escaped into the jungle. On our side two wounded; one seriously, one slightly."

"That is as well as we could expect, Marshall. Of course, most of them got over the wall at the back. You see, all our plans were disarranged by finding them in such unexpected strength. Had we been able to thrash them by ourselves, the Punjaubies would have cut off the retreat in that direction. As it was, that part of the business is a failure."

The Sergeant presently returned.

"There are 340 in the streets, sir," he reported; "and I reckon there are another 20 or 30 killed in the houses, but I have not searched them yet."

"That is sufficiently close; upwards of 400 is good enough.

"Now, Mr. Marshall, set the men to work making stretchers to carry the wounded.

"Mr. Herbert, will you tell off a party of your men to dig a large grave outside the village for the killed, and a small one apart for Mr. Anstruther? Poor fellow, I am sorry indeed at his loss; he would have made a fine officer.

"Sergeant Hugging, take a party and search the village for provisions. We have got bread, but lay hands on any fowls or goats that you can find, and there may be some sheep."

While this party was away, another tore down the woodwork of an empty house, and fires were soon burning, an abundance of fowl and goats having been obtained. The cavalry had by this time come in.

While the meal was being cooked the British and Punjaub dead were carried out to the spot where the grave had been dug. The troops had a hearty meal, and then marched out from the village. They were drawn up round the graves, and the bodies were laid reverently in them. Captain Mallett said a few words over them; the earth was then shovelled in and levelled, and the troops marched to a wood a mile distant, where they halted until the heat of the day was over. They returned by the direct road to the camp, which they reached at midnight.

All concerned gained great credit for the heavy blow that had been inflicted on the mutineers, and the affair was highly spoken of in the Brigadier's report to the Commander in Chief. Shortly afterwards Mallett's name appeared in general orders as promoted to a brevet Majority, pending a confirmation by the home authorities.

Two days after the return of the little column, the brigade marched and joined the force collected at Cawnpore for the final operation against Lucknow, and on the 3rd of March reached the Commander in Chief at the Dil Koosha, which had been captured with the same ease as on the occasion of the former advance.

They found that while the main body had gathered there, 6,000 men under Sir James Outram had crossed the Goomtee from the Alum Bagh, and, after defeating two serious attacks by the enemy, had taken up a position at Chinhut. On the 9th, Sir Colin Campbell captured the Martiniere with trifling loss. On the 11th General Outram pushed his advance as far as the iron bridge, and established batteries commanding the passage of the stone bridge also. On the 12th the Imambarra was breached and stormed, and the troops pressed so hotly on the flying enemy that they entered the Kaiser Bagh, the strongest fortified palace in the city, and drove the enemy from it.

The —th was engaged in this action, and Major Mallett was leading his company to the assault on the Imambarra when a shot brought him to the ground. When he recovered his senses he found himself in a chamber that had been hastily converted into a hospital, with the regimental doctor leaning over him.

"What has happened?" he asked.

"You have been hit, Mallett, and have had a very close shave of it, indeed; but as it is, you will soon be about again."

"Where was I hit? I don't feel any pain."

"You were hit in the neck, about half an inch above the collarbone, and the ball has gone through the muscles of the neck; and beyond the fact that you won't be able to turn your head for some time, you will be none the worse for it. An inch further to the right, or an inch lower or higher, and it would have been fatal. It was not one of the enemy who did you this service, for the ball went up from behind, and came out in front; it is evidently a random shot from one of our own fellows."

"I am always more afraid of a shot from behind than I am of one in front when I am leading the company, doctor. The men get so excited that they blaze away anyhow, and in the smoke are just as likely to hit an officer two or three paces ahead of them as an enemy. How long have I been insensible?"

"You were brought in here half an hour ago, and I don't suppose that you had lain many minutes on the ground before you were picked up."

"Have we taken the Imambarra?"

"Yes, and what is better still, our fellows rushed into the Kaiser Bagh at the heels of the enemy. We got the news ten minutes ago."

"That is good indeed. We anticipated desperate fighting before we took that."

"Yes, it was an unlucky shot, Mallett, that knocked you out of your share in the loot. We have always heard that the place was full of treasure and jewels."

"If there is no one else who wants your attention, doctor, I advise you to join the regiment there for an hour or two. As for me, I care nothing about the loot. There are plenty of fellows who will benefit by it more than I should, and I give up my share willingly."

The doctor shook his head.

"I am afraid I cannot do that; but, between ourselves, I have let Ferguson slip away, and he is to divide what he gets with me."

"Have we any wounded?"

"I don't know yet. The whole thing was done so suddenly that the loss cannot have been heavy. I was in the rear of the brigade when you were brought in, and as the case at first looked bad, I got some of the stretcher men with me to burst open the door of this house and established a dozen temporary beds here. As you see, there are only four others tenanted, and they are all hopeless cases. No doubt the rest have all been carried off to the rear, as only the men who helped me would have known of this place.

"Now that you have come round, I will send a couple of hospital orderlies in here and be off myself to the hospital in the rear. I will look in again this evening."

In a short time the doctor returned with an orderly.

"I cannot find another now," he said, "but one will be enough. Here is a flask of brandy, and he will find you water somewhere. There is nothing to be done for any of you at present, except to give you drink when you want it."

Two hours later Marshall came in.

"Thank God you are not dangerously hurt, Mallett," he said. "I only heard that you were down three-quarters of an hour ago, when I ran against Armstrong in the Kaiser Bagh. He told me that he had seen you fall at the beginning of the fight, and I got leave from the Colonel to look for you. At the hospital, no one seemed to know anything about you, but I luckily came across Jefferies, who told me where to find you, and that your wound was not serious, so I hurried back here. He said that you would be taken to the hospital this evening."

"Yes, I am in luck again. Like the last it is only a flesh wound, though it is rather worse, for I expect that I shall have to go about with a stiff neck for some weeks to come, and it is disgusting being laid up in the middle of an affair like this. Have we lost many fellows?"

"No. Scobell is the only officer killed. Hunter, Groves and Parkinson are wounded—Parkinson, they say, seriously. We have twenty-two rank and file killed, and twenty or thirty wounded. I have not seen the returns."

"And how about the loot, Marshall?" Mallett said, with a smile. "Was that all humbug?"

"It is stupendous. We were among the first at the Kaiser Bagh, and I don't believe that there is a man who has not got his pockets stuffed with gold coins. There were chests and chests full. They did not bother about the jewels—I think they took them for coloured glass. I kept my eyes open, and picked up enough to pay my debt to you five times over."

"I am heartily glad of that, Marshall. Don't let it slip through your fingers again."

"That you may be sure I won't. I shall send them all home to our agent to sell, and have the money put by for purchasing my next step. I have had my lesson, and it will last me for life.

"Well, I must be going now, old man. The Colonel did not like letting me go, as of course the men want looking after, and the Pandies may make an effort to drive us out of the Kaiser Bagh again; so goodbye. If I can get away this evening I will come to see you at the hospital."

A week later Frank Mallett was sitting in a chair by his bedside. The fighting was all over, and a strange quiet had succeeded the long roar of battle. His neck was strapped up with bandages, and save that he was unable to move his head in the slightest degree, he felt well enough to take his place with the regiment again. Many of his fellow officers dropped in from time to time for a short chat, but the duty was heavy. All open resistance had ceased, but the troops were engaged in searching the houses, and turning out all rough characters who had made Lucknow their centre, and had no visible means of subsistence. Large gangs of the lower class population were set to work to bury the dead, which would otherwise have rendered the city uninhabitable. Strong guards were posted at night, alike to prevent soldiers from wandering in search of loot and to prevent fanatics from making sudden attacks.

"There is a wounded man in the hospital across the road who wants to see you, Mallett," the surgeon said one morning. "He belongs to your company, but as he only came out with the last draft, and was transferred only on the day that the fighting began, I don't suppose you know him. He said I was to tell you his name was George Lechmere, though he enlisted as John Hilton."

"I seem to know the name, doctor, though I don't remember at present where I came across him. I suppose I can go in to see him?"

"Oh, yes, there is no objection whatever. Your wound is doing as well as can be; though, of course, you are still weak from loss of blood. I shall send you up this afternoon to the hospital just established in the park of the Dil Koosha. We shall get you all out as soon as we can, for the stench of this town at present is dreadful, and wounds cannot be expected to do well in such a poisoned atmosphere."

"Is this man badly hit, doctor?"

"Very dangerously. I have scarcely a hope of saving him, and think it probable that he may not live another twenty-four hours. Of course, he may take a change for the better. I will take you to him. I have finished here now."

"It must have been a bad time for you, doctor," Mallett said, as they went across.

"Tremendously hard, but most interesting. I had not had more than two hours' sleep at a time since the fighting began, till last night, and then I could not keep up any longer. Of course, it has been the same with us all, and the heat has made it very trying. I am particularly anxious to get the wounded well out of the place, for now that the excitement is over I expect an outbreak of fever or dysentery.

"There, that is your man in the corner bed over there."

Mallett went over to the bedside, and looked at the wounded man. His face was drawn and pinched, his eyes sunken in his head, his face deadly pale, and his hair matted with perspiration.

"Do you know me, Captain Mallett?"

"No, lad, I cannot say that I do, though when the doctor told me your name it seemed familiar to me. Very likely I should have recognised you if I had met you a week since, but, you see, we are both altered a good deal from the effect of our wounds."

"I am the son of Farmer Lechmere, your tenant."

"Good heavens! man. You don't mean to say you are Lechmere's eldest son, George! What in the world brought you to this?"

"You did," the man said, sternly. "Your villainy brought me here."

Frank Mallett gave a start of astonishment that cost him so violent a twinge in his wound that he almost cried out with sudden pain.

"What wild idea have you got into your head, my poor fellow?" he said soothingly. "I am conscious of having done no wrong to you or yours. I saw your father and mother on the afternoon before I came away. They made no complaint of anything."

"No, they were contented enough. Do you know, Captain Mallett, that I loved Martha Bennett?"

"No. I have been so little at home of recent years that I know very little of the private affairs of my tenants, but I remember her, of course, and I was grieved to learn by a letter from Sir John Greendale the other day that in some strange way she was missing."

"Who knew that better than yourself?" the man said, raising himself on his elbow, and fixing a look of such deadly hatred upon Mallett, that the latter involuntarily drew back a step.

"I saw you laughing and talking to her in front of her father's house. I heard you with her in their garden the evening before you left and she disappeared, and it was my voice you heard in the lane. Had I known that you were going that night, I would have followed you and killed you, and saved her. The next morning you were both gone. I waited a time and then went to the depot of your regiment and enlisted. I had failed to save her, but at least I could avenge her. That bullet was mine, and had you not stumbled over a Pandy's body, I suppose, just as I pulled my trigger, you would have been a dead man.

"I did not know that I had failed, and, rushing forward with my company, was in the thickest of the fight. I wanted to be killed, but no shot struck me, and at last, when chasing a Pandy along a passage in the Kaiser Bagh, he turned and levelled his piece at me. Mine was loaded, and I could have shot him down as he turned, but I stood and let him have his shot. When I found myself here I was sorry that he had not finished me at once, but when I heard that you were alive, and likely to recover, I thanked him in my heart that he had left me a few more days of life, that I could let you know that it was I who had fired, and that Martha's wrong had not been wholly unavenged."

He sank back exhausted on to the pillow. Frank Mallett had made no attempt to interrupt him: the sudden agony of his wound and his astonishment at this strange accusation had given him so grave a shock that he leaned against the wall behind him in silent wonder.

"Hello! Mallett, what the deuce is the matter with you?" the surgeon exclaimed, as, looking up from a patient over whom he was bending a short distance away, his eyes fell on the officer's face. "You look as if you were going to faint, man.

"Here, orderly, some brandy and water, quickly!"

Frank drank some of the brandy and water and sat down for a few minutes. Then, when he saw the surgeon at the other end of the room, he got up and went across to Lechmere's bed.

"There is some terrible mistake, Lechmere," he said, quietly. "I swear to you on my honour as a gentleman that you are altogether wrong. From the moment that I got into my dog cart at Bennett's I never saw Martha again. I know nothing whatever of this talk in the garden. Did you think you saw me as well as heard me?"

"No, you were on one side of that high wall and I on the other, but I heard enough to know who it was. You told her that you had to go abroad at once, but that if she would come out there you would put her in charge of someone until you could marry her. You told her that she could not stay where she was long, and I knew what that meant. I suppose she is at Calcutta still waiting, for of course she could not have come out with you. I suppose that she is breaking her heart there now—if she is not dead, as I hope she is."

"Did you hear the word Calcutta or India mentioned, Lechmere?"

"No, I did not, but I heard quite enough. Everyone knew that you were going in a day or two, and that was enough for me after what I had seen in the afternoon."

"You saw nothing in the afternoon," Captain Mallett said, angrily. "The girl's father and mother were at home. We were all chatting together until we came out. She came to the trap with me while they stood at the open window. It was not more than a minute before I drove off. I have not spoken to the girl half a dozen times since she was a little child.

"Why, man, if everyone took such insane fancies in his head as you do, no man would dare to speak to a woman at all.

"However," he went on in an altered voice, "this is not a time for anger. You are very ill, Lechmere, but the doctor has not given you up, and I trust that you will yet get round and will be able to prove to your own satisfaction that, whatever has happened to this poor girl, I, at least, am wholly innocent of it. But should you not get over this hurt, I should not like you to go to your grave believing that I had done you this great wrong. I speak to you as to a dying man, and having no interest in deceiving you, and I swear to you before Heaven that I know absolutely nothing of this. I, too, may fall from a rebel shot before long, and I thank God that I can meet you before Him as an innocent man in this matter.

"I must be going, for I see the doctor coming to fetch me. Goodbye, lad, we may not meet again, though I trust we shall; but if not, I give you my full forgiveness for that shot you fired at me. It was the result of a strange mistake, but had I acted as you believed, I should have well deserved the death you intended for me."

"Confound it, Mallett, there seems no end of mischief from your visit here. In the first place, you were nearly knocked over yourself, and now there is this man lying insensible. So for goodness' sake get off to your room again, and lie down and keep yourself quiet for the rest of the day. I shall have you demoralising the whole ward if you stay here."

Captain Mallett walked back with a much feebler and less steady step than that with which he had entered the hospital. He had some doubts whether the man who had made this strange accusation and had so nearly taken his life was really sane, and whether he had not altogether imagined the conversation which he declared he had heard in the garden. He remembered now the sudden way in which George Lechmere had turned round and gone away when he saw him saying goodbye to Martha, and how she had shrugged her shoulders in contempt.

The man must either be mad, or of a frightfully jealous disposition, to conjure up harm out of such an incident: and one who would do so might well, when his brain was on fire, conjure up this imaginary conversation. Still, he might have heard some man talking to her. From what Sir John had said, she did leave the house and go into the garden about that hour, and she certainly never returned.

He remembered all about George Lechmere now. He had the reputation of being the best judge of cattle in the neighbourhood, and a thoroughly steady fellow, but he could see no resemblance in the shrunk and wasted face to that he remembered.

That evening both the officers and men in the hospital were carried away to the new one outside the town. When the doctor came in before they were moved, he told Mallett that the man he had seen had recovered from his swoon.

"He was very nearly gone," he said, "but we managed to get him round, and it seems to me that he has been better since. I don't know what he said to you or you to him, and I don't want to know; but he seems to have got something off his mind. He is less feverish than he was, and I have really some faint hopes of pulling him through, especially as he will now be in a more healthful atmosphere."

It was a comfort indeed to all the wounded when late that evening they lay on beds in the hospital marquees. The air seemed deliciously cool and fresh, and there was a feeling of quiet and restfulness that was impossible in the town, with the constant movement of troops, the sound of falling masonry, the dust and fetid odour of decay.

A week later the surgeon told Mallett that he had now hopes that the soldier he was interested in would recover.

"The chances were a hundred to one against him," he said, "but the one chance has come off."

"Will he be fit for service again, doctor?"

"Yes, I don't see why he should not be, though it will be a long time before he can carry his kit and arms on a long day's march. It is hot enough now, but we have not got to the worst by a long way, and as there is still a vast amount of work to be done, I expect that the regiment will be off again before long."

"Well, at any rate, I shall be able to go with you, doctor."

"I don't quite say that, Mallett," the doctor said, doubtfully. "In another fortnight your wound will be healed so that you will be capable of ordinary duty, but certainly not long marches. If you do go you will have to ride. There must be no more marching with your company for some time."

A week later orders were issued, under which the regiment was appointed to form part of the force which, under the command of General Walpole, was to undertake a campaign against Rohilcund, a district in which the great majority of the rebels who had escaped from Lucknow had now established themselves. Unfortunately, the extent of the city and the necessity for the employment of a large proportion of the British force in the actual assault, had prevented anything like a complete investment of the town, and the consequence had been that after the fall of the Kaiser Bagh, by far the greater portion of the rebel force in the city had been able to march away without molestation.

Before leaving, Mallett had an interview with George Lechmere, who was now out of danger.

"I should have known you now, Lechmere," he said, as he came to his bedside. "Of course you are still greatly changed, but you are getting back your old expression, and I hope that in the course of two or three months you will be able to take your place in the ranks again."

"I don't know, sir. I ain't fit to stay with the regiment, and have thought of being invalided home and then buying my discharge. I know you have said nothing as to how you got that wound, not even to the doctor; for if you had done so there is not a man in hospital who would have spoken to me. But how could I join the regiment again? knowing that if there was any suspicion of what I had done, every man would draw away from me, and that there would be nothing for me to do but to put a bullet in my head."

"But no one ever will know it. It was a mad act, and I believe you were partly mad at the time."

"I think so myself now that I look back. I think now that I must have been mad all along. It never once entered my mind to doubt that it was you, and now I see plainly enough that except what the man said about going away—and anyone might have said that—there was not a shadow of ground or suspicion against you. But even if I had never had that suspicion I should have left home.

"Why, sir, I know that my own father and mother suspected that I killed her. I resented it at the time. I felt hard and bitter against it, but as I have been lying here I have come to see that I brought their suspicions upon myself by my own conduct, and that they had a thousand times better ground for suspecting me than I had for suspecting you.

"All that happened was my fault. Martha cared for me once, but it was my cursed jealousy that drove her from me. She was gay and light hearted, and it was natural for her to take her pleasure, which was harmless enough if I had not made a grievance of it. If I had not driven her from me she would have been my wife long before harm came to her; but it was as well that it was not so, for as I was then I know I should have made her life a hell.

"I did it all and I have been punished for it. Even at the end she might never have gone off if I had not shouted out and tried to climb the wall. She must have recognised my voice, and, knowing that I had her secret, feared that I might kill her and him too, and so she went. She would not have gone as she did, without even a bonnet or a shawl, if it had not been for that."

"Then you don't think, as most people there do, that she was murdered?"

"Not a bit, sir. I never thought so for a moment. She went straight away with that man. I think now I know who it was."

"Never mind about that, Lechmere. You know what the Bible says, 'Vengeance is mine, saith the Lord,' and whoever it may be, leave him safely in God's hands."

"Yes, sir, I shall try to act up to that. I was fool enough to think that I could avenge her, and a nice business I made of it."

"Well, I think it is nonsense of you to think of leaving the regiment. There is work to be done here. There is the work of punishing men who have committed the most atrocious crimes. There is the work of winning back India for England. Every Englishman out here, who can carry a weapon, ought to remain at his post until the work is done.

"As to this wound of mine, that is a matter between us only. As I have told you, I have altogether forgiven you, and am not even disposed greatly to blame you, thinking, as you did, that I was responsible for that poor girl's flight. I shall never mention it to a soul. I have already put it out of my mind, therefore it is as if it had never been done, and there is no reason whatever why you should shrink from companionship with your comrades. I shall think much better of you for doing your duty like a man, than if you went home again and shrank from it."

"You are too good, sir, altogether too good."

"Nonsense, man. Besides, you have to remember that you have not gone unpunished. Had it not been for your feeling, after you had, as you believed, killed me, you never would have stood and let that Sepoy shoot you; so that all the pain that you have been going through, and may still have to go through before you are quite cured, is a punishment that you have yourself accepted. After a man has once been punished for a crime there is an end of it, and you need grieve no further over it; but it will be a lesson that I hope and believe you will never forget.

"Hackett, who has been my soldier servant for the last five years, was killed in the fight in the Kaiser Bagh. If you like, when you rejoin, I shall apply for you in his stead. It will make your work a good deal easier for you, and I should like to have the son of one of my old tenants about me."

The man burst into tears.

"There, don't let's say anything more about it," Mallett went on, taking the thin hand of the soldier in his. "We will consider it settled, and I shall look out for you in a couple of months, so get well as quick as you can, and don't worry yourself by thinking of the past. I must be off now, for I have to take down a party of convalescents to rejoin this evening.

"Goodbye, lad," and without waiting for any reply, he turned and left the marquee.

Chapter 5

"It is little more than two years and a half since I left, Lechmere, but it seems almost a lifetime."

"It does seem a time, Major. We must have marched thousands of miles, and I could not say how many times we have been engaged. There has not been a week that we have not had a fight, and sometimes two or three of them."

"Well, thank God, we are back again. Still I am glad to have been through it."

"So am I, sir. It will be something to look back on, and it is curious to think that while we have been seeing and doing so much, father and my brother Bob have just been going about over the farm, and seeing to the cattle, and looking after the animals day in and day out, without ever going away save to market two or three times a month at Chippenham."

"And you have quite made up your mind to stay with me, Lechmere?"

"Quite, sir. Short of your turning me out, there is nothing that would get me away from you. No one could be happier than I have been, ever since I rejoined after that wound. It has not been like master and servant, sir. You have just treated me as if you had been the squire and I had been your tenant's son, and that nothing had ever come between us. You have made a man of me again, and I only wish that I had more opportunities of showing you how I feel it."

"You have had opportunities enough, and you have made the most of them. You were by my side when I entered that house where there were a score of desperate rebels, and it would have gone hard with us if aid had not come up. You stood over me when I was knocked down by that charge of rebel cavalry, and got half a dozen wounds before the Hussars swept down and drove them back."

"I was well paid for that, sir," the man said with a smile.

"Yes, you got the Victoria Cross, and no man ever won it more fairly. But, after all, it was not so much by such things as these that you showed your feelings, Lechmere, as by your constant and faithful service, and by the care with which you looked after me. Still, as I told you before, I don't like standing in your way. In the natural course of things you would have had your father's farm, and there is now no reason why you should not go back there."

"No, sir. Since we heard that that poor girl came back home and died, there is no reason why I should not go back to the old place, but I don't like to. Two years of such a life as we have been leading does not fit one for farm work. Brother Bob stopped and took my place while I went soldiering, and even if I were willing to go back to it, which I am not, it would not be fair to him for me to step in just as if nothing had happened. But, anyhow, I shall be glad to be back again at the old place and see them all. Father and mother will know now that they suspected me wrongly. But they were not to blame. Mad as I was then, I might have done it if I had had the chance."

"Well, Lechmere, you know well that I shall be always glad to have you with me as long as you are willing to stay. Perhaps the time will come when you may wish to make a home for yourself, and you may be sure that the first farm on the estate that falls vacant shall be yours, or, as that does not very often happen, I will see that you get a good one somewhere in the neighbourhood."

The man shook his head, and without answering went on unpack.ng his master's portmanteau. They were at the Hummums Hotel, in Covent Garden, and had arrived half an hour before by the evening train, having come overland from Marseilles.

Two years' soldiering had greatly altered George Lechmere. He had lost the heavy step caused by tramping over ploughed fields, and was a well set-up, alert and smart-looking soldier; and although now in civilian clothes—for his master had bought him out of the service when he sent in his own papers—no one could avoid seeing that he had served, for in addition to the military carriage there was the evidence of two deep scars on his face, the handiwork of the mutineers' sabres on the day when he had stood over his master surrounded by rebel horse. His complexion was deeply bronzed by the sun, and there was that steady but watchful expression in his eyes that is characteristic of men who have gone through long and dangerous service.

"I shall stay two or three days in town," Major Mallett said. "I must get an entire refit before I go down. You had better come round with me to the tailor's tomorrow, the first thing after breakfast. You will want three or four suits, too."

"Yes, sir. And besides, they would like to know down there when you are coming home. They are sure to want to give you a welcome."

"And you, too, Lechmere. I am sure that all your old friends will give you as hearty a welcome as they will give me. Indeed, it ought to be a good deal heartier, for you have been living among them all your life, while I have been away for the most part ever since I was a boy."

Four days later they went down to Chippenham. Mr. Norton, the steward, was on the platform when the train came in.

"Welcome home again, sir," he said warmly, as Frank stepped from the carriage. "We were all glad, indeed, when we heard that you were back safe, and were coming down among us."

"I am glad enough to be back again, Norton," Frank Mallett said; as he shook the man's hand. "We had warm work of it for a bit, but at the end, when the excitement was over, one got pretty tired of it.

"This is George Lechmere, Norton," the Major said, as he went along with the agent to where George was standing with the pile of luggage. "You have heard how gallantly he behaved, and how he saved my life at the risk of his own."

"How are you, George?" the agent said, as he shook hands with him. "I should hardly have known you. Indeed, I am sure I should not have done so if I had met you in the street. You seem to have grown taller and altogether different."

"I have lost flesh a bit, Mr. Norton, and I have learnt to stand upright, and I shall be some time before I get rid of this paint the sun has given me."

"Yes, you are as brown as a berry, George. We saw in the gazette about your getting the Victoria Cross in saving the squire's life. I can tell you every man on the estate felt proud of you.

"Are you ready to be off, sir?"

"Yes. I suppose you have got the dog cart outside, as I asked you?"

"Well, no, sir," the agent said, in a tone of some embarrassment. "You see the tenants had made up their minds that you ought to come in a different sort of style, and so without asking me about it they ordered an open carriage to be here to meet you. I knew nothing about it until last night. The dog cart is here and will take up your luggage."

"Well, I suppose it cannot be helped," Mallett laughed. "Of course, they meant it kindly."

"I will see the luggage got in the dog cart, and come over with it," Lechmere said.

"You can see it into the dog cart, George, but you must come with me. I have got to put up with it, and you must, too."

He stood chatting with Mr. Norton on the platform till George returned, and said that the luggage was all packed, and that the dog cart had gone on ahead. There was an amused look on his face, which was explained when, on going out, Mallett found an open carriage with four horses, with postilions in new purple silk jackets and orange caps, and large rosettes of the same colour at the horses' heads.

"Bless me," said the Major, in a tone of dismay. "I shall feel as if I were a candidate for the county."

"They are the family colours, you see, sir."

"Yes, I know, Norton, and the Conservative colours, too. Well, it cannot be helped, and it does not make much difference after all.

"There will be no fuss when I get there I hope, Norton," he went on, as he took his place, and Lechmere climbed up into the seat behind.

"Well, sir," the agent said, apologetically, "there is an arch or two. You see, the tenants wanted to do the thing properly, and the school children will be on the lawn, and there are going to be some bonfires in the evening, and they have got a big box of fireworks down from London. Why, sir, it would be strange if they did not give you a welcome after going through all that, and being wounded three times and getting so much credit. Why, it wouldn't be English, sir."

"I suppose it's all right," Mallett said, resignedly; "and, indeed, Norton, one cannot help being pleased at seeing one's tenants glad to have one home again."

In half-an-hour's drive they arrived at the boundary of the estate. Here an arch had been erected, and a score of the tenants and tenants' sons, assembled on horseback, gave a loud cheer as the carriage drove up, and as it died away one shouted:

"Why, that is George Lechmere behind. Give him a cheer, too!" and again a hearty shout went up.

The carriage stopped, and Major Mallett said a few words, thanking them heartily for the welcome they had given him, and assuring them what pleasure it was to him to be back again.

"I thank you, also," he concluded, "for the cheer that you have given to my faithful comrade and friend, George Lechmere. As you all know, he saved my life at the risk of his own, and has received the greatest honour a soldier can gain—the Victoria Cross. You have a good right to be proud of him, as one of yourselves, and to give him a hearty welcome."

The carriage then drove on again, the farmers riding close behind as an escort. At the entrance of the drive up to the house another and larger arch had been erected. Here the rest of the tenants and the women were collected, and there was another hearty greeting, and another speech from Mallett.

Then they drove up to the house, where a number of the gentry had assembled to welcome him. After shaking hands and chatting with these for a short time, Frank went round among the tenants, saying a few words to each. When he had done this he invited them all to a dinner on the lawn that day week, and then went into the house, where the steward had prepared a meal.

Among the familiar faces, Frank missed those he would most gladly have seen. He had a year before received a letter from Lady Greendale, telling him of Sir John's sudden death, and had learned from the steward during the drive that she and her daughter were in London.

"They went there a month ago," he said. "A year had passed after Sir John's death, and people say that it is not likely that they will be much at home again for some time. Lady Greendale has high connections in London, as you know, sir."

"Yes, she was a daughter of Lord Huntinglen, Norton."

"Yes, sir. They always went up to town for the season; and they say Lady Greendale liked London better than the country; and now that Miss Bertha is out—for she was presented at Court a fortnight ago—people think they won't be much down at Greendale for the present."

"Has Miss Greendale grown up pretty? I thought she would, but, of course, when I went away she was only a girl, not fully developed."

"She is a beautiful young lady, sir. Everyone says she is quite the belle of the county. Folks reckon she will make a great match. She is very well liked, too; pleasant and nice without a bit of pride about her, and very high spirited; and, I should say, full of fun, though of course the place has been pretty well shut up for the last year. For four months after Sir John's death they went away travelling, and were only at home for a few weeks before they went up to London the other day, in time for the first Drawing Room."

"I suppose we shall not see much of you for a time, Mallett?" one of his friends said, as they sat at luncheon.

"No, I don't suppose I shall be able to settle down for a bit. After the life I have led, I am afraid that I shall find the time hang heavily on my hands, alone here."

"You must bring home a wife, Major Mallett," one of the ladies said.

"That is looking quite into the dim future, Mrs. Herbert," he laughed. "You see, since I first went on active service I have been removed altogether from feminine attractions. Of course I have been thinking it over, but for the present my inclination turns towards yachting. I have always been fond of the water, and had a strong wish to go to sea when I was a boy, but that aspiration was not encouraged. However, I can follow my bent now. Norton has been piling up money for me in my absence, and I can afford myself the luxury of a big yacht. Of course I shall be in no hurry about it. I shall either build or buy a biggish craft, for racing in summer, and cruising in winter."

"That means that you won't be here at all, Major Mallett."

"Oh, no, it does not mean that, I can assure you. I shall run down for a month three or four times a year; say for shooting in September or October, and for hunting a month or two later on; besides, I have to renew my acquaintance with my tenants and see that everything is going on comfortably. I expect that I shall spend four or five months every year on the estate."

"Till you settle down for good?"

"Yes, till I settle down for good," he laughed. "I suppose it will have to be someday."

"Then you don't think of passing much time in London, Mallett?"

"No, indeed. Fortunately my father sold his town house three years ago. He did not care about going up, and of course it was of no use to me. I have never had any opportunities for society, and my present idea is that it would bore me horribly. But I'll dare say that I shall be there for a month or so in the season.

"Of course, there is my club to go to, and plenty of men one knows; but even if I had a longing for society, I know no one in what are termed fashionable circles, and so should be outside what is called the world."

"Oh, you would soon get over that, Major Mallett. Why, Lady Greendale would introduce you everywhere."

"It is not likely I shall trouble her to do that," Mallett answered.

Frank had told George Lechmere that, as soon as they arrived, he would be at liberty to go off at once to his father and mother.

the house, an unusual thing at that time of day with the former, but he had said at breakfast to his son:

"You must look after things by yourself today, lad. The Squire said yesterday that he would come over sometime, and I would not be out when he came, not for a twenty pound note."

He and his wife came to the door when they saw Frank coming across the field towards the house.

"Well, Lechmere," the latter said, when he came up. "I am glad to see you and your dame looking so well and hearty. I had not time to say more than a word to you yesterday, and I wanted to have a comfortable talk with you both. I wrote you a line telling you how gallantly George had behaved, and how he had saved my life; but I had to write the day afterwards, and my head was still ringing from the sabre cut that had for a time knocked all the sense out of me, and therefore I had to cut it very short. How gallantly he defended my life against a dozen of the enemy's cavalry was shown by the fact that he received the Victoria Cross, and I can tell you that such an immense number of brave deeds were performed during the Mutiny that George's must be considered an extraordinary act of bravery to have obtained for him that honour."

By this time they had entered the farmhouse parlour. George had not followed them in, but on inquiring where he was likely to find Bob, had gone off to join him.

"I was proud to hear it at the time, Squire; and when it was in the papers that our George had got the Victoria Cross, and all our neighbours came in to congratulate us, we felt prouder still. Up to the time when we got your letter, we did not know for sure where he was. He had said he meant to enlist, and from the humour that he was in when he went away we guessed it to be in some regiment where he could get to the wars. We felt the more glad, as you may guess, from the fact that both the Missus and I had wronged him in our thoughts. We learnt that before we got the news, and it was not until we knew that we had been wrong that either of us opened our lips about it, though each of us knew what the other thought."

"I know what you mean, Lechmere. He told me all about it."

"Well, Squire, you may be sure, when we knew that we had wronged him, how the wife and I fretted that we did not know where to write to, nor how to set about finding out where he was, and so you can guess how pleased we were when we heard from you that he was with your regiment, and that he had saved your life at the risk of his own.

"You are not likely to meet him here, Squire. A year ago he happened to be over at Chippenham one market day. There were a dozen of us there, and I can tell you we gave him such a reception that he mounted his horse and rode straight on again. If he hadn't, I believe that we should have horsewhipped him through the town. Three months afterwards his estate was put up for sale, and he has never been down in this part of the country since; not that he was ever here much before. London suited him better. You see, his mother was, as I have heard, the daughter of a banker, and an only child; and even if he hadn't had the estate he would have been a rich man. Anyhow, I am heartily glad that he has left the county."

"I, too, am glad that he has gone, Lechmere. I have not met him for years, but if we had both been down here we must have run against each other sometimes, and after some matters that had passed between us years ago we could scarcely have met on friendly terms. However, as there is nothing beyond mere suspicion against him, he may in this case be innocent. You see, I was suspected unjustly myself, and the same thing may be the case with him."

"That is so, Squire; though I don't think that there is any mistake this time. In fact, I believe she told her mother, though she kept it from her father for fear he would break the law. At any rate, it is a good thing he has gone; for he was a hard landlord, and there was not a good word for him among his tenants."

"That makes the probability of a mistake all the more likely," Frank said. "If I, who as a landlord, as far as I know, have given no grounds for dislike to my tenants, was suspected unjustly; this would be still more likely to be the case with one who was generally unpopular.

"And now, how has the farm been going on since I was away?"

"Just about as usual, Squire. Bob is not such a good judge of horses and cattle as George was, but in other respects I think he knows more. George did not care for reading, and Bob is always at the papers and getting up the last things these scientific chaps have found out; so matters are pretty well squared. Altogether, I have no call to grumble, and I ain't likely, Squire, to have to ask for time on rent day. We were worried sorely about George as long as that matter hung over him; but since that was cleared up, and we heard of his having saved your life, we have been happy again. We got a big shock yesterday, however, when we heard what had happened out there."

"Well, that is all past and over long ago, and we have none of us any cause to regret it. It has done George a great deal of good, and as for me, I might not be here now talking to you if it had not taken place, for it was the memory of that which led George to the desperate action which saved my life. Besides, you see, it has gained for me an attached and faithful friend, for it is as a friend rather than as a servant that I regard your son."

"He will always be that, I am sure, Squire. He told us that you had offered to set him up on a farm, but he is quite right to say no. I don't say that if it had been with somebody else, his mother and I might not have felt rather sore that our eldest boy should have taken to service; but, of course, it is different with you, Squire. It is only natural that a Lechmere should serve a Mallett, seeing that our fathers have been your fathers' tenants for hundreds of years, so that even if all this had not happened we should not have minded. As it is, we are proud that he is with you; and it seems natural that, after wandering about the world and fighting with those black villains out there, he should never be content to go on as he was before, or to settle down to farming."

"It is like man like master, in this case," Mallett laughed. "After I have once been over the estate, and seen all the tenants, and learned that everyone is satisfied and everything going on well, I shall very soon begin to feel restless, and shall be running off somewhere. You see, I have never been broken in to a country life. I have no idea of becoming an absentee; but I think a month or two together will be as much as I can stand, at any rate as long as I am a bachelor."

"That is just what I was saying, Squire," the farmer's wife said, speaking for the first time—for during the first portion of the conversation she had been crying quietly, and had since been busying herself in placing decanters and glasses and a huge homemade cake on the table. "We all hope that you will soon bring a mistress home. I said only this morning that you would never be settling down until you did.

"And now, will you take a glass of wine and a slice of cake, Squire?"

"Thank you, Mrs. Lechmere, I will; especially a piece of your cake. Many and many a slice of it have I had here when a boy, and famously good it always was."

Major Mallett ate two big slices of cake, drank a glass of wine, and refusing the offer of a second glass, got up to go, saying:

"No, Mrs. Lechmere; I must not treat myself to another glass now. I am going round to four or five other houses before I return to lunch, and I know that the tray will be put on the table everywhere. I can say that I have eaten so much cake here that I cannot eat more. But I know I shall have to drink a glass of wine at each place, and I can assure you that I am not accustomed to tipple in the morning.

"Ah, here come your two sons across the fields. I will meet them at the gate. If I were to begin a regular talk with Bob today, the morning would be gone."

"George has changed wonderfully," Mrs. Lechmere said, as they accompanied him to the gate. "It ain't his face so much, though he is well nigh as brown as that cake, but it is his figure. I should not have known him if he had not come along with Bob. He walks altogether different."

"It is the drilling, Mrs. Lechmere. Yes, it is wonderful how much drill does for a man; and there is a good deal in the cut of the clothes. You see, there is not much difference in the material, but George's were made at a good tailor's in London, and I suppose Bob's were made down here."

Mallett stayed for a few minutes chatting at the gate with Bob, and then, saying that he would certainly come in again before he went up to town, started on a round of calls.

Chapter 6

"And so you have bought a yacht, Major Mallett?"

"Yes; at least she is scarcely a yacht yet. I was going to have one built, but I heard of one that had been ordered by Lord Haverstock, who, they say, has been so hard hit at the Derby that he had to tell Wanhill, the builder, that he could not take her. As the season was getting rather late, the man was glad to sell her a bargain, especially as he had already got a thousand pounds towards her; so I got her for twelve hundred less that Haverstock was to have paid. It suited me admirably, for he has engaged to finish her in six weeks. She is just about the size I wanted, 120 tons, and looks as if she would turn out fast, and a good sea boat. Of course, I shall race a bit with her next year, though I have bought her more for cruising."

"I hope that you and Lady Greendale will favour me with your company, on her first cruise after the season ends. I know it is of no use asking before that."

"I should like it immensely, Major Mallett. It would be delightful. How many can you carry?"

"Eight comfortably. The ladies' cabin has four berths, but will be only really comfortable for three; and there are four other state cabins—that is, three besides my own, but one of them has two berths. Of course, I could put up three or four others in the saloon for a couple of days, but for a cruise of three weeks or a month it would be too many for comfort. We could not seat that number at table without crowding, and I doubt whether the cooking arrangements would be altogether satisfactory.

"Of course, we shall want two more ladies. I will leave the selection of those to you and Lady Greendale, for, except yourselves, I know no ladies; though, of course, I could get plenty of men."

"That will be delightful," Bertha said; "but I dare say that by the time the season is over you will know plenty of ladies that you can ask. You see, you have met so many people here now that, as you have just been grumbling discontentedly, you are out nearly every night."

"Yes," he laughed. "At present, you see, I am regarded rather as an Indian lion; but I shall bid goodbye to London as soon as the yacht is afloat."

"What is her name to be?"

"I have not given it a thought, yet. I only bought her two days ago. It seems to me that it is almost as hard to fix on a name for a yacht as for a race horse."

"Oh! there are so many pretty names that would do for a yacht."

"Yes; but you would be surprised if you knew how many yachts there are of every likely name."

"It ought to be a water bird," the girl said.

"Those are just the names that are most taken."

"Yes; but there are lots of sea birds and water birds, only I cannot think of them."

"Well, you look them out," he laughed. "Here is a Hunt's Yachting List that I bought on my way here. I will leave it with you, and any name that you fix on she shall have. Only, please choose one that only two or three boats, and those not about the same size, have got. It leads to confusion if there are two craft going about of the same name and of about the same size. But I warn you, that it will involve your having to go down to Poole to christen her."

"Do they christen yachts, Major Mallett?"

"I really don't know anything about it," he replied; "but if it is right and proper for ships it must be for yachts; and I should regard the ceremony as being likely to bring good luck to her. When the time comes, I will fix the day to suit your arrangements."

"I will try to come down, Major Mallett, if mamma will agree; but it is a long way to Poole, and somehow one never seems to find an hour to do anything; so I really cannot promise."

"Well, if you cannot manage it, Miss Greendale, I will have her launched without being named and bring her round to Southampton, and then you could go down and christen her there. That would only be a short railway run of a couple of hours after breakfast, and, say, two hours for luncheon there, and to have a look at her, and you could be home by four o'clock in the afternoon."

"That seems more practicable."

Captain Mallett had been three weeks in town. He had called upon Lady Greendale on the day after he had come up, and been received with the greatest cordiality by her and Bertha. The latter, in the two years and a half that he had been away, had grown from a somewhat gawky girl, whose charm lay solely in her expressive eyes and pleasant smile, into a very pretty woman. She was slightly over middle height, and carried herself exceptionally well. Her face was a bright and sunny one, but her eyes were unchanged, and there was an earnestness in their expression which, with a certain resolute curve in the lips, gave character to the laughing brightness of her face. Society had received her warmly, and consequently she was pleased with society. Both for her own sake and as an heiress she was made a deal of, and, though she had been but two months in town, she had already taken her place as one of the recognised belles of the season.

Lady Greendale had a dinner party on the day when Major Mallett called, and was discussing with Bertha whom they could invite to fill up at such short notice a vacancy which had occurred.

"You come at the right moment, Frank," she said, after they had chatted for some time. "We were lamenting just now that we had received this morning a note from a gentleman who was coming to dine with us today, saying that he could not come; but now I regard it as most fortunate, for of course we want you to come to us at once. I suppose you have not made any engagements yet. We shall be sixteen with you, and I think they are all nice people."

"I shall be very happy to come," he said. "I have certainly no engagements. I looked in at the club last night. It was my first appearance there, for my name only came up for election four months ago, and I should have felt very uncomfortable if I had not happened to meet two or three old friends. One of them asked me to dinner for tomorrow. For today I am altogether free."

In the course of the evening Major Mallett received three or four invitations to dances and balls, and, being thus started in society, was soon out every evening. For the first week he enjoyed the novelty of the scene, but very speedily tired of it. At dinners the ladies he took down always wanted him to talk about India; but even this was, in his opinion, preferable to the crush and heat of the dances.

"How men can go on with such a life as this," he said to a friend at the club, "beats me altogether, Colonel. Two or three times in the year one might like to go out to these crowded balls, just to see the dresses and the girls, but to go out night after night is to my mind worse than hunting the rebels through the jungle. It is just as hot and not a hundredth part so exciting. I have only had three weeks of it, and I am positively sick of it already."

"Then why on earth do you accept, Mallett? I took good care not to get into it. What can a man want better than this? A well-cooked dinner, eaten with a chum, and then a quiet rubber; and perhaps once a fortnight or so I go out to a dinner party, which I like well enough as a change. I always get plenty of shooting in winter, and am generally away for three months, but I am always heartily glad to get back again."

"I am afraid I should get as tired of the club as I am of society, Colonel."

"You have plenty of time, lad. I am twenty years your senior. Well, there is plenty before you besides society and club life. Of course, you will marry and settle down, and become a county magistrate and all that sort of thing. Thank goodness, what money came to me came in the shape of consols, and not in that of land. A country life would be exile to me; but, you see, you have left the army much younger than I did. I suppose you are not thirty yet? The Crimea and India ran you fast up the tree."

"No, I am only twenty-eight. You know I was only a brevet Major, and had two more steps to get before I had a regimental majority."

"That makes all the difference, Mallett; and it is absurd, a young fellow of your age crying out against society."

"I don't cry out against it," Mallett laughed. "I simply say that it is out of my line, and I have never been broken into it. I was talking of buying a yacht, or rather of building one."

"What size do you want? I know of one to be had cheap, if you are thinking of a good big craft."

And thus it was that Mallett came to hear of the yawl at Poole.

"I have fixed on the Osprey, Major Mallett," Bertha Greendale said, when he took her down to dinner two days after he had last seen her. "What do you say to that? There are two or three yachts of the same name, but none of them is over thirty tons."

"I think the Osprey is a pretty name, Miss Greendale. I should have accepted the Crocodile if you had suggested it. The name that you have chosen will suit admirably; so henceforth she shall be the Osprey, pending your formally christening her by that name. I might, of course, be hypercritical and point out that, although a fishing eagle, the Osprey can scarcely be called a water bird, inasmuch that it is no swimmer."

"But it is hypercritical even to suggest such a thing," she said, pouting. "The Osprey has to do with the sea. It is strong and swift on the wing, and the sails of the yacht are wings, are they not? Then it is strong and bold, and I am sure your boat will not be afraid to meet a storm. Altogether, I think it is an excellent name."

"I think it a very good name, too."

"You ought to have one for your figurehead."

"Yachts don't have figureheads, else I would certainly have it. At any rate, I will choose an eagle for my racing flag."

"I have never been on board a yacht yet," the girl said. "I think I only know one man who has one, at least a large one; that is Mr. Carthew. Of course you know him; he had a new one this spring—the Phantom. He has won several times this season."

"I saw he had," Frank said, quietly. "Yes, I used to know him, but it's seven or eight years since we met."

"And you don't like him," she said, quickly.

"What makes you think that, Miss Greendale?"

"Oh, I can tell by the tone of your voice."

"I don't think it expressed anything but indifference, as it is such a long time since I met him. But I never fancied him much. I suppose we were not the same sort of men; and then, too, perhaps I am rather prejudiced from the fact that I know that he was considered rather a hard landlord."

"I never heard that," she said.

"No, I dare say you would not hear it, but I fancy it was so. However, he sold his estate, at least so I heard."

"Yes, he told me that he did not care for country life. I have seen him several times since we came up to town. He keeps race horses, you know. His horse was second in the Derby this spring. That takes him a good deal away, else one would meet him more often, for he knows a great many people we do."

"Yes, I know that he races, and is, I believe, rather lucky on the turf."

"You have no inclination that way, Major Mallett?"

"Not a shadow," he said, earnestly. "It is the very last vice I should take to. I have seen many cases, in the service, of young fellows being ruined by betting on the turf. We had one case in my own regiment, in which a man was saved by the skin of his teeth. Happily he had strength of mind and manliness enough to cut it altogether, and is a very promising young officer now, but it was only the fact of our embarking when we did for India that saved him from ruin.

"The man who bets more than he can afford to lose is simply a gambler, whether he does so on racehorses or on cards. I have seen enough of it to hate gambling with all my heart. It has driven more men out of the service than drink has, and the one passion is almost as incurable as the other."

Bertha laughed. "I think that is the first time I have ever heard you express any very strong opinion, Major Mallett. It is quite refreshing to listen to a thorough-going denunciation of anything here in London. In the country, of course, it is different. All sorts of things are heartily abused there; especially, perhaps, the weather, free trade, poaching, and people in whose covers foxes are scarce. But here, in London, no one seems to care much about anything."

"People in your set have no time to do so."

"That is very unkind. They think about amusement."

"They may think about it, but it is all in a very languid fashion. Now, in a country town, when there is a ball or a dance in the neighbourhood, it is quite an excitement; and, at any rate, everyone enters into it heartily. People evidently enjoy the dancing for dancing's sake, and they all look as if they were thoroughly enjoying themselves. Whereas here, people dance as if it was rather a painful duty than otherwise, and there is a general expression of a longing for the whole thing to be over."

"I enjoy the dancing," Bertha said, sturdily. "At least, when I get a really good partner."

"Yes, but then you have only been three months at it. You have not got broken into the business yet."

"Nor have you, Major Mallett."

"No, but while you are an actor in the piece, I am but a spectator, and lookers-on, you know, see most of the game."

"What nonsense! Don't pretend you are getting to be a blase man. I know that you are only about ten years older than I am—not more than nine, I think—and you dance very well, and no doubt you know it."

"I like dancing, I can assure you, where there is room to dance; but I don't call it dancing when you have an area of only a foot square to dance in, and are hustled and bumped more than you would be in a crowded Lord Mayor's show. My training has not suited me for it, and I would rather stand and look on, listen to scraps of conversation, watch the faces of the dancers and of those standing round. It is a study, and I think it shows one of the worst sides of nature. It is quite shocking to see and hear the envy, uncharitableness, the boredom, and the desperate efforts to look cheerful under difficulties, especially among the girls that do not get partners."

"For shame! I am disappointed in you," Bertha said, half in jest, half in earnest. "You are not at all the person I thought you were. Whatever I may have fancied about you, I never imagined you a cynic or a grumbler."

"I suppose it brings out the worst side of my nature, too," he laughed. "When you come down on board the Osprey, Miss Greendale, you will see the other side. I fancy one falls into the tone of one's surroundings. Here I have caught the tone of the bored man of society, there you will see that I shall be a breezy sailor—cheerful in storm or in calm, ready to take my glass and to toast my lass and all the rest of it in true nautical fashion."

"I hope so," she said, gravely. "I shall certainly need something of the sort to correct the very unfavourable impression you have just been giving me. Now let us change the subject. You have not told me yet whether you had any flirtations in India."

"Flirtations!" he repeated. "For once, the small section of womankind that I encountered were above and beyond flirtations.

"I don't think," he went on seriously, "that you in England can quite realise what it was, or that a woman in London society can imagine that there can exist a state of things in which dress and appearance are matters which have altogether ceased to engross the female mind. The white women I saw there were worn and haggard. No matter what their age, they bore on their faces the impress of terrible hardship, terrible danger, and terrible grief and anxiety. Few but had lost someone dear to them, many all whom they cared for. A few had made some pitiful attempt at neatness, but most had lost all thought of self, all care whatever for personal appearance. There was an anxious look in their eyes that was painful to witness."

"I spoke without thinking," the girl said, gravely. "It must have been awful—awful, as you say. It is impossible for us really to imagine quite what it was, or to picture up such scenes as you must have witnessed. I can understand that all this must seem frivolous and contemptible to you."

"No, I don't go so far as that," he smiled. "It is good that there should be butterflies as well as bees; and, at any rate, the women of India, who had the reputation of being as frivolous and pleasure-loving as the rest of their sex, came out nobly and showed a degree of patience under suffering and of heroic courage unsurpassable in history.

"I am afraid," he said, as the hostess gave the signal for the ladies to rise, "you will long look back upon this dinner as one of unprecedented dullness."

"Not dullness," she smiled. "Exceptional certainly, but as something so different from the usual thing, when one talks of nothing but the opera, the theatres and exhibitions, as to deserve to be put down in one's diary by a mark. I won't flatter you by telling you whether a red or a black one."

"Who are the party going to be, Mallett?" his friend Colonel Severn said, as they stood together on the deck of the Osprey early in August. "You guaranteed that it would be a pleasant one when you persuaded me to leave London, for the first time since I retired, before shooting began."

"Well, to begin with, there is Lady Greendale, an eminently pleasant woman. She comes as general chaperon, and I shall consider her under your especial care. You will not find it hard work, for she is an eminently sympathetic woman, ready to chat if you are disposed to talk, to interest herself in other ways if you are not. She has plenty of common sense, is tolerant of tobacco, and a thorough woman of the world, though her headquarters have for years been in the country. With her is her daughter."

"Well, what about her? I have heard of her as having made quite a sensation this season, and between ourselves I had some idea that this party was specially planned on her account."

"To some extent perhaps it was," Frank Mallett laughed. "Bertha Greendale is an old chum of mine. I knew her in very short frocks, for they were near neighbours of ours in the country; and her father, Sir John, was always one of my kindest friends. She was a slip of a girl when I went out to India, and though I thought that she would turn out pretty, I certainly did not expect she would be anything like as good looking as she is. She was always a nice girl, and success so far has not spoiled her.

"Then there is a Miss Sinclair, a great friend of Bertha's; and Jack Hawley of the Guards. I knew him out in the Crimea. The other two are Wilson, who is a clever young barrister, and a particularly pleasant fellow; and his wife, who is a sister of Miss Sinclair; so I think there are the elements of a pleasant party. All the ladies are broken into smoke, for Sir John smoked, and so does Wilson; so that you won't be expected to go forward, as they do on the P and O, whenever you want to enjoy your favourite pipe."

"That is a comfort, anyhow, Mallett. If there is one thing in the world I hate, it is having to go and hunt about for some place to smoke in; and I never accept an invitation to any shooting party unless I know beforehand that smoking is allowed. At what time do you expect the others?"

"They will be down at half-past twelve; they are all coming by the same train, and it was because I knew that you would want to be in a smoking carriage that I told you to come down by the earlier one. And, besides, I thought it well to get you here first. You are the only stranger, as it were. The others are all intimate with each other, and it was as well to post you as to their various relationships."

"One thing, Mallett. I hope Lady Greendale is not in any way a marrying woman. I am not like Mr. Pickwick, afraid of widows, and have perfect confidence in my power to resist temptation; but at the same time it makes all the difference in the world to one's comfort. I am not ass enough to suppose that Lady Greendale would even dream for a moment of setting her cap at a Colonel on half pay, but if a woman is in the marrying line she always expects a certain amount of what you may call delicate attention. It is her daily bread, for she considers that unless every man she comes across evinces a certain amount of admiration, it is a sign that her charms are on the wane, and her chances growing more and more remote."

Mallett laughed. "You can set your mind at ease, for nothing is further from the thoughts of Lady Greendale than re-marriage. She was very happy with her husband."

"The more reason for her marrying again," the Colonel said. "A woman who has been happy with her husband is apt to get the idea into her head that every man will make a good husband; and a confoundedly mistaken idea it is. She is much more likely to marry again than the woman who has had a hard time of it."

"Well, you may be right there, Colonel, but putting aside my conviction that Lady Greendale has no idea of marrying again, is the fact that at present all her thoughts are occupied by her daughter. She is not at all what you would call a managing mother, but I am sure that she has set her heart on Bertha's making a good match, and that the fear that she will succumb to some penniless younger son or other unsuitable partner is at present the dominant feeling in her mind. I don't think she would have agreed to Jack Hawley being of the party, had not Bertha entertained a conviction that he was rather gone on Miss Sinclair, who by the way has, like her sister, money enough to disregard the fact that Jack is hardly in that respect well endowed.

"However, it is time for me to be off; I see the skipper is getting the gig lowered. I suppose you will be content to sit here and smoke your pipe until we come back; and, indeed, seven is as many as the gig will carry with any degree of comfort. The cutter will go ashore to fetch off the luggage, which will probably be of somewhat portentous dimensions."

Two minutes later Mallett took his place in the gig, and was rowed to the shore. He was delighted, with his new purchase. She was an excellent sea boat, and, as he had learned from a short spin with another craft, decidedly fast. He had not, however, entered her for any race.

"There is no hurry," he said to his skipper, when the latter suggested that they should try her at Cowes. "I should like to win my first race, and in the first place we don't know that she is in her best trim. In the next place we must get the crew accustomed to each other and to the craft. I bought her as a cruiser rather than a racer, and don't want to have her full of men, as are most of the racers. It is a heavy expense, and fewer hands accustomed to work well together do just as much work, and more smartly than a crowd. We found, when we sailed round the islands with the Royal Victoria race, that, considering we went under reduced canvas, we held our own very fairly; and I have no doubt that when we get all our light canvas up, the Osprey will give a good account of herself. Our gear is scarcely stretched yet.

"No; I will wait until next season, and then we will make a bold bid for a Queen's Cup."

Frank Mallett reached the platform at Southampton a few minutes before the train came in. The party were on the lookout for him, and alighted in the highest spirits.

"Now, ladies," he said, "the first thing is to point out the luggage. My man here will get it all together, and stand guard over it till two others arrive to get it on board. They will be here in a few minutes. In fact, they ought to be here now."

He looked on with something like dismay while the boxes were picked out and piled together.

"My dear Lady Greendale," he said, "I am afraid you must all have very vague ideas as to the amount of accommodation in a 120-ton yacht. She is not a Cunarder or a P and O. Why, two or three of those trunks would absolutely fill one of her cabins."

"You did not expect, Major Mallett," Bertha said demurely, "that we were coming for a month's cruise with only handbags; especially after telling us that very likely we might not get a chance of getting any washing done all that time."

"Well, I dare say we shall stow them away somewhere. Now, as you have got them all together, we will go down to the boat.

"Now, lads, you had better get a hand cart, and get these things on board as soon as you can."

"Which is the Osprey?" Amy Sinclair asked Bertha, as they took their places in the boat.

Bertha looked with a rather puzzled face at the fleet of yachts.

"That is," she said, confidently, after a moment's hesitation, pointing to one towards which the boat was at the moment heading.

Frank Mallett laughed.

"Really I should have thought, Miss Greendale, that, although making every allowance for feminine vagueness as to boats, you would have known the yacht you christened a month ago; or, at any rate, would not have mistaken a schooner for a yawl, after the patient explanation I gave you on your last visit as to the different rigs. That is the Osprey, a hundred yards lower down."

"Oh, yes, I remember now, that when there is a little mast standing on the stern it is a yawl. These things seem very simple to you, Major Mallett, but they are very puzzling to women, who know nothing about them. Now, I venture to say, that if I were to show you six different materials for frocks, and were to tell you all their names, you would know nothing about them when I showed them to you a month afterwards.

"I suppose the gentleman on board is Colonel Severn."

"Yes, he came down by the train before yours. I thought it better that he should do so, as in the first place, he did not know any of you, and in the next, as you see, we are pretty closely packed as it is."

"What is that flag at the masthead?" Lady Greendale asked. "Bertha said that your flag was going to have an eagle on it."

"That is on my racing flag. Let me impress upon you, ladies, that a racing flag is a square flag, and that that is not a flag at all, but a burgee. Every club has its burgee; as you see, that is a white cross on a blue ground with a crown in the centre, and is the burgee of the Royal Thames, of which I was elected a member last month.

"Here we are. Properly, I ought to be on board first, but I am too wedged in. You and Wilson had better go up first; that will give more room for the ladies to move."

"You have got new steps," Bertha said. "When I came down with Mrs. Wilson to christen the boat we had to climb up nasty steep steps against the side. This is a great deal more comfortable. I was thinking that mamma would have a difficulty in getting up those other things, if it were at all rough."

"Yes, I have had them specially made for the present occasion. Large cruisers always have them, and, at any rate, they are more comfortable for any-sized boats. But they take up rather more room to stow away, and they are really not so handy in a sea, for the boats cannot get so close alongside. Still, no doubt they are more comfortable for ladies. Now it is your turn."

The cruise of the Osprey was in all respects a success. The party was well chosen and pleasant. Colonel Severn and Lady Greendale got on well together. He liked her because she had no objection whatever to his perpetual enjoyment of his pipe. She liked him because he was altogether different from anyone that she had met before; his Indian stories amused her, his views of life were original, and his grumbling at modern ways and modern innovations in no way concealed the fact that in spite of it all he evidently enjoyed life thoroughly.

The Osprey had fine weather as she ran along the south coast, anchoring under Portland for a day, while the party examined the works of the breakwater and paid a visit to the quarries, where the convicts were at work. She put into Torquay, Dartmouth and Plymouth, spending a day in the two former ports and two at the last named. They looked into Fowey, and stopped two days at Falmouth, and then, rounding the Land's End, made for Kingstown. From here they started for the Clyde; but meeting with very heavy weather, went into Belfast Lough.

The Osprey proved to be a fine sea boat, and behaved so well that even Lady Greendale declared she would not be afraid to trust herself on board her in any weather. They sailed up the Clyde as far as Greenock, and then returning, cruised for a fortnight among the islands on the west coast. They had enjoyed their stay at Kingstown so much that they put in there again on their return voyage, shaped their course for Plymouth, and then, without looking into any other port, returned to Southampton.

Jack Hawley and Miss Sinclair had become engaged during the voyage, and the Colonel and Lady Greendale had become so confidential that Frank laughingly asked him if he had changed his views on the subject of matrimony, a suggestion which he indignantly repudiated.

"I should have thought that you knew me better," he said, reproachfully. "I admit that Lady Greendale is a very charming woman, but you don't think that she can imagine for a moment that I have ever entertained any idea of such a thing? You said that I was to amuse her if I could. I have tried my best to keep the old lady as much to myself as possible, so as to enable all you young people to carry out your flirtations to your heart's content. By gad, sir, it would be a nice return for following out your instructions to find myself in such a hole as that."

Frank had some difficulty in persuading the Colonel that his remark was not meant as a serious one, and that there was no fear whatever that Lady Greendale had ever had the slightest reason to suppose that his intentions were not of a most Platonic nature.

"I am heartily glad," the Colonel said, when he was quite pacified, "that Hawley's affair has come off all right. Even if she had not been an heiress I should have said that he was a lucky fellow, for she is an extremely nice and pleasant young woman, without any nonsense about her; still there is no doubt that her fortune will come in very handy for Hawley. As to the girl herself, I think she has made a very good choice. She has plenty of money for both, and as he has managed to keep up on his younger son's portion, he can have no extravagant tastes, and will make her a very good husband. There is no other engagement to be announced, I suppose?"

"As I am the only other unmarried man on board, Colonel, your question is somewhat pointed. No; I hope there may be one of these days, but I don't think that it would be fair to ask her here, where I am her host, and she is under the glamour of the sea. I doubt whether she has the slightest idea of what I want. That is the worst of being very old friends; the relations get so fixed that a woman does not recognise that they can ever be changed. However, I shall try my luck one of these days. I don't think that I shall meet with any serious opposition on her mother's part, if Bertha likes me, but I know that Lady Greendale has very much more ambitious views for her, and has quite set her mind upon her making a good match. No doubt she has a right to expect that she will do so. However, I think she is too fond of Bertha to thwart her, however disappointed she might feel. At present I don't think that she has any more suspicion than Bertha herself of my intentions."

During the voyage Bertha and Amy Sinclair had become quite adroit helmswomen, and one or other was constantly at the tiller when the wind was light. Bertha had learned the names of all the crew, and often went forward to ask questions of the men tending the head sails, becoming a prime favourite with all hands. On arriving at Southampton the rest of the party went up at once to town, while Frank remained behind for a day or two, going round in the yacht to Gosport, where she was to be laid up for the winter.

Chapter 7

"I am so sorry," Bertha Greendale said, "so awfully sorry. I had no idea that you thought of me like that. We were such friends so long ago, and it has been so pleasant since you came home last year, and I like you as if you were a big brother; but I have never thought of you in any other light, and now it seems dreadful to me to give you pain; but I feel sure that I should never come to love you in that way."

And she burst into tears.

"Do not think anything more about it, dear," Frank Mallett said, gently. "I have felt sometimes when we have been together, that you were so kindly and frank and pleasant with me that you could feel as I wanted you to. I ought to have known it always. But I suppose in such cases a man deceives himself and shuts his eyes to facts. You have certainly nothing to blame yourself about. Of course, it is a hard blow, but no doubt I shall get over it as other fellows do. At any rate, I know that we shall always be dear friends, and you need not fear that I shall mope over my misfortune. I shall run up to town for a bit, and as you are going up for the season next week, I shall no doubt often meet you. Don't fret about me. I have been hit pretty hard several times, though not in the same way, and I have always gone through it, and no doubt I shall do so now.

"Goodbye," and when Bertha looked up, he had left the room.

"Oh, mamma," she said, when she went into the room where her mother was sitting, "I am so sorry, so dreadfully sorry. Frank Mallett has asked me to be his wife. I have never thought of such a thing and of course I had to say no."

"I have thought such a thing likely for some time, Bertha, but I thought it best to hold my tongue about it. In such matters the interference of a mother often does more harm than good. I felt sure, by your manner with him, that you had no idea of it; and I must say that much as I like Frank Mallett, I should have been sorry. I have great hopes of your making a really first-class match."

"I could not make a better match," Bertha said, indignantly. "No one could be kinder or nicer than Major Mallett, and we know how brave he is and how he has distinguished himself, and he has a good estate and everything that anyone could wish; only unfortunately I do not love him—at least not in that way. He has never shown me what I should consider any particular attention, and never talked to me in the way men do when they are making love to a girl. Nothing could be nicer, and it was all the nicer because I never thought of this. I suppose it is because he is so different from some of the men I met in town last season, who always seemed to be trying to get round me. No, I know it is not a nice expression, mamma, but you know what I mean."

"I know, my dear," her mother smiled. "Of course you are a very good match, and though I do not want to flatter you, you were one of the belles of the season. Though some of the men you speak of were by no means desirable—younger sons and barristers and that sort of thing—still, there were two or three whom any girl might have been pleased to see at her feet, and who, I am sure from what I saw, only needed but little encouragement from you to be there. I was a little vexed, dear, you see, that you did not give any of them that encouragement; but I understand, of course, that the novelty of your first season carried you away altogether; and that you liked the dancing and the fetes and the opera for themselves, and not because they brought you in contact with men of excellent class. So far as I could see, it was a matter of indifference to you whether the man was a peer with a splendid rent roll, or a younger son without a farthing, so that he was a good dancer and a pleasant companion; but of course after a season or two you will grow wiser."

"I do hope not, mamma," Bertha said, indignantly. "I don't mean to say that it might not be better to marry, as you say, a peer with a good rent roll than a younger son without a penny, other things being equal; that is to say, if one liked them equally; but I hope that I shall never come to like anyone a bit more for being a peer."

Lady Greendale smiled, indulgently.

"It is a natural sentiment, my dear, for a girl of your age and inexperience; but in time you will come to see things in a different light."

Then she changed the subject. "What is Frank going to do? It is fortunate that we are going up to town next week."

"He is going up to town himself tomorrow, and I am sure that you will never hear from him, or from anyone else, what has happened. We shall meet in town as usual, and I am sure that he will be just the same as he was before, and that I shall be a great deal more uncomfortable than he will. It is a very silly affair altogether, I think; and I would give anything if it had not happened."

Lady Greendale did not echo the sentiment. She liked Frank Mallett immensely. He had always been a great favourite of hers, but since she had guessed what Bertha herself had not dreamed of, she had been uncomfortable. It threatened to disturb all the plans she had formed, and she was well contented to learn that she had refused him. Lady Greendale was a thoroughly kind-hearted woman, but she could not forget that she herself might have made, in a worldly sense, a better match than she had; and her ambition had, since Bertha was a child, and still more since she had shown promise of exceptional good looks, been centred on her making a really good match.

Frank went up to town next day, and the Greendales followed him a week later. They did not often meet him in society, as Frank seldom went out; but he called occasionally in the old friendly and unceremonious way. It would have required an acute observer to see any difference in his manner to Bertha, but Lady Greendale noticed it, and the girl herself felt that, although he was no less kind and friendly, there was some impalpable change in his manner, something that she felt, though she could not define it, even to herself.

"Have you had a tiff with Major Mallett, Bertha?" Mrs. Wilson asked one day, when she was alone with her in the drawing room.

Frank had just left, after spending an hour there.

"A tiff, Carrie? No! What put such an idea into your head?"

"My eyes, assisted perhaps by my ears. My dear, do you think that after being with you on the yacht last autumn, I should not notice any change in your manner to each other? I had expected before now to have heard an interesting piece of news; and now I see that things have gone wrong somehow."

"We are just as good friends as we always were," Bertha said, shortly; "every bit."

"You don't mean to say that you have refused him, Bertha?"

"I don't mean to say anything of the sort. I simply say that Major Mallett and I have always been great friends, and we are so now. There is no one that I have a higher regard for."

"Well, Bertha, I do not want to know your secrets, if you do not wish to tell me. All that I can say is that, if you have refused him, you have done a very foolish thing. I don't know any man that a woman might be happier with. When we were out last year with you, Amy and I agreed that it was certain to come off, and thought how well suited you were to each other. Of course, in worldly respects, you might do better; just at present you have the ball at your feet; but choose where you may you will not find a finer fellow than he is. Yes, I told Harry that it was lucky that I had not made that trip on board the Osprey before I was irrevocably captured, for I should certainly have lost my heart to Major Mallett. Well, I am sorry, Bertha, more sorry than I can say; and I am sure that Amy will be, too."

"I said nothing whatever, Carrie, that would justify this little explosion, which I certainly don't intend to answer. I should really feel very vexed, if I were not perfectly sure that you would never tell anyone else of this notion that you have got in your head."

"You may be quite sure of that, Bertha. At least when I say no one else, of course I do not include Harry; but you know him well enough to be certain that it will not go further. I am sure he will be as disappointed as I am. In fact, he will have a small triumph over me, for after the usual manner of men he saw nothing on board the yacht, and has always maintained that it was pure fancy on my part. However, I won't tell anyone else, not even Amy. She can find it out for herself, which you may be sure she will do when she comes back from the continent, if indeed her own happiness with Jack has not blinded her to all sub-lunary matters.

"Well, goodbye, dear. You will forgive my saying that I am disappointed in you, terribly disappointed in you."

"I must try to put up with that, Carrie. I am not aware that you consulted me before you made your own matrimonial arrangements, and perhaps I may be able to manage my own.''

"Well, don't be cross, Bertha. Remember that I am not advising or counselling. I am simply regretting, which perhaps you may do yourself, some day or other."

And with this parting shot she left.

The weeks went on, and when May came and Frank told her that the Osprey was fitted out, and that he would join her in a day or two, Bertha heard the news with satisfaction. The season was a gay one, and she was enjoying herself greatly; the one little drop of bitterness in her cup being that she could no longer enjoy his visits as she formerly did. He had been the one man with whom she was able to talk and laugh quite freely, who was really an old friend, a link not only between her and the past, but between her and her country life.

And now, she thought pettishly, he had spoiled all this, and what annoyed her almost as much was that the change was more in herself than in him. She no longer gave him commissions to execute for her, nor made him her general confidant. She knew that he would be as ready as before to laugh and to sympathise, that he would still gladly execute her commissions, and she felt that he tried hard to make her forget that he had aspired to be something nearer to her than a brotherly friend. She felt that after what he had said they could never stand in quite the same relation as before.

Accustomed as Frank was to read her thoughts, he was not deceived by the expression of regret that she should now see but little of him, as he saw the news was really pleasant to her. She was not aware that it was a conversation that he had had the evening before with Colonel Severn, which had decided him to go down to the Osprey a fortnight earlier than he had intended.

"You are getting to be almost as regular an attendant here, Mallett, as I am. I think you are altogether too young to take regularly to club life. It is all very well for an old fogey like me, but I don't think it a good thing for a young fellow like you to take so early to a bachelor life."

"I don't want to do anything of the sort, Colonel. But I can't stand these crushes in hot rooms; I cannot for the life of me see where the pleasure comes in. I begin to think that I was an ass to leave the army."

"Not at all, lad, not at all. When a man has got a good estate it is much better for him to settle down upon it, and to marry and have children, and all that sort of thing, than it is to remain in the army in times of peace. I had Wilson and Hawley dining with me here yesterday. We had a great chat over the pleasant time we had last year on board your yacht. I don't know when I enjoyed myself so much as I did then. Lady Greendale is a remarkably clever woman, and her daughter is as nice a girl as I have come across for a long time, and without a scrap of nonsense about her. I wonder that she has not become engaged by this time. General Matthews, who, as you know, goes in a good deal for that sort of thing for the sake of his daughters, told me recently that he fancied from what he had heard that Miss Greendale's engagement was likely to be a settled thing before the season was over. He said there were three men making the running—Lord Chilson, the eldest son of the Earl of Sommerlay; George Delamore—his father is in the Cabinet, you know, and he is member for Ponberry; and a man named Carthew, who keeps race horses, and was a neighbour of hers down in the country. He is, I hear, a good-looking fellow, and just the sort of man a girl is likely to fancy. Matthews thought that the chances were in his favour. As you are a neighbour of theirs, too, I suppose you will know him?"

"I knew him at one time, Colonel, but I have not seen him now for a good many years, beyond meeting him two or three times at dinners and so on last season. He was away when I was at home before going out to India, and he had sold his estate before I came back."

"They say he has been very lucky on the turf, and has made a pot of money."

"So I have heard," Frank said; "but, you see, one generally hears of men's good luck, and not of their bad. Besides, many men do most of their real betting through commissioners, especially if they own horses themselves. He is a fellow I don't much care for, and I hope that whomever Miss Greendale may marry, he will not be the man."

"I thought, when you first asked me down last year, that you had got up the party specially for her, Mallett, and that you were going in for the prize yourself. But of course I soon saw that I was mistaken, as you were altogether too good chums for that to come about. I have often noticed that men and girls who are thrown a lot together are often capital friends, but, although just the pair you would think would come together, that they hardly ever do so. I have noticed it over and over again. Well, she is an uncommonly nice girl, whoever gets her."

Frank did not return to town until the end of June.

"I have to congratulate you upon the Osprey's victory," Bertha said, the first time he called to see them. "You may imagine with what interest I read the accounts of the yacht races. I saw you won two on the Thames, and were first once and second once at Southampton."

"Yes, the Osprey has shown herself to be, as I thought, an uncommonly fast boat. We should have had two firsts at Southampton, if the pilot had not cut matters too fine and run us aground just opposite Netley; we were a quarter of an hour before we were off again. We picked up a lot of our lost ground and got a second, but were beaten eight minutes by the winner."

"Have you entered for the Queen's Cup at Ryde?"

"I have not entered yet, but I am going to do so," he said.

"Mamma and I will be down there. Lord Haverley—he is first cousin to mamma, you know—has taken a house there for the month, and he is going to have a large party, and we are going down for Ryde week."

"Yes, and there will be the Victoria Yacht Club ball, and all sorts of gaieties. I have not entered yet, but I am going to do so. The entries do not close till next Saturday."

"You will call and see us, of course, Frank?" Lady Greendale said. "Haverley has a big schooner yacht, and I dare say we shall be a good deal on the water."

"I shall certainly do myself the pleasure of calling, Lady Greendale."

"I warn you, Frank, that Bertha and I will be very disappointed if the Osprey does not win the cup. We regard ourselves as being, to some extent, her proprietors; and it will be a grievous blow to us if you don't win."

"I do not feel by any means sure about it," he said. "I fancy there will be several boats that have not raced yet this season, and as two of them are new ones, there is no saying what they may turn out."

Frank only stayed two days in town. He learned from Jack Hawley that it was reported that Lord Chilson and George Delamore had both been refused by Bertha Greendale.

"Chilson went away suddenly," he said. "As to Delamore, of course as he is a Member he had to stop through the Session, but from what I hear, and as you know I have some good sources of information, I am pretty sure that he has got his conge too. I fancy Carthew is the favourite. As a rule I don't like these men who go in for racing, but he is a deuced-nice fellow. I have seen a good deal of him. He put me up to a good thing for the Derby ten days ago. He gives uncommonly good supper parties, and has asked me several times, but I have not gone to them, for I believe there is a good deal of play afterwards, and I cannot stand unlimited loo."

"Is he lucky himself?" Frank asked.

"No, quite the other way, I hear. I know a man who has been to three or four of his suppers, and he told me that Carthew had lost every time, once or twice pretty heavily."

"Carthew's horse ran second, didn't it, for the Derby?"

"Yes, the betting was twenty to one against him at starting."

"I wonder he did not give that tip as well as the other."

"Well, he did say that he thought it might run into a place, but that he was sure that he had no chance with the favourite. As it turned out, he was nearer winning than he expected; for the favourite went down the day before the race, from 5 to 4 on, to 10 to 1 against. There was a report about that he had gone wrong in some way. Some fellows said that there had been an attempt to get at him, others that he had got a nail in his foot. The general feeling had been that he would win in a canter, but as it was he only beat Carthew's horse by a short head."

"Had Carthew backed his horse to win?"

"He told me that he had only backed it for a hundred, but had put five hundred on it for a place, and as he got six to one against it he came uncommonly well out of it."

"And do you think it likely that Miss Greendale will accept him?"

"Ah! that I cannot say. He has certainly been making very strong running, and if I were a betting man I should not mind laying two to one on the event coming off."

Frank joined the Osprey, which was lying off Portsmouth Harbour, on the following day.

"I am back earlier than I expected, George," he said, as Lechmere met him at the station. "I have got tired of London, and want to be on board again."

"Nothing gone wrong in town, I hope, Major?" George said next day, as he was removing the breakfast things. "You will excuse my asking, but you don't seem to me to be yourself since you came on board."

"Well, yes, George. I am upset, I confess. I am sure you will be sorry, too, when I tell you that it is more than probable that Miss Greendale is going to marry Mr. Carthew."

George put the dish he was holding down on the table with a crash, and stood gazing at Frank in blank dismay.

"Why, sir, I thought," he said, slowly, "that it was going to be you and Miss Greendale. I had always thought so. Excuse me, sir, I don't mean any offence, but that is what we have all thought ever since she came down to christen the yacht."

"There is no offence, George. Yes, I don't mind telling you that I had hoped so myself, but it was not to be. You see, Miss Greendale has known me since she was a child, and she has never thought of me in any other way than as a sort of cousin—someone she liked very much, but had never thought of for a moment as one she could marry. That is all past and gone, but I should be sorry, most sorry, for her to marry Carthew, knowing what I do of him."

"But it must not be, sir," George said, vehemently. "You can never let that sweet young lady marry that black-hearted villain."

"Unfortunately I cannot prevent it, George."

"Why, sir, you would only have to tell her about Martha, and I am sure it would do for his business. Miss Greendale can know nothing about it. So far as I can remember, she was not more than sixteen at the time. I don't suppose Lady Greendale ever heard of it. She knew, of course, of Martha's being missing, because it made quite a stir, but I don't suppose that she heard of her coming back. She was only at home three weeks before she died. There were not many that ever saw her, and father told me that he and the others made it so hot for Carthew one day at Chippenham market that he never came down again, and sold the place soon after. I don't suppose the gentry ever heard anything about it. If they had, Lady Greendale would surely never let her daughter marry him."

"No, I feel sure she would not; but still, George, I don't see that I can possibly interfere in the matter. The story is three years old now, and even if it had only happened yesterday, I, after what has occurred between us, could not come forward as his accuser. It would have the appearance of spite on my side; and besides, I have no proof whatever. He would, of course, deny the whole thing. I do not mean that he would deny that she said so—he could not do that—but he might declare that she had spoken falsely, and might even say that it was an attempt to put another's sin on his shoulders. Moreover, as I told you, I have other reasons for disliking the man, and, on the face of it, it would seem that I had raked up this old story against him, not only from jealousy, but from personal malice.

"No, it is out of the question that I should interfere. I would give everything that I am worth to be able to do so, but it is impossible. If I had full and unquestionable proofs I would go to Lady Greendale and lay the matter before her. But I have no such proofs. There is nothing whatever except that poor girl's word against his."

George's lips closed, and an expression of grim determination came over his face.

"I dare say you are right, Major," he said, after a pause; "but it seems to me hard that Miss Greendale should be sacrificed to a man like that."

Frank did not reply. He had already thought the matter over and over again, and had reached the opinion that he could not interfere. If he had not himself proposed to her, and been refused, he might have moved. Up to that time he had stood in the position of an old friend of the family, and as such could well have spoken to Lady Greendale on a matter that so vitally concerned Bertha's happiness. Now his taking that step would have the appearance of being the interference of a disappointed rival, rather than of a disinterested friend. He went up on deck, sat there for a time, and at last arrived at a conclusion.

"It is my duty. There can be no doubt about that," he said to himself. "If Bertha really loves Carthew, she will believe his denial rather than my accusation, unsupported as it is by a scrap of real evidence. In that case, she will put down my story as a piece of malice and meanness. But, after all, that will matter little. I had better far lose her liking and esteem than my own self respect. I will tell Lady Greendale about this. The responsibility will be off my hands then. She may not view the matter as an absolute bar to Carthew's marrying Bertha—that is her business and Bertha's—but at any rate I shall have done my duty. I will wait, however, until Bertha has accepted him.

"I have made up my mind, George," he said, later on. "If I hear that Miss Greendale has accepted Carthew, I shall go to her mother and tell her the story. I have little hope that it will do much good. It is very hard to make a girl believe anything against the man she loves, until it can be proved beyond doubt, and as Carthew will of course indignantly deny that he had anything to do with it, I expect that it will have no effect whatever, beyond making her dislike me cordially. Still, that cannot be helped. It is clearly my duty not only as her friend, but as the friend of her father and mother. But I wish that the task did not fall upon me."

"I am glad to hear you say that, Major," George said, quietly. "I can see, sir, that, as you say, it would be better if anyone else could do it, but Lady Greendale has known you for so many years that she must surely know that you would never have told her unless you believed the story to be true."

"No doubt she will, George. I hope Miss Greendale will, too; but even if she does not see it in that light I cannot help it. Well, I will go ashore to the clubhouse and find out whether they have heard anything about the entries for the cup."

When he returned he said to the captain:

"I hear that the Phantom has entered, Hawkins. I am told that she has just come off the slips, and that she has had a new suit of racing canvas made by Lapthorne."

"Well, sir, I think that we ought to have a good chance with her. She has shown herself a very fast boat the few times she has been raced, but so have we, and taking the line through boats that we have both sailed against, I think that we ought to be able to beat her."

"I have rather a fancy that we shan't do so, Hawkins. We will do our best, but I have met Mr. Carthew a good many times, for we were at school and college together, and somehow or other he has always managed to beat me."

"Ah! well, we will turn the tables on him this time, sir."

"I hope so, but it has gone so often the other way that I have got to be a little superstitious about it. I would give a good deal to beat him. I should like to win the Queen's Cup, as you know; but even if I didn't win it I should be quite satisfied if I but beat him."

Chapter 8

It was the week of the Ryde Regatta. At that time Ryde disputed with Cowes the glory of being the headquarters of yachting, and the scene was a gay one. Every house in the neighbourhood was crowded with guests, many had been let for the week at fabulous rates, the town was bright with flags, and a great fleet of yachts was moored off the town, extending from the pier westward as far as the hulks. The lawn of the Victoria Yacht Club was gay with ladies, a military band was playing, boats rowed backwards and forwards between the yachts and the clubhouses.

It was the first day of the Regatta, and the Queen's Cup was not to be sailed for until the third. On the previous morning Frank had received a note from Lady Greendale, saying that they had arrived with Lord Haverley's party the day before, and enclosing an invitation from him to dinner that day. He went up to call as soon as he received it, but excused himself from dining on the ground of a previous engagement, as he felt sure that Carthew would be one of the party.

"I suppose, Lady Greendale, it is no use asking you and Bertha to sail in the Osprey on Friday?"

"I should not think of going, Frank. A racing yacht is no place for an old lady. As for Bertha, she is already engaged. Mr. Carthew asked her a fortnight since to sail on the Phantom. Lady Olive Marston and her cousin, Miss Haverley, are also going. I know that it is not very usual for ladies to go on racing yachts, but they are all accustomed to yachting, and Mr. Carthew declares that they won't be in the way in the least."

"I don't see why they should be," Frank said, after a short pause. "Of course, in a small boat it would be different, but in a craft like the Phantom there is plenty of room for two or three ladies without their getting in the way of the crew.

"Well, I must be going," he broke off somewhat hastily, for he saw a group coming down the garden path towards the house.

It consisted of Bertha and two other ladies, Carthew and another man.

"What other evening would suit you, Frank?" Lady Greendale asked as he rose.

"I am afraid I am engaged all through the week, Lady Greendale."

"I am sorry," she said, quietly, "but perhaps it is for the best, Frank."

The door closed behind him just as the party from the garden entered through the French windows.

The next morning George Lechmere went ashore with the steward, when the latter landed to do his marketing. The street up the hill was crowded, and numbers of yachts' sailors were ashore. Stewards with the flat rush baskets, universally used by them, were going from shop to shop; groups of sailors were chatting over the events of the day; and carriages were standing before the fishmongers', poulterers', and fruit and flower shops, while the owners were laying in supplies for their guests. People had driven in from all parts of the island to see the races, and light country carts with eggs, butter, fowls, and fruit were making their way down the steep hill.

George had learnt from a casual remark of Frank's where the house taken by Lord Haverley was situated, and going up the hill turned to the right and kept on until he came to a large house embowered in trees. Breakfast was just over when a servant told Bertha that a gentleman who said his name was George Lechmere wished to speak to her. She went out to him in the hall.

"Well, George," she said, holding out her hand to him frankly, for he was a great favourite of hers; "I suppose you have brought me up a message from Major Mallett?"

"No, Miss Greendale, the Major does not know that I have come to you. It is on my own account that I am here. Could you spare me a quarter of an hour?"

"Certainly, George," she said, in some surprise. "I will come out into the garden. We are likely to have it to ourselves at this hour."

She fetched her hat, and they went out into the garden together. George did not attempt to speak until they reached the other end, where there was a seat in a shady corner.

"Sit down, George," she said.

"Thank you, Miss Greendale, I would rather stand," and he took his place in front of her.

"I have a story to tell you," he said. "It is very painful for me to have to tell it, and it will be painful for you to hear it; but I am sure that you ought to know."

Bertha did not say anything, but looked at him with eyes wide open with surprise.

"I am sure, Miss Greendale," George went on, "that the Major never told you that the bad wound he received at Delhi that all but killed him, was my doing—that he was wounded by a ball from my musket."

"No, George, he certainly never said so. I suppose he was in front of you, and your musket went off accidentally?"

"No, Miss Greendale, I took deliberate aim at him, and it was only the mercy of God that saved his life."

Bertha was too surprised and shocked to speak, and he went on:

"He himself thought that he had been hit by a Sepoy bullet, and it was only when I sent for him, believing that I had received my death wound, that he knew that it was I who had hit him."

"But for what?" she asked. "What made you do this terrible thing? I thought he was liked by his men."

"There was no one liked better, Miss Greendale; he was the most popular officer in the regiment, and if the soldiers had known it, and I had escaped being hung for it, I should have been shot the first time I went into action afterwards. It had nothing to do with the army. I enlisted in his company on purpose to shoot him."

Bertha could hardly believe her ears. She looked at the man earnestly. Surely he could not have been drinking at that time of the morning, and she would have doubted his sanity had it not been for the calm and earnest look in his face. He went on:

"I came here to tell you why I shot at him."

"I don't want to hear," she said, hurriedly. "It is no business of mine. I know that whatever it was Major Mallett must have forgiven you. Besides, you saved his life afterwards."

"Excuse me, Miss Greendale, but it is a matter that concerns you, and I pray you to listen to me. You have heard of Martha Bennett, the poor girl who disappeared four years ago, and who was thought to have been murdered."

"Yes, I remember the talk about it. It was never known who had done it."

"She was not murdered," he said. "She returned some months afterwards, but only to die. It was about the time that Sir John was ill, and naturally you would have heard nothing of it.

"Well, Miss Greendale, I was at one time engaged to Martha. I was of a jealous, passionate disposition, and I did not make enough allowance for her being young and naturally fond of admiration. I quarrelled with her and the engagement was broken off, but I still loved her with all my heart and soul."

Then he went on to tell of how maddened he had been when he had seen her talking to Major Mallett, and of the conversation he had overheard in her father's garden, on the evening before she was missing.

"I jumped at the conclusion at once, Miss Greendale, that it was Captain Mallett, as he was then. He had been round saying goodbye to the tenants that afternoon, and I knew that he was going abroad. What could I suppose but that he had ruined my poor girl, and had persuaded her to go out to join him in India? I waited for a time, while they searched for the body I knew they would never find. My own father and mother, in their hearts, thought that I had murdered her in a fit of jealous rage. At last I made up my mind to enlist in his regiment, to follow him to India, kill him, find her, and bring her home."

"How dreadful!" the girl murmured.

"It was dreadful, Miss Greendale. I believe now that I must have been mad at the time. However, I did it, but at the end failed. Mercifully I was saved from being a murderer. As I told you, I was badly wounded. I thought I was going to die, and the doctor thought so, too. So I sent for Captain Mallett that I might have the satisfaction of letting him know that it was I who fired the shot, and that it was in revenge for the wrong that he had done Martha.

"When I told him I saw by his face, even before he spoke, that I had been wrong. He knew nothing whatever of it. Well, miss, he forgave me — forgave me wholly. He told me that he should never mention it to a soul, and as he has never mentioned it even to you, you may see how well he has kept his word. I wanted to leave the regiment. I felt that I could never mix with my comrades, knowing as I did that I had tried to murder their favourite officer. But the Major would not hear of it. He insisted that I should stay, and, even more, he promised that as soon as I was out of hospital I should be his servant, saying that as the son of an old tenant, he would rather have me than anyone else. You can well imagine, then, Miss Greendale, how willingly I would have given my life for him, and that when the chance came I gladly faced odds to save him.

"Before that I had come to learn who the man was. It was a letter from my father that first gave me the clue; he mentioned that another gentleman had left the neighbourhood and gone abroad, just at the time that Major Mallett did. He was a man who had once made me madly jealous by his attentions to Martha at a fete given to his tenants.

"The Major had the same thought, and he told me that he knew the man was a bad fellow, though he did not say why he thought so. Then I heard that Martha had returned to die, and I learned that she had told her mother the name of her destroyer, who deserted her three months after he had taken her away. When he came back from abroad her father and mine and some others met him at Chippenham market. They attacked him, and I believe would have killed him, had he not ridden off. The next day he went up to London, and a fortnight later his estate was in the market, and he never came into that part of the country again.

"I have told you all this, Miss Greendale, because I have heard that you know the man, and I thought you ought to know what sort of a man he is. His name is Carthew."

Bertha had grown paler and paler as the story went on, and when he ended, she sat still and silent for two or three minutes. Then she said in a low tone:

"Thank you, George. You have done right in telling me this story; it is one that I ought to know. I wonder—" and she stopped.

"You wonder that the Major did not tell you, Miss Greendale. I asked him, myself. When you think it over, you will understand why he could not tell you; for he had no actual proof, save the dying girl's words and what I had seen and heard; and his motive in telling it might have been misunderstood. But he told me that, even at the risk of that, he should feel it his duty, if you became engaged to that villain, to tell the story to Lady Greendale.

"But if he found it hard to speak, there seemed to me no reason why I shouldn't. Except my father and mother and he, no one knows that I was well nigh a murderer. And though he has so generously forgiven me, and I have in a small way tried to show my gratitude to him, it was still painful to me to have to tell the story to anyone else. But I felt that I ought to do it—not for his sake, because he has told me that what I had looked for and what he had so hoped for is not to be—but because I thought that you ought not to be allowed to sacrifice your life to such a man; and partly, too, because I wished to spare my dear master the pain of telling the story, and of perhaps being misunderstood."

"Thank you, George," she said, quietly. "You have done quite right in telling—"

At this moment some voices were heard at the other end of the garden.

"I will be going at once," George said, seizing the opportunity of getting away; and turning, he walked down the garden and left the house.

"Who is your friend, Bertha?" Miss Haverley said, laughingly, as she met Bertha coming slowly down the garden.

"Why—is anything the matter?" she exclaimed, as she caught sight of her face.

"I have become suddenly faint, Hannah," Bertha replied. "I suppose it was the heat yesterday; and it is very warm this morning, too. I am better now, and it will soon pass over. I will go indoors for half an hour, and then I shall be quite right again.

"My friend is no one particular. He is Major Mallett's factotum. He only brought me up a message, but as I know all the men on the Osprey, and have not been on board this season, of course there was a good deal to ask about."

"Well, you must get well as soon as you can," Miss Haverley said. "You know we shall leave in half an hour for the yacht, so as to get under way in time for the start."

At the appointed time, Bertha joined the party below. Her eyes looked heavy and her cheeks were flushed, but she assured Miss Haverley that she felt quite herself now, and that she was sure that the sea air would set her up altogether. The schooner was under way a quarter of an hour before the gun was fired, and sailed east, as the course was twice round the Nab and back.

Yachts were flitting about in all directions, for a light air had only sprung up during the last half hour.

"There is the Phantom," Lord Haverley said. "She has been cruising about the last two days to get her sails stretched, and they look uncommonly well. Carthew told me yesterday that she would be across early this morning, and that he should go round with the race to see how she did. I think you young ladies will have a very good chance of being able to boast that you have sailed in the yacht that won the Queen's Cup. I fancy it lies between her and the Osprey. Mallett is getting up sail, too, I see, but as the Phantom is going with the race, I don't suppose he will. She is a fine craft, though I own I like the cutter rig better. The Phantom will have to allow her time, but not a great deal, for the yawl is the heaviest tonnage.

"There is the starting gun. They are all close together at the line.

"That is a pretty sight, Lady Greendale. Talk about the start of race horses, it is no more to be compared with it than light to dark."

After cruising about for three or four hours, their schooner dropped anchor near the Osprey, which had come in half an hour before.

"Have you ever been on board the Osprey, Lord Haverley?" Bertha asked.

"No, my dear, I don't know that I have ever before been in any port with your friend Major Mallett."

"Well, what do you say to our going on board for a few minutes, on our way to shore? Mamma and I are very fond of her, and I am her godmother, having christened her."

"Godmother and curate coupled in one, eh, Bertha? We will go by all means; that is to say, we cannot invade him in a body, but those of us who know Mallett can go on board, and the gig can come back and take the rest ashore and then come to fetch us."

Accordingly, Lord Haverley and his daughter, Lady Greendale and Bertha, and two others of the party were rowed to the Osprey. Frank saw them coming and met them at the gangway.

"We are taking you by storm, Major," Lord Haverley said, "but Lady Greendale and her daughter claim an almost proprietary interest in the Osprey, because the latter is her godmother. Indeed, we are all naturally interested in her, too, as being one of our cracks. She is a very smart-looking craft, though I think it is a pity that she is not cutter rigged."

"She would look prettier, no doubt," Frank said; "but, you see, though she was built as a racer, and I like a race occasionally, that was not my primary object. I wanted her for cruising, and there is no doubt that a yawl is more handy, and you can work her with fewer hands than you can a cutter of the same size."

They went round the vessel, and then returning on deck, sat down and chatted while waiting for the boat's return.

"I sincerely hope that you will win, Frank, on Friday," Lady Greendale said. "Our sympathies are rather divided, but I hope the Osprey will win."

"Thank you, Lady Greendale, but I am by no means sanguine about it.

"I fancy, Miss Haverley, that you and Miss Greendale will see the winning flag flying overhead when the race is over."

"Why do you think so, Major?" Lord Haverley asked. "The general opinion is that your record is better than that of the Phantom. She has done well in the two or three races she has sailed, but she certainly did not beat the Lesbia or the Mermaid by as much as you did."

"That may be," Frank agreed, "but I regard Carthew as having been born under a lucky star; and though my own opinion is that if the Phantom were in other hands we should beat her, I fancy his luck will pull her through."

Haverley laughed. "I should not have given you credit for being superstitious, Major."

"I don't think that I have many superstitions, but I own to something like it in this case."

Bertha looked earnestly at him. Just before the gig returned from the shore, she and Frank were standing together.

"I am sorry that I shall not have your good wishes tomorrow," he said.

"I have not said that anyone will have my good wishes," she replied. "I shall be on board the Phantom because I was invited there before you asked me, but my hope is that the best yacht will win. I want to speak to you for a minute or two. When can I see you?"

"I can come up tomorrow morning early," he replied. "What time will best suit you?"

"Ten o'clock; please ask for mamma."

The next morning, Lady Greendale and Bertha came together into the sitting room into which Frank had been shown on calling at Lord Haverley's.

"You are early, Frank."

"Yes, Lady Greendale. I am going for a run round the island. It makes me fidgety to sit all day with nothing to do, and I am always contented when I am under sail. As I shan't have time to come in tomorrow morning, for you know we start at nine, I thought that I would drop in this morning, even if the hour was an early one."

After chatting for a few minutes, Lady Greendale made some excuse to leave the room.

"She knew that you were coming, and that I wanted to speak to you," said Bertha.

"Well, what is it—anything of importance?" he asked with a smile.

She hesitated and then went on.

"Some words you spoke yesterday recalled to me something you said nearly four years ago. Do you remember when we sat next to each other in the twilight, the day before you went to India? We were talking about superstitions then, and you told me that you had only one, and said what it was—you remember?"

"I remember," he said, gravely.

"About someone who had beaten you always, and who you thought always would beat you, if you came in contact again. You would not tell me his name. Was it Mr. Carthew?"

"I would not answer the question then, Bertha, and you surely cannot expect me to answer it now."

"I do expect you to answer it."

"Then I must most emphatically decline to do so," he said. "What! do you think that if it were he, I would be so base as to discredit him now? For you must remember that I said that only one of my defeats was due to foul play, that most of the others were simply due to the fact that he was a better man than I was. The matter has long since been forgotten, and, whoever it is, I would not prejudice him in the opinion of anyone by raising up that old story. I have no shadow of proof that it was he who damaged my boat. It might have been the act of some boatman about the place who had laid his money against my winning."

"That is enough," she said quietly. "I did not think that you would tell me whether it was Mr. Carthew, but I was sure that if it were not he you would not hesitate to say so. Thank you, that is all I wanted to see you for. What you said yesterday brought that talk we had so vividly into my mind that I could not resist asking you. It explained what seemed to me at the time to be strange; how it was that you, who are generally so cordial in your manner, were so cold to him when you first met him at our house. I thought that there might be something more serious—" and she looked him full in the face.

"Perhaps I am a prejudiced beggar," he said, with an attempt to smile, and then added somewhat bitterly; "You see things since have not been calculated to make me specially generous in his case."

She did not reply, and after a moment's pause he said, "Well, as Lady Greendale seems to be busy, I will be going."

"You will come to the ball tomorrow evening, won't you?" she asked.

"I suppose I shall have to," he said. "If I win, though mind I feel sure that I shan't, it will seem odd if I don't come. If I lose, it will look as if I sulked."

"You must come," she said, "and you must have a dance with me. You have not been keeping your word, Major Mallett. You said that you would always be the same to me, and you are not. You have never once asked me to dance with you, and you are changed altogether."

"I try to be—I try hard, Bertha; but just at present it is beyond me. I cannot stand by and see you going—" and he stopped abruptly.

"Well, never mind, Bertha. It will all come right in time, but at any rate I cannot stand it at present. Goodbye."

And without giving her time to reply, he hastily left the room.

Bertha stood silent for a minute or two, then quietly followed him out of the room.

The next day Ryde was astir early. It was the Queen's Cup day. Eight yachts were entered: three schooners—the Rhodope, the Isobel, and the Mayflower; four cutters—the Pearl, the Chrysalis, the Alacrity, and the Phantom; and the Osprey, which was the only yawl. It was half-past eight, and all were under way under mainsail and jib.

The Solent was alive with yachts. They were pouring out from Southampton water, they were coming up from Cowes, and some were making their way across from Portsmouth. The day was a fine one for sailing.

"Have you got the same extra hands as last time?" Frank asked the skipper.

"All the same, sir. They all know their work well, and of course if there is anything to be done aloft, our own men go up. I don't think any of them will beat us in smartness."

As the time approached for the start, the racers began to gather in the neighbourhood of the starting line; and as the five-minutes gun fired, the topsail went up, and they began to sail backwards and forwards near it.

As the Phantom crossed under the lee of the Osprey, the three ladies waved their handkerchiefs to Frank, who took off his cap.

"May the best yacht win," Bertha called out, as the vessels flew quickly apart.

"We could not want a better day, George," Frank said. "We can carry everything comfortably, and there is not enough wind to kick up much of a sea. As far as we are concerned, I would rather that the wind had been either north or south, so that we could have laid our course all round; as it is, we shall have the wind almost dead aft till we are round the Nab, then we shall be close-hauled, with perhaps an occasional tack along the back of the island, then free again back. There is no doubt that the cutters have a pull close-hauled. I fancy with this wind the schooners will be out of it; though if it had been a reach the whole way, they would have had a good chance.

"Four minutes are gone."

He was holding his watch in his hand, and after a short pause called out, "Five seconds gone."

The Osprey had a good position at present; though, with the wind aft, this was of comparatively little consequence. She was nearly in a line with the mark boat nearest to the shore, and some hundred and fifty yards from it.

"Haul in the main sheet," Hawkins said quietly, and the men stationed there hauled on the rope until he said, "That will do, we must not go too fast."

He went on, turning to Frank (who had just called out, "Twenty seconds gone"):

"I think that we shall about do."

The latter nodded.

"A bit more, lads," the skipper said ten seconds later. "That will do."

"Fifteen seconds more," Frank said presently.

"Slack away the sheet, slack it away handsomely. Up foresail, that is it," shouted the skipper.

As the boom ran out, and the foresail went up, the Osprey glided on with accelerated speed, and the end of the bowsprit was but a few yards from the starting line when the gun fired.

"Bravo, good start," Frank said, as he looked round for the first time.

The eight yachts were all within a length of each other, and a cheer broke from the boats around as they sped on their way. For a time there was but little difference between them, and then the cutters began to show a little in front. Their long booms gave them an advantage over the schooners and the yawl when before the wind; the spinnaker was not then invented, and the wind was not sufficiently dead aft to enable the schooners to carry their mainsail and foresails, wing and wing; or for the yawl's mizzen to help her.

As they passed Sea View the cutters were a length ahead, the Phantom having a slight advantage over her sisters. They gained no further, for the schooners fell into their wake as soon as they were able to do so, thus robbing them of some of their wind. The Osprey, having the inside station, kept straight on, and came up with the cutters as they were abreast of the end of the island. All were travelling very fast through the water.

"We shall be first round the Nab, sir," Hawkins said in delight. "The schooners are smothering the cutters, but they are not hurting us."

"Give her plenty of room when we get there," Frank said.

The skipper nodded. "I won't risk a foul, sir, you may be sure."

The three ladies on board the Phantom were seated on footstools under the weather bulwark—although as yet the yachts were travelling on an almost even keel. Miss Haverley and Lady Olive uttered exclamations of satisfaction as the Phantom slowly drew ahead of the others, and were loud in their disgust as they saw the effect of the schooner's sail behind them on their own speed.

"I don't call it fair," the former said; "if a vessel cannot sail well herself, that she should be allowed to damage the chances of others. Do you, Bertha?"

"I don't know. I suppose it is equally fair for all, and that we should do the same if a boat had got ahead of us. Still, it is very tiresome, but it is just as bad for the other cutters."

"Look at the Osprey," Lady Olive said soon afterwards. "She is coming up fast; you see, she has nothing behind her. I do believe that she is going to pass us."

"It won't make much difference," Carthew, who was standing close to her, said confidently. "The race won't really begin until we are round the Nab, and after that we shan't hamper each other. I am quite content with the way that we are going."

The Osprey rounded the lightship two lengths ahead, the Phantom came next, three lengths before the Chrysalis, and the others followed in quick succession. The sheets were hauled in, and the yachts were able to lie close-hauled for Ventnor. The three leading boats maintained their respective places, but drew out from each other, and when they passed Ventnor the Osprey was some five lengths ahead of the Phantom.

"Don't be downcast, ladies," Carthew said, gaily. "We have a long way to go yet, and once round the point we shall have to turn till we pass the Needles."

The sea was now getting a good deal rougher. The wind was against tide, and the yachts began to throw the spray over the bows. Bertha was struck with the confidence with which Carthew had spoken, and watched him closely.

"We shall get it a good deal worse off St. Catherine's Head," he went on. "There is a race there even in the calmest weather, and I should advise you to get your wraps ready, for the spray will be flying all over her when we get into it."

They were now working tack and tack, but the Osprey was still improving her position, and as they neared St. Catherine's Head she was a good quarter of a mile to the good. Still Carthew maintained his good temper, but Bertha could see that it was with an effort. He seemed to pay but little attention to the sailing of the Phantom, but kept his eyes intently fixed upon the Osprey.

"I should not be surprised at some of us carrying away a spar before long," he said. "The wind is freshening, and we shall have to shift topsails and jibs, I fancy."

They were now lying far over, and the water was two or three planks up the lee deck. Each time the cutter went about, the ladies carried their footstools up to windward, when the vessel was for a moment on an even keel. When there they were obliged to sit with one hand over the rail, to prevent themselves from sliding down to leeward as the vessel heeled.

"There goes the Chrysalis's topmast," the skipper exclaimed suddenly. "That does for her chance. I think I had better get the jib header ready for hoisting, Mr. Carthew; the spar is bending like a whip."

"Yes, I think you had better get it up at once, captain. It is no use running any risk."

As the Phantom's big topsail came down, the Osprey's was seen to flutter and then to descend.

"He has only been waiting for us," the captain said.

Carthew made no reply. He was still intently watching the craft ahead.

"It is just as well for him," the captain went on. "He will be in the race directly."

Bertha was still watching Carthew's face. Cheerful as his tones were, there was an expression of anxiety in it. Three minutes later, he gave an exclamation as of relief, and a shout rose from the men forward.

Following the direction of his eyes, she saw the bowsprit of the Osprey swing to leeward, and a moment later her topmast fall over her side.

"What did I tell you?" Carthew said, exultingly. "A race is never lost till it is won."

"Oh! I am sorry," Bertha said. "I do think it is hard to lose a race by an accident."

"Every yacht has to abide by its own accidents, Miss Greendale; and carrying away a spar is one of the accidents one counts on. If it were not for that risk, yachts would always carry on too long. It is a matter of judgment and of attention to gear. The loss of a spar is in nine times out of ten the result either of rashness or of inattention.

"However, I am sorry myself; that is to say, I would prefer winning the cup by arriving first at the flag boat. However, I am certainly not disposed to grumble at Fortune just at present."

"I should think not, Mr. Carthew," Lady Olive said. "I am sure I congratulate you very heartily. Of course, I have seen scores of races, and whenever there is any wind someone is always sure to lose a spar, and sometimes two or three will do so. I don't think you need fear any of the boats behind."

"No, yet I don't feel quite safe. I have no fear of any of the cutters, but once round the Needles, it will be a broad reach, and you will see that the schooners will come up fast, and I have to allow them a good bit of time. However, I think we are pretty safe."

Chapter 9

The Phantom presently came along close to the Osprey, and Carthew shouted:

"Is there anything that I can do for you?"

"No, thank you," Frank replied.

Then Bertha called out:

"I am so sorry."

Frank waved his hand in reply. The men were all busy trying to get the wreckage alongside. The cross-trees had been carried away by the fall of the topmast, and her deck forward was littered with gear. The difficulty was greatly increased by the heavy sea in the race.

"As soon as you have got everything on board, Hawkins, we will put a couple of reefs in the mainsail. She will go well enough under that and the foresail. If the mizzen is too much for her, we can take it off."

It was nearly half an hour before all was clear, and the last of the yachts in the race had passed them before the leeward sheet of the foresail was hauled aft, and the Phantom resumed her course. As soon as she did so, the captain came aft with part of the copper bar of the bobstay.

"There has been foul play, sir," he said. "I thought there must have been, for I could not imagine that this bar would have broken unless there had been a flaw in the metal or it had been tampered with. I unshackled it myself, for I thought it was better that the men should not see it until I had told you about it."

"Quite right, Hawkins. Yes, there is no doubt that there has been foul play. The bar has been sawn three-quarters of the way through with a fine saw, and, of course, it went as soon as she began to dip her bowsprit well into it in the race. You see, whoever has done it has poured some acid into it, and darkened the copper, partly perhaps to prevent the colour of the freshly-cut metal from being noticed, and partly to give it the appearance, after it was broken, of being an old cut."

"It cannot have been that, sir, for we were out in quite as rough a sea as this last week, and the bowsprit would have gone then if this cut had been there. Besides, we should have been sure to have noticed it when we went round her to polish up her sides."

"I don't know about that, Hawkins. You see, the cut is from below, and it is only two or three inches above the waterline. It might very well have been there without being noticed. Still, I agree with you, it could not have been there last week, or it must have gone when she put her nose into it then. In point of fact, I have no doubt that it was done last night or the night before. It could easily have been managed. Of course, everyone was below, both here and in the yachts lying round us, and a man might very well have come out in a small boat between one and two o'clock in the morning, and done this without being noticed."

"He might have done that, sir, but we should have heard the grating down in the forecastle."

"I don't know, Hawkins. A fine steel saw, such as burglars use, will work its way through an iron bar almost noiselessly, and I should say that it would go through copper almost as easily as it would through hard wood. It is as well to say nothing to the crew about it, but I think it my duty to lay the matter before the club committee, and they can do as they like about it. Mind, I don't say for a moment that it was done by anyone on board the Phantom. It may have been someone on shore who had laid a bet of a few pounds against us, and wanted to make sure of winning his money. Besides, the Phantom might very well have hoped to have beaten us fairly, for she was just as much fancied as we were. Take it below, and lay it in my cabin, and when we get in unshackle the other bit of the bar, and put it with this."

It was impossible, however, when the bowsprit and bobstay were brought on board, that the crew should have failed to notice the break in the bar, and the news that there had been foul play had at once been passed round. Seeing the angry faces of the men, and the animated talk forward, Frank told the captain to call all hands aft.

"Look here, my men," he said. "I see that you are all aware of what has taken place. It is most disgraceful and unfortunate, and I need hardly say that I am as much vexed as yourselves at losing the Cup, which, but for that, we must have carried off. However, it is one of those cases in which there is nothing to be done, and we should only make things worse by making a fuss about it. We have no ground whatever for believing that it was the work of one of the Phantom's crew, and it is far more likely that it was the work of some longshore loafer who had laid more than he could afford against us. It has partly been our own fault, but we shall know better in future, and your captain will take good care that there shall be an anchor watch set for two or three nights before we sail another race.

"What I have called you up for is to beg of you not to make this an occasion for disputes or quarrels ashore. Hitherto I have been proud of the good behaviour of my crew, and I should be sorry indeed to hear that there was any row ashore between you and the Phantom's men. They at least have nothing to boast of. They have won the Cup, but we have won the honour. We have shown ourselves the better yacht, and should have beaten them by something like a mile, if it had not been for this accident. Therefore it is my express wish and order that you do not show your natural disappointment on shore. You can give the real reason of our defeat, but do not say a word of blame to anyone, for we know not who was the author of the blackguardly act.

"Of course, the matter cannot be kept altogether a secret, for it will be my duty to lay it before the committee. I shall make no protest. If they choose to institute an inquiry they must do so, but I shall take no steps in the matter, and it is unlikely in the extreme that we shall ever know who did it. I shall pay you all winning money, for that you did not win was no fault of yours. One thing I will wager, though I am not a betting man, and that is, that the next time we meet the Phantom we shall beat her, by as much as we should have done today, but for this accident."

The appearance of the Osprey as she sailed into the anchorage, without topmast or bowsprit, excited great attention; and many of the yachtsmen came on board to inquire how the disaster had happened. To save going through the story a score of times, Frank had the broken pieces of the bobstay bar brought up and laid on the deck near the tiller, and in reply to inquiries simply pointed to them, saying:

"I think that tells the tale for itself."

All were full of indignation at the dastardly outrage.

"What are you going to do, Major?"

"I am not going to do anything, except take it ashore and hand it to the Sailing Committee. That it has been cut is certain. As to who cut it, there is no shadow of evidence."

"If I were in Carthew's place," one of them said, "I should decline to take the Cup under such circumstances, and would offer to sail the race over again with you as soon as you had repaired damages."

"I should decline the offer if he made it," he said, quietly. "It is probable that we shall meet in a race again some day, and then we can fight it out, but for the present it is done with. He has won the Queen's Cup, and I must put up with my accidents."

The effect produced by the facts reported to the committee, and their examination of the broken bar, was very great. Such a thing had not been known before in the annals of yachting, and the committee ordered a poster to be instantly printed and stuck up offering a reward of 100 pounds for proof that would lead to the conviction of the author of the outrage.

Frank returned on board at once, and sent off a boat, towing behind it the broken bowsprit and topmast to Cowes, with instructions to Messieurs White to have two fresh spars got ready, by the following afternoon if possible.

He did not go ashore again until he landed, at half-past ten, at the clubhouse. Every window was lit up, and dancing had begun an hour before. Frank at once obtained a partner, in order to avoid having to talk the unpleasant business over with yachting friends.

Presently he sat down by the side of Lady Greendale.

"I am so sorry, Frank," she said. "It does seem hard when you had set your mind on it."

"I had hoped to win," he said, "but it is not as bad as all that after all. It would have been more mortifying to lose because the Osprey was not fast enough, than to lose from an accident, when she had already proved herself to be the best in the race. You know that I never went in for being a racing yachtsman. I look upon racing as being a secondary part of yachting. I can assure you, I don't feel that I am greatly to be pitied. It might have been better, and it might have been a great deal worse."

"Well, I am glad that you take it in that way," she said. "I can assure you that I was greatly upset over it when I heard it."

He sat chatting with her for some time. Presently Bertha was brought back by her partner to her mother's side.

"Thank you for your hail as you passed us, Miss Greendale. It sounded hearty, and really cheered me up, for just at the moment I was in an exceedingly bad temper, I can assure you. You see, my forebodings came true, and luck was against me."

"Not luck," she said, indignantly. "You would have won but for treachery."

"Treachery is rather a hard word," he said. "However, it is of no use crying over spilt milk. I have lost, and shall live to fight another day, I hope; and next time I shall win. Still, you know, there is really nothing to grumble at. I have been fortunate altogether this season, and as I bought the Osprey as a cruiser, I have done a great deal better with her than I could have expected."

At this moment another partner of Bertha's came up, and was about to carry her off, when she said:

"I suppose the Osprey can sail still, Major Mallett?"

"Oh, yes. She is a lame duck, you know, but she can get about all right."

"Well, why don't you ask mamma and me to take a sail with you tomorrow afternoon?"

"I shall be very happy to do so," he said, "but I almost think that you had better wait until she gets her spars. I don't think that they will be finished before tomorrow evening. The men can get to work early in the morning, and we can be here by two o'clock next day."

"No, I think that we will come tomorrow, Major Mallett.

"It will be a novelty to sail in a cripple, won't it, mamma?

"Besides, you know, or you ought to know, that the day after tomorrow is Sunday, and that at present our plans are arranged for going up to town on Monday."

"That being so," Frank said with a smile, "by all means come tomorrow. Will you come to lunch, or afterwards?"

"Afterwards, I think. We will be down at the club landing stage at half-past two."

"Bertha is bent upon taking possession of you tomorrow," Lady Greendale said, smiling, as the girl turned away; "and I shall be glad for her to have a quiet two or three hours out of the racket. A large party is very fatiguing, and I think that it has been too much for her. Yesterday and today she has been quite unlike herself; at one time sitting quiet and saying nothing, at other times rattling away with Miss Haverley and Lady Olive, and absolutely talking down both of them, which I should have thought impossible. She seems to me to be altogether over-excited. I thought it would have been a rest for her to get away for a week from the fag in London, but I am sorry now that we came down altogether. I am a little worried about it, Frank."

"Well, the season is drawing towards its end now, Lady Greendale, and if you can get a short time at home no doubt it will do you good. I did not think that Bertha was looking well when I saw her yesterday."

Frank danced a couple more dances, and then went to Lady Greendale and said:

"Will you make my excuses to Bertha? and tell her that, having shown myself here, so that it might not be thought that I was out of temper at my bad luck, I shall be off. Indeed, I do not feel quite up to entering into the thing. You can understand, dear Lady Greendale, that at present things are going rather hardly with me."

She gave him a sympathetic look. "I can understand, Frank," she said; "but here she comes. You can make your excuses yourself."

"I can quite understand that you don't care about staying," Bertha said, when he repeated what he had said to her mother. "Well, I will give you the next dance, or, what will be nicer, I will sit it out with you. Ah, here is my partner.

"I am afraid I have made a mistake, Mr. Jennings, and have got my card mixed up. Do you mind taking the thirteenth dance instead of this? I shall be very much obliged if you will."

Her partner murmured his assent.

"Thank you," Frank said, as she took his arm. "Now, shall we go out on the balcony, or on the lawn?"

"The lawn, I think. It is a lovely evening, and there is no fear of catching cold.

"I am afraid that you are very disappointed," she went on, as they went out. "I am disappointed, too. I told you I wanted the best yacht to win, and it has not done so."

"Thank you," he replied, quietly. "I should have liked to have won, just this once, but all along I felt that the chances were against me, and that fortune would play me some trick or other."

"It was not fortune. Fortune had nothing to do with it," she said, indignantly. "You were beaten by a crime—by a mean, miserable crime—by the same sort of crime by which you were beaten before."

"I have no reason for supposing that there is any connection."

"Frank," she broke in, suddenly, and he started as for the first time for years she called him by his Christian name, "you are an old friend of ours, and you promised me that you would always be my friend. Do you think that it is right to be trying to throw dust into my eyes? Don't you think, on the contrary, that as a friend you should speak frankly to me?"

Frank was silent for a moment.

"On some subjects, yes, Bertha; on others, what has passed between us makes it very difficult for a man to know what he ought to do. But be assured that if I saw you make any fatal mistake, any mistake at least that I believed to be fatal, I should not hesitate, even if I knew that I should be misunderstood, and that I should forfeit your liking, by so doing. This is just one of the cases when I do not feel justified, as yet, in speaking. Carthew is not my friend, and you know it. If I had had no personal feud—for it has become that with him—I should be more at liberty to speak, but as it is I would rather remain silent. I tell you this now, that you may know, in case I ever do meddle in your affairs, how painful it is for me to do so, and how unwillingly I do it. At any rate, there is nothing whatever to connect the accident that took place today with him. The event is one of a series of successes that he has gained over me. It does not affect me much, for though I should have liked to have won today, I don't feel about such matters as I used to.

"You see, when a man has suffered one heavy defeat, he does not care about how minor skirmishes may go."

They walked up and down in silence for some time, then she said quietly:

"The music has stopped. I think, Frank, that I had better go in again. So you will take us tomorrow?"

"Certainly," he said.

He took her in to Lady Greendale, and then went off to the Osprey. He was feeling in higher spirits than he had done for some time, as he walked up and down the deck for an hour before turning in. It seemed to him that she might not after all accept Carthew, and that he would not be obliged to bring trouble upon her by telling the shameful story.

"It will be all the same, as far as I am concerned," he said to himself, "but I am sure that I could stand her marrying anyone else; which, of course, she will do before long, better than Carthew. I hear whispers that he was hard hit at Ascot, though he gives out that he won. Not that that matters much, but it is never a good lookout for a girl to marry a man who gambles, even though she be rich, and her friends take good care to settle her money upon herself. She evidently suspects that he is at the bottom of this trick, and she would hardly think so if she really cared for him. But if she does think so, I fancy that the winning of the Queen's Cup will cost him dearly.

"I wonder why she has apparently so set her mind on going out with us tomorrow."

Carthew enjoyed his triumph that evening, loudly expressed his indignation and regret at the scandalous affair to which he owed his victory, frankly said that he could hardly have hoped to win the Cup had it not been for that, and expressed his determination to add another hundred pounds to the reward offered by the club for the discovery of the author of the outrage. The men felt that it was hard on a fellow to win the Cup by the breakdown of an opponent in that way, and the ladies admired the sincere way in which he expressed his regrets. He was a good dancer, a good talker, and a handsome man; and as few of them knew Frank, they had no particular interest in his misfortune.

He danced only once with Bertha, who said:

"As the hero of the occasion, Mr. Carthew, you must be generous in your attentions and please everyone."

"I suppose I must obey you, Miss Greendale," he said, "but I had hoped to have had an opportunity of saying something particular to you tonight."

"Really?" she answered innocently. "Well, I shall be at home tomorrow morning, and if you come up about eleven you are sure to find me."

"Miss Greendale is at the other end of the garden, sir," the servant said, as he enquired for her the next morning. "She asked me to tell you if you called that she was there."

With considerable assurance of success, Carthew walked into the garden. She must know what he wanted to say to her, and he had of late felt sure that her answer would be favourable when the question was put. She was sitting on the same bench on which two days before she had heard George Lechmere's story.

"You know what I have come for, Miss Greendale," he began at once. "I think that you know how I feel towards you, and how deeply I love you. I have come to ask you to be my wife."

"Before I answer you, Mr. Carthew," she said, calmly, "I must ask you to listen to a story. It was told me here two days ago by a man named George Lechmere. Do you know him?"

"I seem to have heard his name, though I cannot say where," he replied, surprised at the coolness with which she spoke.

"He is a farmer's son, I believe, and he was an interested party, though not the chief actor of the story. The chief actor, I suppose I should say actress, was Martha Bennett. You know her?"

Carthew stepped back as if he had received a sudden blow. His face paled, and he gave a short gasp.

"I see you know her," she went on. "She was a poor creature, I fancy, and her story is one that has often been told before. She threw away the love of an honest man, and trusted herself to a villain. He betrayed the trust, took her away to America and then cast her off, and she went home to die. Her destroyer did not altogether escape punishment. He was attacked and pelted by her father and his friends in the market place at Chippenham. You see, it all happened in my neighbourhood, and the villain, not daring to show his face in the county again, disposed of his estate."

"You don't believe this infamous lie?" Carthew said hoarsely.

"How do you know that it is an infamous lie, Mr. Carthew? I have mentioned no names. I have simply told you the story of a hapless girl, whom you once knew. Your face is the best witness that I can require of its truth. Thank God I heard it in time. Had it not been for that I might have been fool enough to have given you the answer you wanted, for I own that I liked you. I am sure now that I did not love you, for had I done so, I should not have believed this tale; or if I had believed it, it would have crushed me. But I liked you. I found you pleasanter than other men, and I even fancied that I loved you. Had I not known this story, I might have married you, and been the most miserable woman alive, for a man who could play the villain to a hapless girl, who could stoop to so mean and dastardly an action as to cripple a rival yacht, is a creature so mean, so detestable, that wretched indeed would be the fate of the woman that married him.

"Do not contradict it, sir," she said, rising from her seat now with her face ablaze with indignation. "I was watching you. I had heard that story, and had heard another story of how the boat of an antagonist of yours at Henley had been crippled before a race, and I watched you from the time I came on board. I saw that you were strangely confident; I saw how you were watching for something; I saw the flash of triumph in your face when that something happened; and I was absolutely certain that the same base manoeuvre that had won you your heat at Henley had been repeated in your race for the Queen's Cup.

"I don't think, sir, you will want any more specific answer to your question."

"You will repent this," he panted, his face distorted by a raging disappointment. "I do not contradict your statements. It would be beneath me to do so; but some day you may have cause to regret having made them."

"I may tell you," she said, as she turned, "that it is not my intention to make public the knowledge that I gained of your conduct yesterday. I have no proof save my own absolute conviction, and the knowledge that I have of your past."

He did not look round, but walked at a rapid pace down the garden. Half an hour later the Phantom's anchor was got up, and she sailed for Southampton Water. Beyond giving the necessary order to get under way, Carthew did not speak a word until she anchored off the pier, then he went ashore at once and took the next train for town, sending off a telegram before starting.

When he got home he asked the servant briefly if Mr. Conking had come.

"Yes, sir. He is waiting for you in the dining room."

"Well, Carthew, how have things gone off? I see by the papers this morning that you won the Cup, and also that the Osprey's bobstay burst at the right time, and that a great sensation had been caused by the discovery that there had been foul play.

"Why, what is the matter with you? You look as black as a thundercloud."

"And no wonder. I won the race, but I have lost the girl."

"The deuce you have. Why, I thought that you felt quite certain of that."

"So I did; and it would have come off all right if some infernal fellow had not turned up, and told her about an old affair of mine that I thought buried and forgotten three or four years ago; and it took me so aback that, as she said, my face was the best evidence of the truth of the story. More than that, she declared that she knew that I was at the bottom of the Osprey's business. However, she has no evidence about that; but the other story did the business for me, and the game is all up in that quarter. There never was such bad luck. She as much as told me that, if I had proposed to her before she had heard the story, she would have said yes."

"No chance of her changing her mind?"

"Not a scrap."

"It is an awkward affair for you."

"Horribly awkward. Yes, I have only got fifteen thousand left, and unless things go right at Goodwood I shall be cleaned right out. I calculated that everything would be set right if I married this girl. Things have gone badly of late."

"Yes, your luck has been something awful. It did seem that with the pains that we took, and the way I cleared the ground for you by bribing jockeys and so on, we ought to have made pots of money. Of course, we did pull off some good things, but others we looked on as safe, and went in for heavily, all turned out wrong."

"Well, there will be nothing for me but to get across the Channel unless, as I say, things go right at Goodwood."

"I should not be nervous about it, for unless there is some dark horse I feel sure that your Rosney has got the race in hand."

"Yes, I feel sure of that, too. We have kept him well back all the season, and never let him even get a place. It ought to be a certainty."

Then they sat some time smoking in silence.

"By gad, I have half a mind to carry her off," Carthew broke out, suddenly. "It is the only way that I can see of getting things straightened out. She acknowledged that she liked me before she heard this accursed story, and if I had her to myself I have no doubt that I could make her like me again in spite of it."

"It is a risky thing to carry a woman off in our days," Conkling said, thoughtfully, "and a deuced difficult one to do. I don't see how you are going to set about it, or what in the world you would do with her, and where you would put her when you had got her. I have done some pretty risky things for you in my time, Carthew, but I should not care about trying that. We might both find ourselves in for seven years."

"Well, you would have as much as that for getting at a horse, and I don't know that you wouldn't for bribing a jockey. Still, I see that it is an uncommonly difficult thing."

For five minutes nothing more was said; then Conkling suddenly broke the silence.

"By Jove, I should say that the yacht would be just the thing."

"That is a good idea, Jim; a first-rate idea if it could be worked out. It would want a lot of scheming, but I don't see why it should not be done. If I could once get her on board, I could cruise about with her for any time, until she gave in."

"You would have to get a fresh crew, Carthew. I doubt whether your fellows would stand it."

"No, I suppose some of them might kick. At any rate, I would not trust them. No, I should have to find a fresh crew. Foreigners would be best, but it would look uncommonly rum for the Phantom to be cruising about with a foreign crew. Besides, I know men in almost every port I should put into."

"Couldn't you alter her rig, or something of that sort, so that she could not be recognised? It seems to me that if you were to take her across to some foreign port, pay off the crew there and send them home, then get her altered and ship a foreign crew, you might cruise about as long as you liked, especially abroad, without a soul being any the wiser; and the girl must sooner or later give in, and if she would not you could make her."

"That is a big idea, Jim. Yes, if I once got my lady on board you may be sure that she would have to say yes sooner or later. I don't often forgive, and it would be a triumph to make her pay for the dressing down she gave me this morning. Besides, I am really fond of her, and I could forgive her for that outbreak, which I suppose was natural enough, after we were married, and there is no reason why we should not get on very well together.

"I tell you what, I will go down the first thing tomorrow to Southampton, and will sail at once for Ostend. There I will pay her off, alter her rig, and ship a fresh crew. I will draw my money from the bank. If things go well, I shall be set up again. If they go badly, there will be some long faces at Tattersall's on settling day, but I shall be away, and the money will be enough if we have to cruise for a couple of years, or double that, before she gives in.

"I shall try mild measures for a good bit; be very respectful and repentant and all that. If I find after a time that that does not fetch her, I must try what threats will do. Anyhow, she won't leave until she steps on shore to be married, or safer still, till I can get a clergyman on board to marry us there. Would you like to go with us?"

"If the thing bursts up, there is nothing I should like better."

"You will have to help me carry her off, Jim, and the day that she signs her name Bertha Carthew I will give you a couple of thousand pounds."

"That is a bargain," the man said. "It is a good scheme altogether, if we can hit upon some plan for carrying her away."

"It is of no use to think of that, until we know where she will be. I don't see at present how it is to be done, but I know that there is always a way if one can think of it. You telegraph to me every day Poste Restante, Ostend, or wherever I am stopping. I will send you the name of the hotel I put up at directly I get there. You had better send someone down at once to Ryde to let you know what she is doing, and when she comes up to town; it is just on the cards that they may not come for a bit, but may go for a cruise in Mallett's yacht, as they did last autumn. Anyhow, let me know, and if I telegraph for you to come over, cross by the next boat.

"Likely enough I may run over myself as soon as I get the business there going all right; but of course I shall stay there if I can. I should get it done in half the time if I were present to push things on. Of course, you will run down and see how the horse is getting on, and pick up any information that you can, and let me know about it."

"I will put that into good hands, Carthew. It is better that I should stay here and watch things at Tattersall's; then I can keep you informed how things are looking every day, and be ready to start as soon as I get your telegram. But, of course, you won't do anything until after the race is run."

"No, I feel as safe as a man can as to Rosney, but even if he wins I shall carry my idea out. I have had enough of the turf, and burnt my fingers enough over it, and I shall be glad to settle down as a country gentleman again. If I lose I shall make a private sale of all my horses before I leave the course. That ought to bring me in another seven or eight thousand pounds for our trip."

Chapter 10

"There is the Phantom getting under way," the skipper said, as his turn up and down the deck brought him close to Frank.

"So she is. I saw her owner go ashore less than an hour ago."

"Yes; he came on board again five minutes ago. The men began to bustle about directly he got on deck. I do hope they won't put in again as long as we are here. The hands are as savage as bulls, and though they remembered what you told them, and there were no rows on shore last night, I shall be glad when we ain't in the same port with the Phantom, for I am sure that if two or three men of each crew were to drop in to the same pub, there would be a fight in no time. And really I could not blame them. It is not in human nature to lose a race like that without feeling very sore over it. I hope she is off. Anyhow, as we are going to Cowes this evening, it will be a day or two before the hands are likely to run against each other, and that will give them time to cool down a bit.

"There is one thing. I bet the Phantom won't enter against us at Cowes. If we were to give them a handsome beating there, it would show everyone that they would have had no chance of winning the Cup if it had not been for the accident."

"No, I don't suppose that we shall meet again this season, and indeed I don't know that I shall do any more racing myself, except that I shall feel it as a sort of duty to enter for the Squadron's open race.

"I think, by the course she is laying, that the Phantom is off to Southampton. Perhaps she is going to meet somebody there. Anyhow, she is not likely to be back until we have started for Cowes."

Frank sat for some time with the paper in his hand, but, although he glanced at it occasionally, his mind took in nothing of its contents. Again and again he watched the Phantom. Yes, she was certainly going to Southampton Water.

From what Bertha had said to him the evening before, he had received a strong hope that she would reject Carthew. Nothing was more probable than that he should have gone ashore that morning, fresh from his victory, to put the question to her, and his speedy return and his order to make sail as soon as he got on deck certainly pointed to the fact that she had refused him.

A load of care seemed to be lifted from Frank's mind. From the first, when he had found that Carthew was a visitor at Lady Greendale's, he had been uncomfortable. He knew the man's persevering nature, and recognised his power of pleasing when he desired to do so. He was satisfied that, when he himself was refused, the reason Bertha gave him was, as far as she knew, the true one; but he had since thought that possibly she might then, although unsuspected by herself, have been to some extent under the spell of Carthew's influence. When she had declined two unexceptional offers, he had been almost convinced that Carthew, when the time came, would receive a more favourable answer. But he had watched them closely on the few occasions when he had seen them together in society, and, certain as he had felt at other times, he had come away somewhat puzzled, and said to himself:

"She is captivated by his manner, as any girl might be, but I doubt whether she loves him."

This impression, however, had always died out in a short time, and he had somehow come to accept the general opinion unquestioningly, that she would accept Carthew when he proposed. He had been prepared to face the alternative of either suffering her to marry a scoundrel, or of taking a step more repugnant to him, which would probably end by an entire breach of his friendship with the Greendales, that of telling them this story. He was therefore delighted to find that the difficulty had been solved by Bertha herself without his intervention, and felt absolutely grateful for the accident which had cost him the Queen's Cup, but had at the same time opened Bertha's eyes to the man's true character. Soon after two o'clock he went ashore in the gig, and at the half hour Lady Greendale and Bertha came down.

"The Osprey looks like a bird shorn of its wings," he said, as he handed them into the boat; "and though the men have made everything as tidy as they could, the two missing spars quite spoil her appearance."

"That does not matter in the least, Frank," Lady Greendale said. "We know how she looks when she is at her best. We shall enjoy a quiet sail in her just as much as if she were in apple-pie order."

"You look fagged, Lady Greendale, though you are pretty well accustomed to gaiety in town."

Lady Greendale did indeed look worn and worried. For the last two or three days, Bertha's manner had puzzled her and caused her some vague anxiety. That morning the girl had come in from the garden and told her that she had just refused Mr. Carthew, and, although she had never been pleased at the idea of Bertha's marrying him, the refusal had come as a shock.

Personally she liked him. She believed him to be very well off, but she had expected Bertha to do much better, and she by no means approved of his fondness for the turf. She had been deeply disappointed at the girl's refusal of Lord Chilson, on whom she had quite set her mind. The second offer had also been a good one. Still, she had reconciled herself to the thought of Bertha's marrying Carthew. His connection with the turf had certainly brought him into contact with a great many good men, he was to be met everywhere, and she could hardly wonder that Bertha should have been taken with his good looks and the brilliancy of his conversation. The refusal, then, came to her not only as an absolute surprise, but as a shock.

She considered that Bertha had certainly given him, as well as everyone else, reason to suppose that she intended to accept him. Many of her intimate friends had spoken to her as if the affair was already a settled matter, and when it became known that Bertha had refused him, she would be set down as a flirt, and it would certainly injure her prospects of making the sort of match that she desired. She had said something of all this to the girl, and had only received the reply:

"I know what I am doing, mamma. I can understand that you thought I was going to marry him. I thought so myself, but something has happened that has opened my eyes, and I have every reason to be thankful that it has. I dare say you think that I have behaved very badly, and I am sorry; but I am sure that I am doing right now."

"What have you discovered, Bertha? I don't understand you at all."

"I don't suppose you do, mamma. I cannot tell you what it is. I told him that I would not tell anybody."

"But you don't seem to mind, Bertha; that is what puzzles me. A girl who has made up her mind to accept a man, and who finds out something that seems to her so bad that she rejects him, would naturally be distressed and upset. You seem to treat it as if it were a matter of no importance."

"I don't quite understand it myself, mamma. I suppose that my eyes have been opened altogether. At any rate, I feel that I have had a very narrow escape. I was certainly very much worried when I first learned about this, two days ago, and I was even distressed; but I think that I have got over the worry, and I am sure that I have quite got over the distress."

"Then you cannot have cared for him," Lady Greendale said, emphatically.

"That is just the conclusion that I have arrived at myself, mamma," Bertha said, calmly. "I certainly thought that I did, and now I feel sure that I was mistaken altogether."

Lady Greendale could say nothing further.

"I had better send off a note to Frank, my dear," she said, plaintively. "Of course you are not thinking of going out sailing after this."

"Indeed, I am, mamma. Why shouldn't we? Of course I am not going to say anything here of what has happened. If he chooses to talk about it he can, but I don't suppose that he will. It is just the end of the season, and we need not go back to town at all, and next spring everyone will have forgotten all about it. You know what people will say: 'I thought that Greendale girl was going to marry Carthew. I suppose nothing has come of it. Did she refuse him I wonder, or did he change his mind?' And there will be an end of it. The end of the season wipes a sponge over everything. People start afresh, and, as somebody says—Tennyson, isn't it? or Longfellow?—they 'let the dead past bury its dead.'"

Lady Greendale lifted her hands in mild despair, put on her things, and went down to the boat with Bertha.

"I have brought a book, mamma," the latter said as they went down. "I shall tell Frank about this, though I shall tell no one else. I always knew that he did not like Mr. Carthew. So you can amuse yourself reading while we are talking."

"You are a curious girl, Bertha," her mother said, resignedly. "I used to think that I understood you; now I feel that I don't understand you at all."

"I don't know that I understand myself, mamma, but I know enough of myself to see that I am not so wise as I thought I was, and somebody says that 'When you first discover you are a fool it is the first step towards being wise,' or something of the sort.

"There is Major Mallett standing at the landing, and there is the gig. I think that she is the prettiest boat here."

The mainsail was hoisted by the time they reached the side of the yacht, and the anchor hove short, so that in two or three minutes they were under way.

"She looks very nice," Lady Greendale said. "I thought that she would look much worse."

"You should have seen her yesterday, mamma, when we passed her, with the jagged stumps of the topmast and bowsprit and all her ropes in disorder, the sails hanging down in the water and the wreckage alongside. I could have cried when I saw her. At any rate, she looks very neat and trim now.

"Where is the Phantom, Major Mallett?"

"She got under way at eleven o'clock, and has gone up to Southampton," he replied, quietly, but with a half-interrogatory glance towards her.

She gave a little nod, and took a chair a short distance from that in which Lady Greendale had seated herself.

"Has he gone for good?" Frank asked, as he sat down beside her.

"Of course he has," she said. "You don't suppose, after what I told you last night, that I was going to accept him."

"I hoped not," he said, gravely. "You cannot tell what a relief it has been to me. Of course, dear, you will understand that so long as you were to marry a man who would be likely to make you happy I was content, but I could not bear to think of your marrying a man I knew to be altogether unworthy of you."

"You know very well," she said, "that you never intended to let me marry him. As I said to you last night, I feel very much aggrieved, Major Mallett. You had said you would be my friend, and yet you let this go on when you could have stopped it at once. You let me get talked about with that man, and you would have gone on letting me get still more talked about before you interfered. That was not kind or friendly of you."

"But, Bertha," he remonstrated, "the fact that we had not been friends, and that he had beaten me in a variety of matters, was no reason in the world why I should interfere, still less why you should not marry him. When I was stupid enough to tell you that story, years ago, I stated that I had no grounds for saying that it was he who played that trick upon my boat, and it would have been most unfair on my part to have brought that story up again."

"Quite so, but there was the other story."

"What other story?" Frank asked in great surprise.

"The story that George Lechmere came and told me two days ago," she said, gravely.

"George Lechmere! You don't mean to say—"

"I do mean to say so. He behaved like a real friend, and came to tell me the story of Martha Bennett.

"He told me," she went on, as he was about to speak, "that you had made up your mind to tell mamma about it, directly you heard that I was engaged to Mr. Carthew. That would have been something, but would hardly have been fair to me. If I had once been engaged to him, it would have been very hard to break it off, and naturally it would have been much greater pain to me then than it has been now."

"I felt that. But you see, Bertha, until you did accept him, I had no right to assume that you would do so. At least so I understood it, and I did not feel that in my position I was called upon to interfere until I learned that you were really in danger of what I considered wrecking your life's happiness."

"I understand that," she said, gently, "and I know that you acted for the best. But there are other things you have not told me, Major Mallett—other things that George Lechmere has told me. Did you think that it would have been of no interest to me to know that you had forgiven the man who tried to take your life; and, more than that, had restored his self respect, taken him as your servant, treated him as a friend?"

The tears stood in her eyes now.

"Don't you think, Frank, that was a thing that I might have been interested to know—a thing that would raise you immeasurably in the eyes of a woman—that would show her vastly more of your real character than she could know by meeting you from day to day as a friend?"

"It was his secret and not mine, Bertha. It was known to but him and me. Never was a man more repentant or more bitterly regretful for a fault— that was in my eyes scarcely a fault at all—except that he had too rashly assumed me to be the author of the ruin of the girl he loved. The poor fellow had been half maddened, and was scarce responsible for his actions. He had already suffered terribly, and the least I could do was to endeavour to restore his self respect by showing him that I had entirely forgiven him. Any kindness that I have shown him he has repaid ten-fold, not only by saving my life, but in becoming my most sincere and attached friend. I promised him that I would tell no one, and I have never done so, and no one to this day knows it, save his father and mother.

"How then could I tell even you? You must see yourself that it was impossible that I could tell you. Besides, the story was of no interest save to him and me; and above all, as I said, it was his secret and not mine."

"I see that now," she said. "Still, I am so sorry, so very sorry, that I did not know it before.

"You see, Frank," she went on, after a pause; "we women have to make or unmake our lives very much in the dark. No one helps us, and if we have not a brother to do so, we are groping in the dark. Look at me. Here was I, believing that Mr. Carthew, whom I met everywhere in society, was, except that he kept race horses and bet heavily, as good as other men. He was very pleasant, very good looking, generally liked, and infinitely more amusing than most men one meets. How was I to tell what he really was?

"On the other hand, there were you, my dear friend, who, I knew, had shown yourself a very brave soldier, and whom also everyone liked and spoke well of, but of whose real character I did not know much, except on the side that was always presented to me; and now I find you capable of what I consider a grand act of generosity."

"You overrate the matter altogether, Bertha. The man shot me by mistake. The fellow he took me for richly deserved shooting. When he found it was a mistake, the poor fellow was bitterly sorry for it. Surely, there was nothing more to be said about it."

The girl sat silent for some time.

"Well, it is all cleared up now," she said at last. "There is no reason why we should not be friends as of old."

"None whatever," he said. "There has been only—" and he stopped short.

"Only what, Frank?"

"Nothing," he said. "We will be just as we were, Bertha. I will try and be the good elder brother, and scold you and look after you, and warn you, if it should be necessary, until you get under other guidance."

"It will be some time," she said, quietly, "before that happens. I have had a sharp lesson."

"And did you really care for him much, Bertha?"

"I don't think that I really cared for him at all," she said. "That is not the lesson that I was thinking of."

He saw the colour mount into her cheeks as she twisted the handkerchief she held into a knot. Then, turning to him, she said:

"Frank, are you never going to give me a chance again?"

He could not misunderstand her.

"Do you mean—can you mean, Bertha?" he said, in a low tone. "Do you mean that if I ask you the same question again you will give me a different answer?"

"I did not know then," she said. "I had never thought of it. You took me altogether by surprise, and what I said I thought was true. Afterwards I knew that I had been mistaken. I hoped that you would ask me again, but you did not, and I soon felt that you never would. You tried hard to be as you were before, but you were not the same, and I was not the same. Then I did not seem to care. There were three men who wanted me. I did not care much which it was, but I would not have anyone say that I had married for position—I hated the idea of that—and so I would have taken the third. He was bright and pleasant, and all that sort of thing, and I thought that I could be happy with him, until George Lechmere opened my eyes. Then, of course, that was over; but his story showed me still more what a fool I had been, what a heart I had thrown away, and I said, 'I will at least make an effort to undo the past. I will not let my chance of happiness go away from me merely from false pride. If he loves me still he will forgive me. If not, at least I shall not, all through my life, feel that I might have made it different could I have brought myself to speak a word.'"

"I love you as much as ever," Frank said, taking her hand. "I love you more for speaking as you have. I can hardly believe my happiness. Can it be that you really love me, Bertha?"

"I think I have proved it, Frank. I do love you. I have known it for some time, but it seemed all too late. It was a grief rather than a pleasure. Every time you came it was a pain to me, for I felt that I had lost you; and it was only when I learned, two days ago, how you could forgive, and that at the same time I could free myself from the chain I had allowed to be wound round me, and which I don't think I could otherwise have broken, that I made up my mind that it should not be my fault if things were not put right between us.

"Now let us tell mother."

Her hand was still in his, and they went across the deck together.

"Mamma," she said, "please put down that book. I have a piece of news for you. Frank and I are going to be married."

Lady Greendale sat for a moment, speechless in astonishment. She knew that Bertha had wished to tell him that she had refused Carthew's offer, but that this would come of it she had never dreamt. A year before she had approved of Bertha's rejection of Frank, but since then much had happened. Bertha had shown that she would not marry for position only, and that she would be likely to take her own way entirely in the matter; and, although this was a downfall to the hopes that she had once entertained, Lady Greendale was herself very fond of Frank, and it was at any rate better than having Bertha marry a man of whose real means she was ignorant, and who, as everyone knew, bet heavily on the turf. These ideas flashed rapidly through her mind, and holding out one hand to each, she said:

"There is no one to whom I could more confidently entrust her happiness, Frank. God bless you both."

Then she betook herself to her pocket handkerchief, for her tears came easily, and on this occasion she herself could hardly have said whether they were the result of pleasure in Bertha's happiness, or regret at the downfall of the air castles she had once built.

"I think, Bertha, our best plan will be to go below now," Frank suggested, quietly.

"What for?" Bertha asked, shyly.

The thing had been done. She felt radiantly happy, but more shocked at her own boldness than she had been when she perpetrated it.

"Well, my dear, I thought that perhaps you would rather not kiss me in sight of the whole crew, and certainly I shan't be able to restrain myself much longer."

"Then, in that case," she said, demurely, "perhaps we had better go below."

It was half an hour before they came on deck again.

"Well, my dears," Lady Greendale said, "the more I think of it the better I am pleased. As far as I am concerned, nothing could be nicer. I shall have Bertha within a short drive of me, and it won't be like losing her.

"Do you know, Bertha, your father said to me once, 'I would give anything if some day Frank Mallett and our Bertha were to take a fancy to each other. There is nothing I should like more than to have her settled near us, and there is no one I know more likely to make her happy than he would be.' I am sure, dear, that you will be glad to know that your engagement would have had his approval, as it has mine."

Bertha bent down and kissed her mother, with tears standing in her eyes.

"It will be a great pleasure to us both to have you so near us," Frank said, earnestly. "You know that, having lost my own mother so long ago, I have always looked upon you as more of a mother than anyone else, and have always felt almost as much at home in your house as in my own.

"Now, let us sit down and talk it over quietly. In the first place, I propose that on Monday, when you leave Lord Haverley's, you shall both come here for a time. The Solent will be very pleasant for the next fortnight, and we can then take a fortnight's cruise west, and, if you like, land at Plymouth, and go straight home."

"I should be very glad," Lady Greendale said at once, rejoiced at the thought that she would thus avoid the necessity of answering any questions about Bertha; "and there will be no occasion at all to speak of this at my cousin's. There might be all sorts of questions asked, and expressions of surprise, and so on. It will be quite time enough to write to our friends after we have been comfortably settled at home for a time. We can talk over all that afterwards."

"Yes, and I should think, Lady Greendale, that it would save the trouble of two letters if, while mentioning that Bertha is engaged to your neighbour, Major Mallett, you could add that the marriage will come off in the course of a few weeks.

"Don't you think so, Bertha?"

"Certainly not," she said, saucily. "It will be quite time to talk about that a long time hence."

"Well, I will put off talking about it for a short time, but, you see, I have had a year's waiting already."

Very pleasant was the three hours' cruise. No one gave a thought of the missing topmast and bowsprit. There was a nice sailing breeze, and, clipped as her wings were, the Osprey was still faster than the majority of the yachts.

As soon as the two ladies had been put ashore, Frank sailed for Cowes. It was too late when they got there for anything to be done that evening, but Frank went ashore with the captain, and found that the spars were all ready to receive the iron work and sheaves from the old ones; and as these had been towed up to the yard to be in readiness, Messieurs White promised that they would arrange for a few hands to come to work early, and that the spars should be brought off by half-past eight on Monday morning.

As soon as he had returned in the gig, after putting the ladies ashore at Ryde, Frank had called George Lechmere to him.

"It is all right, George, thanks to your interview with Miss Greendale. It was a bold step to take, but it was the best possible thing, and succeeded splendidly, and everything is to be as I wish it."

"I am glad, indeed, to hear it, Major, and I hoped that you would have something of the sort to tell me. There was a look about you both that I took to mean that things were going on well."

"Yes, George. At first, when she told me that you had told her about that affair at Delhi, I felt that there was really no occasion for you to have said anything about it; but it did me a great deal of good. She made much more of it than there was any occasion for; but, you know, when women are inclined to take a pleasant view of a thing, they will magnify molehills into mountains."

"I thought that it would do good, Major. I don't mean that it would do you any good, but that it would do good generally. I had to tell the other story, and that came naturally with it; and, at any rate, she could not but see that there was a deal of difference between the nature of the man who had been so good to me, and that of that scoundrel."

"That is just the effect it did have. Well, don't say anything about it forward, at present. The men shall be told later on."

By one o'clock on Monday the Osprey was back at Ryde, and at two o'clock the dinghy went ashore with the mate and two of the hands, who waited a quarter of an hour till a vehicle brought down the ladies' luggage. Soon afterwards Frank went ashore in the gig, and brought Lady Greendale and Bertha off.

As they went down to their cabin, Bertha, looking into the saloon, saw George Lechmere preparing the tea tray to bring it up on deck. She at once went to him.

"I did not thank you before," she said, holding out her hand; "but I thank you now, and shall thank you all my life. You did me the greatest service."

"I am glad, indeed, Miss Greendale, that it was so; for I know that the Major would never have been a happy man if this had not come about."

For the next fortnight the Osprey was cruising along the coast, getting as far as Torquay, and returning to Cowes. Frank did not enter her for any of the races. Lady Greendale, although a fair sailor, grew nervous when the yacht heeled over far, and even Bertha did not care for racing, the memory of the last race being too fresh in her mind for her to wish to take part in another for the present.

Chapter 11

"That is an uncommonly pretty trading schooner, Bertha," Frank Mallett said, as he rose from his chair to get a better look at a craft that was passing along to the eastward. "I suppose she must be in the fruit trade, and must just have arrived from the Levant. I should not be surprised if she had been a yacht at one time. She is not carrying much sail, but she is going along fast. I think they would have done better if they had rigged her as a fore-and-aft schooner instead of putting those heavy yards on the foremast. That broad band of white round her spoils her appearance; her jib boom is unusually long, and she must carry a tremendous spread of canvas in light winds. I should think that she must be full up to the hatches, for she is very low in the water for a trader."

The Osprey was lying in the outside tier of yachts off Cowes. The party that had been on board her for the regatta had broken up a week before, and only Lady Greendale and Bertha remained on board. The former had not been well for some days, and had had her maid down from town as soon as the cabins were empty. It had been proposed, indeed, that she and Bertha should return to town, but, being unwilling to cut short the girl's pleasure, she said that she should do better on board than in London; and, moreover, she did not feel equal to travelling. She was attended by a doctor in Cowes, and the Osprey only took short sails each day, generally down to the Needles and back, or out to the Nab.

"Yes, she is a nice-looking boat," Bertha agreed, "and if her sails were white and her ropes neat and trim, she would look like a yacht, except for those big yards."

"Her skipper must be a lubber to have the ropes hanging about like that. Of course, he may have had bad weather in crossing the bay, but if he had any pride in the craft, he might at least have got her into a good deal better trim while coming in from the Needles. Still, all that could be remedied in an hour's work, and certainly she is as pretty a trader as ever I saw. How did your mother seem this afternoon, Bertha?"

"About the same, I think. I don't feel at all anxious about her, because I have often seen her like this before. I think really, Frank, that she is quite well enough to go up to town; but she knows that I am enjoying myself so much that she does not like to take me away. I have no doubt that she will find herself better by Saturday, when, you know, we arranged some time back that we would go up. You won't be long before you come, will you?"

"Certainly not. Directly you have landed I shall take the Osprey to Gosport, and lay her up there. I need not stop to see that done. I can trust Hawkins to see her stripped and everything taken on shore; and, of course, the people at the yard are responsible for hauling her up. I shall probably be in town the same evening; but, if you like, and think that your mother is only stopping for you, we will go across to Southampton at once."

"Oh, no, I am sure that she would not like that; and I don't want to lose my last three days here. Of course, when we get home at the end of next week, and you are settled down there, too, you will be a great deal over at Greendale, but it won't be as it is here."

"Not by a long way. However, we shall be able to look forward to the spring, Bertha, when I shall have you all to myself on board, and we shall go on a long cruise together; though I do think that it is ridiculous that I should have to wait until then."

"Not at all ridiculous, sir. You say that you are perfectly happy—and everyone says that an engagement is the happiest time in one's life—and besides, it is partly your own fault; you have made me so fond of the Osprey that I have quite made up my mind that nothing could possibly be so nice as to spend our honeymoon on board her, and to go where we like, and to do as we like, without being bothered by meeting people one does not care for. And, besides, if you should get tired of my company, we might ask Jack Harley and Amy to come to us for a month or so."

"I don't think that it will be necessary for us to do that," he laughed. "Starting as we shall in the middle of March, we shan't find it too hot in the Mediterranean before we turn our head homewards; and I think we shall find plenty to amuse us between Gibraltar and Jaffa."

"No, three months won't be too much, Frank. Tomorrow is the dinner at the clubhouse, isn't it?"

"Yes. I should be sorry to miss that, for having only been just elected a member of the Squadron, I should like to put in an appearance at the first set dinner."

"Of course, Frank. I certainly should not like you to miss it."

The next evening Frank went ashore to dine at the club. An hour and a half later a yacht's boat came off.

"I have a note for Miss Greendale," the man in the stern said, as she came alongside; "I am to give it to her myself."

Bertha was summoned, and, much surprised, came on deck.

The man handed up the note to her. She took it into the companion, where a light was burning; her name and that of the yacht were in straggling handwriting that she scarcely recognised as Frank's.

She tore it open.

"My Darling: I have had a nasty accident, having been knocked down just as I landed. I am at present at Dr. Maddison's. I wish you would come ashore at once. It is nothing very serious, but if you did not see me you might think that it was. Don't agitate your mother, but bring Anna with you. The boat that brings this note will take you ashore."

Bertha gave a little gasp, and then summoning up her courage, ran down into the cabin.

"Mamma, dear, you must spare me and Anna for half an hour. I have just had a note from Frank. He has been knocked down and hurt. He says that it is nothing very serious, and he only writes to me to come ashore so that I can assure myself. I won't stop more than a quarter of an hour. If I find that he is worse than I expect, I will send Anna off to you with a message."

Scarcely listening to what her mother said in reply, she ran into her cabin, told Anna to put on her hat and shawl to go ashore with her, and in a minute descended to the boat with her maid. It was a four-oared gig, and the helmsman had taken his place in the stern behind them.

Bertha sat cold and still without speaking. She was sure that Frank must be more seriously hurt than he had said, or he would have had himself taken off to the yacht instead of to the surgeon's. The shaky and almost illegible handwriting showed the difficulty he must have had in holding the pencil.

The boat made its way through the fleet till it reached the shallow water which they had to cross on their way to the shore. Here, with the exception of a few small craft, the water was clear of yachts.

Suddenly the long line of lights along the shore disappeared, and something thick, heavy and soft fell over Bertha's head. An arm was thrown round her, and Anna pressed tightly against her. In vain she struggled. There was a faint, strange smell, and she lost consciousness.

An hour passed without her return to the yacht, and Lady Greendale began to fear that she had found Frank too ill to leave, and had forgotten to send Anna back with the message. At last she touched the bell.

"Will you tell the captain that I want to speak to him?"

"Captain," she said. "I am much alarmed about Major Mallett. That boat that came off here an hour ago brought a note for my daughter, saying that he had been hurt, and she went ashore with her maid to see him. She said that she would be back in a short time, and that if she found that he was badly hurt she would send her maid back with a message to me. She has been gone for more than an hour, and I wish you would take a boat and go ashore, find out how the Major is, and bring me back word at once. He is at Dr. Maddison's. You know the house."

The skipper hurried away with a serious face. A little more than a minute after he had left the cabin Lady Greendale heard the rattle of the blocks of the falls. The boat was little more than half an hour away. Lady Greendale, in her anxiety, had told the steward to let her know when it was coming alongside, and went up on deck to get the news as quickly as possible.

"It is a rum affair altogether, my lady," Hawkins said, as he stepped on deck. "I went to the doctor's, and he has seen nothing whatever of the Major, and Miss Greendale and her maid have not been to his house at all."

Lady Greendale stood for a moment speechless with surprise and consternation.

"This is most extraordinary," she said at last. "What can it mean? You are sure that there is no mistake, captain? It was to Dr. Maddison's house she went."

"Yes, my lady, there ain't no mistake about that. I have been there to fetch medicine for you two or three times. Besides, I saw the doctor myself."

"Major Mallett must have been taken to some other doctor's," she said, "and must have made a mistake and put in the name of Dr. Maddison. His house is some little distance from the club. There may be another doctor's nearer. What is to be done?"

"I am sure I do not know, my lady," the captain said, in perplexity.

"Where can my daughter and her maid be?" Lady Greendale went on. "They went ashore to go to Dr. Maddison's."

"Perhaps, my lady, they might have heard as they went ashore that the Major was somewhere else, or some messenger might have been waiting at the landing stage to take them there direct."

"That must be it, I suppose; but it is all very strange. I think the best thing, captain, will be for you to go to the club. They are sure to know there about the accident, and where he is. You see, the landing stage is close to the club, and he might have been just going in when he was knocked down—by a carriage, I suppose."

"Like enough he is at the club still, my lady. At any rate, I will go there in the first place and find out. There is sure to be a crowd about the gates listening to the music—they have got a band over from Newport—so that if they do not know anything at the club, there are sure to be some people outside who saw the accident, and will know where the Major was taken. Anyhow, I won't come back without news."

Even to Lady Greendale, anxious and alarmed as she was, it did not seem long before the steward came down with the news that the boat was just alongside. This time she was too agitated to go up. She heard someone come running down the companion, and a moment later, to her astonishment, Frank Mallett himself came in. He looked pale and excited.

"What is all this, Lady Greendale?" he exclaimed. "The skipper tells me that a letter came here saying that I had been hurt and taken to Dr. Maddison's, and that Bertha and her maid went off at once, and have not returned, though it is more than two hours since they went. I have not been hurt. I wrote no letter to Bertha, but was at dinner at the club when the skipper came for me. What is it all about?"

"I don't know, Frank. I cannot even think," Lady Greendale said in an agitated voice. "What can it all mean and where can Bertha be?" and she burst into tears.

"I don't know. I can't think," Frank said, slowly.

He stood silent for a minute or two, and then went on.

"I cannot suggest anything. I will go ashore at once. The waterman at our landing stage must have noticed if two ladies got out there. He could hardly have helped doing so, for it would be curious, their coming ashore alone after dark. Then I will go to the other landing places and ask there. There are always boys hanging about to earn a few pence by taking care of boats. I will be back as soon as I can."

The boat was still alongside, and the men stretched to their oars. Th a very few minutes they were at the club landing stage. The waterman here declared that no ladies whatever, unaccompanied by gentlemen, had landed after dark.

"I must have seen them, sir," he said, "for you see I go down to help out every party that arrives here. They must have gone to one of the other landing places."

But at neither of these could he obtain any information. There were several boys at each of them who had been there for hours, and they were unanimous in declaring that no ladies had landed there after dark at all. He then walked up and down between the watch house and the club.

He had, when he landed, intended to go to the police office as soon as he had inquired at the landing stages—the natural impulse of an Englishman who has suffered loss or wrong—but the more he thought it over the more inexpedient did such a course seem to him. It was highly improbable—indeed, it seemed to him impossible—that they could do more than he had in the matter. The passage of two ladies through the crowded streets would scarcely have attracted the attention of anyone, and any idea of violence being used was out of the question. If they had landed, which he now regarded as very improbable, they must have at least gone willingly to the place where they believed they should find him, and unless every house in Cowes was searched from top to bottom there was no chance of finding them, carefully hidden away as they would be. He could not see, therefore, that the police could at present be of any utility whatever. It might be necessary finally to obtain the aid of the police, but in that case it was Scotland Yard and not Cowes that the matter must be laid before; and even this should be only a last resort, for above all things it was necessary for Bertha's sake that the matter should be kept a profound secret, and, once in the hands of the police, it would be in all the papers the next day. If the aid of detectives was to be called in, it would be far better to put it into the hands of a private detective.

Having made up his mind upon this point, he returned to the yacht.

"I am sorry to say that I have no news," he said to Lady Greendale, who was lying on the couch, worn out with weeping. "I have ascertained almost beyond doubt that they did not land at the club stage or either of the other two landing places."

"What can it be?" she sobbed. "What can have become of them?"

"I am afraid there is little doubt that they have been carried off," he replied. "I can see no other possible solution of it."

"But who can have done such a thing?"

"Ah! that is another matter. I have been thinking it over and over, and there is only one man that I know capable of such a dastardly action. At present I won't mention his name, even to you; but I will soon be on his track. Do not give way, Lady Greendale; even he is not capable of injuring her, and no doubt she will be restored to you safe and sound. But we shall need patience. Ah! there is a boat coming alongside."

He ran up on deck. It proved, however, to be only a shore boat, bringing off George Lechmere, who, having met a comrade in the town, had asked leave to spend the evening with him. He was, of course, ignorant of all that had happened since he had left, and Frank told him.

"I have no doubt whatever that she has been carried off," he said, "and there is only one man who could have done it."

"That villain, Carthew," George Lechmere exclaimed.

"Yes, he is the man I suspect, George. I heard this evening that he had been hit tremendously hard on the turf at Goodwood. He would think that if he could force Miss Greendale to marry him it would retrieve his fortune, and would, moreover, satisfy his vindictive spirit for the manner in which she had rejected him, and in addition give him another triumph over me."

"That is it, sir. I have no doubt that that is it. But his yacht is not here—at least I have not seen her."

"No, I am sure that she is not here; but I believe, for all that, that Miss Greendale must have been taken on board a yacht. They never would have dared to land her in Cowes. Of course, I made inquiries as a matter of form at the landing places, but as she knew the way to Dr. Maddison's, and as the streets were full of people at the time she landed, they could never have attempted to use violence, especially as she had her maid with her. On the other hand, it would have been comparatively easy to manage it in the case of a yacht. They had but to row alongside, to seize and gag them before they had time to utter a cry, and then to carry them below. The Phantom is not here—at any rate, was not here this afternoon, but there is no reason why Carthew should not have chartered a yacht for the purpose. Ask the skipper to come aft."

"Captain," he said, when Hawkins came aft, "what men went ashore this afternoon?"

"Harris and Williams and Marvel, sir. They went ashore in the dinghy, and Harris went to the doctor's for that medicine."

"Ask them to come here."

"Did anyone speak to you, Harris," he went on, as the three men came aft, "while you were ashore today?—I mean anyone that you did not know."

"No, sir," the man said, promptly. "Leastwise, the only chap that spoke to me was a gent as was standing on the steps by the watch house as I went down to the boat, and he only says to me, 'I noticed you go in to Dr. Maddison's, my man. There is nothing the matter with my friend, Major Mallett, I hope.'

"'No, sir,' says I, 'he is all right. I was just getting a bottle of medicine for an old lady on board.'

"That was all that passed between us."

"Thank you, Harris. That is just what I wanted to know."

After the men had gone forward again, he said to the captain:

"I have a strong conviction, Hawkins, indeed I am almost certain, that Miss Greendale has been carried off to one of the yachts here, but whether it is a large one or a small one I have not the slightest idea. The question is, what is to be done? It is past eleven now, and it is impossible to go round the fleet and make enquiries. Besides, the craft may have made off already. They would have been sure to have placed her in the outside tier, so as to get up anchor as soon as they had Miss Greendale on board."

"We might get out the boats, sir, and lie off and see if any yachts set sail," the skipper suggested.

"That would be of no use, Hawkins. You could not stop them. Even if you hailed to know what yacht it was, they might give you a false name.

"One thing I have been thinking of that can be done. I wish, in the first place, that you would ask all the men if anyone has noticed among the yacht sailors in the streets one with the name of the Phantom on his jersey. Some of them may have been paid off, for she has not been raced since Ryde. In any case, I want two of the men to go ashore, the first thing in the morning, and hang about all day, if necessary, in hopes of finding one of the Phantom's crew. If they do find one, bring him off at once, and tell him that he will be well paid for his trouble.

"By the way, you may as well ask Harris what the gentleman was like who spoke to him at the landing place."

He walked slowly backwards and forwards with George Lechmere, without exchanging a word, until in five minutes Hawkins returned.

"It was a clean-shaven man who spoke to Harris, sir; he judged him to be about forty. He wore a sort of yachting dress, and he was rather short and thin. About the other matter Rawlins says that he noticed when he was ashore yesterday two of the Phantom's men strolling about. Being a Cowes man himself, he knew them both, but as they were not alone he just passed the time of day and went on without stopping."

"Does he know where they live? I don't think it at all likely they would be on leave now, or that he would find either of them at home tomorrow morning; but it is possible that he might do so. At any rate it is worth trying. It is curious that two of them should be here when we have seen nothing of the Phantom since the race for the cup, unless, of course, her owner has laid her up, which is hardly likely. If she had been anywhere about here she would have entered for the race yesterday."

"I will send Rawlins and one of the other Cowes men ashore at six o'clock, Major. If they don't meet the men, they are safe to be able to find out where they live."

"And tell them and the others, Hawkins, that on no account whatever is a word to be said on shore as to the disappearance of Miss Greendale. It is of great importance that no one should obtain the slightest hint of what has taken place."

When the captain had again gone forward, Frank went down, and with some difficulty persuaded Lady Greendale to go to bed.

"We can do nothing more tonight," he said. "You may well imagine that if I saw the least chance of doing any good I should not be standing here, but nothing can be done till morning."

Having seen her to her stateroom, he returned to the deck, where he had told George Lechmere to wait for him.

"It is enough to drive one mad, George," he said, as he joined him; "to think that somewhere among all those yachts Miss Greendale may be held a prisoner."

"I can quite understand that, Major, by what I feel myself. I have seen so much of Miss Greendale, and she has always been so kind to me, knowing that you considered that I had saved your life, and knowing about that other thing, that I feel as if I could do anything for her. And I feel it all the more because it is the scoundrel I owed such a deep debt to before. But I hardly think that she can be on board one of the yachts here."

"I feel convinced that she is not, George. They could hardly keep her gagged all this time, and at night a scream would be heard though the skylights were closed."

"No, sir; if she was put on board here I feel sure that they would have got up sail at once."

"That is just what I feel. Likely enough they had the mainsail already up and the chain short, and directly the boat was up at the davits they would have got up the anchor and been off. They may be twenty miles away by this time; though whether east or west one has no means of even guessing. The wind is nearly due north, and they may have gone either way, or have made for Cherbourg or Havre. It depends partly upon her size. If she is a small craft, they can't get far beyond that range. If she is a large one, she may have gone anywhere. The worst of it is that unless we can get some clue as to her size we can do absolutely nothing. A good many yachts went off today both east and west, and by the end of the week the whole fleet will be scattered, and even if we do get the size of the yacht, I don't see that we can do anything unless we can get her name too.

"If we could do that, we could act at once. I should run up to town, lay the case before the authorities at Scotland Yard, and get them to telegraph to every port in the kingdom, that upon her putting in there the vessel was at once to be searched for two ladies who were believed to have been forcibly carried away in her."

"And have those on board arrested, I suppose, Major?"

"Well, that would have to be thought over, George. Carthew could not be brought to punishment without the whole affair being made public. That is the thing above all others to be avoided."

"Yes, I see that, sir; and yet it seems hard that he should go off unpunished again."

"He would not go unpunished, you may be sure," Frank said, grimly; "for if the fellow ever showed his face in London again, I would thrash him to within an inch of his life. However, sure as I feel, it is possible that I am mistaken. Miss Greendale is known to be an only daughter, and an heiress, and some other impecunious scamp may have conceived the idea of making a bold stroke for her fortune. It is not likely, but it is possible."

Until morning broke, the two men paced the deck together. Scarcely a word was spoken. Frank was in vain endeavouring to think what course had best be taken, if the search for the men of the phantom turned out unavailing. George was brooding over the old wrong he had suffered, and longing to avenge that and the present one.

"Thank God, the night is over," Frank said at last; "and I have thoroughly tired myself. I have thought until I am stupid. Now I will lie down on one of the sofas, and perhaps I may forget it all for a few hours."

Sleep, however, did not come to him, and at seven o'clock he was on deck again.

"The men went ashore at six, sir," the skipper said. "I expect they will be back again before long."

Ten minutes later the dinghy came out between two yachts ahead.

"Rawlins is not on board," the skipper said, as they came close. "I told him to send off the instant they got any news whatever. That is Simpson in the stern."

"Well, Simpson, what news?" Frank asked as she rowed alongside.

"Well, sir, we have found out as how all the Phantom's crew are ashore. Some of the chaps told us that they came back a fortnight ago, the crew having been paid off. Rawlins said that I'd better come off and tell you that. He has gone off to look one of them up, and bring him off in a shore boat. He knows where he lives, and I expect we shall have him alongside in a few minutes."

"Do you think that is good news or bad, sir?" George Lechmere asked.

"I think that it is bad rather than good," Frank said. "Before, it seemed to me that, whatever the craft was in which she was carried away, she would probably be transferred to the Phantom, which might be lying in Portland or in Dover, or be cruising outside the island; and if I had heard nothing of the Phantom I should have searched for her. However, I suppose that the scoundrel thought that he could not trust a crew of Cowes men to take part in a business like this. But we shall know more when Rawlins comes off."

In half an hour the shore boat came alongside with Rawlins and a sailor with a Phantom jersey on.

"So you have all been paid off, my lad?" Frank said to the sailor as he stepped on deck.

"Yes sir. It all came sudden like. We had expected that she would be out for another month, at least. However, as each man got a month's pay, we had nothing to grumble about; although it did seem strange that even the skipper should not have had a hint of what Mr. Carthew intended, till he called him into his cabin and paid him his money."

"And where is she laid up?"

"Well, sir, she is at Ostend. I don't know whether she is going to be hauled up there, or only dismantled and left to float in the dock. The governor told the skipper that he thought he might go to the Mediterranean in December, but that till then he should not be able to use her. It seemed a rum thing leaving her out there instead of having her hauled up at Southampton or Gosport, and specially that he should not have kept two or three of us on board in charge. But, of course, that was his affair. Mr. Carthew is rather a difficult gentleman to please, and very changeable-like. We had all made sure that we were going to race here after winning the Cup at Ryde; and, indeed, after the race he said as much to the skipper."

"Has he anyone with him?" Frank asked.

"Only one gentleman, sir. I don't know what his name was."

"What was he like?"

"He was a smallish man, and thin, and didn't wear no hair on his face."

"Thank you. Here is a sovereign for your trouble.

"That is something, at any rate, George," he went on, as the man was rowed away. "The whole proceeding is a very strange one, and you see the description of the man with Carthew exactly answers to that of the man who found out from the boat's crew that Dr. Maddison was attending Lady Greendale; and now you see that it is quite possible that the Phantom is somewhere near, or was somewhere near yesterday afternoon. Carthew may have hired a foreign crew, and sailed in her a couple of days after her own crew came over; or he may have hired another craft either abroad or here. At any rate, there is something to do. I will go up to town by the midday train, and then down to Dover, and cross to Ostend tonight."

"Begging your pardon, Major, could not you telegraph to the harbour master at Ostend, asking if the Phantom is there?"

"I might do that, George, but if I go over there I may pick up some clue. I may find out what hotel he stopped at after the crew had left, and if so, whether he crossed to England or left by a train for France. There is no saying what information I may light on. You stay on board here. You can be of no use to me on the journey, and may be of use here. I will telegraph to you from Ostend. Possibly I may want the yacht to sail at once to Dover to meet me there, or you may have to go up to town to do something for me.

"Now I must go down and tell Lady Greendale as much as is necessary. It will, of course, be the best thing for her to go up to town with me, but if she is not well enough for that, of course she must stay on board."

Lady Greendale had just come into the saloon when he went down.

"I think I have got a clue—a very faint one," he said. "I am going up to town at once to follow it up. How are you feeling, Lady Greendale?"

"I have a terrible headache, but that is nothing. Of course, I will go up with you."

"But do you feel equal to it?"

"Oh, yes, quite," she said, feverishly. "What is your clue, Frank?"

"Well, it concerns the yacht in which I believe Bertha has been carried off. At any rate, I feel so certain as to who had a hand in it, that I have no hesitation in telling you that it was Carthew."

"Mr. Carthew! Impossible, Frank. He always seemed to me a particularly pleasant and gentlemanly man."

"He might seem that, but I happen to know other things about him. He is an unmitigated scoundrel. Of course, not a word must be said about it, Lady Greendale. You see that for Bertha's sake we must work quietly. It would never do for the matter to get into the papers."

"It would be too dreadful, Frank. I do think that it would kill me. I will trust it in your hands altogether. I have only one comfort in this dreadful affair, and that is that Bertha has Anna with her."

"That is certainly a great comfort; and it is something in the man's favour that when he enticed her from the yacht with that forged letter he suggested that she should bring her maid."

Chapter 12

Frank Mallet and Lady Greendale crossed to Southampton by the twelve o'clock boat, and arrived in London at three.

"I have been thinking," she said, as they went up, "that it will be better for me to stop in town. I shall have less difficulty in answering questions there than I should have at home. Everyone is leaving now, and in another week there will be scarcely a soul in London I know; and I shall keep down the front blinds, and no one will dream of my being there. I shall only have to mention to Bertha's own maid that my daughter has remained at Cowes, that I have left Anna with her, and that she can wait upon me until she returns. There will be another advantage in it—you can see me whenever you are in town. I shall get your letters a post quicker when you are away, and you can telegraph to me freely; whereas, if you telegraphed to Chippenham, whoever received the message there might mention its contents as curious to someone or other, and then, of course, it would become a matter of common gossip."

Frank agreed that it would certainly be better, and more bearable than having to answer questions about Bertha to every visitor who called on her. He crossed that evening to Ostend, and at ten o'clock next morning George Lechmere received the following message:

"Make inquiries as to small brigantine that looked like converted yacht: had very large yards on foremast. I saw her pass Cowes on Tuesday afternoon. Let Hawkins go to Portsmouth and Southampton. Find out yourself whether she anchored between Osborne and Ryde. If not, inquire at Seaview whether she passed there going east. Telegraph result tomorrow morning to my chambers. Shall cross again tonight."

Lechmere had the gig at once lowered, and started, with four hands at the oars, eastward, while the captain went ashore in the dinghy to leave for Southampton by the next boat. The tide was against Lechmere, who, keeping close in round the point, steered the boat along at the foot of the slopes of Osborne, and kept eastward until he reached the coast-guard station at the mouth of Wootton creek.

"Oh, yes, we noticed her," the boatswain in charge replied in answer to his question. "We saw her, as you say, on Tuesday afternoon, going east.

We could not help noticing her, for she was something out of the way. We should not have thought so much of it, if she had not come back again just before dusk the next day, and anchored a mile to the west. We kept a sharp lookout that night, thinking that she might be trying to smuggle some contraband ashore; but everything was quiet, and next morning she was gone. The man who was on the watch said he thought that he made her out with his night glass going east at about eleven o'clock; but it was a dark night, and it might have been a schooner yacht or a brig."

"You don't happen to know whether she stopped at Ryde the first time she passed?"

"Yes; having been all talking about her, we watched to see if she was going to anchor there or keep on to the east. She lowered a boat as she passed, and two men landed. They threw her up into the wind and waited until the boat came off again. The men did not come back in her. They hoisted the boat up again and went east. She stopped off Seaview; then she came back and sent the boat ashore, and two men went off in her. Of course, I can't say whether they were the same. It was as much as I could do to make out that there were two of them, though our glass is a pretty good one. Is there anything wrong about the craft?"

"Not that I know of; but there was a good deal of curiosity about her among the yachts, she being an out-of-the-way sort of craft; and I fancy there were some bets about her. There was an idea that she was seen going west two days later, and the governor asked me to take the boat and find out whether she had been noticed here or at Ryde. Thank you very much for your information. I have no doubt that it will be sufficient to decide any bets there may be about her."

So saying, he took his seat in the gig again, and rowed back to the Osprey. The skipper returned in the evening.

"No such craft has gone into Southampton or Portsmouth," he said; "so I have had my journey for nothing."

"No, I don't think you have," George replied. "It is something to know that she is not in either of the ports now, and has been to neither of them."

George returned in time to send off a full account of what he had learned from the coast-guardsman by the mail that would be delivered in London that night. On his return to town the next morning, Frank found the letter awaiting him; and at ten o'clock, after wiring to Hawkins and the steward to stock the yacht at once with provisions of all kinds for a long voyage, he went into the city and called upon the secretary at Lloyd's.

After giving his name, he told him that he believed that a young lady had been carried off forcibly in the craft, which he minutely described, and that he was desirous of having a telegram sent to every signal station between Hull and the Land's End, asking if such a craft had passed.

"Of course," he added, "I am ready to defray the expense of the telegrams and replies. She left the Solent late on Wednesday evening, and on Thursday would have been between Beachy Head and Dover, if she had gone that way, and yesterday up the Thames or somewhere between Harwich and Yarmouth."

"Well, Major Mallett, if you will sit down and write the telegram with the description that you have given, I will send it off at once. Then, if you will call again in an hour's time, I have no doubt all the answers will have come in."

"Your craft has gone west," he said when Frank returned. "All the answers the other way are negative. Saint Catherine says: 'Craft answering description was seen well out at sea on Thursday morning.' Portland noticed her in the afternoon, and she was off the Start yesterday morning; the wind was light then; and the Lizard reports seeing her this morning. When abreast of them, she headed south, apparently making a departure, as she could be made out keeping that course as long as seen. These are the four telegrams, so I think that there can be little doubt that she has made for the Mediterranean."

"Thank you very much indeed," Frank said. "Can you tell me if I have any chance of getting similar information from the south?"

"You could get it from Finisterre if she passed within sight, but by her holding on as far west as the Lizard, instead of taking a departure from the Start, it is likely that she will take a more westerly course, and then Cape St. Vincent is the first point where she is likely to be noticed. If not there, she would probably be observed at Tarifa, although, if she kept on the southern side of the Straits, she might not be noticed. I should think that she would do so; she would not be likely to put into Gibraltar, although, from what you tell me, the owner would believe that no suspicion whatever of being concerned in this affair would be likely to rest upon him. But you must bear in mind that it is probable that, as a measure of precaution, he has painted out the white streak, sent down the yards, and converted her into a fore-and-aft schooner; in which case she would attract no attention whatever if she passed without making her number."

"I certainly think that they will convert her back into a schooner yacht, as otherwise there will be a difficulty about papers whenever she enters a port. There is one more thing I wish to ask you. You see, she might not turn into the Mediterranean. She might, for example, make for the West Indies, in which case she would be almost certain to touch at Madeira or Palmas."

"Or possibly at Teneriffe, Major. Of course, we have an agent at each of these places, and I will gladly request them, if a brigantine or schooner looking like her puts in there, to find out if possible where she is bound for, and to let you know at—shall I say Gibraltar? I am afraid it is of no use trying to get the Portuguese authorities to arrest the ship or to search her. You see, to a certain extent it is an extradition case. Still, I will ask them to get it done if possible, though I fear that it is quite beyond their power."

"Thank you very much indeed. It would be an immense thing only to find out that she has gone in that direction. Of course, she may not put in at any of these places, as she is sure to have provisioned for a long voyage, but at any rate I will wait at Gibraltar until I get the letters, unless I can get some clue that she has gone up the Mediterranean.

"Of course, if I don't hear of her at Cape Saint Vincent or Tarifa, I shall try Ceuta and Tangier. If she goes up on the southern side of the Straits, she may anchor off either, and send a boat in to get fresh meat and fruit."

"The Royal mail and the mail down the African coast will start, one tomorrow, the other on Monday, and I will send letters by them to the islands. They are sure to get there before this craft that you are in search of, and our agents will be on the lookout for her. It may not be long before you hear from Madeira, but it may be some time before you get the other letters, as the craft may be anything between three weeks and five in getting there. Of course, I shall mention when she sailed, and they will not write until all chance of her having arrived is passed."

"Would you kindly give me the addresses of your three agents? I will wait for the answer from Madeira, but I am afraid my patience will never hold out until the others can come. It will be giving the schooner a fearfully long start as it is, and as you may suppose I shall be almost mad at having to wait and do nothing."

The secretary wrote the three addresses, and, thanking him very warmly for his kindness and courtesy, Frank went out and despatched a telegram to the skipper, telling him to engage ten extra hands at once, and to buy muskets and cutlasses for the whole crew.

"I shall come down by the twelve o'clock train from town. Be at the steamboat pier to meet me. If all is ready, shall sail at once."

Having despatched this, he drove at once to Lady Greendale's, and told her that he had learnt that the craft in which Bertha had been carried off had sailed for the south, probably the Mediterranean, and that he should start that evening in pursuit.

"It may be a long chase, Lady Greendale, but never fear but that I will bring her back safely. It will be for you to decide whether you will continue to remain here, or go down into the country after a time; but, of course, there is no occasion for you to make up your mind now. I must be off at once, for I have several things to do before I catch the twelve o'clock train."

"God bless you, Frank!" she said. "You are looking terribly worn and fagged."

"I shall be all right when I am once fairly off," he said. "I have not had an hour's sleep for the last two nights, and not much the night before. At first the whole thing seemed hopeless; now that I am fairly on the track and know what I have to do, I shall soon be all right again."

"I don't know what I should have done without you, Frank; and I do believe that you will succeed."

"I have no doubt about it," he said; "so keep your courage up, mother— for you know that you are almost that to me now."

He kissed her affectionately, and then hurried downstairs and drove to his chambers.

Here he packed a portmanteau with Indian suits and underclothing, took his pistol and rifle cases, drove to a gunmaker's in the Strand for a stock of ammunition, called at his bank and cashed a cheque for two thousand pounds, and then drove to Waterloo.

Hawkins and George Lechmere were on the landing stage at Cowes.

"How are things going on, Hawkins?" Frank asked, as he came across the gangway.

"All right, sir. I have had my hands pretty full, sir, since I got your second telegram. Lechmere saw to getting the arms. Of course, he could not help me as to hiring the hands. I think I have got ten first-class men. A few of the yachts have paid off already, and I know something about all of those I have engaged. While I was ashore, the mate looked after getting on board and stowing the goods as they came alongside."

"Quite right, Hawkins. Did you think of ammunition, George?"

"Yes, Major; I was not likely to forget that. I got twenty-five muskets and cutlasses. Luckily they kept them at Pascal Aikey's, for the use of steam yachts going out to the east; and they had ammunition too, so I got fifty rounds for each musket. It is not likely that we shall want to use that much, but it is best to be on the right side."

"I think, sir," Hawkins said, "as it is going to be a long voyage, and as we have doubled our crew, that I had better get another mate. Purvis is a very good man, but he is no navigator; and we shall have to keep watches regularly. I met an old shipmate of mine just now who would be just the man. He commanded the Amphitrite for ten years, and I know that he is a good navigator. He has been up in the Scotch waters since the spring, and was paid off last week. I told him that it might be that I could give him a berth as second mate, and he jumped at it."

"By all means, Hawkins; of course you will want an officer for each watch. You can find him without loss of time, I hope."

"Yes, sir. I have told him to hang about outside the gate here, and I would give him an answer."

"Very well. When you have seen him you will find me at Aikey's. I have to go there to get a lot of charts. I have only those for British waters.

"George, do you see to getting these traps down to the boat. I shall be there in a quarter of an hour. Is there anything else that you can think of, or that you want yourself?"

"Nothing, sir."

"When you go on board, you may as well get your traps in one of the spare cabins aft.

"You had better move, too, captain. You and one of the mates can have the stern cabin. For the present the other mate can have yours, and the steward can sleep in the saloon. That will make more room for the extra hands forward."

"It will be a tight stow, sir," the captain said. "I have ordered ten more hammocks and hooks, but I doubt whether there will be room to sling them all."

"I am sure there won't, Hawkins. You had better put the hooks in the saloon beams, and swing five or six of the hammocks there. We can take the hooks out and stop up the holes when we don't need them any longer. We may be having hot weather before we have done, and I don't want the men crowded too closely forward."

Twenty minutes later Frank came down to the boat with the skipper, carrying a large roll of charts, and a man with a handcart containing a bundle of jerseys and caps, and fifty white duck trousers. A large shore boat was alongside when they reached the Osprey.

"Is this the last lot?" the captain asked the man in charge of the pile of casks and boxes with which it was filled.

"Yes, sir, this is the last batch."

"Get them on deck, Hawkins," Frank said, "and we can get them down and stowed when we are under sail. Get the anchor short at once, the sail covers off and the mainsail up.

"I don't want to lose a minute," he went on, turning to George Lechmere. "I know that an hour or even a day will make no material difference, but I am in a fever to be off."

"Have you found out which way they have gone, Major?"

"I have found out that they have sailed for the south, but whether for the Mediterranean or for the West Indies or South America I have no idea; but I have some hopes of finding out by the time we get to Gibraltar."

"And they have got a three days' start of us?"

"Yes, I can hardly believe that it is not more. It seems to me a fortnight since I went ashore to dine at the club. Three days is a long start, and unless the change of rig has spoiled her, the Phantom is as fast, or very nearly as fast, as we are. We can't hope to catch her up, unless she stops for two or three days in a port, and that she is certain not to do. No, I don't think that there is any chance of our overtaking her until she has got to whatever may be her destination. Of course, what Carthew counts upon is that, in time, he will get Miss Greendale to consent to marry him. That is one reason why I think that he will not go up the Mediterranean. The further he takes her the more hopeless the prospect will seem to her."

"But she will never give in, Major," George Lechmere said, confidently.

"I have no fear of that—no fear whatever, and we may be quite sure that as long as he thinks that he will be able to tire her out he will show himself in his best light, and try to make everything as pleasant for her as is possible under the circumstances. It is only when he loses all hope of her consenting willingly that he will show himself in his true light; and you know, George, he is scoundrel enough for anything. However, I consider that she is perfectly safe for a long time, and I hope to be alongside the craft long before he becomes desperate."

Half an hour later, the anchor was on the rail and the Osprey started on her voyage. The tide being in her favour, she passed the Needles just as it was getting dark. The breeze fell very light, and, although every stitch of canvas was put on, she was still some miles east of Portland when morning broke. As the sun rose the wind freshened a bit, and she moved faster through the water. The hands were mustered and divided into two watches, and the jerseys and red caps served out to the new hands.

"You had better give them the whole of the duck trousers, to fit themselves from, Captain," Frank said. "There are assorted sizes, you know, and when they have suited themselves you can take the other ten pairs into store. You and the mates will want some when we get into warmer climates."

"Are we bound for the Mediterranean?" Hawkins asked.

"To Gibraltar, to begin with. What we shall do afterwards will depend upon what news I get there. We may have to go round the world, for all I know."

"Well, sir, I hope not, for your sake, and the young lady's; but as far as we are concerned, we would as lief go round the world as anything else, though she is not a very big craft for such a journey as that."

"How long will the water tanks hold out?"

"That is where the pinch will come in, sir. I reckon that at ordinary times we might make shift to go on for three weeks without filling up, but, you see, we have twenty hands instead of ten, and that will make all the difference.. I did get ten good-sized casks yesterday morning, and got them filled as well as the tanks. They are stowed away forward, but they won't improve her speed. They have brought her head down over two inches, but, of course, we shall use the water in them first."

"You had better bring them amidships, captain, and stow them round the saloon skylight. Appearances are of no consequence whatever, and the great thing is to get her in her best sailing trim. If bad weather comes on, we must put half in the bow and half in the stern, where we can wedge them in tightly together. It would not do to risk having them rolling about the decks.

"Well, then," he went on, seeing that the captain did not like the thought of having weight at each end of the yacht, "if the weather gets bad we will take the saloon skylight off, and lower them down into it. I can eat my meals on deck or in my stateroom, but the water we must keep. If we get a spell of head winds or calms, we may be three weeks getting to Gib."

"That would be a very good plan, sir, if you can do without the saloon, and don't mind its being littered up."

"Well, I hope we shan't get any bad weather until we get well across the bay, Hawkins. I don't mind the discomfort, but it would stop her speed. We want a wind that will just let us carry all our canvas. We can travel a deal faster so than we can in heavy weather, when we might be obliged to get down the greater part of our canvas and perhaps to lie to.

"It looks like a strong crew, doesn't it?" he went on, as he glanced forward.

"That it does, sir. A craft of this size can do well with more when she is racing, but for a crew it is more than one wants, a good deal; and people would stare if we went into an English port. Still, I don't say that it is not an advantage to be strong-handed if we get heavy weather, and it makes light work of getting up sail or shifting it, and one wants to shift pretty often when he is trying to get high speed out of a craft."

The wind continued fitful, and, in spite of having her racing sails, the Osprey's run to the Start was a long one. It was not until thirty-six hours after getting up anchor that they were abreast of the lighthouse.

"I try to be patient, George," Mallett said, "but it is enough to make a saint swear. We have lost eight or ten hours instead of making a gain, although we had the advantage of coming through the Needles passage, while they had to go round at the back of the island to escape observation."

"Yes, sir, but you know we have often found that sometimes one, sometimes another, makes a gain in these shifty winds; perhaps tomorrow we may be running along fast, and the Phantom be lying without a breath of wind."

"That is so, George. I will try to bear it in mind. There, you see, the skipper is taking the exact bearing of the lighthouse, and we shall soon be heading south."

In five minutes the captain gave the order to the helmsman, and the craft was then laid on her new course.

"The wind is northing a bit," the skipper said as, after giving the helmsman instructions, he came up to Frank. "It has shifted two points round in the last half hour, and you see we have got the boom off a bit. If it goes round a point more we will get the square-sail ready for hoisting. It will help her along rarely when the head-sails cease to be of any good."

Half an hour later the wind had gone round far enough for the square-sail to be used to advantage, and it was accordingly hoisted. The captain then had the barrels brought aft, and ranged along each side of the bulwark.

For eight-and-forty hours the Osprey maintained her speed, leaving all the sailing vessels she overtook far behind her, and keeping for hours abreast of a cargo steamer going in the same direction.

"She is bound for Finisterre," the skipper said, "and we shall pass it some thirty miles to the west, so our courses will gradually draw apart; but we shall see her smoke anyhow until we are pretty nigh abreast of the cape— that is, if the wind holds as it is now. It is falling lighter this afternoon."

Two or three hours later the wind died away altogether, the square-sail was got down, and the skipper then said:

"I will get the topsail down, too, sir. We can easily get it up again, and I will put a smaller jib on her. I don't at all think by the look of the sky that we are going to have a blow. The glass would have altered more if we were, but one never can tell. I would not risk the loss of a spar for anything."

"I should think that you might put a couple of reefs in the mainsail, Hawkins."

"Well, perhaps it would be the best, sir; for a puff that one thinks nothing of, one way or the other, when a craft has way; will take her over wonderfully when it catches her becalmed."

Just as he had finished his dinner, the captain came down and asked Frank to come on deck.

"There is a steamer bearing down on us. I can see both her side lights, and as she is coming in from the west she may not notice our starboard light. It is burning all right, but one never can see these green lights. They are the deceivingest things at a distance. I have just sent down for the man to bring up the riding light, and as it is a first-rate one, if we put it on deck it will light up the mainsail. I have told them to bring up the big horn. That ought to waken them if anything will."

"How far is she off now, Hawkins?"

"About a mile and a half, Major. There are no signs of her altering her course, as she ought to have done by this time if she had made us out. You see, her head light shows up fair and square between her side lights, which shows that she is coming as near as possible on to us. I think that I had better light a blue light."

Frank nodded. The blue light at once blazed out.

"They ought to see that if they are not all asleep," Frank said, as he looked up at the sails standing out white against the dark sky.

"Set to work with that foghorn," the skipper said; and a man began to work the bellows of a great foghorn, which uttered a roar that might have been heard on a still night many miles away. Again and again the roar broke out.

"That has fetched them," the captain said. "She is starboarding her helm to 30 astern of us. There, we have lost her red light, so it is all right. How I should have liked to have been behind the lookout or the officer of the watch with a marlinespike or a capstan bar. I will warrant that they would not have nodded when on watch again for a long time to come.

"Here she comes; she is closer than I thought she was. She will pass within fifty yards of the stern. It is lucky that we had that big horn, Major Mallett, for if we had not woke them up when we did she would have run us down to a certainty."

As the steamer came along, scarcely more than a length astern of the yacht, a yell of execration broke from the sailors gathered forward.

"That was a near shave, George," Frank Mallett said, when the steamer had passed. "It brought me out in a cold sweat at the thought that, if the Osprey were to be run down, there was an end to all chance of rescuing Bertha from that scoundrel's clutches. I don't know that I thought of myself at all. I am a good swimmer, and I suppose she would have stopped to pick us up. It was the Osprey I was thinking of. Even if every life on board had been saved, I don't see how we could have followed up the search without her."

Chapter 13

Three hours later the breeze came. Frank was pacing up and down the deck, when there was a slight creak above. He stopped and looked up.

"Is that the breeze?" he asked the first mate, whose watch it was.

"I think so, sir, though it may be just the heaving from a steamer somewhere. I don't feel any wind; not a breath from any quarter."

There was another and more decided sound above.

"There is no mistake this time," the mate said, as the boom which had been hanging amidships slowly swung over to port. "It's somewhere about the quarter that we expected it from, and coming as gently as a lamb."

Five minutes later there was sufficient breeze to cause her to heel over perceptibly as she moved quietly through the water.

"Hands aft to shake out the reefs," the mate called.

The order was repeated down the fo'castle hatch by one of the two men on the lookout. The rest of the watch, who had been allowed to go below, tumbled up.

The sailors hastened to untie the reef points. All were aware of the nature of the chase in which they were embarked. The whole crew were full of ardour. They felt it as a personal grievance that the young lady to whom their employer was engaged had not only been carried off, but carried off from the deck of the yacht. Moreover, she was very popular with them, as she had often asked them questions and chatted with them when at the helm or when she walked forward. She knew them all by name, and had several times come off from shore with a packet of tobacco for each man in her basket. She had been quick in learning to steer, and her desire to know everything about the yacht had pleased the sailors, who were all delighted when they learned of her engagement to the owner. The new hands, on learning the particulars, had naturally entered to some extent into the feeling of the others, and the alacrity with which every order was obeyed showed the interest felt in the chase.

As soon as the reef points were untied came the order:

"Slack away the reef tackle, and see that the caring will run easy.

"Now up with the throat halliard. That will do.

"Now the gaff a little more. Belay there.

"Now get that topsail up from the sail locker. We won't shift jibs just yet, until we see whether the breeze is going to freshen."

It was not long before the increasing heel of the craft, and rustle of water along her side, told that she was travelling faster.

"The wind is freeing her a bit, sir. It has shifted a good half point in the last ten minutes."

"That is a comfort," Frank said. "You may as well heave the log. I should like to know how she is going before I turn in."

"Seven knots, sir," the mate reported. "That is pretty fair, considering how close-hauled she is."

"Well, I will turn in now. Let me know if there is any change."

At five o'clock Frank was on deck again. Purvis was in charge of the watch now.

"Good morning, sir," he said, touching his hat as Frank came up. "We are going to have a fine day, and the wind is likely to keep steady."

"All right, Purvis. What speed were we going when you heaved the log?"

"Seven and a half, sir. Perry tells me that she has been doing just that ever since the wind sprang up. I reckon that we are pretty well abreast of Finisterre now. We shall have the sun up in a few minutes, and I expect that it will come up behind the land.

"Lambert, go up to the cross-tree and keep a sharp lookout, as the sun comes up, and see if you can make land."

"I can make out the land, sir," the sailor called down as soon as he reached the cross-tree. "It stands well up. I should say that you can see it from deck."

The mate and Frank walked further aft and looked out under the boom. The land was plainly visible against the glow of the sky.

"There it is, sure enough," the mate said. "I looked over there before you came up and could not make it out, but the sky has brightened a lot in the last ten minutes. I should say that it is about five-and-twenty miles away. It is a very bold coast, sir.

"That is Finisterre over the quarter; you see the land breaks off suddenly there. We ought to have made out the light, but of course it is not very bright at this distance, and there was a slight mist on the water when I came up at eight bells."

"I suppose in another forty-eight hours we shall not be far from the southern point of Portugal."

"We shall be there, or thereabouts, by that time if the wind keeps the same strength and in the same quarter. That would make an uncommonly good run of it, considering that we were lying twenty-four hours becalmed. If it had not been for that, we should have been only four days from the Start to Saint Vincent."

The mate's calculations turned out correct, and at seven in the morning they anchored a mile off Cape Saint Vincent. The gig was lowered, and Frank was rowed ashore, taking with him a signal book in which questions were given in several languages, including Spanish. He had purchased it at Cowes before starting.

The signal officer was very polite, and fortunately understood a little English. So Frank managed, with the aid of the book, to make him understand his questions. No craft at all answering to the description had been noticed passing during the last five or six days; certainly no yacht had passed. She might, of course, have gone by after dark.

He showed Frank the record of the ships that had been sighted going east, and of those that had made their numbers as they passed. The Phantom was not among the latter, nor did the rig or approximate tonnage, as guessed, of any of the others, at all correspond with hers.

After thanking the officer, Frank returned to his boat, and half an hour later the Osprey was again under weigh.

At Ceuta, Tarifa, and Tangier there was a similar want of success. Such a craft might have passed, but if so she was either too far away to be noted, or had passed during the night. From Tangier he crossed to Gibraltar, and anchored among the shipping there.

So far everything had gone to confirm his theory that the Phantom would not go up the Mediterranean. Of course, she might have passed the three places, as well as Saint Vincent, at night; or have kept so nearly in the middle of the Strait as to pass without being remarked. Still, the chances were against it, and he regarded it as almost certain that she would have put into one or other of the African ports, as she passed them, for water, fresh meat and fruit.

It was six days after the Osprey passed Saint Vincent before she anchored off Gib. She had made her number as she came in, and in a short time the health officer came out in a boat. The visit was a formal one; the white ensign on her taffrail was in itself sufficient to show her character, and that she must have come straight from England; and the questions asked were few and brief.

"We are ten days out," Frank said. "We have touched at Tarifa, Ceuta, and Tangier, but that is all. The crew are all in good health. Here is the list of them if you wish to examine them."

"As a matter of formality it is better that it should be done," the health officer said.

"I will order them to muster," Frank said, "and while they are doing so, will you come below and take a glass of wine?

"Can you tell me if a craft about this size, a schooner or brigantine, has put in here during the last fortnight? I don't know whether she is still flying yacht colours, or has gone into trade, but at any rate you could see at once that she had been a yacht."

"Certainly no such craft has put in here, Major Mallett. Yours is the first yacht that has come round this season, and as I board every vessel that anchors here, I should certainly have noticed any trader that had formerly been a yacht. The decks and fittings would tell their story at once. Do you know her name?"

"I don't know much about her," Frank said, "but a craft of that kind sailed from Cowes a day or two before I started, and, as I believe, for the Mediterranean. Being about our own size, and heavily sparred for a schooner, I was rather curious to know if I had beaten her. We did not make her out as we came along."

"You must have passed her in the night, I should say, unless, as is likely enough, she did not put in, but kept eastward."

As Frank had touched at Gibraltar three times before, the place had no novelty for him. He, however, went ashore at once to make arrangements for filling up again with water. The steward and George Lechmere accompanied him into the town to purchase fresh meat, fruit and vegetables.

Frank then made his way to the post office. He was scarcely disappointed at finding that there was nothing for him as yet.

The next three days he spent in wandering restlessly over the Rock. As long as the Osprey was under weigh, and doing her best, he was able to curb his anxiety and impatience; but now that she was at anchor he felt absolutely unable to remain quietly on board. Several officers of his acquaintance came off to the Osprey, and he was invited to dine at their mess dinner every night. He, however, declined.

"The fact is, my dear fellow," he said to each, "I am at present waiting with extreme anxiety for news of a most important nature, and until I get it I am so restless and so confoundedly irritable that I am not fit to associate with anyone. When I look in here again I hope that it will be all right, and then I shall be delighted to come to you, and have a chat over our Indian days; but at present I really am not up to it."

His appearance was sufficient to testify that his plea was not a fictitious excuse.

On the fourth day he found a letter awaiting him at the post office. He tore it open, and read:

"Funchal, Madeira, August 30.

"Sir: At the request of Mr. Greenwood I beg to inform you that a brigantine, precisely answering to the description given me, anchored in the roads here on the 21st. She only remained a few hours to take in water and stores. I was at the landing place when the master came on shore. He said that they had had a wonderfully fast voyage from England, having come from the Lizard under seven days, and holding a leading wind all the way. She was flying the Belgian flag, and I learned from the Portuguese official who visited her that her papers were all in order, and that she had been purchased at Ostend from an Englishman only three weeks before, and had been named the Dragon. He did not remember what her English name had been.

"Most unfortunately she had left a few hours before the mail steamer came in, bringing me the letter from Lloyd's. I do not know that I could, in any case, have stopped her; but I think that I could have got the officials to have searched her, and if the ladies had been on board, and had appealed to them for protection, I think the vessel would certainly have been detained; or, at any rate, the authorities would have insisted upon the ladies being set on shore.

"Her papers had the Cape as her destination, though this may, of course, have been only a blind. I regret much that I am unable to give you further information, beyond the fact that there were two male passengers on board. I shall be happy to reply to any communication I may receive from you."

Frank hurried down to the landing place.

"Lay out, men," he said. "I want to be under way in a quarter of an hour."

The men bent to their oars, and the gig flew through the water. There was no one on shore, for Frank had given strict orders that no one was to land, of a morning, until he returned from the post office.

"Get under way at once," he called to the captain, as soon as he came within hailing distance.

There was an instant stir on board. Some of the men ran to the capstan, others began to unlace the sail covers, while some gathered at the davits to hoist the boat up directly she came alongside.

"I have news, lads," Frank said, in a loud voice, as he stepped on board. "She has touched at Madeira."

There was a cheer from the men. It was something to know that a clue had been obtained, and in a wonderfully short time the Osprey was under way, and heading for the point of the bay.

"Then they did not stop them there, Major?" George Lechmere asked, after Frank had stated the news.

"No, the mail did not arrive with the letter in time for Lloyd's agent to act upon it. The Phantom had sailed some hours before. She is still under her square yards, and her name has been changed to the Dragon. She was there on the 21st, and the letter is dated the 30th."

"And today is the 6th," George said. "So he has fifteen days' start of us, besides the distance to Madeira."

"Yes, she must be among the West Indies long before we can hope to overtake her—there, or at some South American port."

"Then you have learnt for certain that she has gone that way, Major?"

"It is not quite certain, but I have no doubt about it. Her papers say that she is bound for the Cape, which is quite enough to show me that she is not going there. I think it is the West Indies rather than South America, for if she went to any Brazilian port, or Monte Video, or Buenos Ayres, she would be much more likely to attract attention than she would in the West Indies, where there are scores of islands and places where she could cruise, or lie hidden as long as she liked.

"Yes, I have no doubt that is her destination. It is a nasty place to have to search, but sooner or later we ought to be able to find her. Fortunately the negroes pretty nearly all speak English, Spanish, or French, and we shall have no difficulty in getting information wherever there is any information to be had."

Four days later the Osprey anchored off Funchal. The dinghy at once put off with six water casks, and Frank was rowed ashore in the gig, and had a talk with his correspondent. The latter, however, could give him no more information than had been contained in his letter, except that the white streak had been painted out, and that the craft carried fourteen hands, all of whom were foreigners. He could give no information as to whether she would be likely to touch at either the Canaries or the Cape de Verde Islands, but was inclined to think that she would not.

"They took a very large stock of water on board," he said, "and a much larger amount of meat, vegetables and fruit than they would have required had they intended to put in there, and meat is a good deal dearer here than it would be at Saint Vincent, or even Teneriffe. I should think from this that they had no intention of putting in there, though they might touch at Saint Helena or Ascension, if they are really on their way to the Cape.

"But after what you tell me, I should think that your idea that they have made for the West. Indies is the correct one. I should say that they were likely to lie up in some quiet and sheltered spot there, for it is the hurricane season now, and no one would be cruising about among the islands if he could help it. There are scores of places where he could lie in shelter and no one be any the wiser, except, perhaps, negro villagers on the shore."

"Yes, I should think that is what he would do," Frank agreed. "How long does the hurricane season last?"

"The worst time is between the middle of September and the middle of November, but you cannot depend upon settled weather until the new year begins."

"Well, hurricane or no hurricane, I shall set out on the search as soon as I get over there."

Two hours later the Osprey was again on her way. The breeze was fresh and steady, and with her square sail set and her mizzen furled she ran along at over nine knots an hour. One day succeeded another, without there being the least occasion to make any shift in the canvas, and it was not until they were within a day's sail of Porto Rico that the wind dropped almost suddenly. Purvis at once ran below.

"The glass has fallen a long way since I looked at it at breakfast," he said, as he returned.

"Then we are in for a blow," the skipper said. "I am new to these latitudes, but wherever you are you know what to do when there is a sudden lull in the wind, and a heavy fall in the glass.

"Now, lads, get her canvas off her."

"All down, captain!"

"Every stitch."

"Andrews, do you and two others get down into the sail locker and bring up the storm jib, the small foresail, trysail, and storm mizzen. If it is a tornado, we shan't want to show much sail to it."

"If we are going to have a tornado, captain, I should recommend that you get the mainsail loose from the hoops, put the cover on, roll it up tightly to the gaff and lash it to the bulwarks on one side, and get the boom off and lash it on the other side."

"That will be a very good plan. The lower we get the weight the better."

When this was done, the topmast was also sent down and lashed by the sail. The barrels, which were now all empty, were lowered down into the saloon, while the trysail was fastened to the hoops ready for hoisting, and all the reefs tied up. A triangular mizzen was then hoisted, and a storm jib.

"We won't get up the foresail at present," the captain said. "I have reefed it right down, sir, but I won't hoist it until we have got the first blow over."

"You had better see that everything is well secured on deck, and if I were you I would put the jib in stops. We can break it out when we like; but from all accounts the first burst of these tornadoes is terrible. I should leave the mizzen on her; that will bring her head up to it, whichever way it comes, and she will lie to under that and the jib."

"Yes, sir; but it is likely enough that we shall have to sail. I have been reading about the tornadoes. I picked up a book at Cowes the day we sailed, when I saw that you were ordering the charts of these seas, and have learnt what is the proper thing to do. The wind is from the southeast at present, which means that the centre of the hurricane lies to the southwest.

"If the wind comes more from the east, as long as we can sail we are to head northwest or else lie to on the port tack. If it shifts more to the south, we are to lie to on the starboard tack."

"That sounds all right, Hawkins. It is very easy to describe what ought to be done, but it is not so easy to do it, when you are in a gale that is almost strong enough to take her mast out of her. I will tell you what I would do. I would break up a couple of those casks, and nail the staves over the skylights, and then nail tarpaulins over them. I have no fear whatever about her weathering the gale, but I expect that for a bit we shall be more under water than above it.

"I see Perry is getting the two anchors below; that will help to ease her. At any rate she will be in good fighting trim. I think we began none too soon. There is a thick mist over the sky, and it looks as dark as pitch ahead."

"There is only one thing more, sir," and the captain shouted:

"All hands get the boats on deck, and see that they are lashed firmly.

"Will you see to getting in the davits out of the sockets, Purvis, and getting them below?

"I ought to have done that before," he went on, apologetically, "but I did not think of it. However, with such a strong crew it won't take five minutes, and we have got that and something to spare, I think."

"You have got the bowsprit reefed, Hawkins?"

"Yes, sir; full reefed."

"There is only one thing more that I can suggest. I fancy that these tornadoes begin with heavy lightning. Get those wire topmast stays, and twist them tightly round the shrouds and lash them there, leaving the ends to drop a fathom or two in the water. In that way I don't think that we need be afraid of the lightning. If it strikes us it will run down the wire shrouds, and then straight into the water."

In five minutes all was in readiness; the boats securely lashed on deck, the davits down below, and the lightning protectors tied tightly to the wire shrouds.

"Now, captain, I think we have done all that we can do. What are you doing now?"

"I am running a life line right round her, sir. It may save more than one life if the seas make a sweep of her."

"You are right, captain. These eighteen-inch bulwarks are no great protection."

Four sailors speedily lashed a three-inch rope four feet above the deck, from the forestay round the shrouds and aft to the mizzen, hove as tight as they could get it and then fastened. While this was being done one of the mates cut up a piece of two-inch rope into several foot lengths, and gave one to each of the men and officers, including Frank and George Lechmere.

"If you tie the middle of that round your chest under the arms, you will have the two ends ready to lash yourself to windward when it gets bad. A couple of twists round anything will keep you safe, however much water may come over her."

"Do you mean to stay on deck, sir?" the skipper asked. "You won't be able to do any good, and the fewer hands there are on deck the less there will be to be anxious about. I shall only keep four hands forward after the first burst is over, and they will be lashed to the shrouds. Purvis will be there with them. Perry and Andrews will take the helm, and I shall stay with them.

"We have battened the fore hatch down. One of the men will be in the after cabin, and if I want to hoist the trysail or make any change I shall give three knocks, and that will be a signal for them to send half a dozen hands up. They will come through the saloon and up the companion. We shan't be able to open the fore hatch."

"Very well, skipper. I will go down when the hands do. We are going to have it soon."

It was now indeed so dark that he could scarcely see the face of the man he was speaking to.

"I really think, captain, that I should send some of them down below at once. If a flash of lightning were to strike the mast, it would probably go down the shrouds harmlessly, but might do frightful damage among the men, crowded as they are up here; or it might blind some of them. Besides, the weight forward is no trifle."

"I think that you are right, sir," and, raising his voice, the captain shouted:

"All hands below except the four men told off. Go down by the companion."

"Would you mind their stopping in the saloon, sir? It would make her more lively than if they all went down into the fo'castle."

"Certainly not, captain;" and accordingly the men were ordered to remain in the saloon.

"You can light your pipes there, my lads," Frank said, as they went down, "and make yourselves as comfortable as you can."

The last man had scarcely disappeared when the captain said:

"Look there, Major Mallett," and looking up Frank saw a ball of phosphorescent light, some eighteen inches in diameter, upon the masthead.

"Plenty of electricity about," he said, cheerfully. "If they are all as harmless as that it won't hurt us."

But as he ceased speaking there was a crash of thunder overhead that made the whole vessel quiver, and at the same instant a flash of lightning, so vivid, that for a minute or two Frank felt absolutely blinded. Without a moment's intermission, flash followed flash, while the crashes of thunder were incessant.

"I think that plan of yours has saved the ship, sir," the captain said, when, after five minutes, the lightning ceased as suddenly as it had begun. "I am sure that a score of those flashes struck the mast, and yet no damage has been done to it, so far as I could see by the last flash. Are you all right there, Purvis?"

"All right," the mate replied. "Scared a bit, I fancy. I know I am myself, but none the worse for it."

"It is coming now, sir," the captain said. "Listen."

Frank could hear a low moaning noise, rapidly growing louder, and then he saw a white line on the water coming along with extraordinary velocity.

"Hard down with the helm, Perry," the captain said.

"Hard down it is, sir."

"Hold on all!" the captain shouted.

A few seconds later the gale struck them. The yacht shook as if in a collision, and heeled over till the water was half up her deck. Then the weight of her lead ballast told, and as the pressure on the mizzen did its work, she gradually came up to the wind, getting on to an almost even keel as she did so.

"Break out the jib and haul in the weather sheet," the captain shouted.

Purvis was expecting this, and although he did not hear the words above the howl of the storm, at once obeyed the order.

"There she is, sir, lying-to like a duck," the skipper shouted in Frank's ear; "and none the worse for it. An ordinary craft would have turned turtle, but I have seen her as far over when she has been racing."

"Well, I will go below now, Hawkins," Frank shouted back. "It is enough to blow the hair off one's head.

"Come down, George, with me. You can be of no use here."

Chapter 14

For eight hours the Osprey struggled with the storm. The sea swept over her decks, and the dinghy was smashed into fragments, but the yacht rode with far greater ease than an ordinary vessel would have done, as, save for her bare mast, the wind had no hold upon her. There were no spars with weight of furled sails to catch the wind and hold her down; she was in perfect trim, and her sharp bows met the waves like a wedge, and suffered them to glide past her with scarce a shock, while the added buoyancy gained by reefing the bowsprit and getting the anchors below lifted her over seas that, as they approached, seemed as if they would make a clean sweep over her.

From time to time Frank went up for a few minutes, lashing himself to the runner to windward. The three men at the helm were all sitting up, lashed to cleats, and sheltering themselves as far as they could by the bulwarks. Movement toward them was impossible. Beyond a wave of the hand, no communication could be held.

Frank could not have ventured out had he not, before going down below for the first time, stretched a rope across the deck in front of the companion, so that before going out he obtained a firm grasp of it, and was by its assistance able to reach the side safely. Each time he went out four of the crew from below followed him and relieved those lashed to the shrouds forward.

The skipper was carrying out the plan he had decided on, and the foresail was hoisted a few feet, the Osprey by its aid gradually edging her way out from the centre of the tornado. The hands as they came down received a stiff glass of grog, and were told to turn in at once. Two hours after the storm broke Purvis came down for a few minutes.

"She is doing splendidly, sir," he said. "I would not have believed if I had not seen it, that any craft of her size could have gone through such a sea as this and shipped so little water. We have had a few big 'uns come on board, but in general she goes over them like a duck. It is hard work forward. You have got to keep your back to it, for you can hardly get your breath if you face it. If it was not for the lashings, it would blow you right away.

"I have been at sea in gales that we thought were big ones, but nothing like this. Of course, with our heavy ballast and bare poles, she don't lie over much. It is the sea and not the wind that affects her, and her low free board is all in her favour. But I believe a ship with a high side and yards and top hamper would be blown down on her beam ends and kept there."

"Do you think that it blows as hard as it did, Purvis?"

"There ain't much difference, sir; but I do think there ain't quite so much weight in it. I expect we are working our way out of it. We have been twice round the compass. It is lucky we had not got down among the islands before we caught it. I would not give much for our chances if we had been there, for these gales gradually wear themselves out as they get farther from the islands."

In six hours the weather had so far moderated that they were able to hoist the reefed foresail, and two hours later the trysail was set with all the reefs in. These were shaken out in a short time, the wind dying away fast. Half the crew had turned into their hammocks some time before, and the regular watch was now set. The motion of the ship, however, was very violent, for there was a heavy tumbling sea still on, the waves having no general direction, but tossing in confused masses and coming on to the deck, now on one side, now on the other.

At midnight Frank also turned in, in his clothes; but he was soon up again, for the motion of the yacht was so violent that he found it next to impossible to keep from being jerked out of his berth. The first mate had had four hours off duty, and had just come up again to relieve the captain.

"It is lucky, sir, that all our gear is nearly new," he said; "for if it had not been, this rolling would have taken the mast out of her. The strain on the shrouds each time that she gets chucked over must be tremendous."

"It would have been better, for this sort of work, if we had had ten feet taken off that stick before we started."

"Well, just for the present it would have been better, sir; but even if we had had time I would not have done it. We should not have much chance of overhauling the Phantom if we clipped our wings."

In another two hours the sea had sensibly moderated. Frank again went down, and this time was able to go to sleep. When he went on deck the sun was some way up, the mainsail was set, and the reefs had been shaken out.

"This is a change for the better, captain."

"It is indeed, sir. I think that we have reason to be proud of the craft. She has gone through a tornado without having suffered the slightest damage, except the loss of the dinghy. I shall be getting the topmast up in another hour. You see, I have got her number-two jib on her and shifted the mizzen, but she is still a bit too lively to make it safe to get up the spar. Like as not, if we did, it would snap off before we could get the stays taut."

"I am terribly anxious about the Phantom," Frank said, "and only trust that she was in a snug harbour on the lee side of one of the islands."

"I hope so, sir. I was thinking of her lots of times when the gale was at its height. If she was, as you say, in a good port, she would be right enough. Of course, if she was out she would run for the nearest shelter."

"If she had no more wind than we had before it came on, she had not much chance of doing that."

"That is true enough, sir; but, you see, the glass gave us notice three hours before we caught it. Besides, they certainly took native pilots on board as soon as they got out here, and these must have got them into some safe place at the first sign of a gale."

"Yes, they must certainly have had a pilot on board," Frank agreed; "and there is every ground to hope that they were snugly at anchor. They were three weeks ahead of us, and must know that it is the hurricane season as well as we do. It is likely that the first thing they did on their arrival was to search for some quiet spot, where they could lie up safely till the bad season was over."

Late on the following afternoon land was seen ahead.

"There is Porto Rico, sir. It may not be quite our nearest point to make, but there are no islands lying outside it; so that it was safer to make for it than for places where the islands seemed to be as thick as peas."

"Yes, and for the same reason it is likely that Carthew made for it. Of course, naturally we should have both gone for either Barbadoes or Antigua, or Barbuda, the most northern of the Leeward Islands; but he would not do so if he intends to keep his Belgian colours flying. And, indeed, it would seem curious that two English gentlemen should be cruising about in a Belgian trader. You may take it that he is certain to put into a port for water and vegetables, just as we have to do. There seem to be at least half a dozen on this side of the island. He may have gone into any of them, but he would be most likely to choose a small place. However, at one or other of them we are likely to get news; and the first thing for us to do is to get a good black pilot, who can talk some English as well as Spanish."

"It is likely we shall have to take three or four of them before we have done. A man here might know the Virgin Islands, and perhaps most of the

Leeward Islands, but he might not know anything east, west, or north of San Domingo. We should certainly want another pilot for the Bahamas, and a third for Cuba and the islands round it, which can be counted almost by the hundred. Then again, none of these would know the islands fringing almost the whole of the coast from Honduras to Trinidad. However, I hope we shall not have to search them. There is an ample cruising ground and any number of hiding places without having to go so far out of the world as that. At any rate, at present he is not likely to have gone far, and I think that he will either have sought some secluded shelter among the Virgin Islands, or on the coast of San Domingo."

When within a few miles of Porto Rico they lay to for the night, and the next morning coasted westward, and dropped anchor in the port of San Juan de Porto Rico.

A quarter of an hour after dropping anchor the port officials came on board. The inspection of the ship's papers was a short formality, the white ensign and the general appearance of the craft showing her at once to be an English yacht, and as she had only touched at Madeira on her way from Gibraltar, and all on board were in good health, she was at once given pratique.

"The first thing to do is to get an interpreter," Frank said, as he was rowed to shore, accompanied by George Lechmere. "The secretary of Lloyd's gave me a list of their agents all over the world. It is a Spanish firm here, and it is probable that none of them speaks English, but if so I have no doubt that by aid of this signal book I shall be able to make them understand what I want. I have a circular letter of introduction from Lloyd's secretary."

He had no difficulty in discovering the place of business of Senor Juan Cordovo, and on sending in his card and the letter of introduction, was at once shown into an inner office. He was received with grave courtesy by the merchant, who, on learning that he did not speak Spanish, touched a bell on his table. A clerk entered, to whom he spoke a few words.

The young man then turned to Frank, and said:

"I speak English, sir. Senor Cordovo wishes me to assure you that all he has is at your disposal, and that he will be happy to assist you in any way that you may point out."

"Please assure Senor Cordovo of my high consideration and gratitude for his offer. Will you inform him that I intend to cruise for some time among the islands, and that I desire to obtain the services of an interpreter, speaking English and Spanish; and if he possesses some knowledge of French, so much the better."

The reply was translated to the merchant, who conversed with the interpreter for two or three minutes. The latter then turned to Frank.

"I have a brother, senor, who, like myself, speaks the three languages. He is at present out of employment, and would, I am sure, be very glad to engage himself to you as your interpreter."

"That would be the very thing," Frank said. "Does he live in the town?"

"Yes, senor. I could fetch him here in a few minutes if Senor Cordovo will permit me to do so."

The merchant at once granted the clerk's request.

"Will you tell Senor Cordovo," Frank said, "that I do not wish to occupy his valuable time, and that I will return here in a quarter of an hour?"

The merchant, however, through the clerk, assured Frank that he would not hear of his leaving, and producing a box of cigars, begged him to seat himself until the arrival of the interpreter. He then said something else to the clerk, and the latter asked Frank if he wanted any supplies for the yacht, as his employer acted as agent for shipping.

"Certainly," Frank said, glad to have the opportunity of repaying the civility shown him. "I require fresh meat, fruit and vegetables, sufficient for twenty-five persons. I shall also be glad if he will arrange for boats to take off water. My barrels and tanks are nearly empty, and I shall want a supply of about a thousand gallons."

While the clerk was absent, Frank, with the assistance of the signal book, kept up a somewhat disjointed conversation with the Spaniard. The clerk was, however, away but a few minutes; and returned with his brother, an intelligent-looking young fellow of seventeen or eighteen. He did not speak English quite as well as the clerk, but sufficiently well for all purposes. Frank asked him his terms, which seemed to him ridiculously low, and a bargain was forthwith arranged.

"Will you ask Senor Cordovo if any other English yacht has been here during the past three weeks or a month? I have a friend on board one, and I fancy that she is cruising out here also."

The merchant replied that no English yacht had touched at the port for some months, and that such visits were extremely rare. He assured him that the stores ordered would be alongside in the course of the afternoon, and expressed his regret when Frank declined his invitation to stay with him for a day or two at his country house.

After renewed thanks, Frank took his departure with his new interpreter, whose name was Pedro. George Lechmere was waiting at the corner of the street.

"I have arranged everything satisfactorily, George. This young man is coming with me as interpreter, and as he speaks both French and Spanish we shall get on well in future.

"When will you be ready to come on board, Pedro?"

"In half an hour, senor."

"You will find my boat at the quay. Take your things down to it. It is a white boat with a British flag at the stern. But I don't want you to go off yet. I have two things I want you to do before you go.

"In the first place, I want a pilot. I want one who knows the Virgin Islands well, and also the coast of San Domingo."

"There will be no difficulty about that, senor."

"In the second place, I want to find out, from the boatmen at the quays, whether a Belgian schooner of seventy or eighty tons has touched here during the last month. She carries large yards on her foremast, and is a very fast-looking craft. She was at one time an English yacht. If she called here, I wish to know whether she sailed east or west, and if possible to obtain an idea as to her destination."

"There was such a vessel here, senor, for I noticed her myself. She only remained a few hours, while her boats took off water and vegetables. I happened to notice her, for having nothing to do I was down at the quays, and the boatmen were talking about her, she being a craft such as is seldom seen now. Some of the old men said that she reminded them of the privateers in the great war. I went down to the boats when they first came ashore. The men only spoke French, and they paid me a dollar to go round with them to make their purchases. They took them, and also the water, off in their own boats; which surprised me, for they were very handsome boats, much more handsome than I have seen in any ship that ever came here. I said that it would cost them but a very small sum to send the barrels off in the native boats, but they insisted upon taking them themselves.

"I don't know which way they sailed, because I went home as soon as they went away from the quay, but the boatmen will be able to tell me."

He went away and talked with some of the negro boatmen, and soon returned, saying that she sailed westward.

"At what time did she sail?"

"It was just getting dark, senor, for they said that they could scarcely make her out, but she certainly went west."

"Well, all you have to do now, Pedro, is to hire a pilot. Get the best man that you can find. I want one who knows every foot of the Virgin Islands. We are going there first. It does not matter so much about his knowing San Domingo, for as we shall probably come back here, we can put him ashore and get another pilot specially for San Domingo. Be sure you get the best man that you can find, whatever his terms are. We will be back again here in half an hour.

"That is satisfactory indeed, George," Frank went on, as they turned away. "Of course, strongly as we believed that he might be here, there was no absolute certainty about it, for he might have gone to the South American ports, or even have headed for the Gulf of Florida. You see he is not only here, but came to the very island we thought that he would most likely make for. As for his going west, no doubt that was merely a ruse. He did not get up anchor until it was getting so dark that he would be able in the course of half an hour to change his course, and make for the Virgin Islands without fear of being observed. I don't suppose that they have any idea whatever of being followed, but they take every precaution in their power to cover up their traces. You noticed, of course, their anxiety that no shore boat should go off to them.

"Well, George, we have succeeded so well thus far, that I feel confident that we shall overhaul them before long. As far as one can see on the chart, most of these Virgin Islands are mere rocks, and the number we shall have to search will not be very great, and if the pilot really knows his business, he ought to be able to take us to every inlet where they would be likely to anchor."

Pedro was awaiting them when they returned to the boat, and was accompanied by a big negro, who, by the grin on his good-natured face, was evidently highly satisfied with the bargain that he had made.

"This is the man, senor," Pedro said. "I met one of the port officers I know, and he told me that he was considered to be the best pilot in the island. He speaks a little English—most of the pilots do, for several of the Virgin Islands belong to your people—and, of course, when he goes down to the Windward Islands—"

"The Windward Islands!" Frank repeated. "Why, they are not anywhere near here."

"I should have said the Leeward Islands, senor. The English call them so, but we and the Danes and the Dutch all call them the Windward Islands."

"Oh, I understand.

"What is your name, my man?"

"Dominique, sar. Me talk English bery well. Me take you to any port you want to go. Me know all de rocks and shoals. Bery plenty dey is, but Dominique knows ebery one of dem."

"That is all right. You are just the man I want. Well, are you ready to go on board at once?"

"Me ready in an hour, sar. Go home now, say goodbye to wife and piccaninnies. Pedro just tell me that boat go off with water in one, two hours. Dominique go off with him. Me like five dollars to give wife to buy tings while me am away."

"All right, Dominique, here you are. Now don't you miss the boat, or we shall quarrel at starting, and I shall send ashore at once and engage someone else."

"Dominique come, sar, that for sure. Me good man; always keep promise."

"Well, here is another couple of dollars, Dominique; that is a present. You give that to the wife, and tell her to buy something for the piccaninnies with it."

So saying, Frank, George Lechmere, and Pedro stepped on board the boat; while the pilot walked off, his black face beaming with satisfaction.

He came off duly with the last water boat, and while the contents of the barrels were being transferred to the tanks—for now that the long run was accomplished there was no longer any necessity for carrying a greater supply than these could hold—Frank had a talk with him.

"Now, Dominique, this is, you know, a yacht cruising about on pleasure."

"Yes, sar, me know dat."

"At the same time," Frank went on, "we have an object in view. Just at present we want to find that schooner or brigantine that put in here nearly a month ago. She carried a heavy spread of canvas on her yards, and lay very low in the water."

The pilot nodded.

"Me remember him, sar; could not make out de craft nohow. Some people said she pirate, but dar ain't no pirates now."

"That is so, Dominique. Still there may be reasons sometimes for wanting to overhaul a vessel, and I have such a reason. What it is, is of no consequence. Pedro tells me that when she got under sail she went west, but as it was just dark when she sailed, she may very well have turned as soon as she was hidden from sight and have gone east; and it seems to me likely that she would, in the first place, have made for one of the Virgin Islands."

"It depends, sar, upon the trade that he wanted to do. Not much trade dere, sar. The trade is done at Tortola, dat English island; and at Saint Thomas or Santa Cruz, dem Danish islands; all de oders do little trade."

"Yes, Dominique, but I don't think that she wants to trade at all. What she wants to do is to lie up quietly, where she would not be noticed."

"Plenty of places in the islands for dat, sar."

"Did they take a pilot here?"

Dominique shook his head.

"No, sar; several offers, but no take. If want to hide, they no want pilot from here; they take up a fisherman among the islands, to show dem good place. But plenty of places much better in San Domingo or Cuba. Why dey stop Virgin Islands? Little places, many got no water, no food, no noting but bare rock."

"I think that they would go in there, because, as the hurricane season had begun when they got here, they would think it better to run into the port."

"Hurricane not bad here, sar; bery bad down at what English call Leeward Islands. Have dem sometimes here, not bery often; had one four days ago, one ob de worse me remember. We not likely to have another dis year."

"That is satisfactory, Dominique, We got caught in it the other day, and I don't want to meet another. Well, you understand what I want. To begin with, to search all the places a vessel that did not want to attract notice would be likely to lie up in. We want to question people as to whether she has been seen, and if we don't find her, to hear whether, when last seen, she was sailing in the direction of the Leeward Islands, or going west."

"Me find out, sar," the negro said, confidently. "Someone sure to have seen her."

"Well, you had better come below. I have got a chart, and you shall mark all the islands where there are any bays that she would be likely to take shelter in, and we can then see the order in which we had better take them."

This was a little beyond Dominique's English, but Pedro explained it to him, and at Frank's request went below with them; Frank telling Hawkins to weigh anchor as soon as the tanks were filled and the stores were on board. He had, before he came off, returned to Senor Cordovo and paid for all the things supplied.

Going through the islands, one by one, Dominique made a cross against all that possessed harbours or inlets, that would each have to be examined.

"Tortola is the least likely of the places for them to go," Frank said, "as it is a British island."

"Not many people dar, sar. Most people in town. De rest of island rock, all hills broken up, many good harbours."

"What is its size, Dominique?"

"Twelve miles long, sar. Two miles wide."

"Well, that is not a great deal to search, if we have to examine every inch of the coast. How many people are there?"

"Two, three hundred white men. Dey live in de town most all. Two, three thousand blacks."

"Well, we will begin with the others. I should think that in a fortnight we ought to be able to do them all."

The next twelve days were occupied in a fruitless search. Every fishing boat was overhauled and questioned, and Frank and Pedro went ashore to every group of huts. The only fact that they learned, was that a schooner answering to the description had been seen some time before. The information respecting her was, however, very vague; for some asserted that she was sailing one way, some another; and Frank concluded that she had cruised about for some days, before deciding where to lie up. It was at Tortola that they first gained any useful information. Many vessels had, during the last six weeks, entered one or other of the deep creeks, and one of them had laid up for nearly a month in a narrow inlet with but one or two negro huts on shore. It was undoubtedly the Phantom, or rather the Dragon, for the negroes had noticed that name on her stern. She had sailed on the day after the hurricane, and, as they learned from shore villages at other points, had gone west.

"Well, it is a comfort to think that even if we had sailed direct here from Porto Rico we should not have caught her," Frank said to George Lechmere. "She had left here two days before we got there. I suppose they have someone on board who has been in the islands before, for certainly the harbours are the best in the group. No doubt they got some fishermen to bring them into the creek. Well, there is nothing to do but to turn her head west. It is but forty-eight hours' sail to San Domingo, and I fancy that it is likely that he will have stopped there. You see on the chart that there are numberless bays, and there would be no fear of questions being asked by the blacks. If we don't find him there we must try Cuba; but San Domingo is by far the most likely place for him to choose for his headquarters, and there are at least four biggish rivers he could sail up, beside a score of smaller ones.

"I should say that we had better try the south and west first. The coast is a great deal more indented there than it is to the north. There seem to be any number of creeks and bays. I should think that he would be likely to make one of these his headquarters, and spend his time cruising about."

Although Dominique professed a thorough knowledge of the coast of San Domingo and Hayti, Frank could see that he was not so absolutely certain as he was of the Virgin Islands, and he told him to land at villages as he passed along, and bring fishermen off acquainted with the waters in their locality.

"Dat am de safest way for sure, sar," Dominique said. "Dis chile know de coast bery well, can pilot ship into town of San Domingo or any oder port that ships go to, but he could not say for certain where all de rocks and shoals are along places where de ships neber go in."

Three days later the Osprey, after sailing along the northern shore, arrived at Porto Rico and, passing through the Mona channel between that island and San Domingo, dropped anchor in the port of the capital. Dominique went ashore with Pedro, and spent some hours in boarding coasting craft and questioning negroes whether they had seen the brigantine. Several of them had noticed her. She had been cruising off the coast, and had put in at the mouth of the Nieve, and at Jaquemel on the south coast of Hayti. They heard of her, too, in the deep bay at the west of the island between Capes Dame Marie and La Move. Some had seen her sailing one way, some another; she had evidently been, as Frank had expected, cruising about.

Pedro put down the dates of the times at which she had been seen, but negroes are very vague as to time, and beyond the fact that some had seen her about a week before, while in other cases it was nearer a fortnight, he could ascertain nothing with certainty. So far as he could learn, she had only put into three ports, although the coasters he boarded came from some twenty different localities.

"I fancy that it is as I expected," Frank said. "They have one regular headquarters to which they return frequently. It may be some very secluded spot. It may be up one of these small rivers marked on the chart—there are a score of them between Cape la Move and here. She does not seem to have been seen as far east as this. Of course, she has not put in here, because there are some eight or ten foreign ships here now. Every one of these twenty rivers has plenty of water for vessels of her draught for some miles up. I fancy our best chance will be to meet her cruising."

"The worst of that would be, Major," George Lechmere said, "that she would know us, and if she sails as well as she used to do, we should not catch her before night came on—if she had seven or eight miles' start—especially if we both had the wind aft."

"That is just what I am afraid of. I have no doubt that we could beat her easily working to windward in her present rig, but I am by no means certain that she could not run away from us if we were both free; and if she once recognised us there is no saying where she might go to after she had shaken us off. Certainly she would not stay in these waters.

"The question is, how can we disguise ourselves? If we took down our mizzen and dirtied the rest of our sails, it would not be much of a disguise. Nothing but a yacht carries anything like as big a mainsail as ours, and our big jib and foresail, and the straight bowsprit would tell the tale. Of course, we could fasten some wooden battens along her side, and stretch canvas over them, and paint it black, and so raise her side three feet, but even then the narrowness of her hull, seen end on as it would be, in comparison to the height of the mast and spread of canvas, would strike Carthew at once."

"We could follow his example, sir, and make her into a brig. I dare say we could get it done in a week."

"That might spoil her sailing, and as soon as he found that we were in chase of him, he would at once suspect that something was wrong. That would, of all things, be the worst, especially if he found—which would be just as likely as not—that he had the legs of us.

"I believe the most certain way of all would be to search for her in the boats. If we were to paint the gig black, so that it would not attract attention, give a coating of grey paint to the oars, and hire a black crew, we could coast along and stop at every village, and search every bay, and row far enough up each river to find some village or hut where we could learn whether the Phantom has been in the habit of going up there. It would take some time, of course, but it might be a good deal of time saved in the long run. We could do a great deal of sailing. The gig stands well up to canvas when the crew are sitting in the bottom, and we could fit her out with a native rig.

"From here to Cape La Move, following the indentations, must be somewhere between five and six hundred miles, perhaps more than that. The breeze is regular, and with a sail we ought to make from forty to fifty miles a day—say forty—so that in three weeks we should thoroughly have searched the coast, even allowing for putting in three or four times a day to make inquiries. The yacht must follow, keeping a few miles astern. At any rate she must not pass us.

"At night when she anchors she must have two head lights, one at the crosstrees and one at the topmast head. I shall be on the lookout for her, and we will take some blue lights and some red lights with us. Every night I will burn a blue light, say at nine o'clock. A man in the crosstrees will make it out twenty miles away, and that will tell them where I am, and that I don't want them. If I burn a red light it will be a signal for the yacht to come and pick me up."

"Then you will go in the boat yourself, Major?"

"Yes, I must be doing something. I shall take Pedro with me, and perhaps Dominique. We can get another pilot here. Dominique is a shrewd fellow, and can get more out of the negroes than Pedro can. Certainly, that will be the best plan, and will avoid the necessity of spoiling the yacht's speed, which may be of vital importance to us at a critical moment.

"Call Dominique down. I will send him ashore at once with Pedro, to get hold of a good pilot and four good negro boatmen, and a native sail. I think that is all we want."

Chapter 15

As soon as the dinghy, with Dominique and Pedro, had left the side of the yacht; the captain, by Frank's orders, set four men to work to paint the gig black, while others gave a coat of dull lead colour to the varnished oars. The order was received with much surprise by the men, who audibly expressed their regret at seeing their brightly varnished boat and oars thus disfigured.

After about three hours on shore, the dinghy returned loaded with fruit and vegetables, which Pedro had purchased, and a native mast and sail. The former was at once cut so as to step in the gig. The sail was hoisted, and was then taken in hand by one of the crew, who was a fair sailmaker, to be altered so as to stand flatter. Half an hour later the new pilot and four powerful negroes came alongside in a shore boat.

It was now late in the afternoon, so the start was postponed until the next morning. A few other arrangements were made as to signalling, and it was settled that if Frank showed a red light, a rocket should be sent up from the yacht, to show that the signal had been observed, and that they were getting up sail. They were to keep their lights up, so that Frank could make them out as they came up, and put off to meet them.

George Lechmere saw to the preparations for victualling the gig. Two large hampers of fresh provisions were placed on board, and two four-and-a-half gallon kegs of water. A bundle of rugs was placed in the stern sheets, and the boat's flagstaff was fixed in its place in the stern. The yard of the sail was at night to be lashed from the mast to the staff at a height of four feet above the gunwale, and across this the sail was to be thrown to act as a tent. A kettle, frying pan, plates, knives and forks were put in forward, and a box of signal lights under the seat aft. Canisters of tea, sugar, coffee, and all necessaries had been stowed away in the hamper, together with a plentiful supply of tobacco; and a bag of twenty-eight pounds of flour, wrapped up in tarpaulin, was placed under one of the thwarts.

As soon as it was daylight, anchor was got up, and when the yacht had sailed for seven or eight miles to the west, the gig was lowered, and the four black boatmen took their places in her. Frank took the rudder lines, and Dominique sat near him. The sail was then hoisted, and as the wind was light, the boatmen got out their oars and shot ahead of the Osprey, directing their course obliquely towards the shore.

It was not necessary to land at the coast villages here, as it was morally certain that the Phantom had not touched anywhere within twenty or thirty miles of San Domingo, and she would hardly have entered any of the narrow rivers at night. Nevertheless, they did not pass any of these without rowing up them. When some native huts were reached, Dominique closely questioned the negroes.

The pilot had, by this time, been informed of the cause of their search for the Phantom, which had, until they left San Domingo, been a profound mystery to him. Frank, however, being now fully convinced both of the negro's trustworthiness, and of his readiness to do all in his power to assist, thought it as well to confide in him, and when they were together in the boat, informed him that the brigantine they were searching for had carried off a young lady and her maid from England.

"That man must be a rascal," the negro said, angrily. "What do he want dat lady for, sar? He love her bery much?"

"No, Dominique, what he loves is her fortune. She is rich. He has gambled away a fine property, and wants her money to set him on his legs again."

"Bery bad fellow dat," the pilot said, shaking his head earnestly. "Ought to be hung, dat chap. Dominique do all he can to help you, sar. Do more now for you and dat young lady. We find him for suah. You tink there will be any fighting, sar?"

"I think it likely that he will show fight when we come up with him, but you see I have a very strong crew, and I have arms for them all."

"Dat good. Me wonder often why you have so many men. Nothing for half of dem to do. Now me understand. Well, sar, if there be any fighting, you see me fight. You gib me cutlass; me fight like debil."

"Thank you, Dominique," Frank said, warmly, though with some difficulty repressing a smile. "I shall count on you if we have to use force. As far as I am concerned, I own that I should prefer that they did resist, for I should like nothing better than to stand face to face with that villain, each of us armed with a cutlass."

"If he know you here, he go up river, get plenty of black men fight for him. Black fellow bery foolish. Give him little present he fight."

"I had not thought of that, Dominique. Yes, if he has made some creek his headquarters he might, as you say, get the people to take his side by giving them presents; that is, if he knew that we were here. However, at present he cannot dream that we are after him, and if we can but come upon him unawares we shall make short work of him."

No news whatever was obtained of the schooner until the headland of La Catarina was passed, but at the large village of Azua they learned that she had anchored for a night in the bay five days before. She had been seen to sail out, and certainly had not turned into the river Niova.

Touching at every village and exploring every inlet, Frank continued his course until, after rounding the bold promontory of La Beata, he reached the bay at the head of which stands Jaquemel.

Every two or three days they had communicated with the Osprey and slept on board her, leaving her at anchor with her sails down until they had gone some ten miles in advance. She had at times been obliged to keep at some distance from the shore, owing to the dangers from rocks and shoals. The pilot on board would have taken her through, but Frank was unwilling to encounter any risk, unless absolutely necessary.

At Jaquemel he learnt that the schooner had put in there a fortnight before, but neither there nor at any point after leaving Azua had she been seen since that time. She had sailed west.

The next night, after looking in at Bainette, some twenty miles beyond Jaquemel, Frank rejoined the Osprey.

The gig was hoisted up, and they sailed round the point of Gravois, the coast intervening being so rocky and dangerous that, although there was a passage through the shoals to the town of St. Louis, Frank felt certain that the schooner would not be in there. The coast from here to Cape Dame Marie was high and precipitous, with no indentations where a ship could lie concealed, and the voyage was continued in the yacht as far as this cape. They were now at the entrance of the great bay of Hayti.

"I take it as pretty certain," Frank said, as he, George Lechmere, the skipper, and Dominique bent over the chart; "that the schooner is somewhere in this bay. She has certainly not made her headquarters anywhere along the south coast. In the first place, she has seldom been seen, and in the second we have examined it thoroughly. Therefore I take it that she is somewhere here, unless, of course, she has sailed for Cuba. But I don't see why she should have done that. The coast there is a good deal more dangerous than that of San Domingo. He could not want a better place for cruising about than this bay. You see, it is about ninety miles across the mouth, and over a hundred to Port au Prince, with indentations and harbours all round, and with the island of Genarve, some forty miles long, to run behind in the centre. He could get everything he wants at Port au Prince, or at Petit Gouve, which looks a good-sized place.

"I should say, in the first place, that we could not do better than run down at night to the island of Genarve, and anchor close under it. From there we shall see him if he comes out of Port au Prince, or Petit Gouve, whichever side he may take; and by getting on to an elevated spot have a view of pretty nearly the whole bay. Looking at it at present, the two most likely spots for him to make his headquarters are in that very sheltered inlet behind the point of Halle on the north side, or in the equally sheltered bay and inlet under the Bec de Marsouin on the south. From Genarve we ought to be able to see him coming out of either of them. It is not above five-and-twenty miles from the island to the Bec de Marsouin, and forty to the point of Halle. We might not see him come out from there, but we should soon make him out if he were coming down from Port au Prince."

It was agreed that this was the best plan to adopt. It might lead to their sighting the schooner in a day or two, while to row round the bay and search every inlet in it would take them a fortnight. From Genarve, too, a forty-mile sail in the gig would take them into Port au Prince, which the brigantine might possibly have made its headquarters. Accordingly, after waiting until nightfall, they got up sail, and anchored at six in the morning in a small bay in the island of Genarve. Here they would not be likely to attract the notice of any ship passing up to Port au Prince, unless, which was very unlikely, one came along close to the shore.

As soon as the anchor was dropped, both boats rowed to shore. Frank, George Lechmere, Pedro, and four sailors, with a basket of provisions, started at once for the highest point in the island, some four miles distant. Dominique went along the shore with two sailors, to make inquiries at any villages they came to.

On reaching the top of the hill, Frank saw that, as he had expected, it commanded an extensive view over the bay on each side of the island, which was but some six miles across. A village could be seen on the northern shore, some three miles distant; and to this Pedro, with one of the sailors, was at once despatched. Both parties rejoined Frank soon after midday. The schooner had been noticed passing the island several times, but much more often on the southern side than on the northern. The negroes on that side were all agreed that she generally kept on the southern side of the passage, and that more than once she had been seen coming from the south shore, and passing the western point of the island on her way north.

"That looks as if she came from Petit Gouve, or the bay of Mitaquane, or that under the Bec de Marsouin," Frank said.

"Dat is it, sar," Dominique agreed. "If she want to go north side of bay from Port au Prince, she would have gone either side of island. I expect she lie under de Bec. Fine, safe place dat, no town there, plenty of wood all round, and villages where she get fruit and vegetables; sure to be little stream where she can get water."

The watch was maintained until sunset, but, although a powerful telescope had been brought up, no vessel at all corresponding to the appearance of the brigantine was made out.

At six o'clock the next morning Frank was again at the lookout, and scarcely had he turned his telescope to the south shore than he saw the brigantine come out from behind the Bec de Marsouin and head towards the west. The wind was blowing from that quarter, and after a few minutes' deliberation, Frank told the men to follow him, and dashed down the hill. In half an hour he reached the shore opposite the yacht, and at his shout the dinghy, which was lying at her stern, at once rowed ashore.

"Get up the anchor, captain, and make sail. I have seen her. She has just come out from the Bec, and is making west. As the wind is against her, it seems to me that he would never choose that direction to cruise in unless he was starting for Cuba, and I dare not let the opportunity slip. If he once gets clear away we may have months of work before we find him again, and as the wind now is, I am sure that we can overhaul him long before he can make Cuba. Indeed, as we lie, we are nearer to that coast than he is, and can certainly cut him off."

In five minutes the Osprey was under way, with all sail set. The wind was nearly due west, and as Cuba lay to the north of that point, she had an advantage that quite counter-balanced that gained by the start the Phantom had obtained. In two hours the lookout at the head of the mast shouted down that he could perceive the brigantine's topsail.

"She is sailing in towards the land on that side," he said. "She has evidently made a tack out, and is now on the starboard tack again."

"It will be a long leg and a short one with her, sir," the skipper said. "I think that if we were in her place we could just manage to lay our course along the coast, but with those square yards of hers, she cannot go as close to the wind as we can. As it is, we can lay our course to cut her off."

"It would be rather a close pinch to do so before she gets to the head of the bay," Frank said.

"Yes, sir, and I don't suppose that we shall overhaul her before that, but we certainly shan't be far behind her by the time she gets there. I think that we shall cut her off if the wind holds as it does now. At any rate, if she should get there first, we should certainly lie between her and Cuba, and she will have either to run back, or to round the cape, or to run east or south. I wish the wind would freshen; but I fancy that it is more likely to die away. Still, she is walking along well at present."

Even Frank, anxious as he was, could not but feel satisfied as he looked at the water glancing past her side. She was heeling well over, and the rustle of water at her bow could be heard where they were standing near the tiller. Andrews, the best helmsman on board the yacht, held the tiller rope, and Perry was standing beside him.

From time to time Frank went up to the crosstrees.

"We are drawing in upon her fast," he said, "but she is travelling well, too; much better than I should have thought she would have done with that rig. I think she has got a better wind than we have. She has only made one short tack in for the last two hours."

The captain's prognostication as to the wind was verified, and to Frank's intense annoyance it gradually died away, and headed them so much that they could no longer lie their course.

"What shall we do, sir? Shall we hold across to the south shore and work along by it, as the schooner is doing, or shall we go about at once?"

"Go about at once, Hawkins. You see we can see her topsails from the deck; and of course she can see ours. I don't suppose she has paid any attention to us yet, and if we stand away on the other tack we shall soon drop her altogether; while if we hold on she will, when we reach that shore, be three or four miles behind us. Of course, she will have a full view of us."

They sailed on the port tack for an hour and then came round again. The brigantine could no longer be seen from the deck, and could only just be made out from the crosstrees.

"I think on this tack," the skipper said, as he stood by the compass after she had gone round, "we shall make the point, and I think that we shall make it ahead of her."

"I think so too, Hawkins. What pace is she going now?"

"Not much more than four knots, sir."

"My only fear is that we shan't get near her before it is dark."

"I think that we have plenty of time for that, sir. You see we got up anchor at half-past six, and it is just twelve o'clock now. Another five hours should take us up to her if the wind holds at this."

By two o'clock the topsails of the brigantine could be again made out from the deck. She was still working along shore, and was on their port bow.

"Another three hours and we shall be alongside of her," the skipper said; "and if I am not mistaken we shall come out ahead of her."

"There is one advantage in the course we are taking, Hawkins. Viewing us, as she will, pretty nearly end on till we get nearly abreast of her, she won't be able to make out our rig clearly."

By four o'clock they were within five miles of the brigantine. The wind then freshened, and laying her course as she did, while the brigantine was obliged to make frequent tacks, the Osprey ran down fast towards her.

"They must have their eyes on us by this time," the captain said. "Though they cannot be sure that it is the Osprey, they can see that she is a yawl of over a hundred tons, and as they cannot doubt that we are chasing them, they won't be long in guessing who we are. Shall we get the arms up, sir?"

"Yes, you may as well do so. The muskets can be loaded and laid by the bulwarks, but they are not to be touched until I give the order. No doubt they also are armed. I am anxious not to fire a shot if it can be helped, and once alongside we are strong enough to overpower them with our cutlasses only. With the five blacks we are now double their strength, and even Carthew may see the uselessness of offering any resistance."

They ran down until they were within a mile of the shore, not being now more than a beam off the brigantine. Two female figures had some time before been made out on her deck, but they had now disappeared. It was evident that the Osprey was being closely watched by those on board the brigantine. Presently two or three men were seen to run aft.

"They are going to tack again, sir. If they do they will come right out to us."

Frank made no reply, but stood with his glass fixed on the brigantine. Suddenly he exclaimed:

"Round with her, Hawkins!"

"Up with your helm, Andrews. Hard up, man!" the skipper shouted, as he himself ran to slack out the main sheet. Four men ran aft to assist him.

"That will do," he said, as she fell off fast from the wind. "Now, then, gather in the main sheet, ready for a jibe. Slack off the starboard runner; a couple of hands aft and get the square sail out of the locker.

"Mr. Purvis, get the yard across her, lower her down ready for the sail, and see that the braces and guys are all right.

"Now in with the sheet, lads, handsomely. That will do, that is it. Over she goes. Slack out the sheet steadily."

"She is round, too," Frank said, as the boom went off nearly square. "We have gained, and she is not more than half a mile away."

The manoeuvre had, in fact, brought the yachts nearer to each other. Both had their booms over to starboard.

"Quick with that square sail," Frank shouted. "She is drawing away from us fast."

Two minutes later the square sail was hoisted, and the foot boomed out on the port side. Every eye was now fixed on the brigantine, but to their disappointment they saw that she was still, though very much more slowly, drawing ahead.

"That is just what I feared," Frank said, in a tone of deep vexation. "With those big yards I was certain that she would leave us when running ahead before the wind. However, there is no fear of our leaving her. What are we doing now? Seven knots?"

"About that, sir, and she is doing a knot better."

"What do you think that she will do now, Hawkins?"

"I don't see what she has got to do, sir. If she were to get five miles ahead of us, and then haul her wind, she would know that she could not go away from us, for we should be to windward; and we are evidently a good bit faster than she is when we are both close hauled. The only other thing that I can see for her to do is to run straight on to Port au Prince. At the rate we are going now she would be in soon after daylight tomorrow. We should be seven or eight miles astern of her, and he might think that we should not venture to board her there."

"I don't think that he would rely on that, Hawkins. Now that he knows who we are, he will guess that we shall stick at nothing. What I am afraid of is that he will lower a boat and row Miss Greendale and her maid ashore. He might do it either there, or, what would be much more likely, row ashore to some quiet place during the night, take his friend and two or three of his men with him, and leave the rest to sail her to Port au Prince."

"I don't think that the wind is going to hold," the skipper said, looking astern. "I reckon that it will drop, as it generally does, at sunset. It is not blowing so hard now as it did just before we wore round."

In half an hour, indeed, it fell so light that the Osprey was standing through the water only at three and a half knots an hour. The light wind suited the Phantom, with her great sail spread. She had now increased her lead to a mile and a half, and was evidently leaving them fast.

"There is only one thing to be done, George. We must board them in boats."

"I am ready, Major; but it will be a rather risky business."

Frank looked at him in surprise.

"I don't mean for us, sir," George said, with a smile, "but for Miss Greendale. You may be sure that those fellows will fight hard, and as we come up behind we shall get it hot. Now, sir, if anything happens to you, you must remember that the Osprey will be as good as useless towards helping her. You as her owner might be able to justify what we are doing, but if you were gone there would be no one to take the lead. Carthew would only have to sail into Port au Prince and denounce us as pirates. I hear from the pilot that these niggers have got some armed ships, and they might sink us as soon as we came into the harbour, and then there would be an end to any chance of Miss Greendale getting her liberty."

"That is true enough, George, but I think that it must be risked. Now that he knows we are here, he has nothing to do but to send her ashore under the charge of his friend and two or three of the sailors, and take her up into the hills. Or he might go with her himself, which is perhaps more likely. Then when we came up with her at Port au Prince the skipper would simply deny that there had ever been any ladies on board, and would swear that he had only carried out two gentlemen passengers, as his papers would show, and might declare that he had landed them at Porto Rico. Of course, they are certain to fight now, for they can do so without risk, as they can swear that they took us for a pirate.

"How many do you think that the gig will carry, Hawkins?"

"Well, sir, you might put nine in her. You brought ten off at Southampton; but if you remember, it put her very low in the water, and we should run a good deal heavier than your party then."

"Yes, I think that we had better take only nine. If we overload her she will row so heavily that we shall be a long time overhauling them."

"I am not quite sure that we shall overhaul them anyhow, sir. Look at those clouds coming over the hills. They are travelling fast, and I should say that we are likely to have a squall. No doubt they get them here pretty often with such high land all round."

"Well, we must chance that, Hawkins. If one does come you must pick us up as we come along. I agree with you; it does look as if we should have a squall. It may not be anything very serious, but anyhow, if it comes it will take her along a great deal faster than we can row.

"Purvis, I suppose that the dinghy will carry seven?"

"Yes, she will do that easily."

"Very well, we can but try; that will give sixteen of us, which is about their strength. You must remain on board. Purvis shall command the dinghy; Lechmere will go with me. Pick out thirteen hands. You and Perry can manage with seven and the five negroes, but keep a sharp lookout for that squall. Remember that you will have very short warning. We are only a mile from the shore, and as it is coming down from the hills you may not see it on the water until it is quite close to you."

The boats were lowered, and the men, armed with musket and cutlass, took their places. Frank and George Lechmere each had a cutlass and a revolver buckled to the waist.

"Now give way, lads," Frank said. "She is about two miles ahead of us, and we ought to overtake her in half an hour."

It was now getting dusk, the light fading out suddenly as the clouds spread over the sky. Frank's last orders to the skipper before leaving were:

"Edge her in, Hawkins, until you are dead astern of the brigantine. Then if the squall comes down before we reach her, we shall be right in your track."

"I have put a lighted lantern into the stern sheets of each boat, sir, and have thrown a bit of sail cloth over them, so that if she leaves you behind, and you hold it up, there won't be any fear of our missing you."

The men rowed hard, but the gig had to stop frequently to let the dinghy come up. They gained, however, fast upon the brig, and in half an hour were but a few hundred yards astern. Then came a hail from the brigantine in French:

"Keep off or we will sink you!"

No reply was made. They were but two hundred yards away when there were two bright flashes from the stern of the brigantine, and a shower of bullets splashed round the boats. There were two or three cries of pain, and George Lechmere felt Frank give a sudden start.

"Are you hit, sir?"

"I have got a bullet in my left shoulder, George, but it is of no consequence.

"Row on, lads," he shouted. "We shall be alongside before they have time to load again.

"I never thought of their having guns, though," he went on, as the men recovered from their surprise, and dashed on again with a cheer. "By the sharp crack they must be brass. I suppose he picked up a couple of small guns at Ostend, thinking that they might be useful to him in these waters."

A splattering fire of musketry now broke out from the brigantine. They had lessened their distance by half when they saw the brigantine, without apparent cause, heel over. Farther and farther she went until her lee rail was under water.

The firing instantly ceased, and there were loud shouts on board; then, as she came up into the wind, the square yards were let fall, and the crew ran up the ratlines to secure the sails. Simultaneously the foresail came down, then her head payed off again, and she darted away like an arrow from the boats.

These, however, had ceased rowing. Frank, as he saw the brigantine bowing over, had shouted to Purvis to put the boat's head to the wind, doing the same himself. A few seconds afterwards the squall struck them with such force that some of the oars were wrenched from the hands of the men, who were unprepared for the attack.

"Steady, men, steady!" Frank shouted. "It won't last long. Keep on rowing, so as to hold the boat where you are, till the yacht comes along. It won't be many minutes before she is here."

In little over a quarter of an hour she was seen approaching, and Frank saw that, in spite of the efforts of the men at the oars, the boats had been blown some distance to leeward. However, as soon as the lanterns were held up the Osprey altered her course, and the captain, taking her still further to leeward, threw her head up to the wind until they rowed alongside her.

Frank had by this time learned that one of the men in the bow had been killed, and that three besides himself had been wounded. Two were wounded on board the dinghy.

"So they have got some guns," the skipper said, as they climbed on deck. "No one hurt, I hope?"

"There is one killed, I am sorry to say, and five wounded," Frank replied; "but none of them seriously. I have got a bullet in my shoulder, but that is of no great consequence. So you got through it all right?"

"Yes, sir, it looked so nasty that I got the square-sail off her and the topsail on deck before it struck us, and as we ran the foresail down just as it came we were all right, and only just got the water on deck. It was as well, though, that we were lying becalmed. As it was, she jumped away directly she felt it. I was just able to see the brigantine, and it seemed to me that she had a narrow escape of turning turtle."

"Yes, they were too much occupied with us to be keeping a sharp lookout at the sky, and if it had been a little stronger it would have been a close case with her. Thank God that it was no worse. Can you make her out still?"

"Yes, sir, I can see her plainly enough with my glasses."

In a quarter of an hour the strength of the squall was spent. The wind then veered round to its former quarter, taking the Osprey along at the rate of some five knots an hour.

The wounded were now attended to. George Lechmere found that the ball had broken Frank's collarbone and gone out behind. Both he and Frank had had sufficient experience to know what should be done, and after bathing the wound, and with the assistance of two sailors, who pulled the arm into its place, George applied some splints to the broken bone to keep it firm, and then bandaged it and the arm.

One of the sailors had a wound in the cheek, the ball in its passage carrying off part of the ear. One of the men sitting in the bow had a broken arm, but only one of the others was seriously hurt. Frank went on deck again as soon as his shoulder was bandaged and his left arm strapped tightly to his side.

"I suppose that she is still gaining on us, Hawkins?"

"Yes, she is dropping us. I reckon she has gone fast, sir, fully half a knot, though we have got all sail set."

"There is one comfort," Frank said. "The coast from here as far as the Bec is so precipitous, that they won't have a chance of putting the boat ashore until they get past that point, and by the time they are there daylight will have broken."

Chapter 16

The stars were bright, and with the aid of a night glass the brigantine was kept in sight; the sailors relieving each other at the masthead every half hour. Frank would have stayed on deck all night, had not George Lechmere persuaded him to go below.

"Look here, Major," he said. "It is like enough that we may have a stiff bit of fighting tomorrow. Now we know that those fellows have guns, though they may be but two or three pounders, and it is clear that it is not going to be altogether such a one-sided job as we looked for. You have had a long day already, sir. You have got an ugly wound, and if you don't lie down and keep yourself quiet, you won't be fit to do your share in any fighting tomorrow; and I reckon that you would like to be in the front of this skirmish. You know in India wounds inflamed very soon if one did not keep quiet with them, and I expect that it is just the same here.

"It is not as if you could do any good on deck. The men are just as anxious to catch that brigantine as you are. They were hot enough before, but now that one of their mates has been killed, and five or six wounded, I believe that they would go round the world rather than let her slip through their hands. I shall be up and down all night, Major, and the captain and both mates will be up, too, and I promise that we will let you know if there is anything to tell you."

"Well, I will lie down, George, but I know that I shall get no sleep. Still, perhaps, it will be better for me to keep my arm quite quiet."

He was already without his coat, for that had been cut from the neck down to the wrist, to enable George to get at the wound. He kicked off his light canvas shoes, and George helped him to lie down in his berth.

"You will be sure to let me know if she changes her course or anything?"

"I promise you that I will come straight down, Major."

Three quarters of an hour later, George stole noiselessly down and peeped into the stateroom. He had turned down the swinging lamp before he went up, but there was enough light to enable him to see that his master had fallen off to sleep. He took the news up to Hawkins, who at once gave orders that no noise whatever was to be made. The men still moved about the deck, but all went barefooted.

"The wind keeps just the same," Hawkins said. "I can't make it more than three and a half knots through the water. I would give a year's pay if it would go round dead ahead of us; we should soon pick her up then. As it is, she keeps crawling away. However, we can make her out, on such a night as this, a good deal further than she is likely to get before morning. Besides, we shall be having the moon up soon, and as we are steering pretty nearly east, it will show her up famously.

"Now I will give you the same advice that you gave the governor. You had much better lie down for a bit. Purvis has gone down for a sleep, Perry will go down when he comes up at twelve, and I shall get an hour or two myself later on."

"I won't go down," George said, "but I will bring a couple of blankets up and lie down aft. I promised the Major that I would let him know if there was any change in the wind, or in the brigantine's course, so wake me directly there is anything to tell him. I have put his bell within reach. I have no doubt I shall hear it through that open skylight if he rings; but if not, wake me at once."

"All right. Trust us for that."

Twice during the night George got up and went below. The first time Frank had not moved. The second he found that the tumbler of lime juice and water, on the table at the side of the bunk, was nearly half emptied; and that his master had again gone off to sleep and was breathing quietly and regularly.

"He is going on all right," he said to Hawkins, when he went up. "There is no fever yet, anyhow, for he has drunk only half that glass of lime juice. If he had been feverish he would not have stopped until he had got to the bottom of it."

When George next woke, the morning was breaking.

"Anything new?" he asked Purvis, who was now at the tiller.

"Nothing whatever. The governor has not rung his bell. The wind is just as it was, neither better nor worse, and the brigantine is eight miles ahead of us."

George went forward to have a look at her.

"I think I had better wake him," he said to himself. "He will have had nine hours of it, and he won't like it if I don't let him know that it is daylight. I will get two or three fresh limes squeezed, and then go in to him."

This time Frank opened his eyes as he entered.

"Morning is breaking, Major, and everything is as it was. I hope that you are feeling better for your sleep. Let me help you up. Here is a tumbler of fresh lime juice."

"I feel right enough, George. I can scarcely believe that it is morning. How I have slept—and I fancied that I should not have gone off at all."

Drinking off the lime juice, Frank at once followed Lechmere on deck, and after a word or two with Purvis hurried forward.

"She is a long way ahead," he said, with a tone of disappointment.

"The mate reckoned it between seven and eight miles, Major."

"How far is she from the Bec?"

"I don't know, sir. I did not ask Purvis."

Frank went aft and repeated the question.

"I fancy that that is the Bec, the furthermost point that we can see," Purvis said, "and I reckon that she is about halfway to it."

"Keep her a point or two out, Purvis. The line of shore is pretty straight beyond that, and I want of all things not to lose sight of her for a moment. I would give a good deal to know what she is going to do. I cannot think that she is going to try to go round the southeast point of the island, for if she were she would have laid her head that way before."

The Osprey edged out until they opened the line of coast beyond the headland, and then kept her course again. There was a trifle more wind as the sun rose higher, and the yacht went fully a knot faster through the water. In less than two hours the brigantine was abreast of the headland. Presently Frank exclaimed:

"She is hauling in her wind."

"That she is, sir," Hawkins, who had just come on deck, exclaimed. "She surely cannot be going to run into the bay."

"She can be going to do nothing else," Frank said. "What on earth does she mean by it? No doubt that scoundrel is going to land with Miss Greendale, but why should he leave the Phantom at our mercy, when he could have sent her on to Port au Prince?"

"I cannot think what he is doing, sir; but he must have some game on, or he would never act like that."

"Of course, he may have arranged to go with the lady to some place up in the hills; but why should he sacrifice the yacht?"

"It is a rum start anyhow, and I cannot make head or tail of it. Of course you will capture her, sir?"

"I don't know, Hawkins. It is one thing to attack her when she has Miss Greendale on board, but if she has gone ashore it would be very like an act of piracy."

"Yes, sir. But then, you see, they fired into our boat, and killed one of our men, and wounded you and four or five others."

"That is right enough, Hawkins, but we cannot deny that they did it in self defence. Of course, we know that they must have recognised us, and knew what our errand was, but her captain and crew would be ready to swear that they didn't, and that they were convinced by our actions that we were pirates. At any rate, you may be sure that the blacks would retain both craft, and that we should be held prisoners for some considerable time, while Miss Greendale would be a captive in the hands of Carthew. I should attack the brigantine if I knew her to be on board, and should be justified in doing so, even if it cost a dozen lives to capture her; but I don't think I should be justified in risking a single life in attacking the brigantine if she were not on board. To do so would, in the first place, be a distinct act of piracy; and in the second, if we got possession of the brigantine we should have gained nothing by it."

"We might burn her, sir."

"Yes, we might, and run the risk of being hung for it. We might take her into Port au Prince, but we have no absolute evidence against her. We could not swear that we had positive knowledge that Miss Greendale was on board, and certain as I am that the female figures I made out on the deck were she and her maid, they were very much too far away to recognise them, and the skipper might swear that they were two negresses to whom he was giving a passage.

"Moreover, if I took the brigantine I should only cut off Carthew's escape in that direction. His power over Miss Greendale would be just as great, if he had her up among those mountains among the blacks, as it was when he had her on board. I can see that I have made a horrible mess of the whole business, and that is the only thing that I can see. Yesterday I thought it was the best thing to start on a direct chase, as it seemed absolutely certain to me that we should overhaul and capture her. Now I see that it was the worst thing I could have done, and that I ought to have waited until I could take her in the bay."

"But you see, Major," said George Lechmere, who was standing by, "if we had gone on searching with the boat, before we had made an examination of the whole bay, there would be no knowing where she had gone, and it might have been months before we could have got fairly on her track again."

"No, we acted for the best; but things have turned out badly, and I feel more hopelessly at sea, as to what we had better do next, than I have done since the day I got to Ostend. At any rate, there is nothing to be done until we have got a fair sight of the brigantine."

It seemed, to all on board, that the Osprey had never sailed so sluggishly as she did for the next hour and a half. As they expected, no craft was to be seen on the waters of the bay as they rounded the point, but Dominique and the other pilot had been closely questioned, and both asserted that at the upper end of the bay there was a branch that curved round "like dat, sar," the latter said, half closing his little finger.

Progress up the bay was so slow that the boats were lowered, and the yacht was towed to the mouth of the curved branch. Here they were completely landlocked, and the breeze died away altogether.

"How long is this bend, Jake?" Frank asked the second pilot in French.

"Two miles, sir; perhaps two miles and a half."

"Deep water everywhere?"

"Plenty of water; can anchor close to shore. Country boats run in here very often if bad weather comes on. Foreign ships never come here. They always run on to the town."

"You told us that there were a few huts at the end."

"Yes, sir. There is a village there, two others near."

The crew had all armed themselves, and the muskets were again placed ready for use.

"You had better go round, Hawkins," Frank said, "and tell them that on no account is a shot to be fired unless I give orders. Tell the men that I am just as anxious to fight as they are, and that if they give us a shadow of excuse we will board them."

"I went round among the men half an hour ago, sir, and told them how the land lay, and Lechmere has been doing the same. They all want to fight, but I have made them see that it might be a very awkward business for us all."

The men in the boats were told to take it easy, and it was the best part of an hour before they saw, on turning the last bend, the brigantine lying at anchor a little more than a quarter of a mile away.

"She looks full of men," Frank exclaimed, as turned his glasses upon her.

"Yes, sir," said the captain, who was using a powerful telescope, "they are blacks. There must be fifty of them beside the crew, and as far as I can see most of them are armed."

"That explains why he came in here, Hawkins. They have been using this place for the last three weeks, and no doubt have made good friends with the negroes. I dare say Carthew has spent his money freely on them.

"Well, this settles it. We would attack them at sea without hesitation, however many blacks there might be on board, but to do so now would be the height of folly. Five of our men are certainly not fit for fighting, so that their strength in whites is nearly equal to ours. They have got those two little cannon, which would probably reduce our number a bit before we got alongside, and with fifty blacks to help them it is very doubtful whether we should be able to take them by boarding. Certainly we could not do so without very heavy loss.

"We will anchor about two hundred and fifty yards outside her. As long as she lies quiet there we will leave her alone. If she tries to make off we will board her at once. Anchor with the kedge; that will hold her here. Have a buoy on the cable and have it ready to slip at a moment's notice, and the sails all ready to hoist."

"Easy rowing," the captain called to the men in the boats, "and come alongside. We have plenty of way on her to take up a berth."

In two or three minutes the anchor was dropped and the sails lowered.

"Now I will row across to her," Frank said, "and tell them that I don't want to attack them, but I am determined to search their craft."

"No, Major," George Lechmere said, firmly. "We are not going to let you throw away your life, and you have no right to do it—at any rate not until after Miss Greendale is rescued. You may be sure of one thing: that Carthew has left orders before going on shore that you are to be shot if you come within range. He will know that if you are killed there will be an end of the trouble. I will go myself, sir."

Frank made no answer for a minute or two. Then he said:

"In that case you would be shot instead of me. If Carthew is on shore, as I feel sure he is, the others won't know you from me. I agree with you that I cannot afford to risk my life just now, and yet we must search that brigantine."

"Me go, sar," Dominique, who was standing by, said suddenly. "Me take two black fellows in dinghy. Dey no fire at us. Me go dere, tell captain dat you no want to have to kill him and all his crew, but dat you got to search dat craft. If he let search be made, den no harm come of it. If he say no, den we take yacht alongside and kill every man jack. Say dat white sailors all furious, because dey fire at us yesterday, and want bad to have fight."

"Very well, Dominique. It can do no harm anyhow, and as I feel sure that the lady has been taken ashore, I don't see why they should refuse."

Accordingly, Dominique called to two of the negro boatmen to get into the dinghy, and took his seat in the stern. When the boat was halfway between the two vessels there was a hail in French:

"What do you want? If you come nearer we will fire."

"What want to fire for?" Dominique shouted back. "Me pilot, me no capture ship, single handed. Me want to speak to captain."

It was evident the answer was understood, for no reply came for a minute or two.

"Well, come along then."

The words could be heard perfectly on board the yacht.

"The skipper talks English, George. I thought that he would do so. Carthew was sure to have shipped someone who could understand him. I don't suppose his French is any better than mine."

The dinghy was rowed to within ten yards of the brigantine.

"Now, what message have you brought me from that pirate?"

"Him no pirate at all. You know dat bery well, massa captain. Dat English yacht; anyone see dat with half an eye. De gentleman there says you have a lady on board dat has been carried off."

"Then he is a liar!" the Belgian said. "There is no woman on board at all!"

"Well, sar, dat am a matter ob opinion. English gentleman tink dat you hab. You say no. Dat prove bery easy. De gentleman say he wants to search ship. If as you say, she is no here, den ob course no reason for you to say no to dat. If on de other hand you say no, den he quite sure he right, and he come and search whether you like it or no. Den der big fight. Bery strong crew on board dat yacht. Plenty guns, men all bery savage, cause you kill one of der fellows last night. Dey want to fight bad, and if dey come dey kill many. What de use of dat, sar? Why say won't let search if lady not here?

Nothing to fight about. But if you not let us see she not here, den we board de ship, and when we take her we burn her."

The Belgian stood for two or three minutes without answering. They had seen that there were two or three and twenty men on board the Osprey, and they were by no means sure that this was the entire number. There were three blacks, and there might be a number of them lying down behind the bulwarks or kept below. The issue of a fight seemed to him doubtful. He was by no means sure that his men would fight hard in a cause in which they had no personal interest; and as for the blacks, they would not count for much in a hand-to-hand fight with English sailors.

He had received no orders as to what to do in such a contingency. Presently he turned to three of his men and said in French:

"Go to that stern cabin, and see that there is nothing about that would show that it has been occupied. They have asked to search us. Let them come and find nothing. Things will go quietly. If not, they say they will attack us and kill every man on board and burn the ship, and as we do not know how many men they may have on board, and as they can do us no harm by looking round, if there is nothing for them to find, we had best let them do it. But mind, the orders hold good. If the owner of that troublesome craft comes alongside, you are to pour in a volley and kill him and the sailors with him. That will make so many less to fight if it comes to fighting. But the owner tells me that if he is once killed there will be an end of it."

He then went to the side, and said to Dominique:

"There is nothing for you to find here. We are an honest trader, and there is nothing worth a pirate's stealing. But in order to show you that I am speaking the truth, I have no objection to two hands coming on board and going through her. We have nothing to hide."

Dominique rowed back to the yacht.

"Dey will let her be searched, sar."

"I thought they would," Frank said; "and of course that is a sign that there is no one there."

"I will go, sir," the skipper said, "as we agreed. He would give anything to get rid of you, and you might be met with a volley when you came alongside. And now there ain't no use in running risks. If they have been told what you are like, they cannot mistake me for you. You are pretty near a foot taller, and you are better than ten years younger, and I haven't any hair on my face. I will go through her. I am sure the lady ain't there, or they would not let me. Still, I will make sure. There are no hiding places in a yacht where anyone could be stowed away, and of course she is, like us, chock full of ballast up to the floor. I shan't be many minutes about it, sir. Dominique may as well go with me. He can stay on deck while I go below, and may pick up something from the black fellows there."

"You may as well take him, Hawkins; but you may be very sure that they won't give him a chance to speak to anyone."

The captain stepped into the boat and was rowed to the yacht. He and Dominique stepped on to the deck and were lost sight of among the blacks. In ten minutes they appeared at the gangway again, and stepped into their boat. Another minute and she was alongside the Osprey.

"Of course, you found nothing, Hawkins."

"Nothing whatever, sir. Anything the lady may have left behind had been stowed away in lockers. I looked about to see if I could sight a bit of ribbon or some other woman's fal-lal, but they had gone ever it carefully. Two of the other state cabins had been occupied. There were men's clothes hanging there. Of course, I looked into every cupboard where as much as a child could have been stowed away, and looked round the forecastle. Anyhow, there is no woman there now.

"Dominique had to go round with me. The captain evidently did not want to give him a chance of speaking to anyone. The mate and two of the sailors posted themselves at the gangway, so that the two blacks should not be able to talk to the niggers on board. And now, sir, what is to be done next?"

"We will go below and talk it over, captain.

"You come down, too, George. Yes, and Dominique. He may be useful.

"Now, Hawkins," he went on, when they had taken their seats at the table, "of course, I have been thinking it over all the morning, and I have come to the conclusion that our only chance now is to fight them with their own weapons. As long as we lie here there is no chance whatever of Miss Greendale being brought on board again, so the chase now has got to be carried on on land. If we go to work the right way, there is no reason why we should not be able to trace her. I propose to take Lechmere and Dominique and the four black boatmen. If we stain our faces a little, and put on a pair of duck trousers, white shirts, red sashes, and these broad straw hats I bought at San Domingo, we shall look just like the half-caste planters we saw in the streets there. I should take Pedro, too, but you will want him to translate anything you have to say to Jake.

"I propose that as soon as it is dark tonight we muffle the oars of the dinghy, and row away and land lower down, say a mile or so; and then make off up into the hills before tomorrow morning. Dominique will try to find out something by inquiring at some of the huts of the blacks. They are not likely to know, but if he offers them a handsome reward to obtain news for him, they will go down to the villages and ferret out something. The people there would not be likely to know where they have been taken, but they would be able to point out the direction in which they went on starting. Then we could follow that up, and inquire again.

"We might take a couple of the villagers with us. Belonging here, they would have more chance of getting news from other blacks than strangers would have."

"Don't you think, sir, that it would be as well to have four or five men with you?" Hawkins said. "There is no doubt this fellow that you are after is a desperate chap, and he may have got a strong body of these blacks as a guard. He might suspect that, after having pursued him all this way, you might try to follow him on land. You could put the men in hiding somewhere every day while you were making inquiries, and they would be mighty handy if it came to fighting, which it seems to me it is pretty sure to do before you see the lady off."

"Well, perhaps it would be best, Hawkins; and, as you say, by keeping them hid all day I don't see that they could increase our difficulties. But then, you see, you will want all your hands here; for if the brigantine sails, whether by night or day, you are to sail too, and to keep close to her wherever she goes. It is not likely that Carthew and Miss Greendale will be on board, but he may very well send orders down to the brigantine to get up the anchor. He would know that we should stick to her, as Miss Greendale might have been taken on board again at night. In that way he would get rid of us from here, and would calculate that we should get tired of following the brigantine in time, or that she would be able to give us the slip, and would then make for some place where he could join her again. So my orders to you will be to stick to her, but not to interfere with her in any way, unless, by any chance, you should discover that Miss Greendale is really on board. In that case I authorise you to board and capture her. They won't have the blacks on board, and as the wounded are going on all right, and three of them, anyhow, will be able to lend a hand in a couple of days, you will be a match for them; especially as they will soon make up their minds that you don't mean to attack them, and you will get a chance of running alongside and taking them by surprise."

"Well, sir, I think that we can do that with four hands less than we have now. You see, there are nineteen and the two mates and myself. Say two of the wounded won't be able to lend a hand, that makes us twenty, to say nothing of Jake and Pedro. So, even if you took four hands, we should be pretty even in numbers; and if our men could not each whip two Belgians, they had better give up the sea."

"Yes, I have no doubt that they could do that, and were it not for Carthew and his friend I would not hesitate to take eight men. I don't know about the other, but you may be sure that Carthew will fight hard. He is playing a desperate game. Still, I think that I might take four, especially as I think the chance of Miss Greendale's being brought on board, until he believes that we have left these waters, is very small.

"Very well, then, that is settled. The five blacks, Lechmere and myself, and four of the sailors, will make a strong party. Serve muskets and cutlasses out to the blacks; and the same, with a brace of pistols, to each of the hands that go with us. While we are away let two of the men dress up in my white duck shirts and jackets, and in white straw hats. Let them always keep aft, and sit about in the deck chairs, and always go down below by the main companion. That will make them think that I am still on board; while if there is no one on the deck aft they will soon guess that we have landed.

"You understand all that we have been saying, Dominique?"

"Me understand, sar, and tink him bery good plan. Me suah to find out which way dat rascal hab gone. Plenty of black fellows glad to earn two dollar to guide us. Dey no money here. Two dollars big sum to them."

"All right, Dominique, but we won't stick at two dollars. If it were necessary I would pay two hundred cheerfully for news."

"We find dem widout dat," the black said, confidently. "Not good offer too much. If black man offered two dollars he bery glad. If offered twenty he begin to say to himself, 'Dis bery good affair; perhaps someone else give forty.'"

"There is something in that, Dominique. Anyhow I shall leave that part of the business to you. As a rule, I shall keep in hiding with the boatmen and sailors all day. I shall be no good for asking questions, for I don't know much French, and the dialect the negroes of these islands speak is beyond me altogether. I cannot understand the boatmen at all."

"Black men here bad, sar; not like dem in de other islands. Here dey tink themselves better than white men; bery ignorant fellows, sar. Most of dem lost religion, and go back to fetish. Bery bad dat. All sorts of bad things in dat affair. Kill children and women to make fetish. Bad people, sar, and dey are worse here than at San Domingo."

There was nothing to do all day, but to sit on deck and watch the brigantine. Most of the blacks had been landed, and only three or four sailors remained on watch on deck. Frank and George Lechmere, in their broad straw hats, sat and smoked in the deck chairs; the former's eyes wandering over the mountains as if in search of something that might point out Bertha's hiding place. The hills were for the most part covered with trees, with here and there a little clearing and a patch of cultivated ground, with two or three huts in the centre. With the glasses solitary huts could be seen, half hidden by trees, here and there; and an occasional little wreath of light smoke curling up showed that there were others entirely hidden in the forest.

"Don't you think, Major," George Lechmere said after a long pause, "that it would be a good thing to have the gig every night at some point agreed on, such as the spot where we land? You see, sir, there is no saying what may happen. We may have to make a running fight of it, and it would be very handy to have the boat to fall back upon."

"Yes, I think that a good idea, George. I will tell Hawkins to send it ashore, say at ten o'clock every night. There is no chance whatever of our being down before that. They are sure to have taken her a long distance up the hills; and though, of course, one cannot say at present, it is pretty certain that we shall have to attack after dark.

"It is important that we should land where there is some sort of a path. I noticed one or two such places as we came along. We may as well get into the dinghy and row down and choose a spot now. Of course, they will be watching from the brigantine, but when they see the same number that went come back again, they will suppose that we have only gone for a row, or perhaps to get a shot at anything we come across. We may as well take a couple of guns with us."

A mile down the inlet they came upon just the spot they were searching for. The shore was level for a few yards from the water's edge, and from here there was a well-marked path going up the slope behind.

"We will fix upon this spot, George. It will be easy for the boats to find it in the dark, from that big tree close to the water's edge. Now we will paddle about for half an hour before we go back."

An hour later they returned to the yacht, and George began at once to make arrangements for the landing.

Chapter 17

"I Should keep watch and watch regularly, Hawkins. I do not say that it is likely, but it is quite possible that they may make an attempt to surprise us, cut all our throats, and then sink the Osprey. He might attack with his boats, and with a lot of native craft. At any rate, it is worth while keeping half the crew always on deck. Be sure and light the cabin as usual. They would suspect that I was away if they did not see the saloon skylights lit up.

"There is no saying when I may be back. It may be three nights, it may be six, or, for all that I know, it may be longer than that. You may be sure that if I get a clue I shall follow it up wherever it leads me."

The strictest silence was maintained among the men. The two men at the oars were told to row very slowly, and above all things to avoid splashing. The boat was exceedingly low in the water, much too low for safety except in perfectly calm water; as, including the two men at the oars, there were thirteen on board.

Frank had thought it, however, inadvisable to take the dinghy also, for this was lying behind the stern, and it might have been noticed had they pulled her up to the gangway. The gig had been purposely left on the side hidden from the brigantine, and as they rowed away pains were taken to keep the yacht in a line with her. They held on this course, indeed, until they were close in to the shore, and then kept in under its shelter until the curve hid them altogether.

"Be very careful as you row back, lads, and go very slowly. A ripple on this smooth water might very well be noticed by them, even if they could not make out a boat."

"Ay, ay, sir, we will be careful."

They had brought a lantern with them, covered with canvas, except for a few inches in front.

"Me take him, sar, and go first," Dominique said. "Den if we meet anyone you all stop quiet, and me go on and talk with them."

Frank followed Dominique, George keeping beside him where there was room for two to walk abreast, at other times falling just behind. Then came the sailors, and the four black boatmen were in the rear. They had been told that, in case they were halted, and heard Dominique in conversation, they were to pass quietly through the others, and be ready to join him and help him if necessary. With the exception of Dominique, Frank and George Lechmere, all carried muskets. The pilot declined to take one.

"Me neber fired off gun in my life, sar. Me more afraid of gun than of dose rascals. Dominique fight with um sword; dat plenty good for him."

The path mounted the hill until they were, as Frank thought, some three hundred feet above the water. Here the ground was cultivated, and after walking for ten minutes they saw two or three lights in front.

"You stop here, sar," Dominique said, handing the lantern to Frank. "Me go on and see how best get round de village. Must not be seen here. If native boat come in at night suah to go up to end ob water, and land at village dere."

The negro soon returned, and said that the cultivated land extended on both sides of the village, and there was no difficulty in crossing it. The village was passed quietly, and when it was once well behind them they came down upon the path again, which was much larger and better marked than it had been before. After following it for half a mile, they came upon a road, which led obliquely up from the water, and ran somewhat inland.

"This is no doubt the road from the village at the head of the arm of the bay. They have probably come along here, though they may have turned more directly into the hills. That is the first point to find out, Dominique."

"Yes, sar, next village we see me go in wid two ob de boatmen and ask a few questions."

Following the path along for another few hundred yards, they saw a road ahead of them. Here they halted, and two of the blacks handed over their muskets and cutlasses to the care of the sailors. Dominique also left his cutlass behind him, and as he went on gave instructions to his two companions.

"Now look here," he said in negro French, "don't you say much. I will do the talking, but just say a word or two if they ask questions. Mind we three belong to the brigantine. I am the pilot. The captain has given me a message to send to his friends who have gone up into the hills. He asked me to take it, but I am not sure about the way. I am ready to pay well for a guide. I expect that they will say that the ladies came along, but that they do not know how they went afterwards. Then we ask him to come as guide, and promise to pay him very well."

By this time they were close to the hut, which, as Dominique assured himself before knocking at the door, stood alone. There was an old man and woman inside, and a boy of about seventeen. Dominique took off his hat as he entered, and said in French:

"Excuse me for disturbing you so late. I am the pilot of a vessel now in the bay, and have been sent by the captain to carry an important message to a gentleman who landed with another and two ladies and some armed men. He did not give me sufficient directions to find him, and I thought that if they passed along here you might be able to put me in the way."

"They came along here between eleven and twelve, I think. We saw them," the old man said, "and we heard afterwards that the ladies were being taken away because the ship was, they thought, going to be attacked by a pirate that had followed them. The people from the villages went to help fight, for the gentleman had bought many things and had paid well for them, and each man was promised a dollar if there was no fighting, and four dollars if they helped beat off the pirate."

"Yes, that was so," Dominique said, "but it seems that it was a mistake. Still we had cause for alarm, for the other vessel followed us strangely. However, it is all explained now, and I have been sent with this message, because the captain thought that if he sent a white sailor they would not give him the information."

"Do you know, Sebastian?" the old man asked his son.

"Yes, they turned off to the right two miles further on."

"Look here, boy," Dominique said, "we were promised twenty dollars if we took the message straight. Now, if you will go with us and find out, we will give you five of them. As we are strangers to the people here, they might not answer our questions; but if you go and say that you have to carry the message, no doubt they will tell you which way they have gone."

The lad jumped up.

"I will go with you," he said; "but perhaps when we get there you will not give me the money."

"Look here," Dominique said, taking three dollars from his pocket. "I will leave these with your father, and will hand you the other two as soon as we get within sight of the place where they are."

The lad was quite satisfied. Five dollars was more than he could earn by two months' work. As soon as they went out, Dominique whispered to one of the boatmen to go back and tell Frank what had taken place, and to beg him to follow at some distance behind. Whenever they took a fresh turning, one of the boatmen would always be left until he came up.

Frank had some difficulty in understanding the boatman's French, and it was rather by his gestures than his words that he gathered his meaning. As soon as the message was given the negro hurried on until he overtook Dominique.

"I am sorry now that we did not bring Pedro," Frank said. "However, I think we made out what he had to say. Dominique has got someone to go with him to do the questioning, as he arranged with me; and he will leave one or other of the men every time he turns off from the road he is following. That will be a very good arrangement. So far we have been most fortunate. We know now that we are following them, and it will be hard if we don't manage to keep the clue now that we have once got hold of it."

When they came to the road that branched off to the right, the other boatman was waiting. He pointed up the road and then ran on silently ahead. No fresh turn was made for a long distance. Twice they were stopped by one of the blacks, who managed to inform them that Dominique and the guide were making inquiries at a hut ahead.

The road had now become a mere track, and was continually mounting. Other tracks had branched off, leading, Frank supposed, to small hill villages. After going some ten miles, the lad told Dominique that it was useless for him to go further, for that there were no more huts near the track. Beyond the fact that the two women were on horseback when they passed the last hut, nothing was learned there.

"It is of no use to go further," the guide said. "There are no houses near here to inquire at, and there are three or four more paths that turn off from here. We must stop until morning, and then I will go on alone and make inquiries of shepherds and cottagers; but, you see, I thought that we should find them tonight. If I work all day tomorrow, I shall expect three more dollars."

"You shall have them," Dominique said. "Here is my blanket. I will share one with one of my boatmen."

The lad at once lay down and pulled the blanket over his head. As soon as he did so, Dominique motioned to the two boatmen to do the same, and then went back along the track until he met Frank's party. As the hills were for the most part covered with trees almost up to their summits, Frank and his party had only to turn a short distance off from the path, on receiving Dominique's news that the guide had stopped.

"It is half past one," Frank said, holding the lantern, which the pilot had left with them, to his watch. "We shall get four hours' sleep. You had better serve a tot of grog all round, George. It will keep out the damp night air."

One of the blacks was carrying a basket, and each of the men had brought a water bottle and pannikin.

"Put some water in it, lads," Frank said, "and it would be a good thing to eat a bit of biscuit with it."

Dominique had told Frank that the guide had made some remark about the two blacks dropping behind so often, and the latter took out his handkerchief, tore it into eight pieces, and gave it to him.

"Wherever you turn off, Dominique, drop one of these pieces on the path. That will be quite sufficient."

"Yes, sar; but you see we don't know when we start up path whether it be right path or no. We go up one, if find dat hit not de one dey go, den come back again and try anoder. What we to do?"

After thinking for some little time, Frank suggested that Dominique's best way would be to tell the guide that he was footsore, and that as several paths would have to be searched, he and one of the men would sit down there. The other would accompany the boy, and bring down word when the right path had been discovered.

As soon as it became light Frank, without rousing the men, went out into the path and moved cautiously up it. He had but just started when he saw Dominique coming towards him.

"All right, sar. Boy gone on; he hunt about. When he find he send Sam back to fetch me. De oder stay with him."

"Oh, you have sent both with him."

"Yes, sar, me thought it better. If only one man go, when he come back, boy could talk to people. Perhaps talk too much, so sent both men."

"That was the best plan, no doubt," Frank agreed. "I will join the men, and remain there until you come for me."

"Dat best thing, sar. People might come along, better dey not see you."

It was twelve o'clock before Dominique joined the waiting group in the wood.

"They have been a long time finding the track, Dominique."

"Yes, sar, bery long time. Dey try four tracks, all wrong. Den dey try 'nother. Sam say boy tell him try that last, because bad track; lead ober hills, to place where Obi man live. Black fellow no like to go there. Bad men there; steal children away, make sacrifice to fetish. All people here believe that Obi man bery strong. Dey send presents to him to make rain or to kill enemy, but dey no like go near him demselves. Dere was a hut a little up dat road. Party went by dere yesterday. No more houses on road. Sam say boy wait dere till he bring me back to him; den go home. Not like to go further; say can't miss way dat path. Leads straight to Obi man's place. Fetish on road strike people dead dat go dar without leab ob Obi man."

"That will suit us well altogether," Frank said. "How far is it to where the guide is?"

"One and a half hours' walk."

"Then we will be off at once."

All were glad to be on the move again, and in spite of the heat they proceeded at a rapid pace, until the boatman, Sam, said that they were close to the spot where he had left his companions with the guide. The rest then entered the wood, and Dominique went on with the boatman.

Ten minutes later a young negro came down the path. They had no doubt that it was the guide. Dominique arrived two or three minutes later.

"I suppose that was the guide that went down," Frank said, as he stepped out.

"Dat him, sar," he said. "Quite sure path go to Obi man's place. It was miles away in centre of hills. I pretend want him to go on. He said no go for thousand dollars. So me pay him his money, and he go back. He tell me no use hunt for friends if Obi man hab not giben dem leab to go and see him. Den the fetish change dem all into snakes. If he gib leab and not know dat me and oder two men were friends, den de fetish change us into snakes."

"Well, there is one comfort, Dominique, we shall be able to march boldly along without being afraid of meeting anyone."

"Yes, sar. Sam be a little frightened, but not much. Not believe much in San Domingo about fetish. Dey better dan dese Hayti people. Still Sam not like it."

"I suppose you told him that he was a fool, Dominique?"

"Yes, sar. Me tell him, too, dat white man tink nothing ob Obi man. Hang him by neck if he tries fetish against dem."

Having picked up Sam, they proceeded at a brisk pace along the path, Frank leading the way with George Lechmere.

"You see," he said, "Carthew must have been uneasy in his mind all along. I have no doubt that directly he put into the bay, and decided to make this his headquarters, he set about preparing some place where he could carry them off to, and where there would be very little chance of their being traced. Down at the village by the water he heard of this Obi man. He has evidently great power in this part of the island. These fellows are all great rascals, and Carthew may have either gone or sent to him, and made arrangements that he and a party should if necessary be allowed to establish a camp in the valley where this fellow lives; of course, promising him a handsome present. He could have chosen no safer place. Following hard as we have done on his track, we have obtained a clue; but it is not probable that any of the natives whom Dominique has questioned has the smallest idea that the party were going towards this fetish man's place. In fact, the only man that could know it was the negro at that last hut, and you may be sure that were he questioned by any searching party he would not dare to give any information that might excite the anger of this man.

"It is likely enough that this fellow has a gang of men with him, bound to him partly by interest and partly by superstitious fears. We shall probably have to reckon with these fellows in addition to Carthew's own force. He seems to have taken ten or twelve of the blacks from the village with him. They would have no fear of going when he told them that he was under the special protection of the fetish man. Then, you see, he has four of his own sailors, his friend and himself; so that we have an equal number of white men and five negroes against his ten or twelve and the fetishman's gang.

"However, I hope that we shall have the advantage of a surprise. If so, I think that we may feel pretty confident that we shall, at any rate, in the first place, carry off Miss Greendale and her maid. The danger won't be in the attack, but in the retreat. That Obi fellow may raise the whole country against us. There is one thing—the population is scanty up here, and it won't be until we get down towards the lower ground that they will be able to muster strongly enough to be really formidable; but we may have to fight hard to get down to the boats. You see, it is a twenty miles' march. We shan't be able to go very fast, for, although Miss Greendale and her maid might keep up well for some distance, they would be worn out long before we got to the shore, while the black fellows would be able to travel by other paths, and to arouse the villagers as they went, and make it very hot indeed for us."

"There is one thing—we shall have the advantage of darkness, Major, and in the woods it would be difficult for them to know how fast we were going. We might strike off into other paths, and, if necessary, carry Miss Greendale and her maid. We could make a couple of litters for them, and, with four to a litter, could travel along at a good rate of speed."

In another three hours, they found that the path was descending into a deep and narrow valley. On the way they passed many of the fetish signs, so terrible to the negro's imagination. Pieces of blue string, with feathers and rags attached to them, were stretched across the path. Clumps of feathers hung suspended from the trees. Flat stones, with berries, shells, and crooked pieces of wood, were nailed against the trunks of the trees.

At first the four negro boatmen showed signs of terror on approaching these mysterious symbols, and grew pale with fright when Frank broke the strings that barred the path; but when they saw that no evil resulted from the audacious act, and that no avenging bolt fell upon his head, they mustered up courage, and in time even grinned as the sailors made jeering remarks at the mysterious emblems.

As soon as they began to descend into the valley, and it was evident that they were nearing their destination, Frank halted.

"Now, Dominique, do you object to go down and find out all about it? I am quite ready to go, but you are less likely to be noticed than I am. There is no hurry, for we don't wish to move until within an hour of sunset, or perhaps two hours. There is no fear of our meeting with any interruption until we get back to the point where we started this morning, and it would be as well, therefore, to be back there just before dark."

"Me go, sar. Me strip. Dat best; not seen so easy among de trees."

"Quite right, Dominique. What we want to find out is the exact position of the camp and the hut, for no doubt they built a hut of some sort, where Miss Greendale is; and see how we can best get as close to it as possible. Then it would be as well to find out what sort of village this Obi man has got, and how many men it probably contains. But don't risk anything to do this. Our object is to surprise Carthew's camp, and we must take our chance as to the blacks. If you were seen, and an alarm given, Carthew might carry Miss Greendale off again. So don't mind about the Obi village, unless you are sure that you can obtain a view of it without risk of being seen."

"Me manage dat, sar," the negro said, confidently. "Dey not on de lookout. Me crawl up among de trees and see eberyting; no fear whatsomeber."

Dominique stripped and started down the path, while the rest retired into the shelter of the trees. An anxious two hours passed, the party listening intently for any sound that might tell of Dominique's being discovered. All, however, remained quiet, except that they were once or twice startled by the loud beating of a drum, and the deep blasts from the fetish horn. At the end of that time there was a general exclamation of relief as Dominique stepped in from among the trees.

"Well, Dominique, what have you found?" Frank exclaimed as he started to his feet.

"Me found eberyting, sar. First come to village. Not bery big, twenty or thirty men dere. Den a hundred yards furder tree huts stand. Dey new huts, but not built last night, leaves all dead, built eight or ten days ago. Me crawl on tomack among de trees, and lay and watch. In de furder hut two white lady. Dey come in and out, dey talk togeder, de oders not go near them. Next hut to them, twenty, thirty yards away, two white men. Dey sit on log and smoke cigar. In de next hut four white sailor. Den a little distance away, twelve black fellows sit round fire and cook food. Plenty of goats down in valley, good gardens and lots of bananas."

"How did the white ladies seem?"

"Not seem anyting particular, sar. Dey neber look in de direction ob oders. Just talk togeder bery quiet. Me see dere lips move, but hear no voice. Hear de voice of men quite plain."

"How close can we get without being seen?"

"About fifty yards, sar. Huts put near stream under big trees. Trees not tick just dar; little way lower down banana trees run down to edge ob stream. If can get round de village on dat side widout being seen, can go through bananas, den dash across de stream and run for de ladies. Can get dere before de oders. Besides, if dey run dat way we shoot dem down."

"Thank God, that is all satisfactory," Frank said. "But it is hard having to wait here another five hours before doing anything."

"We are ready to go and pitch into them at once, sir," one of the sailors said. "You have only to say the word."

"Thank you, lads, but we must wait till within an hour or two of sunset. I expect that we shall have to fight our way back, and we shall want darkness to help us. It would be folly to risk anything, just as success seems certain after these months of searching. Still, it is hard to have to wait.

"It is getting on to twelve o'clock. You had better get that basket out and have your dinners."

The next four hours seemed to him interminable. The sailors and negroes had gone to sleep as soon as they had finished their meal and smoked a pipe. Frank moved about restlessly, sometimes smoking in short, sharp puffs, sometimes letting his pipe go out every minute and relighting it mechanically, and constantly consulting his watch. At last he sat down on a fallen tree, and remained there without making the slightest motion, until George Lechmere said:

"I think it is time now, Major."

"Thank goodness for that, George. I made up my mind that I would not look at my watch again until it was time.

"Now, lads, before we start listen to my final orders. If we are discovered as we go past the village, we shall turn off at once and make straight for the camp. Don't waste a shot on the blacks. They are not likely to have time to gather to oppose us, but cut down anyone that gets in your way. When we are through the village make straight to the farthest hut. Don't fire a shot till we have got between that and the next, and then go straight at Carthew and his gang. If I should fall, Lechmere will take the command. If he, too, should fall, you are to gather round the ladies and fight your way down to the landing place. Take Dominique's advice as to paths and so on. He and his men know a good deal better than you do—but remember, the great duty is to take the ladies on board safe.

"The moment you get them there, tell the captain my orders are that you are to man the two boats, row straight at the brigantine, drive the crew overboard and sink her. Then you are to sail for England with Miss Greendale. The brigantine must be sunk, for if Carthew gets down there he will fill her with blacks and sail in pursuit; and as there is not much difference in speed between the two boats, she might overtake you if you carried away anything. You must get rid of her before you sail.

"What have you got there, George?"

"Two stretchers, Major. Dominique and I have been making them for the last two hours. We can leave them here, sir, by the side of the path, and pick them up as we come along back."

A couple of minutes later the party started. They followed the path down until nearly at the bottom of the hill. Here the trees grew thinner, and Dominique, who was leading, turned to the right. They made their way noiselessly through the wood, Dominique taking them a much wider circuit round the village than he himself had made, and bringing them out from the trees at the lower end of the plantation of bananas.

Hitherto they had been walking in single file, but Frank now passed along the order for them to close up.

"Keep together as well as you can," he said, when they were assembled; "and mind how you pass between the trees. If you set these big trees waving, it might be noticed at once."

Very cautiously they stole forward until they reached the edge by the stream. Frank looked through the trees. Four white sailors were lying on the ground, smoking, in front of their hut. Carthew and his companion were stretched in two hammocks hung from the tree under which their hut stood. Bertha and her maid had retired into their bower.

"Now, lads," he said, as with his revolver in his right hand he prepared for the rush. "Don't cheer, but run silently forward. The moment they catch sight of us you can give a cheer.

"Now!" and he sprang forward into the stream, which was but ankle deep.

The splash, as the whole party followed him, at once attracted the attention of the sailors; who leaped to their feet with a shout, and ran into their hut, while at the same moment Carthew and his companion sprang from their hammocks, paused for a moment in surprise at the men rushing towards them, and then also ran into their hut, Carthew shouting to the blacks to take to their arms.

"Go straight at them, George," Frank shouted, running himself directly towards the nearest hut, just as Bertha, startled at the noise, came to its entrance.

She stood for an instant in astonishment, then with a scream of joy ran a step or two and fell forward into his arms.

"Thank God, I have found you at last," he said. "Wait here a moment, darling. I will be back directly. Go into the hut until I come."

But Bertha was too overpowered with surprise and delight to heed his words, and Frank handed her to her maid, who had run out behind her.

"Take her in," he said, as he carried her to the entrance of the hut, "and stay there until I come again."

Then he ran after his party. A wild hubbub had burst forth. Muskets and pistols were cracking. Carthew, as he ran out of the hut, discharged his pistol at the sailors, but in his surprise and excitement missed them; and before he had time to level another, George Lechmere bounded upon him, and with a shout of "This is for Martha Bennett," brought his cutlass down upon his head.

He fell like a log, and at the same moment one of the sailors shot his companion. Then they dashed against the Belgian sailors, who had been joined by the blacks.

"Give them a volley, lads!" George shouted.

The four sailors fired, as a moment later did the boatmen, and then cutlass in hand rushed upon them.

Just as they reached them Frank arrived. There was but a moment's resistance. Two of the sailors had fallen under the volley, a third was cut down, and the fourth, as well as the blacks, fled towards the village. Here the Obi drum was beating fiercely.

"Load again, lads," Frank shouted. "Two of you come back with me."

He ran with them back to the end hut, but Bertha had now recovered from her first shock.

"Come, darling," he said, "there is not a moment to lose. We must get out of this as soon as we can.

"Come along, Anna.

"Thompson, do you look after her. I will see to Miss Greendale."

Just as they reached the others, a volley was fired from the village by the blacks of Carthew's party, who were armed with muskets. Then they, with thirty other negroes, rushed out with loud shouts.

"Don't fire until they are close," Frank shouted. "Now let them have it."

The volley poured into them, at but ten paces distance, had a deadly effect. The blacks paused for a moment, and the rescuing party, led by George Lechmere and Dominique, rushed at them. The sailors' pistols cracked out, and then they charged, cutlass in hand.

For a moment the blacks stood, but the fierce attack was too much for them, and they again fled to the village.

"Stop, Dominique!" Frank shouted, for the big pilot, who had already cut down three of his opponents, was hotly pursuing them. "We must make for the path at once."

Chapter 18

In a couple of minutes they had gained it.

"Anyone hurt?" Frank asked.

One of the boatmen had an arm broken by a bullet, and two of the sailors had received spear wounds at the hands of the villagers. They were not serious, however, and leaving George Lechmere to cover the rear, they started up the path; Dominique, as usual, leading the way, Frank following behind him with Bertha, who had hitherto not spoken a word.

"Am I dreaming?" she asked now, in a tone of bewilderment. "Is it really you, Frank?"

"You are not dreaming, dear, and it is certainly I—Frank Mallett. Now tell me how you got on."

"As well as might be, Frank, but it was a terrible time. Please do not talk about it yet. But how is it that you are here? It seems a miracle.

"Oh, how ill you are looking! And your arm is in a sling, too."

"That is nothing," he said; "merely a broken collarbone. As to my looking ill, you must remember, I have had almost as anxious a time as you."

"Then it was the Osprey, after all," she exclaimed, suddenly, "that we saw the last day that we were out sailing. We were on deck, and I was not noticing—I did not notice much then—when Anna said to me, 'That looks like an English yacht, miss. I am sure Mr. Carthew thinks she is chasing us.'

"Then I got up and looked round. I could not see for certain, but it did look like a yacht, and I thought that it was about the size of the Osprey. Those two men were standing with their backs to us looking at it through their glasses, and Carthew happened to turn round and saw me standing up, and at once said: 'You must go below. I believe that is a pirate chasing us.'

"I said that it was nothing to me if it was. One pirate was just as good as another. Then he said that if I would not go down he should be obliged to use force, and called four men aft. So as it was of no use resisting, we went down. Presently we felt that the course had been changed. Late in the evening we heard them fire the two guns, and then some musket shots. Later on the man came down and told us that the pirates had tried to attack us in their boats, and that they had beaten them off, and that there was no further danger. But for all that I could see that he was troubled."

"That was when I was hit, dear. We had not reckoned on the two guns, and with only the gig and dinghy, with one man killed and five of us wounded, it was too stiff a business, though we should have persevered, but that squall came down on us from the hills, and the Phantom, moreover, left us standing still. We believed that we should come up with the schooner in the morning."

"But how did you come here, Frank? How did you know where we had been taken?"

"It is a long story, dear. We started in pursuit four days after you had been carried off. I will tell you all about it when we get safe again on board the yacht. I am afraid we shall have some trouble yet. Now if you are quite recovered from your surprise, do you feel equal to hurrying on? Every moment is of importance."

"Oh, yes," she said. "He will be after us."

"He won't," Frank said. "George Lechmere cut him down. Whether he killed him or not I cannot say, but I don't fancy anyhow that he will be able to take up the chase. It is that rascally Obi man I am afraid of. He has great power over the people, and may raise the whole country to attack us."

"I am ready to run as fast as you like, Frank."

"We may as well go at a trot for a bit."

Then raising his voice, he said:

"We will go at double, lads, now.

"Put your arm on my shoulder, Bertha, and we can fancy that we are going to waltz."

"I feel so happy that I want to cry, Frank," she said as they started.

"Don't do that until you get on board the Osprey."

As they passed the spot where they had halted, George Lechmere told two of the blacks to pick up the stretchers and carry them along. They were merely two light poles, with a wattle work formed of giant creepers worked for some six feet in length between them.

"What are those for?" Bertha asked, as she passed them.

"Those are to carry you and Anna along when you get exhausted. It is twenty miles to the coast, you know."

"I feel as if I could walk any distance to get on board the Osprey again."

"I have no doubt that you have the spirit, Bertha, but I question whether you have the strength; especially after being over three months without any exercise at all. I felt it myself yesterday, although we did little more than ten miles."

"Oh, but then you have been wounded. And you do look so ill, Frank."

"I dare say the wound had a little to do with it," he said; "but of course the climate is trying too; though it is cooler up on the hills than it is in that bay."

"Now, Frank, the first question of all is—How is my mother? What did she do when I was missing? It must have been awful for her."

"Of course, it was a terrible anxiety, Bertha, but she bore it better than would be expected, especially as she had not been well before."

"It troubled me more, Frank, than even my own affairs. As soon as I had time to think at all, I could not imagine what she would do, and the only comfort was that she had you to look after her."

"No doubt it was a comfort, dear, that she had someone to lean upon a little.

"Halt!" he broke off suddenly, as there was the sound of a stick breaking among the trees close by. "Stand to your arms, men, and gather closely.

"Bertha, do you and Anna take your place in the centre, and please lie down."

"I cannot do that, Frank," she said, positively. "Here you are all risking your lives for us, and now you want me to put myself quite safe while you are all in danger."

"I want to be able to fight, Bertha, free of anxiety, and to be able to devote my whole attention to the work. This I can't do if I know that you are exposed to bullets."

"Well, I can't lie down anyhow, Frank; but Anna and I will crouch down if you say that we must when they begin to fire."

They were silent for two or three minutes, and no sounds were heard in the wood.

"We shall be attacked sooner or later," Frank said quietly to the men. "We will take to the trees on our right if we are attacked from the left, and to those on the left if they come at us from the right. If we are attacked on both sides at once, take to the right.

"George, do you and Harrison and Jones get behind trees, next to the path. It will be your business to prevent anyone from passing on that side. I, with the other two, will take post behind trees facing the other way. The four boatmen with Dominique will shelter themselves in the bushes between us, with Miss Greendale and her maid in the middle. They will be the reserve, and if a rush is made from either side, they will at once advance and beat it back.

"You understand, Dominique?"

"Me understand, sar. If those fellows come we charge at them. These fellows no used to shoot, sar. Better give muskets to others. We do best with our swords."

"That is the best plan.

"You take one of the muskets, George, and give one to Harrison. The two men on my side had better have the others, as I can't use one.

"You understand, lads. These will be spare arms. Keep them in reserve if possible, so as to check the fellows when they make a rush. Now do you all understand?

"You explain it to your men, Dominique.

"Now we will go on again, and at the double. It will be as much as those fellows can do to keep up with us in this thick wood."

Ten minutes passed. Then there was a loud shout and the blowing of a deep horn on their left, followed by a yell from the wood on both sides.

"To the right," Frank shouted, and the party ran in among the trees.

"Get in among that undergrowth with Anna," he said to Bertha.

"Gather there, Dominique, with your men. We shall want you directly. They are sure to make a rush at first.

"Now, lads, one of you take that tree; the other the one to the right," and he placed himself behind one between them. On glancing round he saw that George had already posted his two men, and had taken up his station between them.

"All hands kneel down," he said. "These bushes will hide us from their sight. If we stand up we may be hit by shots from behind."

A moment later there was a general discharge of firearms round them, and then some forty negroes rushed at them.

"On your feet now, men," Frank shouted. "Take steady aim and bring down a man with each shot."

A cheer broke from the sailors. Four shots were fired from Frank's side, and five from George Lechmere's, and with them came the cracks of Frank's revolver, followed almost directly afterwards by those of the pistols carried by the men, and George Lechmere's revolver.

Scarce a shot missed. Ten of the negroes fell, and those attacking from the right turned and bolted among the trees. The negroes on the left, however, inspired by the roaring of the horns and the shrieking yells of the Obi man, came on with greater determination and dashed across the path.

"Now, Dominique, at them!" Frank shouted, as with the two sailors he rushed across.

The numbers now were not very uneven. Of the twenty negroes on that side, five had fallen under the musketry and pistol fire, and two others were wounded; and as Frank's party and the blacks fell upon them they hesitated. The struggle was not doubtful for a moment. Six of the negroes were cut down, and the rest fled.

"Don't pursue them, men," Frank shouted; and the sailors at once drew off, but Dominique and his black boatmen still pursued hotly, overtaking and cutting down three more of their assailants.

"All is over for the present," Frank said, going to the spot where Bertha and Anna were crouching. "Not one of us is hurt as far as I know, and we have accounted for sixteen or seventeen of these rascals."

Bertha got up. She was a little pale, but perfectly calm and quiet.

"It is horrid, being hidden like that when you are all fighting, Frank," she said, reproachfully.

"We were hidden, too, till they came at us," he said; "and very lucky it was, for some of us would probably have been hit, bad shots though they are."

"No, Frank, not before all these men," she remonstrated.

"What do I care for the men?" he laughed. "Do you think if they had their sweethearts with them they would mind who was looking on?

"There, I must be content with that for the present. We must push on again."

Dominique had returned now with his men, and the party started again at a trot, as soon as the firearms had all been reloaded.

"We shan't have any more trouble, shall we?" Bertha asked.

"Not for the present," he said. "We have fairly routed the blacks who came here with you, and the villagers, and they certainly won't attack us again until they are largely reinforced; which they cannot be until we get down towards the sea, for there are no villages of any size in the hills."

After keeping up the pace for a mile, Frank ordered the men to drop into a walk again.

"Now, Frank, about my mother?" Bertha asked again as soon as she had got her breath; and Frank related all that had taken place up to the time that the Osprey sailed.

"Then she is all alone in town? It must be terrible for her, waiting there without any news of me. It is a pity that she did not go home. It would not have mattered about me, and it would have been so much better for her among her old friends. They would all have sympathised with her so much."

"I quite agreed with her, Bertha, and think still that it was better that she should stay in London. I am sure the sympathy would do her harm rather than good. As it is, now she will be kept up by the belief that she is doing all in her power for you, by saving you from the hideous amount of talk and chatter there would be if this affair were known."

"Of course, it would be horrid, Frank, and perhaps you are right, but it must be an awful trial."

"I have done all I could to set her mind at rest," Frank said. "I wrote to her directly I arrived at Gibraltar, and again as soon as I got the letter from Madeira saying that the brigantine had touched there. I wrote from Madeira again with what news I could pick up, and again from Porto Rico, from the Virgin Islands, and from San Domingo. Of course, from there I was able to say that the scent was getting hot, and that I had no doubt I should not be long before I fell in with the brigantine. Then I sent another letter from Jaquemel. That seems to me a long time ago, for we have done so much since; but it is not more than ten days back. We will post another letter the first time that we touch anywhere, on the off chance of its going home by a mail steamer, and getting there before us."

"It was wonderful your finding out that I had been carried off in the Phantom. That was what troubled me most, except about mother. I did not see how you could guess that the brigantine we had both noticed the day before was the Phantom. I felt sure that you would suspect who it was, but I could not see how you would connect the two together."

"You see, I did not guess it at first," he replied. "I felt sure that it was Carthew from the first minute when I found that you had not landed, and it was just the luck of finding out that the Phantom's crew had returned, and that they had been paid off at Ostend, that put me on the track. Of course, directly I heard that she had been altered and turned into a brigantine, I felt sure that she was the craft that we had noticed; and as soon as I learned through Lloyd's that she had sailed south from the Lizard, I felt certain that she must have gone up the Mediterranean, or to the West Indies. I felt sure it was the latter. However, it was a great relief when I got a letter from Lloyd's agent at Madeira, telling me that the brigantine had touched there, and I felt certain that I should hear of you either here or at one of the South American ports."

They kept on until they reached the hut at the point where the path forked. It was found to be empty.

"Open the basket," Frank said. "We must have a meal before we go further. We have come about half the distance.

"Now, Bertha, there is the bay, you see, and it is all downhill, which is a comfort. Do you feel tired, dear?"

"Not tired," she said, "but my feet are aching a bit. You see, I had thin deck shoes on when we were hurried ashore, and they are not good for walking long distances in."

"Well, we will have a quarter of an hour's rest," he said. "It is getting dark fast, and by the time we go on it will be night, and will be a great deal cooler than it has been."

"I can go on at once if you like," she said.

"No, dear; there is no use in hurrying. We may as well stop half an hour as a quarter. Don't you hear that?"

The girl listened.

"It is a horn, is it not?" she asked, after a pause.

"Yes, I can hear it in half a dozen directions," he said. "That scoundrel of an Obi man is down there ahead of us, and that unearthly row he and his followers are making will rouse up all the villagers within hearing. We will try to give him the slip. I intend to take the path we came by for four or five miles, and then to strike off by one to the right, and hit the main road to Port au Prince, a good bit to the east of where we quitted it. The country is all cultivated there, and we will strike down towards the bay and make our way through the fields, and if we have luck we may be able to get down to the place where the gig will be waiting for us without meeting any of them."

"Oh, I do hope there will be no more fighting, Frank! You may not all get off as well as you did last time."

"We must take our chance of that, dear. At any rate the country will be open, and we shall be able to keep in a solid body, and I have no doubt that we shall be able to beat them off."

"Could we not go down to the shore, and get a boat somewhere, and row to the yacht?"

"Yes, we might manage that, perhaps. That is a capital idea, Bertha. There is a place called Nipes, twelve or fourteen miles east of our inlet. It won't be very much further to go, for we have been bearing eastward all the way here. Making sure that we shall go straight for the yacht, they will gather in that direction first, and won't think of giving the alarm so far east. There was a path, if I remember right, that came up from that direction a quarter of a mile further on. We will turn off by it."

As soon as the meal was over they started again. They found the path Frank had spoken of, and followed it down until they came among trees. Then Dominique lighted his lantern again.

For a time the two women kept on travelling, but after five miles Bertha was compelled to stop and take off her shoes altogether. For two miles further she refused the offers to carry her, but at last was forced to own that she could go no further.

The two litters were at once brought up, and the four sailors, Dominique and the three uninjured boatmen, lifted them and went along at a trot, George Lechmere leading the way with a lantern. The weight of the girls, divided between four strong men, was a mere trifle, and they now made much more rapid progress than they had before, and in three quarters of an hour arrived at Nipes.

As they got to the little town, Bertha and Anna got out and walked, so as to attract as little attention as possible among the negroes in the streets. Dominique answered all questions, stating that they were a party belonging to a ship in Marsouin Bay, that they had been on a sporting expedition over the hills, and had lost their way, and now wanted a boat to take them back.

As soon as they reached the strand half a dozen were offered to them. Dominique chose the one that looked the fastest. He told the boatman that the ladies were very tired, and they wanted to get back as soon as possible, and he must, therefore, engage ten men to row, as the wind was so slight as to be useless.

As he did not haggle about terms, the bargain was speedily concluded, and in a few minutes they put off. The men, animated by the handsome rate of pay they were to receive, rowed hard, and in a little over two hours they entered the inlet at the end of which the Osprey was lying. As they neared the end the boatmen were surprised at seeing a large number of people with torches on the rising ground, and something like panic seized them when they heard the Obi horns sounding. They dropped their oars at once.

"Tell them to row on, Dominique," Frank said, "and to keep close along the opposite side. Tell them that if they don't do so we will shoot them. No; tell them that we will chuck them overboard and row on ourselves."

"There is the place where we landed," Frank said presently to Bertha (the men had resumed their rowing), "just under where you see that clump of torches."

"Ah, there is our boat," he broke off suddenly, as it appeared in the line of the reflection of the torches on the water.

It was half a mile away, lying a few hundred yards from shore. He took out the dog whistle that he used when coming down to the landing stage to summon the boat from the yacht, and blew it. There was a stir in the boat, and a moment later it was speeding towards them.

"Row on, Dominique. She will pick us up in no time."

And long before they reached the Osprey the gig was alongside.

"Thank God that you are back, sir," they cried as they came abreast. "We have been in terrible anxiety about you. Have you succeeded, sir?"

"Don't cheer. I want to get back to the yacht before they know that we are here. Yes, thank God, I have succeeded. Miss Greendale and her maid are on board."

A low cheer, which even his order could not entirely suppress, came from the three men in the boat. The mate was himself rowing stroke.

"We did not dare bring any more hands, sir," he said. "There has been such a hubbub on shore for the last hour and a half that we thought it likely that they and the Phantom's people might be going to attack us. We rowed to the landing at ten o'clock, as you ordered us, but in a short time a party of men came along close to the water, and as soon as they saw us they opened fire on us, and we had to row off sharp. We have been lying off here since. We did not see how you could get down through that lot, but we thought it better to wait. I did think there was just a hope that you might make your way down to the coast somewhere else and come on in a shore boat."

"Well, here we are, sir."

As he spoke they came alongside the Osprey.

"Is it you, sir?" Hawkins asked eagerly.

"Look here, lads," Frank replied, standing up, "above all things I don't want any cheering, or any noise whatever. I don't want them to know that we have got on board. I know that you will all rejoice with me, for I have brought off Miss Greendale, and none of our party except one of the boatmen has been wounded in any way seriously."

There was a murmur of deep satisfaction from the crew. As Bertha stepped on deck the men crowded round with low exclamations of "God bless you, miss! This is a good day indeed for us!"

Bertha, in reply to the greeting, shook hands all round.

"I see you have not put out the lights in the cabin yet, Hawkins. I will just go down with Miss Greendale and see that she is comfortable, and then I will come up again."

"Oh, Frank!" the girl exclaimed, bursting into tears as they entered the saloon, "this is happiness indeed. I feel at home already."

Frank remained with her for three or four minutes.

"Now, dear, take possession of your old cabin again. No doubt Anna is there already. She had better share it with you.

"Now I must go up and finish with the Phantom at once. Do not be afraid, I shall take them by surprise, and there will be very little fighting."

And without waiting for remonstrance he hurried on deck.

"Are the men armed, Hawkins?"

"That they are, sir. We have been expecting an attack every minute. There have been three or four shore boats going off to the brigantine within the last quarter of an hour."

"I am going to be beforehand with them, Hawkins."

"They've got both those guns pointing this way, sir."

"I am not coming from this way to attack them, Hawkins. I am going to put all hands in that native craft I came in, row off a little distance from this side, then make a circuit, and come down on the other side of them. I will leave George Lechmere here with four men, with three muskets apiece, so that if they should start before we get there they can keep them off until we arrive. If I can get a few of the boatmen to enlist I will do so."

He spoke to Dominique, who went to the side and asked:

"If any of you are disposed to stop here to guard the craft for a quarter of an hour, in case she is attacked, the gentleman here will pay twenty dollars a man; but remember that you may have to fight."

The whole crew rose. Twenty dollars was a fortune to them.

"Come on board, then," Dominique said.

"I don't know whether these fellows are to be trusted, George, but I hope you won't be attacked. Keep these fifteen muskets for yourselves. Put four apiece by the bulwarks and station yourselves by them. Keep your eyes on these boatmen, put the oars of the boat handy for them, and let them arm themselves with them. If you are attacked an oar is not a bad weapon for repelling boarders."

"All right, Major. I will station two of them between each of us."

By this time the captain had picked out the four men that were to remain, and had the rest drawn up in readiness to get into the boat.

"Get in quietly, lads," Frank said. "Ten of you man the oars. We will put an end to the Phantom's wanderings tonight."

"That we will, sir," was the hearty rejoinder of the men.

Frank took the tiller, and they rowed straight away from the Osprey for a hundred yards, when Frank steered towards the right bank, where there were no torches, and where all was quiet. The brigantine could be seen plainly, standing up against the glare of the torches on the other side. They rowed three or four hundred yards beyond her, then taking a turn approached her on the side opposite to that facing the Osprey. Three native boats like their own were lying beside her, and there was a crowd of men on her deck.

Frank brought her round alongside of these boats. He had already ordered that firearms were not to be used in the first place.

"I don't want to kill any of these blacks," he said. "They have nothing to do with the affair, and they believe us to be pirates. I expect that we shall get on board unnoticed. Then with a cheer go at them with the flat of your cutlasses. You can use the edge on the whites if they resist. But I expect that the blacks will all jump overboard in a panic, and that then the whites, seeing that they are outnumbered, will surrender."

No one, indeed, noticed them. There was a great hubbub and confusion, and the captain was endeavouring to get them into something like order; when suddenly there was a loud cheer, and Frank's party fell upon them. Yells of terror rose as the sailors, Dominique, and his blacks sprang among them, striking heavily with the flat of their cutlasses, and the sailors using their fists freely. Frank had brought with him a heavy belaying pin, and used it with great effect.

The blacks in the panic fell over each other, and rushing to the side jumped overboard, some into their boats, and some into the water. The white sailors, carried away by the stampede, and separated from each other, were unable to act. The captain, drawing a brace of pistols from his belt, fired one shot, but before he could fire another Frank hurled the iron belaying pin at him. It struck him in the face, and he fell insensible. The Belgian sailors, seeing themselves altogether outnumbered, and without a leader, threw down their arms.

"Tie their hands and feet," Frank ordered, "and bundle them into one of the native boats."

Two of these had pushed off and lay fifty yards away, and the sea was dotted with the heads of swimmers making towards them. The Belgian sailors were placed in the other boat.

"Put their captain in, too," Frank said. "He will come round presently.

"Now four of you jump into our boat and cast her off.

"Captain, will you look about for the oil, and pour it over all the beds, but don't set them on fire until I give the order.

"Now, lads, two of you run below, and get the cushions off the starboard sofa.

"Purvis, get the skylight open on the port side, and wheel the two guns round, and point them down into the cabin. I will train them myself on the same spot just at the back of that seat. They might come off and extinguish the fire, though I don't think they will; but we will make sure by blowing a hole through her side under the water line."

Five minutes were sufficient to make the preparations, and the captain came up and reported that all was ready.

"I have heaped up all the bedding on the floor, sir, and poured plenty of oil over it," he said.

"Very well, then, take two men aft, and begin there and work your way forward, and finish with the fo'c'sle hammocks. You can begin at once."

In a minute there was a glare of light through the stern cabin skylight, while almost at the same moment a dense cloud of smoke poured up the companion. Then the light shone up through the bull's-eyes on deck of the other staterooms. Then the captain and the two hands ran through the saloon forward. Frank went to the fo'castle hatch, and stooping down saw the captain apply the fire to a great heap of bedding.

"That will do, Hawkins," he said. "Come up at once with the men, or you will be suffocated down there."

They ran up on deck, and a minute later a volume of flame burst out through the hatch. Frank went to the guns, and lighting two matches gave one to Hawkins.

"Now," he said, "both together."

The two reports were blended in one, and as the smoke cleared away Frank could see, by the cabin lamp that was still burning, a spurt of water shooting up from a ragged hole at the back of the sofa. Fired at such a short distance, the bullets with which the guns were crammed had struck like solid shot.

"Into the boats, men!" Frank shouted.

"Shall we take these chaps off with us, sir?" the captain said. "They will be keepsakes."

"All right, Hawkins, in with them."

The tongue of fire leaping up from the forecastle, followed by the discharge of the guns, had been the first intimation to those on the Osprey of what had happened. Bertha and her maid ran up on deck at the sound of the cannon.

"What is that?" the former asked, in alarm.

"It is all right, Miss Greendale," George Lechmere said, leaving the side and coming up to her. "The Major has captured the brigantine almost without fighting. There was only one pistol shot fired. I did not hear a single clash of a sword, and the blacks on board jumped straight into the water. I was just coming to call you as you came up. The brigantine is well on fire, you see."

"But I thought I heard the cannon."

"Yes, the Major has fired them down the skylight, so as to make sure of her. Do you see, miss, they are putting the guns in the boat now. They will be back here in a few minutes."

By the time the boat came alongside, the flames from the after skylight had lit the mainsail and were running up the rigging. A minute later they burst out from the companion and the skylight.

"Thank God that is all over, Frank," Bertha said, as they stood together watching the sight.

The inlet was now lit up from side to side. On shore a state of wild excitement prevailed. The boats had reached the shore, and the negroes there had rushed down to hear what had taken place, and to inquire after friends. Above the yells and shouts of the frenzied negroes sounded the deep roar of the horns, and the angry beating of the Obi drums. Numbers of torch bearers were among the crowd, and although nearly half a mile away, the scene could be perfectly made out from the yacht.

The boatmen had received their promised pay as soon as Frank had reached the yacht, and had taken their places in their boat, but Dominique told Frank that they would not go till the Osprey sailed, as they were afraid of being pursued and attacked by the villagers' boats if they did so.

Chapter 19

As Frank stood gazing at the scene, George Lechmere touched him. Frank, looking round, saw that he wished to speak to him privately.

"What is it, George?" he asked, when he had stepped a few paces from Bertha.

"Look there, Major," George said, handing him a field glass. "I thought I had settled old scores with him, but the devil has looked after his own."

"You don't mean to say, George, that it is Carthew again."

"It is he, sure enough, sir. I would have sworn that I had done for him. If I had thought there had been the slightest doubt about it, I would have put a pistol ball through his head."

Frank raised the glass to his eyes. Just where the torches were thickest, he could make out a man's figure raised above the heads of the rest. He was supported on a litter. His head was swathed with bandages. He had raised himself into a sitting position, supported by one arm, while he waved the other passionately. He was evidently haranguing the crowd.

As Frank looked, he saw the figure sink down. Then there was a deep roll of the drum, and a fantastic-looking figure, daubed as it seemed with paint and wearing a huge mask, appeared in his place. The drum and the horns were silent, and the shouting of the negroes was at once hushed. This man, too, harangued the crowd, and when he ceased there was a loud yell and a general movement among the throng. At that moment, Hawkins came up.

"The chain is up and down, sir. Shall I make sail? The wind is very light, but I think that it is enough to take her out."

"Yes, make sail, Hawkins, as quickly as you can. I am afraid that those fellows are coming out to attack us, and I don't want to kill any of the poor devils. There is a small boat coming out from the shore towards that craft. The white sailors are on board, and we shall have them on us, too."

"Up with the anchor," Hawkins shouted. "Make sail at once. Look sharp, my hearties, work with a will, or we shall have those niggers on us again."

Never was sail made on the Osprey more quickly, and by the time that the anchor was apeak all the lower sails were set.

"Shall I tell the blacks to tow their boat behind us?" Hawkins asked Frank, as the yacht began to steal through the water.

"No; let them tow alongside, Hawkins. I don't suppose the people ashore know that we have a native boat with us. If they did, they would be sure that it came from Nipes, and it might set up a feud and cost them their lives, especially as that Obi scoundrel is concerned in the affair."

Then he moved away to George Lechmere.

"Don't say a word about that fellow Carthew," he said. "Miss Greendale thinks he is killed; and it is just as well that she should continue to think that she is safe from him in the future."

"So far as she is concerned, I think that is true; but I would not answer for you, Major. You have ruined his plans, and burned his yacht, and as long as he lives he will never forgive you."

"Well, it is of no use to worry about it now, George; but I expect that we shall hear more about him someday."

"What are they doing, Frank?" Bertha asked, as he rejoined her. "I think that they are getting into the boats again."

"Yes. I fancy they are going to try to take us, but they have no more chance of doing so than they have of flying. The Obi man has worked them up to a state of frenzy, but it will evaporate pretty quickly when they get within range of our muskets."

"But we have got the cannon on board, have we not?"

"Yes; but we did not bring off any ammunition with us. It was the men's idea to bring them as a trophy. However, I have plenty of powder and can load them with bullets; but I certainly won't use them if it can be possibly avoided. I have no grudge against the poor fellows who have been told that we are desperate pirates, and who are only doing what they believe to be a meritorious action in trying to capture us."

In a few minutes six boats put out from the shore. The Osprey was not going through the water more than two miles an hour, though she had every stitch of canvas spread. Frank had the guns taken aft and loaded. As the boats came within the circle of the light of the burning yacht, it could be seen that they were crowded with men, who encouraged themselves with defiant yells and shouts, which excited the derision of the Osprey's crew. When they got within a quarter of a mile they opened a fusillade of musketry, but the balls dropped in the water some distance astern of the yacht. As the boats came nearer, however, they began to drop round her.

"Sit down behind the bulwarks," Frank said. "They are not good shots, but a stray ball might come on board, and there is no use running risks."

By this time he had persuaded Bertha to go below. The boats rowed on until some seventy or eighty yards off the Osprey. The shouting had gradually died away, for the silence on board the yacht oppressed them. There was something unnatural about it, and their superstitious fear of the Obi man disappeared before their dread of the unknown.

As if affected simultaneously by the disquietude of their companions, the rowers all stopped work at the same moment. Dominique had already received instructions, and at once hailed them in French.

"If you value your lives, turn back. We have the guns of the brigantine. They are crammed with bullets and are pointed at you. The owner has but to give the word, and you will all be blown to pieces. He is a good man, and wishes you no harm. We have come here not to quarrel with you poor ignorant black fellows, but to rescue two ladies the villain that ship belongs to had carried off. Therefore, go away back to your wives and families while you are able to, for if you come but one foot nearer not one of you will live to return."

The news, that the Osprey had the cannon from the brigantine on board, came like a thunderbolt upon the negroes. The prospect of a fight with the men who had so easily captured the brigantine was unpleasant enough, but that they were also to encounter cannon was altogether too much for them, and a general shout of "Don't fire; we go back!" rose from the boats.

For a minute or two they lay motionless, afraid even to dip an oar in the water lest it should bring down a storm upon them, but as the Osprey glided slowly away the rearmost boat began to turn round, the others followed her example, and they were soon rowing back even more rapidly than they had come.

"You can cast off that boat, Hawkins, as soon as we are out into the bay," Frank said, and then went down below.

"Our troubles are all over at last, dear, and we can have a quiet talk," he said. "As I expected, the negroes lost heart as soon as they came near, and the threat of a round of grape from the guns finally settled them. They are off for home, and we shall hear no more of them. Now you had best be off to bed at once. You have had a terrible day of it, and it is just two o'clock.

"Ah! that is right," he broke off, as the steward entered carrying a tray with tea things. "I had forgotten all about that necessity. You had better call Anna in; she must want a cup too, poor girl."

"Yes, I should like a cup of tea," Bertha said, as she sat down to the tray, "but I really don't feel so tired as you would think."

"You will feel it all the more afterwards, I am afraid," Frank replied. "The excitement has kept you up."

"Yes, we felt dreadfully tired, didn't we, Anna, before we gave up? But the two hours' row in the boat, and all this excitement here, have made me almost forget it. It seems to me now quite impossible that it can be only about nine hours since you rushed out so suddenly with your men. It seems to me quite far off; further than many things do that happened a week ago. And please to remember that your advice to go to bed is quite as seasonable in your case as in mine."

When he had seen them leave the saloon, Frank went on deck for a last look round.

"I don't think that there is a chance of anything happening before morning, Hawkins, but you will, of course, keep a sharp lookout and let me know."

"I will look out, sir. I have sent the four hands who were with you down to their berths, as soon as the niggers turned back. Lechmere has turned in, too."

"Is the wind freshening at all?"

"Not yet, sir. I don't suppose that we shall get more than we have now till day begins to break. Still, we are crawling on and shall be out in the bay in another quarter of an hour."

When Frank got up at sunrise he found that the yacht was just rounding the point of the bay. He looked behind. No boat was in view.

"Nothing moving, I see," he said as the first mate, who was in charge, came up.

"We have not seen a thing on the water, sir."

"I hardly expected that there would be. It is probable that, as soon as the boats got back, Carthew sent his skipper or mate off with a couple of the men to Port au Prince, to lay a complaint for piracy against me. But, even if they got horses, it would take them a couple of days to get there; that is, if they are not much better riders than the majority of sailors are. Then it is likely that there would be some time lost in formalities, and even if there was a Government steamer lying in the port, it would take her a long time to get up steam. Moreover, I am by no means sure that even Carthew would venture on such an impudent thing as that. It is certain that we should get into a bad scrape for boarding and burning a vessel in Haytian waters, but that is all the harm he could do us. The British Consul would certainly be more likely to believe the story of the owner of a Royal Squadron yacht, backed by that of her captain, mates and crew, and by Miss Greendale and her maid; than the tale of the owner of a vessel that could give no satisfactory explanation for being here. Besides, he will know that before a steamer could start in chase we should be certainly two, or perhaps three, days away, and whether we should make for Jamaica or Bermuda, or round the northwestern point of the bay, and then for England, he could have no clue whatever."

"How shall I lay her course, sir? The wind has freshened already, and we are slipping through the water at a good four knots now."

"We will keep along this side, as far as the Point at any rate. If Carthew has sent for a steamer, he is likely to have ordered a man down to this headland to see which course we are taking. When we have got so far that we cannot be made out from there, we will sail north for Cape la Mole. I think it would be safe enough to lay our course at once, but I do not wish to run the slightest risk that can be avoided."

The wind continued to freshen, and to Frank's satisfaction they were, when Bertha came on deck at eight o'clock, running along the coast at seven knots an hour.

"Have you slept well?" he asked, as he took her hand.

"Yes. I thought when I lay down that it would be impossible for me to sleep at all—it had been such a wonderful day, it was all so strange, so sudden, and so happy—and just as I was thinking so, I suppose I dropped off and slept till Anna woke me three quarters of an hour ago, and told me what time it was.

"Frank, I did not say anything yesterday, not even a single word of thanks, for all that you have done for me; but you know very well that it was not because I did not feel it, but because if I had said anything at all I should have broken down, and that was the very thing that I knew I ought not to do. But you know, don't you, that I shall have all my life to prove how thankful I am."

"I know, dear, and between us surely nothing need be said. I am as thankful that I have been the means of saving you, as you can be that I was almost miraculously enabled to follow your track so successfully."

"Breakfast is ready, sir," the steward announced from the companion.

"Coming, steward.

"I have told them, Bertha, to lay for three. I thought that it would be pleasanter for you to have Anna with you at meals, as I suppose she has taken them with you since you were carried off."

"Thank you," she said, gratefully. "It won't be quite so nice for you, I know, but perhaps it will be better."

"Well, Anna, you are looking very well," Frank said as he sat down.

"You must officiate with the coffee, Bertha. I will see after the eatables."

"Yes, Anna does look well," Bertha said. "She has borne up capitally, ever since the first two days. We have had all our meals together in our cabin."

"Miss Greendale has been a great deal braver than I have, sir," Anna said, quietly. "She has been wonderfully brave, and though she is very good to say that I have borne up well, I know very well that I have not been as brave as I ought; and I could not help breaking down and crying sometimes, for I did think that we should never get home again."

"Except carrying you away, Carthew did not behave altogether so badly, Bertha?"

"No. The first day that we got on board he told me that I was to stay there until I consented to marry him. I told him that in that case I should become a permanent resident on board, but that sooner or later I should be rescued. He only said then, that he hoped that I should change my mind in time. He admitted that his conduct had been inexcusable, but that his love for me had driven him to it, and that he had only won me as many a knight had won a bride before now.

"At first I made sure that, when we put into a port, I should be able somehow to make my condition known; but I realised for the first time what it was going to be, when I saw us stand off the Lizard and lay her head for the south. Up to that time I had scarcely exchanged a word with him. I had said at once that unless I had my meals in my own cabin with Anna, I would eat nothing at all, and he said, quite courteously, I must confess, that I should in all respects do as I pleased, consistent with safety.

"From that time he said 'Good morning,' gravely when I came up on deck with Anna, and made a remark about the weather. I made no reply, and did not speak until he came to me in the morning, and said quietly, 'That is the Lizard astern of us, Miss Greendale. We are bound for the West

Indies, the finest cruising ground in the world, full of quiet little bays where we can anchor for weeks.'

"'It is monstrous,' I said desperately, for I own that for the first time I was really frightened. 'Some day you will be punished for this.'

"'I must risk that,' he said, quietly. 'Of course, at present you are angry. It is natural that you should be so, but in time you will forgive me, and will make allowance for the length to which my affection for you has driven me. It may be six months, it may be ten years, but however long it may be, I can promise you that, save for this initial offence, you will have no cause to complain of me. I am possessed of boundless patience, and can wait for an indefinite time. In the end I feel sure that your heart will soften towards me.'

"That was his tone all along. He was perfectly respectful, perfectly polite. Sometimes for days not a word would be exchanged between us; sometimes he would come up and talk, or rather, try to talk, for it was seldom that he got any answer from me. As a rule I sat in my deck chair with Anna beside me, and he sat on the other side of the deck, or walked up and down, smoking or talking with that man who was with him.

"So it went on till the afternoon when we saw you. As I told you, he made us go down at once. I could see that he was furiously angry and excited. The steward came to our cabin early in the morning, and said that Mr. Carthew requested that we would dress and come up at once. As I was anxious to know what was going on, I did so; and he said when we came on deck, 'I am very sorry, Miss Greendale, but I have to ask you to go on shore with us at once.'

"I had no idea where we were, save that it was somewhere in the island of San Domingo; but I was ready enough to go ashore, thinking that I might see some white people that I could appeal to.

"I did speak to some negroes as we landed, but he said, 'It is of no use your speaking to them, Miss Greendale, for none of them understands any language but his own.'

"I saw that they did not understand me, at any rate. I was frightened when I saw that four of the sailors were going with us, and that a dozen of the blacks, armed with muskets, also formed round us. I said that I would not go afoot, but Carthew answered:

"'It would pain me greatly were I obliged to take such a step; but if you will not go, there is no course open to me but to have you carried. I am sorry that it should be so, but for various reasons it is imperative that you should take up your abode on shore for the present.'

"Seeing that it was useless to resist, I started with him. A short distance on, two blacks came up with the horses, which had evidently been sent for. We mounted, and were taken up among the hills to the place where you found us. Every mile that we went I grew more frightened, for it seemed to me that it was infinitely worse being in his power up in those hills, than on board his yacht, where something might happen by which I might be released from him. Those huts you saw had been built beforehand, so that he had evidently been preparing to take us there if there should be any reason for leaving the yacht. There was bedding and a couple of chairs and a table in ours.

"In the morning, while still speaking politely, he made it evident to me that he considered he could take a stronger tone than before.

"'I assure you, Miss Greendale,' he said, 'that this poor hut is but a temporary affair. I will shortly have a more comfortable one erected for you. You see, your residence here is likely to be a long one, unless you change your mind. Pray do not nourish any idea that you can someday escape me. It is out of the question; and certainly no white man is ever likely to come to this valley, nor is any negro, except those who live in this village. Its head is an Obi man, whose will is law to the negroes. Their belief in his power is unlimited, and I believe that they imagine that he could slay them with the look of his eye, or turn them into frogs or toads by his magic power. I pray you to think the matter over seriously. Why should you waste your life here You did not always regard me as so hateful; and the love that I bear you is unchangeable. Even could you, months or years hence, make your escape, which I regard as impossible, what would your position be if you returned to England? What story would you have to tell? It might be a true one, but would it be believed?'

"'I have my maid, sir,' I said, passionately, 'who would confirm my report of what I have suffered.'

"'No doubt she would,' he said quietly, 'but a maid's testimony as to her mistress's doings does not go for very much. I endeavoured to make the voyage, which I foresaw might be a long one, pleasant to you by requesting you to bring her with you, and I believe that ladies who elope not unfrequently take their maids with them. But we need not discuss that. This valley will be your home, Miss Greendale, until you consent to leave it as my wife. I do not say that I shall always share your solitude here. I shall cruise about, and may even for a time return to England, but that will in no way alter your position. I have been in communication with the Obi gentleman since I first put into the bay, and he has arranged to take charge of your safety while I am away. He is not a pleasant man to look at, and I have no doubt that he is an unmitigated scoundrel—but his powers are unlimited. If he ordered his followers to offer you and your maid as sacrifices to his fetish, they would carry out his orders, not only willingly, but joyfully. He is a gentleman who, like his class, has a keen eye to the main chance, and will, I doubt not, take every precaution to prevent a source of considerable income from escaping him.'

"'You understand,' he went on, in a different manner, 'I do not wish to threaten you—very far from it. I have endeavoured from the time that you set foot on board to make you as comfortable as possible, and to abstain from thrusting myself upon you in the slightest degree, and I shall always pursue the same course. But please understand that nothing will shake my resolution. It will pain me deeply to have to keep you in a place like this, but keep you I must until you consent to be mine. You must see yourself the hopelessness, as well as the folly, of holding out. On the one side is a life wasted here, on the other you will be the wife of a man who loves you above all things; who has risked everything by the step that he has taken, and who, when you consent, will devote his life to your happiness. You will be restored to your friends and to your position, and nought will be known, except that we made a runaway match, as many have done before us. Do not answer now. At any rate I will remain here for a couple of months, and by the end of that time you may see that the alternative is not so terrible a one.'

"Then, without another word, he turned and walked away; and nothing further passed between us until in the afternoon, when you so suddenly arrived."

"Thank God, he behaved better than I should have given him credit for," Frank said, when she had finished. "He must have felt absolutely certain that there was no chance whatever of your rescue, and that in time you would be forced to accept him, or he would hardly have refrained from pushing his suit more urgently. His calculations were well made, and if we had not noticed that brigantine at Cowes, and I had not had the luck to come upon some of his crew and pick up his track, he might have been successful."

"You don't think that I should ever have consented to marry him?" Bertha said, indignantly.

"I am sure that such a thought never entered your head, Bertha; but you cannot tell what the effect of a hopeless captivity would have had upon you. The fellow had judged you well, and he saw that the attitude of respect he adopted would afford him a far better chance of winning you, than roughness or threats would do. But he might have resorted to them afterwards, and you were so wholly and absolutely in his power, that you would almost have been driven to accept the alternative and become his wife."

She shook her head decidedly.

"I would have killed him first," she said. "I suppose some girls would say, 'I would have killed myself;' but I should not have thought of that—at any rate not until I had failed to kill him. Every woman has the same right to defend herself that a man has, and I should have no more felt that I was to blame, if I had killed him, than you would do when you killed a man who had done you no individual harm, in battle."

"We only want mamma here," she said a little later, as she took her seat in a deck chair, "to complete the illusion that we are sailing along somewhere on the Devonshire coast. The hills are higher and more wooded, but the general idea is the same. I suppose I ought to feel it very shocking, cruising about with you, without anyone but Anna with me; but somehow it does not feel so."

"No wonder, dear. You see, we have been looking forward to doing exactly the same thing in the spring."

"I think we had better not talk about that now," she said, flushing. "I intend to make believe, till we get to England, that mamma is down below, and that I may be called at any moment. How long shall we be before we are there?"

"I cannot say, Bertha. I shall have a talk with Hawkins, presently, as to what course we had better take. It may be best to sail to Bermuda. If we find a mail steamer about to start from there, we might go home in it, and get there a fortnight earlier than we should do in the yacht, perhaps more. However, that we can talk over. I can see there may be difficulties, but undoubtedly the sooner you are home the better. You see, we are well in November now.

"What day is it?" he reflected.

"I have lost all count, Frank."

He consulted a pocketbook.

"Today is the twenty-first of November. I should think that if we get favourable winds, we might make Bermuda in a week—ten days at the outside; and if we could catch a steamer a day or two after getting there, you might be able to spend your Christmas at Greendale."

"That would be very nice. The difficulty would be, that I might afterwards meet some of the people who were with us on the steamer."

"It would not be likely," he said. "Still, we can talk it over. At any rate, from the Bermudas we can send a letter to your mother, and set her mind at rest."

The captain and Purvis, consulting the book of sailing directions, came to the conclusion that the passage via the Bermudas would be distinctly the best and shortest. The wind was abeam and steady, and with all sail set the Osprey maintained a speed of nine knots an hour until Bermuda was in sight. They were still undecided as to whether they had better go home by the mail, but it was settled for them by their finding, on entering the port, that the steamer had touched there the day before and gone on the same evening, and that it was not probable that any other steamer would be sailing for England for another ten days.

They stopped only long enough to lay in a store of fresh provisions and water, of which the supply was now beginning to run very short. Indeed, had not the wind been so steady, all hands would have been placed on half rations of water.

Bertha did not land. She was nervously afraid of meeting anyone who might recognise her afterwards, and six hours after entering the port the Osprey was again under way. The wind, as is usual at Barbadoes, was blowing from the southwest; and it held with them the whole way home, so that after a remarkably quick run they dropped anchor off Southampton on the fifteenth of December. Frank had already made all arrangements with the captain to lay up the Osprey at once.

"I shall want her out again in the first week in April, so that she will not be long in winter quarters."

On landing, Frank despatched a telegram to Lady Greendale:

"Returned all safe and well. Just starting for town. Shall be with you about six o'clock."

The train was punctual, and five minutes before six Frank arrived with Bertha at Lady Greendale's. He had already told Bertha that he should not come in.

"It is much better that you should be alone with her for a time. She will have innumerable questions to ask, and would, of course, prefer to have you to herself. I will come round tomorrow morning after breakfast."

Anna had been instructed very carefully, by her mistress, not to say anything of what had happened, and in order that she might avoid questions, George Lechmere had seen her into a cab for Liverpool Street, as she wished to spend a week with some friends at Chelmsford. Then she was to join Bertha at Greendale.

Frank went to his chambers, where George Lechmere had driven with the luggage. The next morning he went early to Lady Greendale's, so early that he found her and Bertha at breakfast.

"My dear Frank," the former said, embracing him warmly, "how can I ever thank you for all that you have done for us! Bertha has been telling me all about how you rescued her. I hear that you were wounded, too."

"The wound was of no great importance, and, as you see, I have thrown aside my sling this morning. Yes, we went through some exciting adventures, which will furnish us with a store of memories all our lives.

"How have you been, Lady Greendale? I am glad to see that, at any rate, you are looking well."

"I have had a terribly anxious time of it, as you may suppose; but your letters were always so bright and hopeful that they helped me wonderfully. The first fortnight was the worst. Your letter from Gibraltar was a great relief, and of course the next, saying that you had heard that the yacht really did touch at Madeira, showed that you were on the right track. When you wrote from Madeira, I sent to Wild's for the largest map of the West Indies that they had, and thus when I got your letters, I was able to follow your course and understand all about it. You are looking better than when I saw you last."

"You should have seen him when I first met him, mamma. I hardly knew him, he looked so thin and worn; but during the last three weeks he has filled out again, and he seems to me to be looking quite himself."

"And Bertha is looking well, too."

"So I ought to do, mamma. I don't think I ever looked very bad, in spite of my troubles, and the splendid voyage we have had would have set anyone up."

"It has been a wonderful comfort to me," Lady Greendale said, "that I have met hardly anyone that I know. The last three weeks or so I have met two or three people, but I only said that I was up in town for a short time. Of course, they asked after you, and I said that you were not with me, as you were spending a short time with some people whom you knew. We intend to go down home tomorrow."

"The best thing that you can do, Lady Greendale. I shall be down for Christmas, and the first week in April, you know, I am to carry her off. So, you see, this excursion of ours has not altered any of our plans."

Chapter 20

Christmas passed off quietly. As soon as it was known that Lady Greendale had returned, the neighbours called, and for the next few months there was the usual round of dinner parties. To all remarks as to the length of time that she had been away, Lady Greendale merely replied that Bertha had been staying among friends, and that as she herself had not been in very good health, she had preferred staying in town, where she could always find a physician close at hand if she needed one.

It was not until they had been back for more than a month, that the engagement between Bertha and Major Mallett was announced by Lady Greendale to her friends, and it was generally supposed that it had but just taken place. The announcement gave great satisfaction, for the general opinion had been that Bertha would get engaged in London, and that Greendale would be virtually lost to the county.

The marriage was to take place in April.

"There is no reason for a long delay," Lady Greendale explained. "They have known each other ever since Bertha was a child. They intend to spend their honeymoon on board Major Mallett's yacht, the Osprey, and will go up the Mediterranean until the heat begins to get too oppressive, when they talk about sailing round the islands, or, at any rate, cruising for some time off the west of Scotland."

About the same time, George Lechmere, in a rather mysterious manner, told Frank that he wished for a few minutes' conversation with him.

"What is it, George? Anything wrong with the cellar?"

"No, sir, it is not that. The fact is that Anna Parsons, Miss Greendale's maid, you know, and I, have settled to get married, too."

"Capital, George, I am heartily glad of it," Frank said, shaking him warmly by the hand.

"I never thought that I should get to care for anyone again, but you see we were thrown a good deal together on the voyage home, and I don't know how it came about, but we had pretty well arranged it before we got back, and now we have settled it altogether."

"I am not surprised to hear it, George. I rather fancied, from what I saw on board, that something was likely to come of it. It is the best thing by far for you."

"Well, sir, as I said, I never thought that I should care for anyone else, but I am sure that I shall make a better husband, now, than I should have done had I married five years ago."

"That I am sure you will. You have had a rough lesson, and it has made a great impression, and I doubt whether your marriage would have been a happy one had you married then, after what you told me of your jealous temper. Now I am sure that neither Anna, nor anyone else, could wish for a better husband than you will make. Well now, what are you thinking of doing, for I suppose you have thought it over well?"

"That is what we cannot quite settle, Major. I should like to stay with you all my life, just as I am."

"I don't see that you could do that—at least, not in your present condition. There is no farm vacant, and if there were one I must give the late tenant's son the option of it. That has always been the rule on the estate. However, we need not settle on that at present. When are you going to get married? I should like it to be at the same time as we are. I am sure that Miss Greendale would be pleased. We both owe you a great deal, and, as you know, I regard you as my closest friend."

"Thank you, Major, but I am sure that neither Anna nor I would care to be married before a church full of grand people, and we have agreed that we won't do it until after you come back from your trip. Miss Bertha has promised Anna that she shall go with her as her maid, and of course, Major, I shall want to go with you."

"Well, you might get married the week before, and still go with us."

George shook his head.

"I think that it would be better the other way, Major. We will go with you as we are, and get married after you come back."

The next day Frank had a long talk with Mr. Norton.

"Well, sir, your plan would suit me very well. Nothing could be better," said the old steward. "In fact, I was going to tell you that I was beginning to find that the outdoor work was getting too much for me, and that though I should be very sorry to give it up altogether, I must either arrange with you to have help, or else find a successor. I am sure that the arrangement you propose would suit me exactly.

"George Lechmere would be just the man for the work. We used to think him the best judge of livestock in the county, and he is a good all-round farmer. If he were to take the work of the home farm off my hands, I could keep on very well with the rest of the estate for another two or three years, and as he would act as my assistant he would, by the end of that time, be quite capable of taking it over altogether. I should then move into Chippenham. We have two married daughters living, and now that we have no one at home, my wife has been saying for some time that she would rather settle there than go on living in the country, and there is really no more occasion for me to go on working. So, as soon as Lechmere has got the whole thing in hand, I shall be quite ready to hand it over to him."

"Well, I am very glad that it is so, Norton. Of course, I should never have made any change until you yourself were perfectly willing to give it up, but as you are willing, I am certainly glad to be able to put him into it. As you know, he saved my life, and has done me many other great services, and I regard him as a friend and want to keep him near me. Of course, he will go into the farmhouse, and after you retire he can either move into yours, or remain there, as he likes. Naturally, as long as you live, Norton, I shall continue the rate of pay you have always had. You were over thirty years with my father, and I should certainly make no difference in that respect."

"Well, George, I have arranged your business," Frank said that evening. "Norton is getting on in life now, and he begins to find his work in winter a little too hard for him, so I have arranged that you are to take the management of the home farm altogether off his hands, and will, of course, establish yourself at the house. You will be a sort of assistant to him in other matters, and get up the work, and in the course of a couple of years, at the outside, he will retire altogether, and you will be steward. If you like you can work the home farm on your own account, but that will be for your consideration. How do you think that you will like that?"

"I should like it above everything, Major, and I am grateful to you, indeed."

"Well, I am glad that you like the arrangement, George. I had it in my mind when I was talking to you two days ago, but until I saw Norton, and found that he was willing to retire, I did not propose it."

Towards the end of February, Lady Greendale and Bertha went up to town for a fortnight, intimating to Frank that they would be so busy with important business that his presence there would not be desired. He, however, travelled with them to London, and then went round to Southampton, where he had a consultation with the firm in whose yard the yacht was laid up, and the head of the great upholstering firm there, and arranged for material alterations in the plans of the cabins, and their redecoration. Everything was to be completed by the beginning of April. He had written to Hawkins to meet him on board.

"You must have everything ready by the fifth," he said. "We shall arrive late in the afternoon, or perhaps in the evening of the fifth, and shall get under way next morning. I hope that you have been able to get the same crew."

"There is no fear of their not all coming, sir, except Purvis. He has been bad all the winter, and I doubt whether he will be able to go with us."

"I am sorry to hear that. Tell him that I shall make him an allowance of a pound a week for the season, and that I shall give him a little pension, of ten shillings a week, as long as he lives. I shall consider that all who went with me on that cruise to the West Indies have a claim upon me."

The time for the wedding approached. There was some consultation, between Frank and Lady Greendale, as to whether the dinner to the tenants should be given on that occasion, or on their return; and it was settled that it would be more convenient to postpone it.

"I am sure they would rather have you and Bertha here, and it would be much more convenient in every way. We have so much to think about now, and there will be so many arrangements to be made."

"I quite agree with you. I will put it all in the hands of Rafters, of Chippenham. I think that it is only right to give it to local people. We shall want two big marquees, one for your tenants and mine and their wives and families, and the other for all the labourers and farm servants."

"And there must be another for all the children," Bertha put in.

"Very well, Bertha.

"Then, of course, we must have a military band and fireworks, and we had better have a big platform put down for those who like to dance, and a lot of shows and things for the elders and children, and a conjurer with a big lucky basket, and things of that sort. Of course, at present one cannot give even an approximate date, but I will tell them that they shall have a fortnight's notice."

"I wonder what has become of Carthew, Major?" George Lechmere said, as he was having a last talk with Frank on the eve of the wedding. "He will gnash his teeth when he sees it in the papers."

"I have thought of him a good many times, George. He is an evil scoundrel, and nothing would please me more than to hear that he was dead. When I remember how many years he kept up his malice against me, for having beaten him in a fight; I know how intense must be his hatred of me, now that I have thwarted all his plans and burned his yacht. It is not that I am afraid of him personally, but there is no saying what form his vengeance will take, for that he will sooner or later try to be revenged I feel absolutely certain."

"I have often thought of it myself, sir. Perhaps he is out in Hayti still."

"No chance of that, George. Miss Greendale said that he told her that he had money sufficient to pay for a ten years' cruise. That may have been a lie, but he must have had money sufficient to last him for some time, anyhow, and you may be sure that he took it on shore with him. He may have died from the effects of that wound you gave him, but if he is alive I have no doubt that he is in England somewhere. Of course, he would not show himself where he was known, having been a heavy defaulter last year; but he may have let his beard grow, and so disguised himself that he would not be easily recognised. As to what he is doing, of course I have not the slightest idea; but we may be quite sure that he is not up to any good.

"Well, George, then it is quite settled that you and Anna are to go off with the luggage directly the wedding is over. You will come ashore with the gig and meet us at eight o'clock at the station, with a carriage to take us down to the boat."

"I will be there, Major, and see that everything is ready for you on board."

When packing up his things in the morning, George Lechmere put aside a pistol and a dagger that he had taken from the sash of a mutineer, whom he had killed in India.

"They are not the sort of things a man generally carries at a wedding," he said, grimly, "but until I know something of what that villain is doing, I mean to keep them handy for use. There is never any saying what he may be up to, and I know well enough that the Major, whatever he says, will never give the matter a thought."

He loaded the pistol and dropped it into his coat pocket. Then he opened his waistcoat, cut a slit in the lining under his left arm, and pushed the dagger down it until it was stopped by the slender steel crosspiece at the handle.

"I will make a neater job of it afterwards," he said to himself. "That will do for the present, and I can get at it in a moment."

The wedding went off as such things generally do. The church was crowded, the girls of the village school lined the path from the gate to the church door, and strewed flowers as the bridal party arrived; and as they drove off to Greendale tenants of both estates, collected in the churchyard, cheered them heartily. There was a large gathering at breakfast, but at last the toasts were all drunk, and the awkward time of waiting over, and at three o'clock Major Mallett and his wife drove off amidst the cheers of the crowd assembled to see them start.

"Thank God that is all over," Frank said heartily as they passed out through the lodge gates.

At half-past eight Captain Hawkins was standing at the landing stage in a furious passion.

"Where can that fellow Jackson have got to?" he said, stamping his foot. "I said that you were all to be back in a quarter of an hour when we landed, and it is three quarters of an hour now. I never knew him to do such a thing before, and I would not have had such a thing happen this evening for any money. What will the Major think when he finds only five men instead of six in the gig, on such an occasion as this? We shall be having them down in a minute or two. Jackson had better not show his face on board after this. It is the most provoking thing I ever knew."

"It ain't his way, captain," one of the men said. "Jackson can go on the spree like the rest of us, but I never knew him to do such a thing all the years I have known him, when there was work to be done; and I am sure he would not do so this evening. He may have got knocked down or run over or something."

"I will take an oar if you like, captain," said a man in a yachtsman's suit, who was loitering near. "I have nothing to do, and may as well row off as do anything else. You can put me on shore in the dinghy afterwards."

"All right, my lad, take number two athwart. It is too dark to see faces, and the owner is not likely to notice that there is a strange hand on board. I will give you half a crown gladly for the job."

The man got into the boat and took his seat.

"Here they come," the captain went on. "We are only just in time. Up-end your oars, lads. We ain't strong enough to cheer, but we will give them a hearty 'God bless you!' as they come down."

George Lechmere came on first, and handed in a bundle of wraps, parasols, and umbrellas. The captain stood at the top of the steps, and as Frank and Bertha came up took off his hat.

"God bless you and your wife, sir," he said, and the men re-echoed the words in a deep chorus.

"Thank you, captain.

"Thank you all, lads, for my wife and myself," Frank said, heartily, and a minute later the boat pushed off.

The tide was running out strong, and they were halfway across it towards the dark mass of yachts, when there was a sudden crash forward.

"What is it?" Frank exclaimed.

"This fellow has stove in the boat, sir," the bow oar exclaimed, and then came a series of hurried exclamations.

Frank had not caught the words, but the rush of water aft told him that something serious had happened.

"Row, men, row!" he shouted.

"Steer to the nearest yacht, Hawkins."

"We shall never get there, sir. She will be full in half a minute."

"Let each man stick to his oar," Frank said, standing up. "We aft will hold on to the boat."

Then he raised his voice in a shout:

"Yachts, ahoy! Send boats; we are sinking!

"Don't be frightened, darling," he said to Bertha. "Keep hold of the gunwale. I can keep you up easily enough until help comes, but it is better to stick to the boat. We must have run against something that has stove her in."

A moment later the water was up to the thwarts, the boat gave a lurch, and then rolled over. Frank threw his arm round Bertha, and as the boat capsized clung to it with his disengaged hand.

"Don't try to get hold of the keel," he said. "It would turn her over again. Just let your hands rest on her, and take hold of the edge of one of the planks.

"That is it, Hawkins. Do you get the other side and just keep her floating as she is. We shall have help in a minute or two.

"Are you all right, George?"

"Yes, I am at her stern. Do you want assistance, sir?"

"No, we are all right, George."

A moment later a man came up beside the Major, and put his hand heavily on his shoulder.

"You won last time, Mallett," he hissed in his ear. "It is my turn now."

The man's weight was pressing him under water, and the boat gave a lurch.

Frank loosed his hold of Bertha with the words, "Hold on, dear, for a minute," and, turning, grappled with his enemy, at the same moment grasping his right wrist as the arm was raised to strike him with a knife.

In a moment both went below the water. They came up beyond the stern, and Frank said:

"Take care of Bertha, George—Carthew—" and then went down again.

Furiously they struggled. They were well matched in strength, but Frank felt that his antagonist was careless of his own life, for he had wound his legs round him, and, unable to wrench his arm from his grasp, was doing his utmost to prevent their coming to the surface.

Suddenly, when he felt that he could no longer retain his breath, he felt arms thrown round them both, and a moment later came to the surface. Then he heard an exclamation of "Thank God!" An arm was raised, and two blows struck rapidly.

Carthew's grasp relaxed, the knife dropped from his hand, and, as Frank shook himself free, he sank under the water.

"Are you all right, Major?" his rescuer said.

"Yes," he gasped.

"Put your hand on my shoulder. The boat is not a length away."

A minute later Frank was beside Bertha again.

"Where have you been, Frank? I was frightened."

"One of the men grasped me," he said, "and I should have turned the boat over if I had not let go. However, thanks to George Lechmere, who came to my rescue, I have shaken him off.

"Ah! here is help."

Three or four boats from the yachts were indeed rowing up. The four clinging to the gig were taken on board by one of them, while the others picked up the men who were floating supported by their oars.

"Don't say a word about it, George," Frank whispered.

The Osprey was lying but two or three hundred yards away, and they were soon alongside.

"This is not the sort of welcome I thought to give you on board, dear," he said, as he helped Bertha on deck, and went down the companion with her.

Anna burst into exclamations of dismay at seeing the dripping figures.

"We have had an accident, Anna," Frank said, cheerfully, "but I don't think that we are any the worse for it. Please take your mistress aft and get her into dry things at once.

"Steward, open one of those bottles of champagne, and give me half a tumbler full."

He hurried after the others with it.

"Please drink this at once, Bertha," he said. "Yes, you shall have some tea directly, but start with this. It will soon put you in a glow. Oh! yes, I am going to have one, too; but a ducking is no odds to me."

Then he ran up on deck.

"You have saved my life again, George, for that scoundrel would have drowned us both."

"I saw the knife in his hand as you went down, and knew that you wanted me more than Miss—I mean Mrs. Mallett did."

"How did you make him let go so quickly?"

"I had a sort of fear that, sooner or later, that villain would be up to something; and had made up my mind that I would always have a weapon handy. This morning I stuck that dagger of mine inside the lining of my waistcoat, so that it might be handy. And it was handy. You were not five yards from me when you went down, and I dived for you, but could not find you at first, and had to come up once for air. Of course, I could not use the dagger until I found which was which, and then I put an end to it."

"Then you killed him, George?"

"I don't think that he will trouble you any more, sir; and if ever a chap deserved his fate that villain did. Why, sir, do you know how it all happened?"

"No, I did not catch what the man at the bow said. There was such a confusion forward."

"He said that he had staved the boat in somehow. He must have taken the place of one of the men on purpose to do it."

"Well, George, I can't say that I'm sorry."

"I am heartily glad, sir. I am no more sorry for killing him than for shooting one of those murderous niggers. Less sorry, a great deal. The man deserved hanging. He was intending to murder you, and perhaps Mrs. Mallett, and I killed him as I should have killed a mad dog that was attacking you."

"Well, say nothing about it at present, George. It would be a great shock to my wife if she were to know it. Now you had better go and change your things at once, as I am going to do. Are all the men rescued?"

"Yes, sir, they are all five on board."

"Hawkins," Frank said, putting his hand in his pocket, "give the men who came to help us a couple of sovereigns each, and tell our men that I don't want them to talk about the affair. I will see you about it again."

Frank was not long in getting into dry clothes, and a few minutes later Bertha came in.

"Are you none the worse for it, dear?"

"Not a bit, Frank. That champagne has thoroughly warmed me. What a sudden affair it all was. Is everyone safe?"

"Yes, they stuck to the oars, and all our crew were picked up. It was a bad start, was it not? But it has never happened to me before, and I hope that it will never happen to me again."

"Some people would be inclined to think this an unlucky beginning," said Bertha, with a slight tone of interrogation.

"I am certainly not one of them," he laughed. "I had only one superstition, and that is at an end. You know what it was, dear, but the spell is broken. He had a long run of minor successes, but I have won the only prize worth having, for which we have been rivals."

Some days later the body of a sailor was washed ashore near Selsey Bill. An inquest was held, and a verdict returned that the man had been murdered by some person or persons unknown; but although the police of Portsmouth, Southampton, Cowes, and Ryde made vigilant inquiries, they were unable to ascertain that any yacht sailor hailing from those ports had suddenly disappeared.

There was much discussion, in the forecastle of the Osprey, as to the identity and motives of the man who had first got into conversation with Jackson, and then asked him to take a drink, which must have been hocussed, for Jackson remembered nothing afterwards. It was evident that the fellow had done it in order to take his place. He had staved in the boat, and, as they supposed, afterwards swam to shore; but the crime seemed so singularly motiveless that they finally put it down as the work of a madman.

It was not until the day before the Osprey anchored again in Cowes, three months later, that Bertha, on expressing some apprehension of further trouble from Carthew, if he had survived the wound George Lechmere gave him, learned the true account of the sinking of the gig, as she went on board at Southampton on her wedding day.